PROMISED IN BLOOD

BROKEN BLOODLINES: BOOK 2

SADIE KINCAID

For all of my readers who fell in love with the vampires of Montridge University and their sweet elementai, they're all waiting for you ...

And they have a few surprises in store ...

Love Sadie x

CONTENT ADVISORY

This book is a dark paranormal romance and contains the following topics which may be sensitive for some readers:

Blood play (well, they are vampires)
Violence
Scenes of an explicit sexual nature

PROLOGUE

NAZEEL DANRAATH—GRAND HEALER OF THE
ORDER OF AZEZAL

"Reading up on your prophecies, my sweet?" Kameen's distinctive low growl makes me jump. I close the ledger of ancient texts and spin around to face him. Pink and silver scars on the left side of his face seem to flicker in the dim illumination from the torches on the wall, the only form of light allowed down here in the library of our ancestors.

"Simply reminding myself of their warnings, my lord and commander," I say with a slight bow.

His eyes narrow with suspicion as he takes a few steps closer. "My lord and commander?"

I drop my head and train my attention on the floor. "That is what you are, is it not?"

Strong fingers grip my chin, and he tilts my head until I am looking into his undeniably handsome face. "You are still mad at me, my sweet?"

I try to wrench from his grip, but he holds me fast with his superior strength. Kameen Nassari. Commander of the Order of Azezal and the most powerful demon alive.

Not to mention, he is the only man I have ever loved. He is the other half of my heart and soul. Yet we disagree on so much. "You grounded me." I spit out the accusation.

"Because you were in Havenwood, Nazeel." His voice vibrates with the remnants of his fury. "I warned you to stay away from the girl."

"But she is—"

"We do not interfere," he barks, cutting me off.

I glare at him. "If she is the chosen one—"

"Then she will not need your help."

I shake free of his grip and push myself onto my tiptoes, the top of my head barely reaching his chin. "She is also your niece, Kameen."

He hisses out a breath. "All the more reason I cannot be seen to interfere. I have already done too much in saving the child."

"Who says we cannot interfere? You know there are others who are aware of her gifts. Those who tried to kill her before she was even born." I ball my hands into fists but force my voice to remain steady. Yelling at him is the least successful way to make him see reason. "The Skotádi grow stronger, and you cannot deny it. If they can interfere, then why cannot we? Who says we must stand back and do nothing?"

His lip curls in a sneer. "The Skotádi represent everything we stand against. Are you forgetting your vows?"

"Vows that we made thousands of years ago, Kameen. To a great man, but a man who is no longer with us."

"The rules of the Order were carved in stone by Azezal

2

himself. They cannot simply be amended to fit your whims, no matter how passionate those whims might make you, my little witch." His eyes flicker with dark desire.

I ignore the warmth spreading through my core, the way it always does when he looks at me like that. It is one of his favorite—and most effective—distraction techniques. But not today. "We are living in different times, Kameen. With different rules. The dragons left the mortal realm, and we did nothing. The Skotádi wiped out an entire species. We sat back and did *nothing*."

"As was our role, Nazeel. We are granted the gift of immortality so we can observe, not act. Not to affect outcomes, merely to witness them. Those who abuse that privilege have no honor, and they shall meet their just fate when the time is right."

I shake my head. "What if I am tired of observing, Kameen? What if I actually want to do something that makes a difference?"

His eyes fill with pain, and he cups my jaw again, this time much more tenderly than before. "To do that, you must leave the Order. And that is not something I would ever allow."

Of course he would never allow it. For that would mean our parting, and he would never tolerate such a thing. And with any other creature, that knowledge may offer leverage, but not with him. There is no use reasoning with Kameen. His stubbornness knows no bounds. He peers over my shoulder at the ancient ledger, his eyes narrowing. "Your mother did such a good job transcribing the ancient scrolls."

Swallowing the lump in my throat, I recall her slender fingers and her beautiful penmanship. How she would spend hours transcribing by candlelight to ensure that the ancient prophecies were not lost to the ravages of time. It was the Prophecies of Fiere which were always the most interesting to me, along with the brave knights who rescued them from the library of Alexandria whilst it burned. As a child, I would dream of the day I would meet such a heroic soul.

I run my fingertips over the mottled scars on the left side of Kameen's face. "How was it that the fire made you more beautiful, my love?"

He lets out a low growl. "It is only you who thinks that, witch."

I slide my hand to the back of his neck and pull him toward me. He acquiesces, allowing me to press a soft kiss on his cheek. "It is only I who matters."

He hums, and his warm breath dusts over my forehead. "Stop meddling, Nazeel. Or I will be forced to stop you."

Regret and guilt wrap around my heart like a vise. "I know, my love." I rest my head on his chest, fully aware that he speaks the truth.

And that I have no choice but to disobey him.

CHAPTER
ONE
OPHELIA

2 DAYS EARLIER

The world around me has changed infinitely. Every color is more vibrant, every sound sharper, each scent stronger and more potent than before. Yet I know, paradoxically, that everything remains exactly the same.

"How are you feeling, little one?" Alexandros's words wash over me, blanketing me in warmth and anchoring me back to the present.

I suck in a deep lungful of air. I have no words to even begin to accurately explain how I'm feeling right now. My head is spinning with new emotions, thoughts, questions. It's hard to believe that it's been a little more than an hour since I was in the library with Cadence. It feels like a lifetime ago. "I don't know. Different. Stronger?"

Alexandros arches an eyebrow. "Powerful?"

That would be an understatement. I feel like I could shoot lightning from the tips of my fingers. I nod and sink my teeth into my bottom lip, feeling both awkward and strangely unrestrained. "Yes. What just happened to me?"

"I believe you just unlocked your powers."

"B-because we had ..." I blush at the thought of saying the word sex to him despite the fact that I'm sitting on his lap and he's still inside me.

"While I would like to think your powers were unlocked because of how well I fucked you, I think learning of your heritage is the true cause."

The memory of what happened—of all those women who were tortured and murdered, the children who were torn from their mother's arms—makes my chest tighten. "The pain."

He pulls me closer. "I know."

"Your pain, Alexandros. I'm so sorry."

"We should get back to the house." He slides himself out of me, and I wince at the burn and the loss of him. I can already feel him closing himself off to me.

The house. The boys. Where are they? "Why can't I hear them?"

He shuffles me back enough that he can zip up his pants, and then he tucks my hair behind my ear. His fingertips tenderly brush over my face. He doesn't have to ask who I'm referring to. "I blocked them."

"You blocked them?"

He nods.

"But why?"

"Can you imagine how much of a distraction they would

have been if they had felt even a fraction of what happened in here?"

I press my lips together and hum my agreement, suppressing a laugh at the thought. "They'd have been breaking the door down to get in here."

"Exactly, agápi mou."

My love. I will never tire of him calling me that. "And you can block them from my head too? How?"

"All bloodborne vampires are born with a gift. Mine lies in the power of my mind."

"Like what? You can—"

"Ophelia," he says, his tone assertive but somehow still gentle. "Not now."

"I'm sorry, but this is all so new and ..." I swallow. "I want to know everything, sir. About what I am. My power. About you. About your family."

I feel his heart ache with sadness as though it were my own. I cannot imagine enduring a betrayal such as the one he experienced. "You will. In good time."

"Do the boys know of your past life? Of your wife and children?"

"No." His response is a soft murmur as he presses his lips against my neck.

I know better than to delve further into that with him right now. It wouldn't do me any good—he isn't going to tell me why he chose to hide such a large part of who he is from them. Besides, I have slightly more immediate concerns. "And they don't know what happened tonight? What we just did?"

He lifts his head, his dark eyes locked on mine once more. "They know nothing of what we did or of what I showed you, but I have no doubt they will have felt your power awakening within you."

A shudder runs down my spine. *My power!* There is so much

to know. My mind is buzzing with a bazillion questions, and I want to ask every single one.

Alexandros runs the pad of his thumb over my lip, anchoring me back to this moment. His touch soothes me, calming the chaos in my brain, and I wonder if that's a part of his power too. There are still so many things I need to know, but most pressing is what we just did and what it means for all of us. Does he not want Axl, Xavier, and Malachi to know? Am I going to be his shameful secret? Locked away in his memories along with the family he lost five centuries ago but who he still mourns every single day?

He places his palm on my cheek, his large hand cupping an entire half of my face. "There are a lot of secrets we will have to keep, agápi mou, but this ..." He presses a soft but possessive kiss on my lips, and I melt into him. "This is not one of them."

TWO

"What the fuck is going on?" Xavier bounces on his toes as we stand on the porch and wait for Ophelia and the professor to return. "You think we should go check on her?"

As much as I'd like to do exactly that, I shake my head. "Alexandros made it clear we were supposed to wait here." The order he gave us fifteen minutes earlier still rings fresh in my head. His tone, as usual, was commanding and gruff, but there was something different about him.

Xavier jogs down the three steps and stands beside Malachi on the grass. "What do you think it is? Something definitely happened to her, didn't it?" He glances back over his shoulder at me. "You both felt it?"

I nod and absentmindedly run my fingertips over the thick veins in my forearm, recalling how they burned with pure fire a short while ago. And without a shadow of a doubt, I know the rush of adrenaline that accompanied it had something to do with Ophelia.

Malachi stares out across the lawn and into the distance. "I think it's her power. Something happened with her power."

"You think it was something to do with the witches? Is that why Alexandros was so mad at her?" Xavier glances anxiously between the two of us. "Because he sounded real pissed when he went to get her, right?"

I nod, my mouth dry and my throat working as I try to swallow.

Xavier spins around, directing all his attention at me, his blue eyes wide with terror. "He wouldn't hurt her, would he? We'd know if she was hurting, right, Axl?"

"Of course he wouldn't hurt her," I assure him, although that same fear already snaked its way into my thoughts too.

"And we'd know if he had," Malachi says, his eyes still focused on a spot in the distance. He cranes his neck. "Here they are."

I follow his gaze to find the unmistakable figures of Ophelia and the professor walking side by side. From here, they both look the same, but everything has changed. I can tell by the closeness of their bodies and the way she steals glances at him every few seconds. And then he looks at her too. Their eyes meet at the perfect moment. Neither looks away.

As they grow closer to the safety of the Dragon houses, away from the potential prying eyes of the college, she slides her tiny hand into his. He doesn't pull away from her, and my heart sinks through my chest. If he's claimed her, what does that mean for us?

I jog down the steps and stand between Malachi and Xavier.

"Do you see that?" Xavier asks, and the same anxiety inside me ripples through each of them too.

"Yeah."

"It'll be okay," Malachi says reassuringly.

Xavier snarls. "I'm not giving her up. He can try to take my fucking head, but he can't have her."

Malachi reaches behind me and squeezes Xavier's shoulder. "It'll be okay," he mutters again. But the sideways glance he shoots my way speaks volumes.

The three of us can do nothing but watch and wait for them to tell us what the hell happened in the past hour.

"Hey." Ophelia gives us a shy smile when they finally reach us.

It's Malachi who responds first. "Hey, sweet girl." I know we all want to touch her, but this is uncharted territory, and none of us dare attempt it while Alexandros is holding onto her hand like he'll never let her go. I stare at him and try to read his expression, but as usual, he gives nothing away, so I focus all my attention on my girl. Her cheeks are flushed, her eyes bright and shining. The curve of her lips is faint, probably because she's feeling as awkward as the rest of us are. Still, she's practically fucking glowing.

"What happened?" Xavier asks.

Ophelia presses her lips together and glances at Alexandros.

He nods toward the house. "Let us go inside."

Xavier and Malachi turn and head toward the door, but the tension in my body solidifies my limbs, and I remain rooted to the spot. My heart is pounding in my chest. Something's different, and I need to know what it is.

My eyes lock on Ophelia's, and she smiles, then slips her

free hand into mine. Her touch soothes a little of the tension in me. Enough to unglue my feet from the ground. With her hand firmly clasped in mine, I follow her and Alexandros into the house.

ALEXANDROS CLEARS HIS THROAT, and we sit on the sofa and watch him, waiting with bated breath for him to talk. A memory of my former life flashes before me. I'm thirteen years old, sitting on the sofa and waiting for my father to tell me that my brother, Frederik, won't be coming home that night, his face unreadable and impassive. The same feelings of fear and trepidation wash over me now.

Ophelia sits on Xavier's lap, his arms banded tightly around her waist like he's scared she might float away.

"I had a family." Alexandros's voice is low and calm, but it's filled with an emotion I don't think I've ever heard from him before. "A wife, Elena, and two daughters, Alyria and Imogen. They were elementai. And they were all murdered in the genocide over five centuries ago."

Malachi shifts beside me. Xavier rests his lips on Ophelia's shoulder, his dark brows knitted with a frown.

I lean forward, sure I misheard him. "You had a wife and kids?"

He nods.

"And you kept that from us? You never once mentioned—"

"There are a lot of things about my past that you are unaware of, Axl." His tone remains calm and controlled, but there is no denying the implicit threat it carries.

"So why are you telling us now?" Xavier asks.

He glances at Ophelia, who smiles at him reassuringly. Some of his tension visibly slips away from his shoulders. "In order for Ophelia to discover who she is, to accurately explain the elementai and what happened to them, I ..." His voice cracks a little, and he clears his throat again. "Their entire history is too long and too complex to explain. I had to show her what happened. And that included what happened to my family."

"So you bonded with Ophelia to show her the truth of her past? You bit her?" Xavier asks, his tone accusatory.

The harsh look Alexandros gives him communicates a clear warning. "Yes."

"And it seemed to unlock my power somehow," she quietly adds.

Alexandros hums his agreement, and he seems to sit up straighter as his eyes fill with something I rarely see from him. Pride.

An unexpected and unfamiliar emotion burns in my chest. It feels a lot like resentment. I have shared almost my entire life with him, yet he has shared nothing of his true self with me, and that stings more than I care to admit. I suddenly understand a little more about Xavier and how he feels at being left out. "Would you have ever told us? If not for Ophelia, would you have always kept us in the dark?"

Malachi places a supportive hand on my thigh. "It doesn't matter how we came to know, only that we do," he says in that soothing tone he's so good at. He threads his thick fingers through Ophelia's slender ones. "What happened with your power, sweet girl?"

She draws in a shaky breath. "When I felt Alexandros's pain ... It was like it tore something open inside me. And then all of this power just poured into me, filling up every part of my body until it reached the tip of every hair on my head." Ophelia's eyes light up now, sparkling with her usual curiosity, but I can feel her nervous excitement. "It's hard to explain, but it was like ... like being hit by lightning and being wrapped in a warm blanket at the same time. It was devastating and euphoric."

I can't take my eyes off her. She's the same feisty girl who tried to stop three vampires from biting one of her classmates. Yet she's somehow radically different. Extraordinary, vibrant energy radiates from her, and it feels like I'm standing too close to the surface of the sun. And I can't help but wonder if we are all about to get burned.

Alexandros clears his throat. "I believe Ophelia can access all four magical elements. If she can master all of them, then ..." He doesn't finish his sentence, but his eyes cloud with worry.

I'm not entirely sure why that's significant, but Malachi's low whistle tells me that it is. "That's pretty impressive, right?" he says.

Alexandros rubs a hand over his jaw. "More than impressive."

"But what does all this actually mean? Ophelia has powers now—so what?" Xavier glances at her and winces. "No offense, Cupcake."

She smiles sweetly. "None taken. I'd kinda like to know myself."

Alexandros clears his throat. "This university is full of magical beings, but Ophelia is not like any one of them. I should have known that showing her the pain of her species would unlock her powers, but ..." He draws a deep breath, the vein in his temple throbbing. We all wait for him to finish speaking while he rubs the spot between his brows. "Perhaps I was careless."

Malachi edges forward, hands clasped between his spread thighs. "But her powers were always meant to be unlocked, right? Isn't that why she has them? To use them?"

"Why were Ophelia's powers bound? And by whom?" Alexandros sighs. "There are too many unanswered questions.

But I am sure of one thing." Pausing, he looks at each of us, his dark eyes full of worry, then continues in a grave tone. "This was inevitable. And now we all must prepare for what this will mean."

Ophelia shifts on Xavier's lap, waves of anxiety rolling off her now. I reach over Malachi and rest my hand on her thigh. "Whatever it means, we've all got you, princess."

"But what *does* it mean, Alexandros?" Xavier asks. "Surely Ophelia getting her powers is a good thing for all of us."

He tips his face to the ceiling and mutters something in Greek that I don't understand. When he looks at us again, his expression is back to its normal unreadable state. "I cannot lie and tell you that the existence of an elementai is not a good thing for our species. Our fates are irrevocably and eternally bound together, and that is both a blessing and a curse."

I squeeze her thigh reassuringly. I can't even begin to imagine how disconcerting this must be for her. It confuses the fuck out of me, and I've spent over two hundred years surrounded by magic. Yet I still don't understand the elementai and their powers.

What I do know—and what I allow to comfort me now—is that the universe bringing Ophelia to me, to all of us, will only ever be a blessing.

THREE

ALEXANDROS

X avier rests his chin on Ophelia's shoulder, his blue eyes glued to my face as he listens, enraptured. It is unlike him to be so curious, and this side of him intrigues me. "So the fates of elementai and vampires are bound. But how?" he asks.

I run my fingers through my beard and suppress a heavy sigh. I never intended to reveal this part of myself to them, having foolishly convinced myself that my past had no place in my future—and, until now at least, it had been irrelevant. Still, this is not a conversation I am prepared for tonight. But when Ophelia catches my eye and smiles, I am reminded how much all our lives are about to change. My boys need to know everything. The whole story. Everything except Lucian. I lack the strength necessary to answer the inevitable questions that will arise concerning him.

I blow out a breath. "Elementai are the only creature strong enough to bear vampire children. That is why they were hunted to extinction and why no vampire has been born in over five hundred years."

Axl and Xavier stare back at me in confusion, and it is Malachi, almost as curious as Ophelia, who probes further. "So who wiped out the elementai? And why didn't the vampires stop them?"

"And why are witches taught that vampires were responsible for the genocide?" Ophelia asks, her eyes wide. "Cadence truly believes it was the vampires."

I sink back against my chair and let out a long breath. "There are four vampire houses. Each of them tolerates the other, but they have never been willing to work together. Over a thousand years ago, three of the houses joined together under the guidance of my father, and vampires began to conquer territories and spaces that other species could only dream of. We infiltrated every organization, every government, every kingdom of any worth. But with the elementai eternally at our sides, the balance of our power was kept in check. Despite this, the witches, wolves, and demons grew more afraid as the centuries passed, and slowly, they began to plot our demise." A fresh wave of despair washes over me, threatening to drown me. But once again, I find Ophelia's bright-blue eyes fixed on mine, and the memory of her taste and her blood in my veins is enough to spur me on.

"In addition, there was a growing faction of bloodborne vampires, mostly from House Chǫma, who were unhappy with the new status quo and the power that House Drakos wielded with the support of Thalassa and Elira. That, along with a growing resentment within the sired vampire community of feeling powerless and being beholden to a master, was the perfect recipe for mutiny." I avoid Ophelia's gaze now. She is no doubt thinking of Lucian at this very moment, and I am beyond grateful to her for not mentioning his name. I have yet to discover exactly how much she learned of my son and his part in the elementai genocide, but that is a conversation we will need to have soon.

"That group of vampires, along with armies of witches, wolves, and demons banded together and targeted us at our weakest point—our eternal devotion to and our species' reliance on the elementai. We were not enough to stop them."

A tear rolls down my cheek, and I brush it away quickly, wishing they had not witnessed such an overt display of emotion from me. But the sting of that betrayal has not lessened during the last five centuries. In fact, the sting of my son's betrayal has only grown.

"And you lost your family," Axl says, his voice cracking with emotion.

I nod, still avoiding Ophelia's gaze.

"Elena, Alyria, and Imogen?" Malachi adds.

To hear their names spoken aloud after so long ... It brings me both pain and comfort. To my relief, Ophelia continues to keep my son's name to herself. I am not ready to open that wound so freely.

"Your wife and daughters were all elementai?" Malachi asks.

"That is correct. Vampire and elementai are the feminine and the masculine in balance. Those who committed such atrocious acts were eventually dealt with, but the damage had already been done. And I truly believe that those who were responsible had no idea of the destruction they would cause, not only to elementai and vampires, but to all magical species."

Malachi's green eyes narrow. "All of them?"

"The elementai were the balance in this world. You cannot simply exterminate an entire species and expect there to be no consequences. Whilst there have been no vampires born, there have also been fewer witches, wolves, and demons. Each species is in decline. The power of the elementai is unmatched, and without their magic to splinter through the bloodlines of every species, then each of them will suffer ... and ultimately end."

"Surely not vampires though. Seeing as we don't *need* to procreate to recreate." Malachi silently implores me to confirm his statement.

"Whilst that is true, there will come a day when the last bloodborne vampire will die, and then so will the species."

"So how does that explain Ophelia?" Xavier lifts his head from her shoulder. "How is she here if there are no elementai left?"

How to even begin to explain Ophelia Hart? It is an impossible task. My eyes fix on hers once again. "She is ..." I wet my lips, searching for the right word. She is so many things. "An anomaly."

Her cheeks flush pink. "I guess I've been called worse."

"But why?" Malachi screws his eyes closed and shakes his head like this is all too much to comprehend. "I mean how can she be an anomaly? How is that possible?"

"There is an ancient bloodline which still carries traces of the elementai gene. Theoretically, it is possible for a witch or even a human to give birth to an elementai, but only if they carry a trace of the bloodline and their mate is incredibly powerful."

"So my parents were powerful?" Ophelia's eyes fill with tears.

"At least one of them was."

"So why did they ...? What happened to them?" she whispers.

I shake my head. "That I do not know. But I cannot imagine that they did not do everything in their power to protect you."

Axl cuts in before she can respond to that. "So Ophelia is the only being in the entire world capable of carrying a vampire baby?"

Ophelia gasps, and it is unnecessary to tune into her thoughts for me to know that she is considering the potential consequences of that for the first time. Her heart rate doubles, and she sinks her fingernails into Xavier's forearm.

I fervently wish that I could ease the anxiety snaking its way through her body, but there is no denying the truth any longer. "Yes. Which is why it is absolutely imperative that nobody discovers who or what you are, Ophelia. There are powerful vampires who, if they found out what you are, would think nothing of ..."

Her blue eyes widen with horror, and I cannot bring myself to finish the sentence that would conjure the image of anyone defiling her in such a way.

Then her hand flies to her stomach, and her regret crashes over us both. "But *you* could? Oh my god, we didn't use any protection." Her voice is little more than a whisper.

I hold out my hand and beckon her to me, and I am unable to stop my heart from swelling when, without hesitation, she climbs out of Xavier's embrace and comes to me. I pull her onto my lap. "We have no need for protection," I assure her. "I know when you are ovulating."

She blinks. "But how?"

I run my nose over her hair, and her sweet candy-scented shampoo floods my senses. "Your scent changes."

The blush on her cheeks races down her neck. "Oh. So you'd never ... right?"

"Not without your consent, little one."

She murmurs with relief and nestles herself against my chest. Her trust in me—which I have done little to earn—is both humbling and exhilarating at the same time.

"Is that why turned vampires are forbidden from turning their own?" Malachi asks, his brow still furrowed. He is trying to process all he has learned these past few minutes, which is perfectly understandable. It is a lot.

"Yes. That was another legacy of the aftermath. The rights of turned vampires were stripped even further to prevent another uprising. This ensured that power remains only with a select few."

Ophelia wriggles on my lap. "But isn't that counterproductive? All turned vampires are beholden to their sire, right? So the power remains with the sire anyway?"

"Imagine ripples on a pond," I begin, channeling my inherent desire to educate. "All it takes is for one bloodborne vampire to decide to turn against his kind and allow his sireds to spawn armies of their own. All in service to him. But whilst all turned vampires are bound to the original sire of their bloodline, their strongest allegiance is always to their immediate sire. So the further one gets from the original bloodborne vampire, the thinner that bond becomes. It is believed that during the time of the elementai genocides, vampires were being turned in such great numbers that the bonds became so weak that they broke entirely.

"So if you think of that pond, those ripples begin to grow and distort exponentially, turning into waves and taking up all of the pond's surface. In the right circumstances, it would not take long for chaos to ensue."

"Wouldn't more vampires be a good thing?" Xavier leans forward, his dark-blue eyes alight with a fascination that I so rarely see in him.

"Not necessarily. It is a fine balance to ensure our species thrives. Too few of us and we risk extinction. But the same is true if we grow too great in number. Nature keeps all species in balance for this very reason. If it did not, then the food chain would simply stop working. Whilst humans are doing their best to usurp this carefully constructed ecosystem, vampires are far more aware of the delicate balance of life."

"But who enforces these laws though?" Ophelia lifts her head from my chest and blinks up at me. Having her in my arms like this feels warm and familiar and so very right.

"The four vampire houses separated once more after the genocide, but they are all bound by ancient vampire law. No matter our differences, we abide by these laws to ensure the ongoing survival of our species. The four heads of the houses along with their most trusted advisers are responsible for enforcing any new laws."

"So who is the head of your house?" she asks. "House Drakos?"

"My father."

Ophelia blinks. "Your father?"

"You seem surprised that I have one."

She shrugs, chewing on her lip. "Surprised he's still alive, I guess. You've never spoken of him is all. I assumed you had no family left."

I suppose I have never spoken of him or my brother with her. After all, this is so new, and I have spoken to her so very little. It should come as no surprise that I did not share with her details of my life that I have barely spoken of to the three vampires I have lived with for hundreds of years. "I have a brother also."

Her eyes widen, and she looks from me to the guys, then back at me.

"Giorgios," Malachi says.

"Yeah, we met him. But why have we never met your father?" Xavier asks, his voice dripping with suspicion.

"Because I do not wish for you to." My tone makes it clear that I have no intention of discussing this issue further, but I can tell by Xavier's expression—I would recognize that stubborn tilt of his jaw from a mile away—that he has no plan to drop it.

"Because you're ashamed of us, right?" he demands, proving my instincts right.

I suppress both my frustration and annoyance even as they prickle beneath my skin. "Because he would tear your head off your shoulders if you gave him even half of the attitude you give me."

Xavier's right eye twitches as he glares at me.

Do not mistake my behavior toward the girl as any sign of weakness, Xavier, I warn him and him alone.

He cracks his neck. *Yes sir!*

Unaware of our private conversation, Malachi chimes in. "Is he a danger to Ophelia?"

I swallow the knot of anxiety that rolls up my throat, but Malachi's question saves Xavier from my wrath. "Yes." I cup her chin in my hand and tilt her head back until her sparkling blue eyes are fixed on my face. "Where you are concerned, he is the most dangerous creature that exists."

"Why?"

"Because he would lock you in a cage and breed you for the next three millennia. He would exploit your power for his own ends, Ophelia. Do you understand me?"

She nods, her lip caught between her teeth. And now all I can think about is burying myself so deep inside her that I will not have to think of anything but her. I stand with her in my arms, and the immediate despair that radiates from my boys makes me pause for a second. Their fear that I will keep her for

23

myself is so palpable I can taste it in the air. And I am so cruel I could do that to them without a moment's hesitation.

Or could I?

I have never been the kind of father they deserve, but perhaps that is because I failed to be even a halfway decent father to my own son. If I had been better, then maybe he would not have betrayed his own blood so cruelly. But regardless of any of that, it is not something I could do to Ophelia. She has already bonded to them, and that means she needs them as much as they need her.

I crush her to my chest and walk toward the door. "Ophelia is staying with me tonight." I have to force out the next words. "But that does not change what you all have."

A current of relief runs through the room like an electric charge, but it is the smile on Ophelia's face as she wraps her arms around my neck that makes the sacrifice of agreeing to share her with them worthwhile.

FOUR
OPHELIA

"Your skin is softer than silk, little one." Alexandros's warm breath dusts over my stomach as he peels off my panties, making goosebumps break out all over my flesh. He presses a soft kiss on my abdomen before he stands tall and towers over me, his dark eyes ablaze with heat and desire.

My legs tremble with anticipation, and his mouth twitches with the hint of a smile. "I am not undressing you for any reason other than I do not allow the wearing of clothes in my bed, Ophelia."

"Oh." My bottom lip juts out before I can stop it. It felt so good to be close to him earlier in his office. Was incredible to be worshipped by him. Because that's what it was—worship. At least that's what it felt like. Yet I already feel his mind closed off to me. Not entirely, but much more than it was before. When he was biting me, when he was inside me, it was like he couldn't stop our link even though I sensed he wanted to. He couldn't keep me out. Having that kind of connection with him made me feel special.

He runs the pad of his thumb over my bottom lip, tugging it down and opening my mouth. "I do worship you. And I know how good it felt. But there will be plenty of time for all of that. Right now, you need to sleep."

How did he know ... "Can you read my mind?" I blurt out.

He nods. "Yes."

Well, that's terrifying. "But how? I thought it was only when I spoke to you."

He dips his head and runs his nose over my jawline, inhaling deeply. "Your scent is intoxicating and addictive, Ophelia." The low growl that comes out of him makes my head spin. How is this my life? "I told you earlier that my power is in my mind."

I nod, recalling how Malachi and Xavier told me that the professor could read minds, I just didn't think he was *this* good at it. "So will you always be able to do that? I mean, can I never have any privacy?"

He hums softly, his fingers trailing over my hipbones before he grabs me roughly and pulls me forward, pressing me flush against his chest. "You will learn to block me out, and I will not always want to be inside your head. But when you are naked and alone with me, yes, I will be inside there."

"Oh."

He arches an eyebrow. "And quite often, inside *you*." He gives me a swat on the ass. "Now get into bed."

I press my lips together to stop my giggle. He's so stern and serious, and I haven't figured out how to act around him yet. For some strange reason, I enjoy him telling me what to do, so I do as he asks. He watches me crawl beneath the covers and pull them up to my chin, then he unfastens a button on his shirt. And now it's my turn to watch. The only part of his body I've seen are his forearms, his head, and obviously his huge ... I cough as my cheeks flush with heat at the memory of seeing him in his office earlier.

He moves swiftly, making quick work of his clothes, and I take in every beautiful inch of his skin. His broad chest, peppered with a faint dusting of dark hair. The pale scars that snake around the left side of his torso, twisting and curling into a point beneath his ribs. I tilt my head and study the marks, wondering how he could have gotten them when vampires heal too quickly to scar.

"Silver can mark a vampire."

Of course, the mind reading. "It can?"

He unbuckles his belt. "If used repeatedly, yes. It is why the ink in Malachi's tattoos is laced with silver."

"Or his body would simply heal and force out the ink?"

"You are a very quick study, Ophelia Hart." He pulls off his belt, and the sound of the leather sliding against the fabric sends a shiver up my spine. An image of me bent over his desk with my panties halfway down my thighs sears itself into my brain. What the ...?

He arches a dark eyebrow. "So you would like to be spanked? I am certain we can arrange that."

"N-no. I don't want to be spanked," I protest, and another image of him punishing me with his belt while I moan loudly comes into focus. I clamp my thighs together because wow, that is hot.

He slides his pants down his thighs—his incredibly muscular, almost-wider-than-my-waist thighs. "It seems like you do."

"I do not. I have no idea where that came from."

He takes off the rest of his clothes along with his shoes and places them neatly on a chair at the foot of the bed. When he stands tall again, I stare at his naked body, mouth hanging open as I drink in the sight of him. He looks like he was carved from marble. His lips curve in the faintest hint of a smirk. "But you enjoyed the visuals, did you not?"

Now my mouth hangs open for a different reason. "You did that? You put those images in my head? How do you do that?"

He moves quickly, sliding beneath the covers before I've even finished speaking. "I can do a lot of things, agápi mou." He pulls me close, nestling my body against his solid form, and without an ounce of resistance, I curl into him like this is the most natural thing in the world.

"I don't like not being able to tell the difference between my own thoughts and the ones you put there," I admit.

He smooths my hair back with his palm and cradles the back of my head. "Your thoughts are your own. I simply evoked an image that you were already considering in that beautiful mind of yours."

"I wasn't imagining you spanking me with your belt until you made me think of it."

Placing his pointer finger beneath my chin, he tips my head back. "If you listened to your own body as closely as I do, Ophelia, you would know that is not true."

He seriously thinks he knows my body better than I do? I roll my eyes, and he narrows his. "You gasped when I took off my belt. Your heart rate increased in that exact moment." He brushes the pad of his thumb over my lip. "I was unable to see the sparkling blue of your eyes because your pupils were so dilated. You do know why your pupils dilate?"

Adrenaline. Fear. Desire. "Of course I do. And I'll remind you that I was watching you undress at the time."

He hums. "Even if I discount the rest of your body language, the increase of blood flow, right here." He slips his hand between my thighs and presses on my clit, sending a shockwave of pleasure ricocheting through my body. "Had already betrayed you. Blood never lies."

Damn! I guess there's no denying that. "How am I ever going to win with you?"

He shakes his head, his eyes twinkling with amusement. "You cannot, little one. I suggest you make your peace with that now."

"So unfair." A wave of exhaustion washes over me, and I rest my head on his chest. "Wait until I figure out how to use these powers, and I might just win occasionally."

"You will win in all the ways that matter, Ophelia." The deep timbre of his voice is so soothing that my eyes flutter closed. Who is this man, and what has he done with Professor Drakos?

Sleep threatens to claim me, and then I remember ... "Why didn't you tell them about Lucian?" I ask in a whisper, not trusting that I'm capable yet of speaking through our bond in such a way that the boys won't hear me.

His muscles tense, but he goes on gently stroking my hair. "You can speak through our bond. Focus on speaking to me, and the boys will not hear."

Why? I ask again.

Because I did not know how to tell them of a betrayal so profound that it changed the essence of my being. A pain so unfathomable and agonizing that the only way to live through it is to bury it so deeply that it can never be found.

I feel his pain. His anger. His betrayal. It threatens to swallow me whole. *I found it.*

I know.

A tear leaks from the corner of my eye. *Was I not supposed to?*

His weary sigh ruffles my hair, but he bands his arms tightly around me and rests his lips on the top of my head. It makes me feel like I'm wrapped in a safe little cocoon where nobody can hurt me. Nobody can hurt us. *I knew it was a risk, but no, you were not supposed to learn of Lucian. Very few people know of his existence.*

I'm sorry. I couldn't help it.

I know, agápi mou. Your powers are greater than I anticipated.

My powers? I don't feel them right now. The lightning that raced through my body earlier seems to have all but dissipated. Perhaps it was a fluke? Perhaps I am not powerful at all.

It was no fluke, Ophelia. But you burned up a lot of energy. You need rest, that is all, he says.

I feel so conflicted. My insides are churning. *So do I have to keep this secret from the boys? What if I can't? I don't want to lie to them, but I don't want to betray your trust either.*

You already kept it from them earlier. You did not reveal that I had a son, even though I heard you think about him. Whether that was intentional or not, you were able to not communicate that thought to them.

I don't know if it was intentional or not either, I admit, feeling so out of my depth that I'm afraid I'll never get a handle on any of this. I yawn loudly.

I would ask that you keep it to yourself for the time being. We will tell them when the time is right.

But what if I—

He cuts me off with a kiss—the kind that has me forgetting what day of the week it is. *If you reveal it unintentionally, Ophelia, then I will not hold you responsible. I know I ask a great deal of you.*

I run my fingers through his thick hair. My brain is clouded with exhaustion, but my body is awakening, sizzling with electricity as his tongue explores my mouth. My limbs instinctively wrap around him. But much too soon, he pulls back and leaves me panting. Wanting more. "Rest now."

I don't have the mental energy to argue with him, so I lay my head on his chest once more and allow sleep to claim me. And I dream of monsters and faces cloaked in shadow that speak to me of fire and blood.

FIVE

MALACHI

orning, sweet girl. Are you awake yet?

Yes, she says in reply. Even the voice in her head is seductive, and I close my eyes and imagine her warm breath on my face. Since Ophelia started living at the house with us, we have all spent the night in the same bed, usually Axl's, unwilling to be parted from her any longer than necessary. Waking up to her sweet smile and her soft little body curled up against mine makes sleeping a much more pleasant activity than it's ever been before. And that only makes the absence of her in our bed this morning all the more acute.

Meet me in the kitchen? she adds.

I'm there. I throw back the covers and jump out of bed,

leaving Xavier snoring softly and Axl grumbling quietly in his sleep. I take the stairs two at a time, and a few seconds later, I'm in the kitchen waiting for her.

I stare at the door that leads to Alexandros's quarters, the part of the house that contains his bedroom and study, my breath held in anticipation as I wait for her to walk through it.

There's no escaping the fact that the professor's choice to bond with her has changed all our lives, and I'm desperate to know exactly how much. My arms physically ache with the need to hold her. I crack my neck as the seconds seem to stretch on like minutes. Finally, the handle turns and the door opens, and she's standing there with her pink messy hair and that beautiful fucking smile on her face. My breath stalls in my lungs, but I'm across the room before she can blink, pulling her into my arms and crushing her to my chest as I bury my face in her hair.

"Morning," she says, laughing.

I nuzzle her neck, letting her scent flood my senses. "Morning, baby."

Snaking her arms around my neck, she tips her head back and allows me better access to her throat. Her submissiveness makes both my fangs and my dick ache to be inside her.

Her stomach growls, and she giggles. "I'm really hungry."

I hum, running my nose along the column of her neck. "Me too."

"For food," she whispers.

I drag my teeth over the pulse fluttering in her throat. "Yeah, me too."

She moans, pressing her body into mine. "I need to eat first."

I grab a handful of her ass and squeeze. "I know. I'll make you some waffles."

She licks her lips. "Mmm. Waffles."

33

I give her ass a hard slap and untangle myself from her embrace, then I head to the fridge to grab the milk before grabbing the rest of the ingredients. Our pantry has never been as well stocked as it is these days. While we all enjoy human food, it's not a necessity for us. However, keeping our elementai properly fed and sustained is our number one priority, given how much we all enjoy fucking her—not to mention feeding on her. She perches herself on a stool at the counter and rests her chin on her hand while she watches me mix the batter.

I catch her eye and grin. "So, you want to talk a little more about last night?"

She squeals, and I can only imagine how many billions of questions must be racing through my curious girl's head. "Yes, so much! But I don't even know where to start."

I shrug. "Start wherever you like, baby."

She presses her lips together, and her brows pinch with a cute-as-fuck frown. "Did you feel any of it? I mean, it was intense."

"I ... no. We all felt something. Like a shift in you maybe. A surge of power. But it was strange. Detached. Like it was you and not you at the same time."

She nods. "The professor blocked you all."

"He does that. I guess it's a lot to have so many people in your head all the time. And bonding is ..." I suck on my top lip.

"Bonding is?" she probes.

"It's special. Intimate. At least it should be. I understand why he wanted you to himself for that."

Her cheeks flush bright pink. "It was special," she whispers.

I stop whisking the batter and give her my full attention. "How did it feel? Bonding with him?"

"Like with you and Axl and Xavier, only a little more ..." She narrows her eyes, deep in thought. "Intense?"

I nod. "That makes sense. He's one of the most powerful vampires in existence."

"Was being turned by him like that?"

I shake my head. "Being bitten is pleasurable. And the more powerful the vampire, the more intoxicating the bite. But being turned is painful. Not something I'd ever want you to go through."

"How painful?"

Painful is an understatement. Even the memory of it makes my knees wobble. "Like being burned up from the inside out and then torn apart before being stitched back together piece by piece."

She shudders. "Ouch."

"Yeah. Not everyone survives it. That's why we have the Trials, to identify the strongest."

"Would you do it again? Knowing what you do now?"

I have asked myself that same question a million times in the past hundred years, and the answer has changed depending on my mood. But right here with her, there is only one right answer, and I feel it in every fiber of my being. "Yes. Without a doubt."

She smiles again, her blue eyes sparkling.

"You need to stop looking at me like that if you want to eat your breakfast before I eat mine, sweet girl."

She giggles and rolls her eyes, and I go back to mixing the batter. She watches me in silence for a few moments before she speaks again, her voice quiet and unsure. "The power was intoxicating, Malachi." She worries her bottom lip. "And I *felt* so much. Like it was about to overwhelm me, and the more I felt, the harder it was to control."

"That makes sense. An elementai's powers are rooted in their emotions."

She nods, and a tear runs down her cheek. "I think it was

feeling his pain that unlocked it. It was like this overwhelming rush. Then ..." Her slender throat works as she swallows. "I felt like I was ..." Her eyes widen. "Invincible. I know that sounds ridiculous, but it was like nothing I've ever experienced. I felt some of the professor's power, and that was exhilarating, and then ..." She sucks in a deep breath. "It was like a fire lighting me up from the inside, but in a good way, you know? It was raw, untamed power. Like it could eat me alive if I let it." Her shiver is laced with fear. And I understand because I feel it too. This changes everything for all of us. And given what the professor told us about elementai, our girl is a target for every bloodborne vampire walking this earth. And *that* scares the living shit out of me.

But I have faith in her strength. Because regardless of her power, she is strong. This tiny pink-haired girl might be the most kindhearted soul I've ever met in my life, but she has a fierceness about her that cannot be denied. "How did you control it?"

"Alexandros told me to focus on my light, and I dunno." She shrugs. "I just instinctively knew what he meant. And so I closed my eyes, and there was this light inside me. I looked into the heart of it and ..." She wrinkles her nose. "Do I sound crazy?"

How could she possibly think that? "I'm a vampire, baby. Standing here in my boxers with a raging boner while I make my elementai girlfriend waffles. Nothing you say could sound crazy to me."

She giggles. "Well, channeling my focus into the light somehow enabled me to isolate my emotions and control the power."

I wink at her. "Sounds like you did good."

She chews on her lip again, worry furrowing her brow.

I round the counter and wrap my arms around her, and she

leans into my chest, nuzzling her cheek against my bare skin. I rest my lips on the top of her head. "It will all be okay."

"I set the professor's office on fire," she whispers.

A laugh bubbles out of me. "You did?"

She laughs too. "Yeah."

I brush her hair back behind her ears. "Was he mad?"

"No. Not even a little."

"You're kind of impossible to get mad at, sweet girl." I kiss her forehead, and the thought of what they were probably doing when that happened has my cock aching again. I glance at the kitchen counter and lick my lips. Yeah, I gotta eat right now. Before I can lift her onto the worktop and enjoy my girl, the door opens.

"You left without waking me," Alexandros says gruffly, running a hand through his thick hair.

She flutters her eyelashes at him. "I didn't want to disturb you."

He grunts and switches on the coffee machine. "Your lessons will start today."

She blinks. "Lessons?"

He's prevented from answering by Axl and Xavier bursting into the room. They make a beeline for our girl, and I let her go so they can hug her. The tension visibly lifts from both of them as soon as they touch her. No matter what happened between her and the professor last night, what we have with her hasn't changed. She needs us as much as we need her, and I know his bond with her wouldn't allow him to deny her that, no matter how badly he might want to.

Xavier grabs her jaw and tilts her head before giving her a long, deep kiss. Then Axl pushes him out of the way and does the same. And now I just want to take her to bed and run my tongue over every single inch of her.

Alexandros clears his throat. "Lessons, Ophelia." His voice is a low command that ensures everyone's attention is now firmly on him.

She wrinkles her cute little nose. "Like my classes? Yeah, I know."

"No." He shakes his head. "Not classes. Lessons."

Her bottom lip juts out, and she plonks herself back on her stool at the island. "What kind of lessons?"

"To learn how to control your power." A smile lights up her face, but before she can speak, Alexandros goes on. "To control your mind. To shield yourself from other beings who would try to manipulate you. To fight. To—"

"To fight?" She barks out a laugh.

My shoulders tense at the thought of my girl having to fight anyone. I will tear out the throat of any being who even tries to touch her. And the thought of anyone causing her harm ... It steals my next breath.

Alexandros scowls. "Yes, fight. Lessons will start this morning."

She shakes her head. "I can't. I have class this morning."

Axl and Xavier look as anxious as I feel.

"Classes are no longer a priority," the professor replies dismissively.

She huffs indignantly. So feisty for someone who's so submissive with her body. "They're a priority for me. I need my degree. I need to—"

Alexandros slams his fist onto the counter. "Keeping the entire world from finding out what and who you are is your priority, Ophelia."

Can't we let her be a regular person for just a little while longer? I plead with him privately.

At least I thought it was private until Ophelia gives me a sharp nudge in the ribs with her elbow. "Hey, don't talk about me like I'm not here!"

I blink at the professor. "How did she ...? I only spoke to you."

Alexandros frowns, his eyes narrowed on Ophelia. Then he pinches the bridge of his nose. "Ophelia is capable of hearing you in my head. Unless I actively tune her out."

Xavier laughs darkly, but Axl gasps. "Ophelia is in *your* head? How the fuck?"

Ophelia's cheeks flush pink. "I didn't mean to be. I just heard it."

Alexandros sighs, pressing his palms on the kitchen counter. "Ophelia's power is already greater than I anticipated. I expect you will not be able to block her out for much longer no matter how hard you try."

Xavier slides an arm around her waist and presses his teeth against her bare shoulder, leaving the imprint of his bite behind. "Fine by me, Cupcake."

Alexandros scrubs a hand over his face. "And to answer your question, Malachi, no. There is no time to waste." He directs all his attention to Ophelia now. "Learning to control your power is the key to keeping you safe. That is your only priority. You have no idea of the importance of what happened last night."

She sucks in a raspy breath that makes her tits heave against the thin fabric of her tank top. Then she shakes her head, and Alexandros's eyes darken at her willful display of defiance. "That's not gonna work for me. I came to college to get my psychology degree. I'm going to be a social worker." His jaw tics as he glares at her. "So my actual classes will take priority," she finishes with a triumphant smile.

Axl swallows nervously. Xavier wraps a protective arm around our girl, and I press myself against her back. Alexandros's eyes remain firmly on her, as dark and dangerous as I have ever seen them.

He rolls his neck, and the vein in his temple throbs. He takes a few seconds before he speaks. "Once the vampire world learns of who you are, it will take more than the four of us to protect you, Ophelia. This is not a request." He glances between Axl, Xavier, and me, and I offer him a reluctant nod of agreement because as much as I want him to be wrong, I know that he's not.

"But I—"

"Ophelia!" The way he roars her name has the windows shaking. He stalks around the island, his entire body seeming to vibrate with rage. Our girl simply tips her chin up and folds her arms over her chest like she's not even the slightest bit intimidated by him. Like she has no idea who the fuck he is and the things he's capable of.

He cups her chin in his hand, turning her head so she's looking up at his scowling face. "This is much bigger than you can imagine. Bigger than you. Than us. You are not the same person you were yesterday, and that means your life is no longer the one it was. Forget your past dreams, Ophelia, because they are gone."

I feel her heart breaking, and it makes me want to throw my arms around her and protect her from it all. But she knows he's right, even if she doesn't want to admit it yet. There is no arguing with the graveness of his tone or the reality of what he's told us.

She tries anyway. "But—"

He squeezes her jaw tighter, cutting off the retort on her lips. "*You* are the most powerful being in this room, Ophelia. Quite possibly the entire world." Her lip quivers. Axl and Xavier glance at me, and I widen my eyes, indicating that I didn't know that either. "There is no escaping that. And allowing you to think for another moment that you have any chance of even a semblance of a normal life, a life where you will become the social worker you dreamed of being, would not only be cruel, it would also be a waste of precious time that we do not have."

A shiver of fear runs through her and into the rest of us. "Can't we just put it back?" she asks, her voice a mere whisper.

Alexandros blinks. *"Put it back?"*

"My power? Wherever it came from. I don't want it. I want to go back to being just regular me."

His lip curls, baring his teeth, and her entire body trembles. Pretty sure my own knees want to give out on me too. "You do not *want it*?" He repeats her words back to her, his tone dripping with incredulity.

She swallows. Her heart rate doubles, but she holds his gaze. "I don't."

"You are the most powerful being born in over two thousand years, and you do not want it?"

She jumps off the stool and stands toe-to-toe with him, jaw tilted defiantly as she glares up into his face. "Will you stop saying that? I am not the most powerful anything. I am Ophelia Hart. Nobody. Nothing." A tear runs down her cheek, and she swats it away. "I don't want any of this."

His scowl deepens. "You asked for this!"

"I did not," she croaks.

The pained expression on his face causes a physical ache in my chest. I've never seen him so vulnerable. So open to being hurt. "You asked me to show you who you are. You begged me, Ophelia." His voice cracks on her name.

She shakes her head. "I didn't ask for this."

His eyes darken, and the rare glimpse of vulnerability we all just witnessed is already long gone, hidden behind the mask once more. "Regardless, it is a burden we all carry now." His tone is as cold and detached as his demeanor.

A sob heaves in her throat, and it makes my chest ache. She opens her mouth, but this time she doesn't have a snappy retort for him. Instead, she rushes from the room. I fight the instinct to run straight after her and allow her a moment to deal with the gravity of everything she's learned.

"She's just scared," Axl says, voicing what the three of us are thinking.

"There is no time to be scared," Alexandros barks back.

Xavier runs a hand through his thick hair. "She just found out she's some kind of superhuman powerhouse who's catnip to every single vampire on the planet. Give her a break."

I half expect Alexandros to tear Xavier's throat out, or at least shoot him one of his don't-you-ever-fucking-speak-to-me-like-that glares, but he does neither. Instead, he turns his attention to the doorway she walked out of. "She has much to learn. Each of you has something to teach her. Her lessons *will* start today."

We all agree, and he jerks his head toward the door. "Go."

Xavier and Axl obey immediately, but I hang back. There's an anxious feeling churning deep in my gut, and I know he knows it too. "It will be okay, right? We can protect her? We can teach her to control her powers, and it will be okay?"

He stares at Axl's and Xavier's retreating backs.

"It will, right?" I ask again.

He turns to face me and rests his hand on the back of my neck. "Go make sure she is okay."

Without argument, I do as he says. If all the years I've spent watching Xavier clash against him have taught me anything, it's that Alexandros Drakos doesn't entertain insubordination lightly.

SIX

XAVIER

Ophelia's cheeks are flaming with indignation. I sit on the bed beside her, and she swats the tears from her eyes and blinks at me. "Sorry if I was an asshat."

I shake my head. "You weren't. You're dealing with some real big fucking changes, Cupcake. You're entitled to throw a hissy fit if you like."

She opens her mouth to protest, but I wink at her, and she rewards me with her sweet-as-apple-fucking-pie smile. "So you're bonded with the professor now too, huh?"

"Yeah. You're not mad, are you?"

Axl flops down on the other side of her. "He's our sire, princess. Why would we be mad?"

I grab her hand and trace my fingertips over her wrist in a circle. "Yeah, it completes our little unit perfectly."

Right on cue, the other member of our unit walks into the room. "You okay, sweet girl?"

She bites down on her juicy bottom lip. "Yeah."

Damn, now I want to bite her. It's been too long already. "Well, I'm not," I say with a dramatic sigh.

She blinks at me. "Why not?"

I can see Malachi and Axl grinning at me in my peripheral vision. They know where this is headed. The same place ninety-nine percent of all interactions on a bed with Ophelia end. I trail my fingertips over her cheek and down her neck, making her shiver. "Because I haven't tasted my little cupcake in ..." I check my watch. "About twenty-four hours now, I reckon."

She rolls her eyes, and my cock twitches. Love my feisty little elementai. "I know you did not just do that, Ophelia Hart." I leap on top of her and pin her hands to her sides while dragging my lips across all the exposed skin of her neck and chest.

She giggles, squirming beneath me, and a few seconds later, Malachi and Axl are lying beside us.

"Clothes need to go." Axl grabs the hem of her T-shirt. I release her arms and allow him to pull the offending item over her head while Malachi takes care of her panties. Not two seconds later, our girl is naked and I have her thighs spread open, my mouth tantalizingly close to her dripping center. The fact that some of Alexandros's cum will also be seeping out of her only makes me more ravenous.

I lick the length of her wet slit, groaning when I taste him on her too. "Fuck me, Cupcake. I hope you hydrated after the professor fucked you because I'm about to drink your cunt dry."

She pants out my name, but her sexy little sounds are cut off by Axl and Malachi. They take turns claiming her mouth while I lick and suck on her deliciously sensitive skin. Whimpers roll in her throat, her blood races through her veins, and my cock leaks with the need to be inside her.

If you make her come now, she is likely to set the room on fire or sink the entire house into a black hole. Alexandros's voice fills my head. *Which is why her lessons are imperative.*

A quick glance at the dejected looks on Axl's and Malachi's faces lets me know they heard him too. Ophelia, however, arches her back and presses her sweet pussy into my mouth, telling me she didn't. There's no way she wouldn't have some kind of smart-ass comeback for that.

I flick the tip of my tongue over her clit, and her needy whine has me feral with the need to sink my fangs into her.

Do not, Xavier! Alexandros's warning rings loud and unmistakable. How the fuck am I supposed to stop now and leave my little cupcake all sad and horny?

I got this, buddy, Malachi tells me. "Didn't you tell me you set the professor's office on fire when he made you come, sweet girl?" he asks, running his fingertips over her abdomen.

A wave of embarrassment washes over her, and I push myself up onto my forearms and stare at her pretty face. Her cheeks are pinker than her hair. Axl goes on nuzzling her neck. "Y-yes." She presses her lips together.

Axl laughs darkly. "Naughty princess."

"I guess we should stop until you can control your power, huh?" I ask, arching one eyebrow.

Her eyes blow wide at the realization of what that means. "I can ..." She presses her lips together. "I can try to control it."

Malachi presses a kiss on her temple. "But what if you can't?"

Her eyes fill with tears. "Was this his idea? To get me to agree to his ridiculous lessons?"

"No." I shake my head. "And believe me, I am as butthurt about not making you come as you are. But he *is* right."

Axl hums his agreement and finally lifts his head from her neck. "If you truly are an elementai and are as powerful as Alexandros says you are, then learning to control your power is the most important thing there is. We can't risk bringing unnecessary attention to you."

A tear rolls down her cheek, and she swats it away. "This feels like I'm being punished for something I have no control over."

Axl trails his fingertips over her jawline. "We would never cause you unnecessary harm, Ophelia. You know this."

I nod my agreement. "And your lack of fear, while admirable, is gonna get us all in a fuckload of trouble. Do you understand what you are? How every bloodborne vampire on this earth would try to take you from us if they discovered you?"

Now she's hurting, and I feel her pain as acutely as my own. "I'm sorry. I've been so selfish. I didn't think of how it would affect you. If they hurt you ..." She chokes on a sob.

She truly has no idea how high the stakes are for us. "Losing you would be the worst kind of pain imaginable, Cupcake. That's all we're worried about."

Tears stream down her cheeks now. "Losing any of you would kill me. I'm sorry that I'm putting you all in danger."

"No," Malachi says. "*You* are not putting anyone in danger, sweet girl. Alexandros warned us what it would mean if we bonded with you, and we all chose this for ourselves. The fact that others will try to take you from us is not on you. Do not for a single second pick up that burden, because it is not yours."

"But doing what I can to keep us all safe is mine though." She sniffs. "And that means doing everything I can to control my powers."

I'm never one to follow the rules or do what's expected of me, but this—this is too fucking important to fuck up. The three of us murmur our agreement, reluctant though it may be.

She wipes her cheeks with the back of her hand and offers us a faint smile. "Damn Alexandros. Is he ever wrong about anything?"

I shake my head. "Nope."

"Better get used to it, baby." Malachi grins at her.

I suck in a deep breath, hoping for some relief for my aching cock and fangs but find none. "I guess we'd better wrap this up."

"No." She runs her fingers through my hair. "I still want to feel close to you all. I need to."

I flash her a wicked grin. It's so sweet that she thought not letting her come meant that we wouldn't be. "Oh, we can torture you by fucking you and not letting you come, but we have time for that later."

"No." She shakes her head again. "I mean I need you to bite me."

Axl runs his nose along her jawline. "I think you're a little too worked up already to let us bite you and it not set you off, princess."

"So, make it hurt," she pleads.

Malachi growls. "No, baby."

Oh, what I wouldn't give to sink my fangs into her sweet flesh right now. "You know we can't, Cupcake."

Her perfect tits heave as she sucks in a rasping breath. "But you can if I want it. You told me that, remember?"

"If we make it hurt, it will *hurt*, Ophelia," Axl warns her.

"I know, but I need it. I need all of you. I feel different, and I need you to be part of it, part of the new me. I need to still be a part of you all." She sniffs again, tears welling in her eyes once more.

She speaks the truth. Her blood races through her veins, calling to me, to each of us. My fangs throb with pulsing need.

But it's Malachi who gives in first. "Okay. If that's what you need. But if it hurts too much ..."

She places her free hand on his cheek. "If it hurts too much, you'll know."

My brothers and I share a quick look, and that is all the additional permission we need. Through our connection, I feel Axl's teeth sink into her throat and Malachi's into the crease of her forearm at the same time I bite down on the creamy skin of her thigh. Her moan is full of pleasure, and the bed starts to rattle.

She asked you to make it hurt. The professor's voice floods my thoughts once more.

And so I do. I clamp my jaws into her flesh, and the trickle of blood becomes a strong, steady flow, coating my tongue and sliding down my throat, lighting up my body with her power. She tastes the same. Her power has always been in her blood, but it's stronger now, more potent in its effect on me. My head spins. My heart races so hard that it might beat out of my chest. Malachi and Axl feel it too. She cries out in pain, but she writhes in part ecstasy as we give her what she needs. Enough to take the edge off the euphoria that threatens to overwhelm her.

The walls shake and the ground vibrates.

"I am!" she shouts.

Who are you yelling at, baby? Malachi asks.

"The professor!" she pants.

And then I hear him in her head, guiding her to find her light and control her emotions. It seems that the pain taps into her power even more than the pleasure. It occurs to me that I can never hear him in Malachi's or Axl's heads, so I shouldn't be able to hear him in hers, but I have no time to unravel what that means. We need to stop our girl from going supernova.

We all ease off a bit. The violent tremors that were wracking her body abate, and the walls stop shaking. And somehow, we find a balance between her pleasure and her pain that doesn't send her powers into overdrive. I suck softly, letting her taste flood my entire being, and like each new time I feed from her, our connection grows deeper and more profound. And when she's given enough, we all stop and stare at the powerful creature lying in our bed, willing to give everything of herself to us, just as we are to her.

~

LEAVING Axl and Malachi to help a temporarily weakened Ophelia get showered and dressed, I head back to the kitchen. She didn't need all three of us, and her naked body in the shower is a little too much temptation for me. I haven't fucked her in two days, and I'm a man on the edge.

Alexandros sits at the breakfast table, nursing a cup of coffee and staring out the window with a scowl on his face.

I sit beside him, and he gives me his full attention. "She has agreed to the lessons, yes?"

I can't help but smirk. "Yep. Seems the prospect of not having any orgasms is a real motivator for our little cupcake. Who'd have guessed it?"

"You know that is not the true reason she is agreeing, Xavier." The way his eyes burn into mine makes heat coil at the base of my spine. Why is everything so goddamn tense between us? And if I didn't know better, I'd say that lately he's shown way more than his usual amount of contempt for me. "We are not all so driven by our basest desires as you are."

And there it is. He can't help himself from putting me in my place. But I shrug off his hurtful comment like I always do. "I guess not."

He sucks on his top lip, his gaze still locked on mine, his eyes blacker than the depths of hell. "She is agreeing because of how she feels about you all. The desire to not put any of you in danger is what truly drives her. Her inherent goodness is what will always drive her. She will always put others before herself. You must remember that."

I know she will, and that scares the fuck out of me. "Can we not train it out of her or something? You know, make her more like ..." I search for a better word than the one I was going to use but don't find one. "Us?"

He draws a deep breath through his nose. "I wish it were possible, but I fear it is not. There are many who have feared that elementai magic could be used for evil. The Skotádi even tried, and whilst evil can harness good magic, it remains inherently pure. It was why the Skotádi fell. Magic is never as powerful when it is used for a purpose it was never intended for."

I feel like I woke up in a whole new universe today. There are so many things I don't know, not just about our world, but also about this man sitting in front of me. I wonder if he was as cold to his real family as he is to us. Perhaps their deaths changed him into the man he is today. I can see how that kind of trauma would be life altering. I want to ask him so many things about who he was, who they were, but I suspect he wouldn't answer me.

"Who are the Skotádi?" I ask instead.

His eyes narrow in suspicion. "You have never shown an interest in this before."

While he might be right, I think it's pretty clear that we are now living in an entirely different reality. "I've never been bonded to the only elementai in existence before."

He nods, and I'm sure I see the faintest flicker of a smile on his lips, but I must be wrong because I can count on the fingers of one hand the number of times he has actually smiled at me. "You have heard me speak of the Order of Azezal, yes?"

I vaguely recall it, so I nod.

"They are the ..." He sucks on his teeth. "For want of a better explanation, observers. They are a group of immortal beings—"

"Like vampires?" We're the only immortal species I'm aware of.

"There are very few vampires amongst their number, but yes vampires, witches, demons, and wolves. They are granted immortality when they devote their lives to the Order."

"And they observe? Like just sit around and watch what happens?"

He tilts his head. "Their role is more than that. They are the keepers of secrets. Those responsible for ensuring that our history is never forgotten. Never lost. They are neither a force for good nor evil."

They sound redundant to me. "So what is the point of them?"

"Do not underestimate the power of knowledge, Xavier. It is the foundation of every civilization that has ever existed, and it is all protected by the Order."

I still don't get it, but philosophy and ancient history have never been my strong suits. "And the Skotádi?"

His jaw tics. "There were some members of the Order who thought that to simply observe was not enough. They wanted to act. To affect change. They believed that there was no point in having such immense power if it cannot be wielded."

"I kinda see their point."

He closes his eyes and takes a breath, and I sense the anger bubbling beneath his skin even if he does not permit me to feel it. I edge my chair back an inch, certain he's about to rip out my throat. But a few seconds later, he opens his eyes and appears his usual calm and unreadable self once more. "To wield great power is a burden not all are fit to carry, Xavier. Sometimes it is harder to do nothing than to act. Those who devoted their life to the Order did so knowing that they could not interfere. But there were members of the Order who grew tired of observing, and they broke off from the Order, forsaking their vows and using their powers for change."

"So, good or bad change?"

"I suppose it depends on your perspective. One man's enemy is another's friend. And at first, I do believe that they at least had honorable intentions. However, it is difficult to wield such unchecked power and not allow it to corrupt. Before long, the Skotádi—initially named such because they wanted to remain secret and act without fear of human detection—became synonymous with darkness for many other reasons."

"Skotádi means darkness in Greek, right?"

He tilts his head to the side. "You know this?"

I recall the number of times I sat in the back of his classroom just to listen to him teach. Engrossed in the way his passion for history changed his speech and his facial expressions. But I haven't done that for decades now. "I picked up a thing or two, I guess."

His brow furrows a little, but not from anger or annoyance for once. If I didn't know better, I'd say he was impressed.

"You remind me so much of someone I used to know, Xavier." His voice is thick, and his eyes are full of something new. Hurt? Longing?

"My girl definitely needs her waffles now," Malachi says as he enters the kitchen, and Alexandros drops his gaze from mine.

I swallow down my regret that our moment was interrupted and force a grin. "Yeah, I'm sure she does."

A second later, Axl walks into the room with Ophelia close behind him. She looks pale, but she has a sweet smile on her face. I pull her onto my lap and bury my face in her hair, inhaling the scent of her shampoo and letting her presence dispel all the negative thoughts swirling in my head.

Alexandros clears his throat. "Have you reconsidered the idea of lessons, Ophelia?"

"You already know I have."

"Good." His tone is stern, and I feel her hurt at his coldness. He can't bear to be vulnerable with any of us for longer than a moment. Like we would ever use it against him. We would all die for him in a fucking heartbeat, and he knows it.

Malachi passes Ophelia a plate of chopped strawberries and banana. "While you wait for your waffles, sweet girl."

She thanks him and pops a strawberry into her mouth. "So what do I do now? Stay here but don't attend classes? Wait for one of these crazy-ass vampires to come find me, and then what?"

Alexandros rests his chin on his hand and swipes his tongue over his bottom lip like he's deep in thought. Eventually, he sighs, and it's deep and weary. "Montridge is the safest place for you right now. The boys have ..." He pauses. "They have duties that they need to attend to, which they cannot simply abandon or too many questions will be asked. And we have allies here, and whilst I do not intend to burden them with the truth before it is absolutely necessary, the time will come when it will become so. For now, you will continue to attend classes as you wish. There is no reason to draw unnecessary attention by having you disappear from campus life."

Her face breaks into a wide smile. "Thank you." Then she purses her lips, and I can picture the millions of questions whizzing through her head. My curious little cupcake. Her eyes dart between Axl, Malachi, and me. "What exactly are your duties?"

"Huh?" Axl grunts.

"What do you guys actually do here? I mean, you obviously don't attend classes." She regards us with suspicion. "Well, except from when you accompany me just to annoy me." Her eyes twinkle with amusement. "So what do you actually do all day?"

Alexandros clears his throat. "They have duties beyond this college, Ophelia. Duties that involve the vampire pledges and ensuring they get the appropriate training to equip them for their chosen careers when they leave this institution."

Her nose wrinkles, and she shakes her head, confused.

Malachi drops a kiss on her head. "We teach them the rules of their trade. We coordinate their assignments from their future employers."

The way her face comes alive with fascination ... Fuck me, I adore her. I could sit with her and answer her questions all day every day and be completely content. Well, as long as we fucked in between, obviously. "What kind of employers?" she asks.

There's an uncomfortable pause, and I suspect that, like me, Axl and Malachi have no idea what we're allowed to tell her. Fortunately, Alexandros finally speaks. "There is no reason Ophelia should not be aware of all our secrets."

Her mouth drops open, and she glances between us all with undisguised glee. "Secrets?"

"We work with the kind of employers who don't recruit from regular colleges, princess," Axl explains. "The Cosa Nostra, the Bratva, the Yakuza, Colombian Cartels. Organized crime groups from every corner of the globe."

"And occasionally the government," Malachi adds with a wink.

"Who are the biggest criminals of all." I snort.

"Wow," Ophelia says. "I knew that Ruby Dragon had some pretty notorious alumni, but I didn't realize you actually trained criminals."

I rest my chin on her shoulder, inhaling the smell of her skin. Even her fruity body wash does little to mask her intoxicating natural scent. I have no idea how she doesn't have a trail of vampires following her around wherever she goes. The thought alone makes a possessive snarl tumble from my lips, and Ophelia strokes my hair. "I didn't mean to judge you. I wasn't. I guess it's kind of cool."

I nip her shoulder. "I know you didn't. I was just distracted, Cupcake. I wasn't growling at you."

Alexandros clears his throat. "But your training will take priority now, Ophelia. You will practice every day. Each of us will train you in a different subject."

She nods, and I don't miss the thrill of excitement that runs through her. He did make that sound kind of fun.

"Every day, Ophelia. Without fail. Understand?"

She bites on her juicy bottom lip and nods once more. "Every day."

While I know it's probably not what Alexandros has in mind, thoughts of all of the fun and filthy ways I may get to train my girl start to race through my head. This is going to be so much fucking fun.

Alexandros stares out the kitchen window, his white shirt straining against the muscles in his broad shoulders and his battered briefcase sitting on the counter beside him.

I chew on my bottom lip, wanting to speak to him, but I'm not sure where we stand. Last night, he was so open with me. So tender and sweet. He appears much more like his usual self this morning though.

"What is it, Ophelia?"

I roll my eyes. Of course he knows I'm standing here. I pluck at a stray thread on the hem of my tank top. "I-I have Greek history today."

He doesn't turn around. "I am well aware."

I don't know what I expected him to say, but I want him to say more than that. "So I guess I'll see you there?"

"If you are continuing with your studies, then yes, you will."

I hoist my backpack onto my shoulder.

"Your lessons will begin immediately after your last class of the day is over."

"With you?" I blink away a tear. How can he treat me so coldly when only a few hours ago I was sleeping in his bed? In his arms!

"We shall see." He drains the remains of his coffee. "You are going to be late for class."

I should ask him what's crawled up his ass this morning, but he's right—I will be late if I don't get moving. And despite everything I've learned in the last twenty-four hours, I wasn't kidding about wanting to finish my degree. We can figure it out. I've hidden my powers, albeit unconsciously, for the last nineteen years. What's another four?

So I leave him to his sour mood and walk out of the kitchen, shouting a goodbye to the boys as I reach the door. The three of them come running down the stairs and shower me with hugs and kisses and offer to walk me to class.

I'm unable to hold back my laugh, and I forget all about Alexandros's coldness as I squirm in Malachi's embrace and tell them I'll be fine walking alone.

I arch an eyebrow when they protest. "I'm the most powerful being on campus, remember?"

"You brought all of us to our knees, sweet girl." Malachi winks and gives me a kiss on the lips.

Xavier and Axl do the same, and then Xavier swats my ass. "Get to class, Cupcake."

~

"HEY, Ophelia. You want to grab some lunch?" I sling my backpack over my shoulder and search my memory for her name but come up empty. We've been in the same class all semester, but this is the first time she's spoken to me. "We're going to Henley's."

I blink at her. She's surrounded by a small group, three girls and a guy, and they all wait expectantly for my reply. Henley's is the most popular hangout for students in Havenwood, and I've never been invited there by anyone other than the guys. "Me?"

She laughs. "Yeah. We're headed there now if you want to join?"

She's being serious, and I'm not sure how I know that, but I do. They're all giving off the same friendly, nonthreatening vibe. I'm tempted to say yes, but I need to find Cadence. I haven't spoken to her since Alexandros dragged me out of the library last night, and I've been kicking myself for not getting her number any of the times we've hung out. "Thanks, but I have to find my friend. Maybe next time?"

"Sure. We go most afternoons. It would be cool if you could hang some time."

I nod, shrugging on my backpack. "Yeah."

The door to the classroom bursts open, and I look up to see Cadence running through it. She stops when she sees me and closes her eyes, appearing to sigh with relief. I say goodbye to the group and head over to her. "I'm so happy to see you," I say, grabbing her hand.

"Girl. What the hell happened last night? I wanted to come over and check on you, but Enora forbade me. Are you okay?"

Her worry is palpable, and I offer her a reassuring smile. "I'm okay. No, I'm good. Really good." Apart from being vampire catnip, anyway. But I don't add that last part.

Despite what Alexandros told me about the witches' role in

the elementai genocide, I trust Cadence. And although I won't share my secrets, I don't want to lose her as a friend.

"You have time for a burrito?" I ask hopefully.

She links her arm through mine. "Yeah, but you gotta tell me why the hell Professor Drakos dragged you out of the library the way he did."

"Yeah. As soon as we grab some food." I press my lips together. I should have come up with a story. Stupid Ophelia! But Alexandros will know what to do. I'm not entirely sure how our bond works, but I assume it must be similar to the one I have with the guys.

Alexandros, can you hear me?

There's no reply. This overwhelming sense of rejection is ridiculous, yet I can't help what I feel when I realize that he's blocking me.

I try the boys instead, calling out to each of them while half listening to Cadence tell me about how Professor Green was acting all mysterious when she told her what happened with Professor Drakos.

What is it, sweet girl? Malachi answers me instantly.

Cadence is asking me what happened after I left the library. She wants to know why Alexandros was so mad. We should have come up with a story.

Hang on, baby. Give me two minutes, okay?

Okay.

I swallow my anxiety and force a smile while I give Cadence my full attention. A short time later, Malachi is back. *Alexandros says to tell her that you were supposed to be having a private tutoring session with him.*

You spoke to him?

Yeah, just now.

A lump forms in my throat. Why wouldn't he speak to me?

Ophelia? Malachi's concerned tone fills my head.

I have to pay more attention to Cadence or she's going to realize I'm lying. Or that I'm having a conversation with a vampire in my head. *You think she'll buy that?*

You can sell it. I believe in you.

His praise fills me with confidence. *Thank you, Kai.*

Any time.

And then he's gone, and I give Cadence my undivided attention once more. This is the first true friendship I've ever had, and I'm not going to let Alexandros's refusal to speak to me distract me from being a good friend.

After we grab food, Cadence and I choose a quiet spot at the back of the dining hall, and my butt has barely touched the seat when she asks again what happened to make Alexandros so mad.

"I mean, he was kind of hot all riled up like that." She blows out a breath and fans herself. "But I was so worried about you, girl. I went straight to Enora, but she said I shouldn't worry about you. I was so relieved to see you today."

I take a bite of my burrito to buy myself a few seconds to get my story straight. It would be so much easier if I could at least tell her about the professor and me. He said we didn't have to keep us a secret, but then he told Malachi to tell Cadence I had a private tutoring session.

Cadence stares at me, her eyes wide in expectation.

I lick a spot of sauce from my lips and hum like this is the most delicious burrito I've ever tasted.

She huffs, but her warm laughter quickly follows. "Spill, girl."

I shrug, wiping my mouth. "It wasn't all that exciting, really. He agreed to give me some private tutoring, and I completely forgot about our session."

She leans back and folds her arms. "Private tutoring?"

I nod. "Yeah. Ancient history fascinates me, and we don't

cover nearly enough of it in class. I wanted to delve a little deeper, you know?"

She waggles her eyebrows at me. "I bet he wanted to delve a little deeper." She snorts a laugh. "Maybe that's why he was so pissed."

My cheeks heat, but I can't help but laugh along with her. "Cadence! He did not."

"You never know. I mean, his vampire offspring sure seem super into you." She presses her lips together like she's revealed something she shouldn't have.

"Yeah. I know that. But he wouldn't be into me. He's my professor."

She lowers her voice. "Lots of the professors fool around with the students here. It's not like a normal college. Especially wolves and vampires. They're all very sexually charged creatures if you know what I mean." She grins. "And you, Ophelia, are hot. Even Sienna has a thing for you, and in all the time I've known her, she's only ever been attracted to other wolves."

"She does not." The heat from my cheeks races down my neck, and I have to shake my head to clear it of the mesmerizing werewolf I met in the library yesterday.

"Anyway." I clear my throat. "You know how he is about not giving private lessons. I guess he agreed because of my friendship with the guys. And then when I forgot ..." I wince, faking embarrassment and hoping she buys my flimsy story.

Cadence pops a fry into her mouth. "Well, I for sure would never forget a private session with that man. He is perfect. And I bet he knows exactly what to do with a woman." She finishes chewing with her eyes closed and lets out a dreamy sigh.

Unexpected jealousy washes over me, but I shove it aside. "Well, I'm not sure he'll offer again after last night."

She eats another french fry and licks her lips. "So did you do it?"

My heart stops beating. "Do what?"

She laughs. "The lesson. Did he calm down enough to give you your private tutoring? Or was he so mad he spanked you over his desk instead?" Another sigh escapes her, and she stares off into the distance. Is she imagining him doing that to her? Oh my word. I have to tell her about us.

Sienna approaches our table before I can find the right words. "Hey, girls," she says. "Can I sit?"

Cadence beams at her. "Sure."

Sienna sits beside me, her thigh lightly resting against mine. Recalling what Cadence told me a few moments ago has nerves fluttering in my abdomen. She tosses her long dark braids over her shoulder and beckons us to lean closer. "Did you hear someone burned down Professor Drakos's office last night?"

Oh dear god. I'm going to die of shame right here at this table.

Cadence gasps. "What? Who? Was he in it? Is he hurt?"

Sienna shakes her head. "Dunno. I heard President Ollenshaw is pissed, and nobody knows what happened."

My eyes dart between the two of them as they speculate about what could have happened, each new theory wilder than the last. And not a single one remotely close to the truth.

"I wonder if he burned it down in a fit of rage after Ophelia missed his tutoring session," Cadence says with a giggle.

I finally snap. "Don't be ridiculous."

Sienna bumps her arm against mine. "Okay, fire starter."

Tears burn behind my eyes, and my throat closes over. "Please don't call me that."

She blinks in surprise. "Okay, I'm sorry."

Despite my inability to make friends, my instincts about people have always been pretty good. And since that day in the kitchen when Professor Drakos told me I was something other than human, I have wondered if maybe whatever powers I had were responsible for that.

Those instincts are telling me now that I should trust these two girls. That I will regret it if I don't. "When I was in high school, there was a huge fire, and people accused me of starting it." I know that I technically did start it. The professor told me as much that day in the faculty library, but he also assured me it wasn't my fault. "And it kind of ruined my life. The only good foster parents I ever had kicked me out, and I had to move into a group home and finish high school online." I've been staring down at my half-eaten burrito the whole time I was talking, and I finally look up at Cadence and Sienna. My stomach twists while I wait for their reaction, and I fervently hope they don't get up and walk away.

I have to swallow a sob when Sienna wraps her arm around my shoulder and gives me a quick but warm sideways hug. "I had no idea that happened to you. I'm so fucking sorry, O."

Cadence reaches across the table and squeezes my hand in hers. "Yeah, girl. It sucks you had to go through that."

"We know you didn't burn down the professor's office," Sienna adds, her lips gently curving at the corners.

I close my eyes and try to melt into my seat. They're the first real friends I've ever had, and I hate keeping things from them

"Probably someone he pissed off at some point." Sienna snags a french fry from Cadence's plate. "You know he's like two thousand years old or something? My dad told me."

"I bet you can upset a lot of people in two thousand years." Cadence lets out a low whistle. "Vampires are the best at pissing people off too."

I bristle at that insult. Cadence may be under the false illusion that vampires killed the elementai, and I can't tell her otherwise, but I'm still not going to listen to her talk crap about them. "They're not," I insist.

Sienna nods her agreement. "I think they get a bad rap from the witches. There are good vampires and bad vampires, but that's the same as any other species."

If Cadence takes any offense at Sienna's comment she doesn't let it show. Instead, she regards my new friend with curiosity. "But you do know that vampires are the only beings who kill humans for food, right?"

I'm about to leap to their defense, but Sienna beats me to it. "They don't, actually. They feed on them, but there's no evidence it causes any lasting harm. Vampires haven't gone around hunting humans for centuries. Not since long before the genocide."

Searing pain blooms deep inside my chest, and I struggle to catch my breath.

Cadence frowns. "The genocide they were responsible for?"

Before I can stop myself, I blurt, "No they weren't!"

Cadence's frown deepens, and Sienna speaks up again. "She's right."

"B-but ..." She looks at Sienna, then me, then back at Sienna. "It's fact. Historical fact."

Sienna tilts her head to the side. "History as recorded by the winning side. Vampires lost the war. They didn't get to write the history of what happened. They were so decimated by the loss of the elementai that they were too busy seeking revenge or licking their wounds to argue with the story that our ancestors wove."

Cadence shakes her head. "That makes no sense."

"It makes all the sense, C. Why would vampires wipe out their other halves? The only species capable of bearing their children? Yes, a handful of vampires did play a part, but it was the witches and the wolves who drove the campaign."

I stare at Sienna with open admiration. "How do you know all this?"

"My father. He used to have private tutoring with Professor Drakos too." She arches an eyebrow, her lips quirked at the corner.

Oh god. She knows.

"But all witches are taught something different," Cadence says, eyes still narrowed with suspicion. "Are you telling me my parents and all my teachers have been lying to me?"

"No." Sienna shakes her head. "They have simply given you their acceptable version of the truth. It doesn't mean it's the right one."

Cadence sits back in her chair. "Well, I'm not—I don't buy that. But I do know that vampires are misogynistic and—"

Sienna snorts, cutting our friend off. "Vampires do not hate women. They revered the elementai."

Hearing her say that makes me think about my four vampires—all of whom are bonded to me and incapable of harming me. All of whom I realize I could never live without.

Cadence has fallen silent, arms crossed over her chest and her face lined with concentration. I can't imagine the inner turmoil she must be feeling right now. I wish I knew what to say to make her feel better, but I'm still trying to wrap my head around all of this myself.

"You dated that vampire sophomore year, remember?" Sienna nudges Cadence's arm playfully. "And I *know* he loved women. He couldn't get enough of you if I recall. And you told me he had a tongue that could make you hear choirs of angels."

Cadence presses her lips together as though she's stifling a laugh. And then a second later, a giggle bubbles from her lips.

Their laughter washes over me in a warm, comforting wave, making me realize that there is power in every connection. There's something special about the friendship I'm forming with these two incredible women who are powerful in their own right.

And that's a type of magic too.

EIGHT

ALEXANDROS

A s I expected he would be, President Ollenshaw is waiting outside my office when I arrive. He taps his foot impatiently while muttering something under his breath, but upon seeing me, he offers a tight smile and pushes his wire-rimmed spectacles up his nose.

"Alexandros." He says my name almost apologetically. "I heard reports of ..." He clears his throat.

"A fire?" I offer.

He nods, seemingly grateful to have been saved from his temporary discomfort. Jerome Ollenshaw might be the president of Montridge, but he is merely a figurehead—a fact of which he is acutely aware. An unremarkable man in his late fifties, if only in appearance, is a much easier sell to the humans and their families than a wolf with a temper as fragile as his ego or a six-foot-eight demon whose eyes glow red when he gets pissed—as were the case with the previous two deans of Montridge.

"I wouldn't bother you with such matters. Only ... People will talk, Alexandros. Uncontained fires on campus grounds are not permitted. Not since the incident in the woods." He winces as though troubled by the memory, but I suspect he is giving me a warning of sorts. At least as close as he will ever come to censure when it comes to me. Vampires were responsible for that particular fiasco too.

With a curt nod of acknowledgment, I remove the key from my jacket pocket and unlock the door. The smell of smoke still lingers, clinging to the scorched books and charred wooden shelves. My desk remains untouched by the flames, sitting stoically in the center of the room as it always has.

Jerome shuffles into the room behind me. "Is this something I need to worry about?"

I stoop to pick a book up from the floor and run my fingertips over the blackened leather binding. An unexpected knot of regret unfurls in my chest. The books themselves held no particular value to me, but this is a reminder of what I did. Of the danger I put her in.

Jerome clears his throat once more, and I shake my head. "There is nothing to be concerned about. I simply had a visit from an old fire demon acquaintance of mine."

"Did you have some kind of altercation?" His tone is tinged with suspicion.

My eyes dart to the deep fingernail scratches on my desk, the ones made by my own hands when I was inside her. The beast inside me flickers to life with a low growl when I recall how good it felt to finally claim her. My blood heats at the memory, most of it hurtling toward my cock as the recollection —her taste, her scent, her submission—almost overwhelms me.

"No." There is a crack in my voice, and I have no doubt he hears it.

He steps toward my desk and runs his forefinger over one of the deep grooves in the wood. "It was a pleasant visit, then?" He fails to suppress a chuckle.

I twist my neck from side to side and draw in a breath, trying to rid my mind of the images of her sitting on my lap while I fed from her and fucked her. But they are burned into my consciousness for eternity and refuse to budge. My fangs protract, and I unconsciously flick my tongue over the tips. I want to sink inside her right now. Need to feel her skin on mine. I burn to taste her, have both her blood and her cum coating my tongue.

"Alexandros." Jerome's voice cuts through my inner thoughts, and I realize he has been talking to me.

I give him my full attention, managing to push thoughts of Ophelia to the side, but I am unable to rid myself of them entirely. "Apologies, Jerome. I was distracted. You were saying?"

His gray eyes twinkle with amusement. "I was asking if you enjoyed your friend's visit, but I guess from your distracted state and the mess in your office that it either went very well or terribly. Which is it? I have known a fire demon or two in my time."

My eyes narrow. I have known Jerome for forty years, ever since I personally chose him to take over from his predecessor, but we have barely spoken two words that were not directly related to the curriculum during that entire time. And now is not the time to start bonding over sexual conquests. I want him out of here so that I can focus on thoughts of Ophelia without having to endure his small talk. "It was pleasant enough. But I will ensure this mess is taken care of, and I can assure you that this will not happen again."

He nods, his lips pressed together in a thin line now as he slips back into president mode. "I appreciate that, Alexandros." He places his hand over his heart. "I know that your family built this institution, and it is a great honor to be the president of this fine university. But that doesn't mean I can play favorites. I have parents and the student body and the school board to answer to."

"I am aware of that, Jerome."

"Of course you are. I'm sure it's no different from the days when you held my esteemed title." He raises his eyebrows, clearly trying to remain friendly, but there is an edge to his tone now that always creeps in when he is reminded of the fact that I once held his position. The role was undesirable to me then and equally so now, and I stepped down after two short years. However, he is well aware I could take it back if I so chose, and that never fails to make him feel threatened in my presence.

"You are doing a fair job, Jerome. There will be no more incidents like the one which occurred last night."

He raises his hand like he is going to clap me on the back, but he quickly drops it again, having wisely thought better of it. "I will leave you to deal with this mess. Good day, Professor."

I give him a curt nod. "Good day, Dr. Ollenshaw."

I KNEW she would be in here, sitting in her usual spot—two seats from the end of the second row—but I am still unprepared for what the sight of her does to me. I have always found it difficult not to watch her. Not to stare at her beauty as she listens to me so intently, her brow furrowed in concentration. Not to let my gaze linger on the pale skin of her decolletage, or the way her breasts strain against the thin material that covers them. She sees me, and her bright-blue eyes widen, brimming with excitement and hope when they land on mine.

Hi, she says, speaking freely through our bond.

All the blood in my body is already heading south. The enduring memory of what we did last night, of how incredible it felt to sink into all the parts of her, is enough to have desire coursing through me like it is my lifeblood. I avert my gaze from hers and bark an order for the students still standing to take their seats.

Ophelia's resulting sadness is acute. I do not need to look at her to know that her eyes are brimming with tears. Her blood still flows through my veins, and it calls to me now, demanding that I taste her again. Our bond is a new one, but it is stronger than any I have ever felt before. In ancient times, when there was little to do but fuck and fight, I would have taken her to my bed, and we would not have left it for weeks except to get her sustenance. We would have taken our fill until the beasts inside us both were sated.

But times are different now. We have so many responsibilities. And I suspect the beast that Ophelia Hart has awoken within me will never be sated. So all I can do for now is avoid looking at her, block her sweet voice from my thoughts, and not think about any of the things I would like to do to her once I get her home.

After class, I wait until most of the students have filtered out before raising my voice enough for her to hear me. "Miss Hart, may I speak with you about your paper?"

She stops in her tracks and glares at me defiantly. "I have somewhere to be, Professor," she grits out.

Yes you do, little one. I growl the warning inside her head but keep my outward tone calm and neutral. "It will not take but a few moments of your time."

She sighs, shrugging her backpack onto her shoulder. When another student stops to ask me about the midterm, Ophelia taps her foot impatiently. I curl my hands into fists, stopping myself from putting her over my knee and punishing her for her insolence.

I watch the rest of my students file out of the room, aware of Ophelia's eyes on me and her growing anger. I am still actively tuning her out, counting down the seconds until that door closes and we are alone. Every cell in my body vibrates with the desire to scream at her meandering classmates to move faster and stop with their inane chatter, but I remain silent. However, as soon as the last one leaves and the door swings closed, I turn and face the object of my torment.

"Who do you—" she starts.

With a hand wrapped around her slender throat, I push her against the wall and cut off her question by sealing my lips over hers. She resists me, but I am undeterred, forcing my way into her defiant mouth until she submits. It takes no more than few seconds before she is whimpering softly and flicking her tongue against mine. She rakes her fingers through my hair, pulling me closer. I lift her and wrap her legs around my waist, pressing her flat to the wall. Grinding into the heat radiating from her damp panties, I try to find a semblance of relief for the throbbing ache in my shaft.

When I am certain of her compliance, I break our kiss and allow her to draw a breath.

"Why did you ignore me, and why can't I speak to you through our bond?" she asks through a series of pants, but there is no fire in her tone now, only sadness.

I rub my nose over her cheek and inhale her uniquely addictive scent. "It was the only way to get through this class, Ophelia."

"But it wasn't just in class. I tried to speak to you earlier today about Cadence, and you didn't answer me."

That she thinks I would purposely ignore her stings more than I could have anticipated. I lower the guard I had in place and speak through our bond. *I was in Thucydides Library. I did not answer you because our bond will not work there. Malachi sought me out to ask my counsel, but had I known you were calling for me, I would have left the library and answered you myself.*

Relief floods her, and she gives me a sweet smile. *But why couldn't you get through class without ignoring me? I've been in your class all semester.*

Yes, but I was not bonded to you before. I did not have such intimate knowledge of the sweetest of temptations only a few feet away from me. Had I so much as looked at you today, I might have remembered all too clearly what happened between us last night.

And why would that have been so bad?

I huff a laugh. *Because then it would have been incredibly difficult and incredibly painful to restrain myself. Would you like all your classmates to watch me fuck you? Perhaps I could have sat you on my podium and made them watch me eat your pussy instead?*

She gasps, but the scent of her arousal grows stronger. My fangs protract with the need to take her. To taste her. But she has given enough blood this day. "You wouldn't do that though, would you?" Her words come out as a string of breathy moans that do nothing to sate the desire burning through my veins.

"I would rather not, little one. But make no mistake, it is what I want to do whenever you are near. So if I am ever cold toward you, know that it is because I am fighting an internal battle to keep my hands off you."

The skin on her neck and chest pinkens the way it does when she is aroused, and she wraps her arms around my neck. "I like having your hands on me."

A feral growl rumbles from my chest. I am a mere breath away from taking her here in my classroom. "I know that I told you last night that it is unnecessary to keep us a secret, but I should have been clearer. We need not keep it a secret from our kind, but from the humans, we must. A professor dating his nineteen-year-old student is not good for the reputation of the college."

She sighs. "Or for the reputation of Ophelia. I don't really want everyone to know I'm ..." She rolls her lips together, and the flush on her neck creeps over her cheeks.

I arch an eyebrow. "Screwing your professor?"

She feigns indignation, mischief sparkling in her eyes. "Well, yes. Although I could be doing that right now." She glances down at our bodies pressed together. "But I'm not."

"And you shall not until you can learn to control your power a little better. Dr. Ollenshaw has already been asking questions regarding my office. I had to tell him I met up with an old fire demon acquaintance of mine."

Jealousy flares from her and almost makes me laugh, but it is quickly replaced by her frustration. "That doesn't seem very fair."

My mouth trails down the column of her throat, taunting us both with the promise of the sweet relief that would come from me biting her. "I agree. I can think of no greater punishment than me not fucking you."

She curls her fingers in the hair at the nape of my neck and rubs herself against me. "But it's a punishment for you too, if you really think about it. You know, staying away from me, not to mention my vamp-nip blood, could be hazardous for you."

I dust my lips over her ear and laugh softly. "I was talking about me, Ophelia. And I will not feed from you again today. Your vamp-nip blood is safe for now. But if you are so concerned about my welfare, perhaps I do need to fuck you." I unfasten my belt and my slacks and free myself before she has a chance to protest. "I think we will be fine so long as you get nowhere close to orgasm."

I tug her panties aside and line the crown of my shaft up with her wet heat. "That also doesn't seem very fair," she says, whimpering.

"Nothing in life is fair, Ophelia." I drive inside her with one smooth stroke, and she cries out, throwing her head back. I cradle it with my palm just in time to stop her from smacking it against the wall. "You are not going to burn down the history building, are you, Ophelia?"

She shakes her head.

I pull out and drive inside her again, making her bite down on her lip. "Can you see your light?"

"Y-yes."

She is learning quickly. That she can find her center already is a strong sign of her abilities, and it fills me with pride. "Good girl. Focus on that whilst I fuck you."

"What if I do something?" she asks, her voice trembling. "What if I can't stop it?"

"I can feel you. I will not let you get too close." She is right—this is unfair. This is all about my pleasure and has nothing to do with hers, but I must do everything I can to prevent her from unleashing her powers in here, and I am incapable of stopping this. In this moment, if I were forced to choose between walking away from her or letting her burn this entire campus to ash, there would still only be one option. And that would be me inside of her.

I pay close attention to her body. Her erratic breathing. Her racing heart. Her arousal coating my cock with every thrust. And I am careful to keep her from getting anywhere close to the edge. She is already more in control than she was last night.

"Alexandros," she whines, her muscles squeezing my cock so tightly that my own release is only seconds away.

I rest my forehead against hers. "I know, little one. I will teach you how to control your power, and then I will make it up to you. All the orgasms you desire."

Her face lights up with a smile that almost makes my knees buckle. "You promise?"

"I promise." I pull out slowly and savor the desperate whimpers I wring from her body before driving back inside and losing myself in the sweet oblivion of Ophelia.

NINE

XAVIER

Ophelia pulls her hair into a ponytail while she waits for the leftover moussaka to finish heating in the microwave. Even from a few feet away, I can clearly see the pulse fluttering on the underside of her jaw. My fangs ache to taste her. I fed from her this morning, but it may as well have been weeks ago for how much I need her now. With four vampires drinking her blood every day, we need to be careful about how much we take.

"I can feel you watching me, Xavier," she says, giggling.

I smirk. "I am always watching you, Cupcake."

Flashing me a coy smile over her shoulder, she flutters her eyelashes. My beautiful little slut.

"Little and often, Xavier," Alexandros says, reminding me of the agreement we made yesterday after Ophelia left for class. We will all feed from her each day because going longer than that without a taste of her blood feels like torture, but we will only take small sips, at least until she's stronger. Who knows what her new powers are going to hold? She healed much faster from our bites this morning than she has previously.

I study him from across the table. "Are you reading my mind?" Not that it's a big deal, I have nothing to hide from him, it's just that he usually doesn't.

He arches an eyebrow. "I do not need to read your mind to know what you are thinking." He licks his lips. *And make no mistake ... I am thinking about it too.*

I snort a laugh.

"What are you making, sweet girl?" Malachi steps up behind her, wraps his arms around her waist, and drops a kiss on the back of her neck.

Axl takes a seat beside me and rolls his eyes. *Such a sap for her.*

"I heard that," Malachi snaps.

Axl leans back in his chair and puts his feet on the table. "Yeah, you were supposed to, nutsack."

"We are at the table." Alexandros scowls at Axl's feet, and Axl swiftly drops them to the floor. I flash him a shit-eating grin, grateful to not be the one getting roasted for a change.

Ophelia squeals, and I look up to see Malachi nuzzling her neck and tickling her. "Stop!" She lets out a loud, infectious giggle as she squirms in his arms.

He burrows his hand beneath her top and carries on. "But you're so ticklish."

"Kai!" she shrieks with laughter now, twisting in his embrace and planting her hands on his chest. A split second later, Malachi slams into the wall on the other side of the room.

"Oh my god, Malachi!" Ophelia gasps, her eyes darting between him and her hands held in front of her face.

Malachi, sprawled on the floor and looking as confused as I am, rubs the back of his head.

"W-what happened?" Ophelia asks, her voice filled with panic. "I just pushed him away."

When it comes to size, Malachi is by far the largest and strongest of the three of us, and the dude just got thrown clear across the room by our tiny cupcake.

Alexandros pushes back his chair and goes to Ophelia. He takes her hands and examines them. "Did you channel your power, Ophelia?"

She shakes her head. "I-I don't know."

He presses his lips together the way he does when he's deep in thought. "Did it feel like when you started the fire?"

Her cheeks flush bright pink. "No," she whispers.

Humming, he turns her hands over and inspects her palms. "I did not feel anything from you."

"I just pushed him away and ... Usually, he wouldn't budge an inch." She chews on her lip and looks past the professor at Malachi, who jumps to his feet and rubs the back of his head again. "Are you okay?"

"I'm fine. Just shocked." He winks at her.

A thrill of excitement shoots through my veins. "This is going to make fight lessons so much more fucking fun." We were going to start yesterday, but Ophelia was feeling over-whelmed with her upcoming midterms, so Alexandros decided to have us kick off the weekend with lessons after she's done with class today. Images of me pinning my little cupcake have my dick twitching in my pants already.

"Axl will provide Ophelia's combat training," Alexandros says without taking his eyes off her.

I roll my eyes. Of course it's fucking golden boy who gets to manhandle our girl in the name of "teaching" her. It's Axl's turn to flash me a shit-eating grin. Dickface.

"Wait. Not me?" Malachi asks with a frown.

"You are stronger, Malachi, but Axl is a better strategist. Fighting is about more than strength."

What the hell? I jump to my feet. "I'm a fucking strategist! Who plans all the obstacles for the Hunt? Me!"

Alexandros sighs and rolls his neck, and I shut my mouth. I don't want to piss him off any further. Even if this is all fucking kinds of unfair. He directs his attention back to Malachi. "You will be my TA for the rest of the semester. That gives you full unrestricted access to Thucydides Library. You will be able to take Ophelia with you so you can both study our history. Ancient magic, the Skotádi, the Order, elementai genocide. All of it."

Malachi grins, and Ophelia squeals with delight. I suppress a snort. They're such fucking nerds. Hot-as-fuck nerds who I want to bite and fuck into oblivion, but still nerds.

But my amusement doesn't outweigh my irritation. "So Kai is your TA, and Axl teaches Ophelia to fight. What about me? I sit on my ass and watch?"

Alexandros sighs, and I know I've poked the bear, but I don't give a fuck anymore. I'm tired of this shit. Tired of never being good enough for him. Without waiting for his answer, I kick my chair to the floor and stalk out of the kitchen.

A few seconds later, I find myself pinned to the wall in the hallway with his hand around my throat, his expression carefully and terrifyingly blank. I should have known he wouldn't let that slide. "You will watch your tone when you address me, Xavier." His tone is deathly quiet, the threat implicit.

I growl, wanting to fight back. Wanting to sink my teeth into his neck and tear out his throat. So often, I piss him off on purpose, needing his reaction to show me that he at least feels *something*. As much as I want to resist, instinct makes me submit. "Yes sir."

His jaw tics, and his dark eyes bore into my soul. My pulse throbs beneath the pressure of his hand on my throat. My fangs ache to taste him. My skin burns where his touches mine, and I know that he can feel what he does to me. I fucking hate that he does this to me when I mean so little to him. I want to close my eyes and break the connection, but I can't. His tongue darts out, and he moistens his lips as he breathes heavily through his nose. "You are infuriating, Xavier."

Tell me something I don't know.

"You will assist me in teaching Ophelia to channel her powers and control her mind."

I'll *assist* him? So I'm being given a pity role? What the actual fuck? Clearly he heard all that because he squeezes my throat tighter and slams my head back against the wall. "Controlling her mind is the key to controlling her power, Xavier. It is *the* most important thing she can do. I would not risk Ophelia's teaching to assuage your fragile ego. I do not do pity." That's actually true. So what is this, then? I blink at him, my throat raw from the pressure of his grip. "Despite your many flaws, Xavier, you are far more skilled than your brothers when it comes to controlling your mind."

Was that a fucking compliment?

"It is the truth," he says.

I can't help the rush of pride I feel at his words, and I hate the fact that he must feel it too. He releases his grip on me, and I rub at my burning throat. "I trust you will treat this with the utmost seriousness?"

His need to clarify that stings and takes the edge off his previous compliment. "Ophelia's safety is everything to me."

He nods, his glare softening at the mention of her name. "Do not let me down."

"I won't." My voice cracks, and I tell myself it's because my throat is raw, but we both know that's not why. We both know that I would rather die than let either of them down.

CHAPTER

TEN

AXL

Fuck me, she makes me hard as granite. I adjust my cock while I watch her walk across the lawn toward me, her hips swaying with every step she takes. Her tiny little skirt swishes over the creamy skin of her thighs, and perhaps it's because I am all too aware of the tempting delights that lie underneath, but I'm practically drooling by the time she reaches me.

"Are you ready for your first lesson, princess?"

She glances down at my cock straining against my zipper and folds her arms across her chest. "Are you?"

I arch an eyebrow. "Getting to put my hands on you and pin you to the dirt, yeah, pretty much."

"I'm not gonna make it easy for you though." Her lips twitch. "You saw what I did to Malachi earlier."

My hungry gaze roams up and down her body. "I did, and knowing I don't have to be so gentle with you is going to make this all the better."

She takes a step closer, fluttering her eyelashes as she stares up at me. Her eyes are so vibrantly blue, like none I've ever seen before. I swear I could fall into them and never want to escape. "You won't hurt me though, will you?" Her voice is timid, and her bottom lip wobbles.

I tuck her hair behind her ear. She's too fucking cute. "Aw. I won't hu—"

She hooks her leg around my ankle, and before I know it, I'm staring up at her from the ground. The element of surprise was on her side, but I still can't believe she managed to take me down. She dives on top of me like a wildcat. Straddling me, she grabs my wrists and pins them above my head. I could throw her off with ease, but I don't want to. Not yet.

I grin at her. "That was a cheap shot."

"Hey, a girl's gotta do what a girl's gotta do. Especially when it comes to wrestling a giant wall of hot vampire muscle."

I arch an eyebrow. "And what if they're not hot?"

She giggles. "Then it wouldn't be as much fun, I guess."

I roll her over and pin her to the ground the way she just had me. She squirms, but I hold her in place easily. "If any vampire other than us ever comes anywhere near you, princess, you kick him in the nutsack, and then you run. You got me?"

She sinks her teeth into her lower lip, taunting me because she knows how much I want to sink mine into every part of her.

"Ophelia?" I growl in warning.

She nods. "Okay."

I lick my fangs, aching to bite her and fuck her here on the grass. "What do you do?"

She grins. "Kick him in the nutsack and run."

"That's my girl." I give her a quick kiss on her pouty pink lips before I jump up and brush the grass from my sweats.

She holds out her hand like she wants me to help her. I shake my head. "After that little stunt you just pulled, you're on your own."

She gasps in a show of outrage. "So ungentlemanly of you."

I bare my fangs. "There is nothing gentlemanly about any of the things I'd like to do to you. Now get up. I'm going to teach you some basics."

I SLAM OPHELIA DOWN, and her back hits the grass with a thud. She's surprisingly good at fighting, and not all of that comes down to her newfound strength. She's quick and agile too, but more than that, she's smart. She anticipates a move before I make it, and not only because of our bond.

She gasps for breath, and her pert tits heave against my chest. The gentle throb in my cock turns to a deep, pulsing ache.

With a grunt, I wedge myself between her thighs, spreading them wide with my hips and pinning her body to the ground with the weight of mine. "Do you yield, princess?"

She wiggles halfheartedly beneath me, and all she accomplishes is to rub her hot pussy over me, making us both groan in frustration. Surely the professor won't be mad if our lesson ends with fucking, right? We've been out here for over half an hour. I've taught her some cool self-defense moves, and now I want to show her *my* moves. All the ones that involve me being inside her sexy little body.

"Do you?" I ask again, pinning her hands above her head.

She shakes her head and bucks her hips, but despite her increase in strength, she's unable to move me.

I run my tongue over the tip of my fangs and suppress a growl. "I guess I'll just have to find another way to force your submission." Her eyes shimmer with desire. "Oh, you like the sound of that?"

"Yeah." She pants out the word.

"Shame you're not allowed to come though. You know, on account of you setting the professor's office on fire and all."

"I think that actually happened before he made me ..." Her cheeks turn a deep-pink hue, and she giggles rather than finish her sentence.

I rock my hips, rubbing my aching cock over her pussy. "Before he made you what?"

She presses her lips together, and I grind harder, making sure she feels every solid inch of me. And when she starts to whimper, I ask her again. "What did he make you do, princess? Say the word for me."

"C-come," she mewls, trying to jerk her wrists from my grip.

I lean down and nip the skin on her neck, making her yelp. "You're a naughty girl, Ophelia." I pin her wrists with one hand and free my throbbing dick with the other. "And I'm desperate to be inside your tight pussy."

She wraps her legs around my waist, pulling me closer, encouraging me to fuck her out here on the lawn. We're behind a hedge, so I'm not worried anyone will get a glimpse of what's mine. Because she is mine. While she is also theirs, I was the first to claim her. The first man to ever be inside her. To taste her and bond with her.

And nobody will ever take that from me. From us.

Snaking my hand beneath her skirt, I feel for her panties and grunt with relief when my fingers skate over the damp fabric.

"Axl," she groans, bucking her hips and chasing her own relief, and I wish I could give her more. More than the pleasure that will come from me sinking my cock into her. But it's too dangerous, and I'm not stupid enough to incur the professor's epic wrath. Even if it might be worth it to hear my name on her lips when I make her come. "I need you."

I trail my lips along the skin of her neck. "I know, princess. I've got you." I nudge the crown of my cock at her tight entrance until she's whimpering with desperation, and then I tease her a little more, pulling guttural cries from her throat that rock me to my core.

"You're so hot and tight, Ophelia. You drive me crazy with the need to fuck you, do you know that?"

"Then do it," she pleads.

I rest my forehead against hers, staring into her bright-blue eyes as I sink deep inside her with one smooth thrust.

She cries out, tipping her head back while her pussy spasms around me. Her heart rate picks up, and the earth trembles beneath her. I slide out of her, easing her back down. "I think this might be a bad idea."

She sinks her teeth into her lip, her eyes brimming with tears. "I know."

"You know I want to fuck you more than I want my next breath, though, don't you?"

A sweet but tremulous smile lights up her face. "Yes."

I let out a long, slow breath. "Seems like lessons are over for today."

"This one is. I have to meet Xavier and the professor in his study as soon as I'm done here."

I guess I'd better let her leave then. With a gargantuan amount of effort, I tear my body away from hers and force my dick back into my sweats before I hold out my hand and pull her up.

"Looks like you can be a gentleman after all, Axl," she says, sweet and seductive.

I give her a hard slap on the ass. "Go inside before I change my mind, princess. And next time, please dress appropriately for our lesson."

"I guess I can dig out some old sweatpants from some-where." She gives me a soft peck on the cheek, and then she heads into the house, her ass swaying seductively like she knows my eyes are glued to her every motion.

I guess I can be a gentleman. For her, anyway. I will always be anything she wants me to be.

CHAPTER

ELEVEN

XAVIER

"Ready for your next lesson, Cupcake?"

She ties her long pink hair up with a hairband and nods.

I grab her ponytail, yanking her head back and running my nose along the column of her throat. "You are such a fucking distraction, Ophelia."

Her giggle is cut off by Alexandros's deep voice. "This is not the kind of lesson we are teaching, Xavier."

I glance over my shoulder, my fingers still tangled in Ophelia's hair. "I didn't realize you'd be joining us."

He rolls up his shirt sleeves, revealing powerful forearms

89

lined with thick veins. The kind I'd like to trace my tongue over before sinking my teeth into.

His dark eyes narrow. "I said you would be assisting me, did I not?"

"Yeah, but ... I didn't realize that meant we'd be teaching together." I assumed he'd simply tell me what to do. I don't voice that last part, but I figure he hears it anyway because he scowls at me.

"Before we start, there is something important to understand about your power, Ophelia, and that is its source. You and Malachi will research it more thoroughly. But before we start this part of your training, it would help you both to have a basic understanding of an elementai's powers."

I release her hair, and she nods, eyes wide with excitement.

"Take a seat." He gestures to the sofa and sits in the armchair. "Tell me what you understand of an elementai. Either of you."

Ophelia glances at me, so I answer first. "Only what Kai has told me. They don't need spells like witches do because they channel magic directly from the elements."

"Yeah, that's kind of what I thought," Ophelia says. "Except they don't need the element to channel? That's where I get confused."

The whole thing confuses the hell out of me. "I don't get how that makes them so powerful though. Demons and vampires are born with power. It's inherent. So how is a being that has to channel power stronger than that?" I squeeze my girl's hand in mine, and she flashes me a sweet smile.

"Yeah, I don't get that either."

Alexandros draws a breath through his nose, a deep one that makes his nostrils flare. "It is difficult to explain." His eyes land on the ficus tree that Malachi lovingly tends to. He grabs it and places it on the coffee table between us. "The elements themselves are a source of great power. Tsunamis have been known to decimate entire cities. A tornado can wipe out everything in its path. Earthquakes and wildfires—all proof of the raw, inherent power to be found within the elements. Vampires are born with magic in their blood. This power is directly linked to one of the elements and comes from a bloodline so old that no one knows of its origin. But each vampire house has magic derived from their elemental bloodline. For House Drakos, our powers are borne from fire. For several millennia before I was born, this meant control over fire, but it evolved as we did. Now, for sons of House Drakos, it is more common to have power over the mind."

I lean forward in my seat, my curiosity for our history piqued in a way that it never has been before. Learning about what makes us who we are brings me closer to knowing more about our girl, and that means I'm all in.

"How is that linked to fire?" Ophelia asks.

"Fire is emotion. Passion, anger, jealousy, destruction. To control someone's mind is to control their emotions. And when a vampire bonds with an elementai, whichever power they have mastery over also permeates that bloodline. It was why elementai with mastery over two elements were so highly prized."

Ophelia rubs her temples. "So their children would take on the power of the other elements too?"

He shakes his head. "No. Not for vampire or elementai children. My mother had mastery over air and water. However, this simply strengthens our bloodline powers rather than changes them. So House Drakos, which has all four elements in its bloodline, is much stronger than Houses Chóma, Elira, and Thalassa, which only have two or three."

I frown. "So elementai can cause natural disasters and stuff? Start fires? Knock someone over with a wave? I understand how they can make vampires stronger, but I still don't get why that makes them these super powerful beings."

"You are looking at this too literally, Xavier," he explains. His tone is patient and calm, reminding me how good of a teacher he is. He takes a small amount of soil from the ficus pot and holds it in the palm of his hand. "Earth is inherently powerful. It gives life. It has a raging ball of energy at its core. Elementai who have mastery over earth have access to this power." He runs a fingertip through the dirt in his palm. "Witches who can channel earth do so through the use of spells, but an elementai has it running through their veins." He looks up at Ophelia. "The deep ancient power, the one that heals you when we bite you—do you feel that?"

She closes her eyes, and a smile spreads across her face. "Yes."

"That is the earth line within you, Ophelia. Witches and elementai with mastery over earth are usually great healers."

I knew there was something special about the cupcake, but I never for one minute imagined she had the kind of power the professor is talking about. And the way he's speaking, the emotion in his eyes when he looks at her—I don't think I've ever seen him like this before. I never thought I'd bear witness to Alexandros Drakos being awed by anything, and yet here we are.

Ophelia claps her hands on her knees and leans forward in her seat, her excitement filling the room. "And how about water and air? Your mom's powers?"

"To manipulate air is to be able to create forcefields or mask one's presence. It is also linked to movement and speed. My brother's power of teleportation is rooted in air magic he inherited from our mother. Water is life-giving. The root of creation. But all of the elements are a source of great magic, and if tapped into correctly, they are all a source of immense power."

My mind is buzzing with so much new information it feels like it's about to explode, and I suddenly realize why Ophelia never stops asking questions. The desire to know the answers is overwhelming. "And Ophelia has power over fire too, right?"

He nods. "Fire is often considered the most dangerous and therefore strongest element because of its raw, violent potential. It is why House Drakos has reigned in the vampire world for as long as our history has been recorded."

I sense a hesitation and perhaps a sadness in him. "But you don't think that though? About fire?"

He glances at the palm of his hand once more. "I believe that the earth is the key to the most ancient of powers. It was here before water, before fire, before air, and even when the earth as we know it is done, parts of it will live in the cosmos for eternity."

I'm sure I see a glimpse of the man he was before he lost his family. An unexpected lump forms in my throat.

"That's kind of beautiful," Ophelia whispers.

Alexandros places the soil back into the pot and dusts off his hands. When he looks up again, his eyes are cold and unreadable. "Time to learn how to control those powers, little one. Once you know how to control them, there will be no limit to what you will be able to do."

Shivers of excitement and fear race through my veins, lighting up my insides. My little cupcake is going to be unstoppable. My gaze rakes over the side of her face until it lands on the fluttering pulse in her throat. Flicking my tongue over my fangs, I bask in the vibrant memory of her power running through me when I bite her.

"But wait. You said the most sought-after elementai had power over two elements, right?" Ophelia asks, and I don't miss the tremor in her voice.

He nods.

"But you think I can tap into all four?"

"Perhaps." He sucks on his top lip, his brow furrowed. "But we will not know for sure until your training is underway. It may be that because your powers were bound for so long that the elements are somehow crossing over. Maybe you are only channeling one or two but it appears as four."

"Has that ever happened to anyone before? Being able to channel all four?" I ask.

He's silent for a few seconds. "Only once," he finally says. "And that was Azezal himself."

Holy shit! "The guy they named that Order after?"

Alexandros gives me a single shake of his head. "It was he who founded the Order. That is why it is so named."

"So what happened to him? He wasn't an elementai, because they're only female, right?" Ophelia asks.

"He was a demon. He died almost two thousand years ago, and some say he was around three thousand years old when he finally perished."

Ophelia gasps. "Demons can live that long?"

He steeples his hands beneath his chin. "Perhaps longer."

My mind races with a billion questions, but I ask the most pressing first. "If he was so powerful, how did he die?"

The professor's dark eyes narrow. "You are not so obtuse that you do not understand that the more power a being wields, the more enemies they curate, are you, Xavier?"

I growl, lacing my fingers through Ophelia's and gripping her hand protectively in mine. I'm pissed at him for calling me stupid, but that's overridden by the fear that comes with the realization that he's right. How many will come after our girl once they know the kind of magic she possesses?

"So his enemies killed him?" Ophelia asks, her voice quiet but still full of awe.

Alexandros lets out a heavy sigh. "We are not here to

discuss history. You will research the finer details with Malachi. But yes. Despite his power, Azezal was eventually betrayed and killed. Some would say ..." He runs his tongue over his bottom lip and shakes his head.

I edge forward, needing more. "Some would say what?"

"Some would say that after three thousand years, he simply had enough of living. So he established the Order, and then he allowed his enemies to topple him."

I blow out a breath, and we sit in silence for a moment. Alexandros stares at Ophelia, and I allow my eyes to wander to her too. She's so fucking sweet, so kind and trusting, and while those are things I love about her, they're not the kind of attributes that will serve her well in our world. Because our pint-sized little elementai is probably the most powerful creature who ever fucking lived, and we can pretend it might not be true, but we all know it is.

Ophelia's mouth hangs open, and for the longest time, she only stares at him. Eventually, she speaks, and her voice is weak and quiet—the opposite of her. "But what does that mean? For me? For us?"

He stands and glares at her. "It means training, Ophelia. Lots and lots of training."

TWELVE

ALEXANDROS

My brother's blue eyes remind me so much of our mother's. Long-forgotten memories swim through my mind, bombarding me with images of the life I closed the door on after the loss of my wife and daughters. For five hundred years, those memories have lain dormant.

But now they linger close to the surface, ready to break free at the slightest hint of encouragement. Surely it is Ophelia's doing. My mind is sharper than it was before too, and my ability to hear other's thoughts has been magnified. As if allowing her inside has somehow heightened the potential of my power whilst unlocking its secrets.

"Alexandros," Giorgios says, reminding me that he is

waiting for an explanation as to why I have again summoned him to Montridge.

I shake my head, and the memories wash away like water circling a drain. "I have something to tell you."

He rolls his eyes. "I suspected as much given that you summoned me here. But what is it?"

I lick my bottom lip and avoid his scrutinizing gaze. Will he think me more a fool for giving into temptation or for protesting so adamantly that I would resist? I suppose his opinion matters very little, although he would be right either way. But I do wonder if he suspects. Does he have any inkling that I have bonded with an elementai? Her effect on my entire being has been so profound, I am certain he must have sensed something.

Yet four full days have passed since I bonded with her, and I have not heard from him. Surely he would have contacted me if he suspected. I clear my throat. "I bonded with Ophelia."

He blinks at me, his mouth agape, and then he simply stares. The silence hangs heavy between us. Judging by his reaction, I would say he had no idea that was why I called him here, which is a huge relief. That means our father would not have felt it either.

"Are you going to say something, Giorgios?"

He snaps his mouth closed and takes a deep breath before he speaks. "You bonded with the elementai girl?"

I tilt my head, scrutinizing his features: the slight pinch between his thick, dark brows, the barely detectable narrowing of his sapphire-blue eyes. "Yes."

His right eyelid twitches. "When?"

I lean forward in my seat, hands clasped between my thighs as though being closer to him will allow me to read him more easily. This is not the reaction I was expecting—not that I truly know what I anticipated. But it was not this. "Are you disappointed in me, brother?"

He runs his tongue over his top teeth and gives a brief shake of his head. When his eyes lock on mine again, there is no trace of the disappointment or suspicion I thought I just saw in them. "No, Alexandros. I am merely surprised by your change of heart. And so quickly too."

I wince. It was not all that long ago when we sat in these same chairs and I swore I would never bond with her. He was so sure even then that I was fooling myself, so his reaction now is particularly unsettling. "And I am surprised by yours."

He frowns. "How so?"

"When we spoke last, whilst you did not say I was fooling myself, you certainly gave the impression you believed such. Did you not?" In fact, he practically encouraged me to bite her and claim her for my own.

His nostrils flare on a deep breath. "I suppose you convinced me with your steadfast conviction that this was not what you intended." He leans across the void between us and places his hand on mine. "But make no mistake. I am happy for you, brother."

Appeased by his explanation, I offer him a nod of thanks.

"What was she like?" His voice contains a low rumble that I suspect is purely instinctual.

I frown, confused by his question. "In what way?"

"She is the first elementai born in half a millennium. You told me you believe she has mastery over three elements, possibly all four. So tell me, what did she taste like?" He licks his lips.

In the entirety of our long existence, we have never compared notes on sexual conquests, and even if that is not what this is, his question is uncomfortably intimate. And whilst the connection Ophelia and I share goes far beyond our sexual relationship, to discuss her taste in such a way feels disrespect-ful. "I can tell you that the experience of bonding with her was like nothing I have ever felt before, Giorgios, but her taste will remain between Ophelia, my boys, and me." I add a growl of warning, and he thankfully heeds it.

"So it was different from bonding with Elena?" His eyes sparkle with curiosity once more, and I wonder if my posses-siveness over Ophelia caused me to misinterpret his previous question.

I recall bonding with Elena. How her blood warmed my insides, and her inherent goodness made me want to be a better man for her. My feelings for her—safe and stable—came from a place of loyalty and honor.

But biting Ophelia—

Pure fire. A raging inferno of passion that burns within my blood still. I will be any kind of man, better or worse, to keep her at my side until the end of my days. I will bring the entire universe to ruination if it means I get to keep her. My feelings for her are dangerous and addictive, and they are born from a place so deep inside my soul that I know I could never lose her without losing myself. "I cannot compare the two, brother. It would be like comparing night and day."

"But you loved Elena, did you not? You told me you loved her, Alexandros."

His voice cracks on her name, as though he is reliving the heartbreak he experienced when our father and Elena's chose me rather than him as her suitor. Despite the magic blocking our bond within the library walls, his pain assaults me anew, the ache every bit as excruciating as it was a thousand years ago. A testament to our mother and the example of integrity she provided us, Giorgios made the choice to put his feelings aside for the good of our family name. But before he took that honor-able step back, he made me promise that I would love her always. It is a promise I have kept. "I did love her, Giorgios. I do still."

My words ring with the strength of their truth, although I now know it was not Elena who was meant for me. She is not the other half of my soul. She was never supposed to be mine.

The bond I had with Elena, whilst not destined, still carried all the markings of a vampire–elementai bond and therefore gave me the privilege of knowing her feelings as if they were my own. That is how I know how deeply she cared for my brother. But she never felt for him the love he so desired. Never looked at him with the heat of a lover's embrace. She thought of Giorgios as if he were as much her brother as he was mine.

And yet.

Perhaps she was always destined to belong to Giorgios. If I am to believe the legends, every creature alive has a fated mate. Elena was not mine. Was she his? There is no way to know, which means I will forever live with the question of whether I prevented him from living his own destiny. The idea that I may have taken from him that which I have found with Ophelia cuts me with a million guilt-poisoned blades. "I am sorry, brother."

He dismisses me with a wave of his hand, his shoulders stiff and his countenance impassive; however, his pain still lingers close to the surface. "It was our father's will. Neither of us were prepared to disappoint him back then. And it made our family all the stronger." He rubs a hand over his beard. "For a time, at least."

Bone-crushing despair threatens to drown me, but I remain unfaltering in the face of my brother's outward stoicism. "Until the elementai bloodlines were no more."

"Except they have returned now. Perhaps the girl is only the first of many."

Unable to dash his hopes, I nod. "Perhaps."

"If our father learns of her existence, she will surely be the first of many. He will breed her like a common broodmare."

The thought of my kindhearted, trusting elementai being used in such a way has bile burning my esophagus. "He can never discover her identity, Giorgios. Never."

The lines of his face soften into a reassuring expression. "I have no idea how we will keep her a secret forever, brother, but we shall certainly try."

I press my lips together and lean back in my chair. I have no idea either, but keeping her from him is imperative. Even after she learns how to control her powers, she will be a target. But someone knows about her. Someone who is responsible for her being here at Montridge.

"We need to find out about her past," I tell him. "Perhaps then we can better understand how to protect her. If someone else even suspects what she is, they are a danger to her whether they mean her harm or not."

He nods solemnly. "How much information do you have thus far?"

I recount the information Osiris obtained for me at the beginning of the semester. "That was as much as he could find, and I do not wish to have him continue digging into Ophelia's past. I would rather we keep her identity between us for a long as possible."

He absentmindedly hums his agreement. "So the only people who know about her are you, me, and your boys?"

"As far as I am aware. But there is clearly someone else out there who is aware that she is something special. Perhaps not elementai, but something." The puzzle of Ophelia Hart extends farther than the eye can see, and there are still far too many pieces missing. "There was also an incident a few weeks ago." I rub my temples, annoyed at myself for not following up on it sooner.

He raises an eyebrow. "Oh?"

"A girl who used to bully Ophelia transferred here after the semester started. She toyed with her for a few weeks and then lured her off campus, planning to kill her. At the time, I thought it extreme for a human to go to such lengths, but not unheard of. At some point, the girl received an anonymous note with the name of a vampire who could help her be rid of her Ophelia problem."

He tips his chin. "Which vampire?"

Ronan King. While I am satisfied that he has no knowledge of Ophelia's true identity, that he put his dirty hands on her will not go unpunished, but that is for another day. "A commander of Onyx. He was merely a pawn."

"And the girl? Where is she? Perhaps she knows more."

"She was disposed of accordingly. Axl, Xavier, and Malachi swore she knew nothing more than what she told them about the anonymous note. However, they sensed there was something not right about her." I comb my memories. "Rotten, I believe is the word they used to describe her scent and her blood."

He recoils, his nose wrinkling.

"Perhaps she was under the influence of some dark magic?" I offer.

"It is entirely possible. But if that is the case, then it is surely a certainty that someone knows of Ophelia's true identity. For why else would someone who possesses dark magic take an interest in a teenage girl who appears, for all intents and purposes, to be human?"

That thought has crossed my mind as well, but I am unconvinced they—whoever *they* are—know that she is an elementai. If anyone possessed such knowledge, we would be fending off attack after attack to get to her. "But why would they want her dead? Surely they would prefer to manipulate her powers somehow. And is whoever arranged for her to attend Montridge the same person who wanted her dead? Or are there two different motives at play here?"

He runs his fingertips over the dark hair on his chin. "It is a puzzle to be sure."

"One we must solve as soon as possible, Giorgios."

"Would you consider sending the girl away?" he asks, worry lining his features. "At least until we can determine the threat to her?"

A snarl rumbles in my chest. "And where would you suggest I send her, Giorgios?"

"I do not know." He pinches the spot between his brows and shakes his head. He is quiet for the space of several heartbeats, but when he speaks again, his posture and voice are confident. "I still have my mountain fortress in the foothills of Tibet. She would surely be safe there. You could send one of your sireds with her for company."

"The boys have responsibilities here, and I will not send her away." I manage, just barely, to keep the rage invoked by his suggestion from my tone. The mere thought of spending a single day without her fills me with panic.

He sighs. "Then you come with her, Alexandros. For she is surely an easy target here if what you have told me is true. Do not put her at risk unnecessarily."

Anger prickles beneath my skin, bristling to be let out. "I would *never* risk her safety." For a few seconds, I let those words fill the space between us, ensuring his understanding that I will not abide such accusations. "But if I leave here, then questions will be asked. Not only by Dr. Ollenshaw and other faculty members and students, but by our father. It would draw far too much unnecessary attention. Do not think that I have failed to consider the option of taking her far away from here."

He holds his hands up in surrender, banking the fury I have

been directing his way. "If she cannot leave, we must make haste to determine what, if any, threats there are to her safety. If you cannot leave this campus, then you must do what you can from within these walls, and I will pick up on the trail that Osiris left."

"Thank you, Giorgios."

He stands and puts a hand on my shoulder. "We will protect her, brother. I give you my word." As he walks away, he glances back at me over his shoulder, a pensive look on his face. My thoughts are already on her and what she is doing at this very moment.

It is Monday, and if I remember correctly, she should be in her algebra class. I wonder what she would do if I summoned her to my office instead. The desire to spend the rest of my afternoon losing myself in her beautiful body is almost too strong to resist. I can think of no better way to counter the emotional toll of my conversation with Giorgios.

Yet my better judgment prevails, and I chase the images from my head. I have a stack of test papers to grade, and if I begin summoning Ophelia to me every time I get the urge to touch her, then she would never leave my side.

And that would certainly draw unnecessary attention.

THIRTEEN

XAVIER

The scent of his cologne combined with the rich blood that runs so tantalizingly close to his skin is enough to have my mouth watering as soon as I walk into Alexandros's study.

He stands shirtless, staring out the window with his back to me, every muscle in his back taut and full of raw, potent power. Thin silvery scars snake around his left side. He places his hands into the pockets of his dress pants, causing those muscles to flex, each hardened ridge illuminated by the overhead light.

"Where is Ophelia?" he asks without turning his head.

"On her way back from class. Axl's with her."

"She is late."

I drop into the seat in front of his desk and brush the hair from my eyes so it doesn't obstruct my impressive view. "Yeah, but Professor Underwood wanted to speak to her about her test before the break starts tomorrow."

He turns and runs a hand over his beard, staring at a spot over my shoulder for a few seconds before he changes the subject. "How was last night?"

"As smooth as can be expected." I give him a quick rundown of the job two of our seniors were tasked with by their soon-to-be employers, the Russian Bratva. "Two wounded. The target was acquired and delivered to the Pakhan. I believe he was impressed," I say in conclusion.

He nods. "And how are Ophelia's lessons coming along?"

Is that a trick question? We do the lessons with her together.

He sucks on his top lip and stares at me, waiting for my answer. I clear my throat and sit up straighter in my chair. "Axl said her fighting is improving. She knocked him on his ass a few times yesterday, although he claims he let her. But she's getting stronger every day." I subconsciously rub my left wrist, which she accidentally fractured yesterday when I was teasing her and she tried to get away from me. "Is that a part of her power too? She's almost as strong as we are."

He hums. "I believe she takes on the powers of those she is bonded with."

I guess that explains her sudden freakish strength then.

He takes a seat, his dark eyes boring into mine. "And our lessons? How do you think they are going?"

I shift uncomfortably in my seat. This feels like a test that I am not at all prepared for.

"You are always so suspicious of my motives, Xavier. It is a simple question, is it not?"

I chew on the inside of my cheek while I take a minute to

think. Test or not, I guess all I can give him is the truth. "I, uh, think she's doing great. She can already tune into your mind, can't she? And from the little I know about your power, that's some kind of epic feat."

His eyes narrow, and he leans forward and rests his elbows on his desk. "You think you know little about my power?"

Shit, did I fail already? I suck on my teeth, thinking. "I guess I feel like I don't know a whole lot about you at all if I'm honest."

I brace myself for his ice-cold stare, the one that makes me feel entirely worthless, but he simply hums to himself. "You are correct; she is doing well," he finally says. "Her powers are growing exponentially, and that is a very good thing."

"Yeah. The sooner she gets a handle on them, the sooner the poor girl can get her rocks off. She's like a pressure cooker right now." I bark out a laugh, but he doesn't join me. Composing myself, I blow out a long breath. Is it hot in here?

"And you, Xavier? Are the lessons helping you at all?"

What the hell does that mean? Does he think I need lessons too? Is that why he asked me to help him? I bristle. "Are they supposed to?"

The heat of his gaze has a bead of sweat running down the channel of my spine. "Not *supposed* to, but that is not what I asked."

I glance at my watch. Where the fuck is Ophelia? He's still staring at me, his expression unreadable while he waits for my answer. "I guess that helping Ophelia learn how to tune people out and listening to you teach her, in particular ..." My skin heats under his scrutiny, and I inwardly curse myself for being such a fucking idiot. But it's true—in teaching her, he has taught me too. I clear my throat. "Well, I guess that's helped me sharpen my own skills, you know."

He tilts his head. "How?"

Jesus fucking Christ, what does he want from me? Does he take some sick pleasure in making me squirm?

"I want you to simply answer the question, Xavier. And no, I take zero pleasure in your discomfort."

"I fucking hate that mind-reading thing you do," I snap. Ordinarily, I don't, but right now …

"So you know a lot more about my powers than most. Now answer the question. How have you honed your skills?"

"I can tune Axl and Malachi out more easily. I can communicate with only Ophelia if I want to, even when they're in the room with us, but I know they haven't learned to do that yet. I can just …" I search for the words. "I can close the world out a little easier too. Does that make sense?"

"Perfect." I'm sure his lips twitch in a smile, but before we can go any further, the hurricane that is Ophelia Hart blows into the room.

"I'm so sorry I'm late," she blurts, all smiles and pink-haired sweetness.

"I do not tolerate tardiness, Ophelia," he says, his tone mild enough, but it still carries a strong warning.

She keeps on smiling at him anyway. "I know, but Dr. Underwood wasn't happy with my test grade, and he wanted to give me the opportunity to retake it after Thanksgiving break." Ophelia perches sideways on my lap, and I wrap my arms around her, burying my nose in her hair. My cupcake. "I missed a few classes when I first started living here, remember?"

I smirk. Those first few days after we bonded, we barely let her leave our beds.

He watches her intently. "I recall all too well. The house shook all the way down to the foundation."

"Well, that's not happening again any time soon, is it?" She huffs, blowing some hair from her eyes.

In seconds, Alexandros is on his feet and around his desk

with her jaw cupped in his hand. "If you want to come so desperately, Ophelia, then arrive on time for your lessons." The dangerous rumble in his voice sends a shudder down both our spines.

"Yes sir," she purrs.

His right eye twitches, and he rubs his thumb over her bottom lip, tugging it down until her mouth opens, and then he stares at her like he's contemplating what to do with her gorgeous, wide-open, expectant mouth. I know what I'd like to do with it.

But he releases her and steps back. "Xavier is going to take today's lesson."

I am?

She blinks at him. "You're leaving?"

"Today you are going to work on closing off your mind to others, and Xavier is more than capable of assisting you with that task."

Was that a compliment?

Through the window, I watch the clouds obscure the sun. A steady drizzle begins to fall, and her lower lip quivers. "I really am sorry I was late."

He bends down and drops a lingering kiss on her forehead. "This is not a punishment, Ophelia." He waits until she gives him a shaky nod before continuing. "Do as Xavier says, and behave yourselves in my study."

He walks out and leaves us alone, and I'm left wondering what the hell to do now because he's taken the lead in all our sessions so far. Now it's just me, and I'm no teacher.

She spins on my lap so she's straddling me and wraps her arms around my neck. Her eyes rake over my face, and she licks her lips. "So ... what do we do now?"

Bend you over his desk and fuck you is the answer that immediately springs to mind, but I don't voice it.

Every opportunity is a learning opportunity, Xavier, Alexandros says.

I stare into her shining blue eyes while I speak to him. *You're seriously giving me permission to fuck Ophelia over your desk?*

You do not need my permission to do anything with Ophelia. I am trusting you to deliver her lesson. Whatever means you choose to employ in pursuit of that goal is up to you. But do not sacrifice her learning for your own selfish needs.

She grinds herself over my cock, which is now hard and aching—its usual state around her. Fucking her would be giving into her needs too, right?

Damn him for putting his fucking faith in me. When did that happen? I think I prefer being the fuckup he expects little to nothing from.

With a sigh and a gargantuan effort, I lift her from my lap and set her on her feet. "We have work to do, Cupcake."

She rolls her eyes, and I jump up and wrap a hand around her slender throat, enjoying the feel of it working beneath my palm. "Rolling your eyes is only going to make this lesson longer and harder, Ophelia."

She licks her lips. "Longer and harder sounds good to me."

I growl, part frustration and part desperation. She's a horny elementai who needs a good fucking, and I know she's trying to break me. If the professor were here, she'd be all well-behaved and studious, but with me ... I lick my lips and press them to her ear. Two can play at this game. "I know you want me to fuck you, sweet little Ophelia. So eager for me to fill your greedy cunt with my cock." She gasps, and I slip my hand beneath her skirt. After tugging aside her panties, I slide a fingertip through her center. "Already dripping wet for me."

She presses her lips together, stifling a moan.

"But only good girls who do their lessons get fucked." I

place my finger into my mouth and suck her sweet juices from the tip.

She glares at me defiantly, and it makes me want her even more. I want to watch as her body submits to mine, because it would. She always submits.

I tip her chin up with my forefinger, the same one I just sucked clean. "Are you ready?"

"Always."

FOURTEEN

MALACHI

Δράκος Σπίτι

I stare at the top of Ophelia's head where a hint of her dark roots peek through the vibrant pink of her hair. She hasn't colored it since shortly after she moved in, and I'll never forget how the shower looked like someone had ravaged Barbie against the tiles before Ophelia scrubbed it clean.

She glances up from the book on her lap. "What are you smiling at?"

I guess I do have a goofy grin on my face. "I can't help smiling when I'm watching you, sweet girl. Especially when you're reading and you sit with your legs crossed like that. Because when I use this angle"—I tilt my head to the side—"I can see your pretty pink panties."

Her cheeks flush pink now too.

"And that little damp spot on them too." I rearrange my aching dick in my jeans.

"I do not have a damp spot," she angry-whispers.

"Yeah you do, baby. And I know how much you enjoy reading." Leaning forward, I slide my hand beneath her tiny skirt and brush the tip of my forefinger over said spot. "But please tell me this is all for me."

She bites on her lip, giving a quick glance around the faculty library. As usual, it's almost empty, and I'm not worried about anyone seeing us in our cozy little corner. "We're supposed to be studying."

I pull her panties aside and swipe my knuckles through her wet pussy. "I am studying. Discovering exactly what makes my girl wet."

"I mean studying witchcraft." She holds up her book of ancient spells as proof of what we *should* be doing.

I suck on my top lip and stare into her incredible blue eyes. It's been less than a week since we started her lessons, and watching her learn so quickly and so greedily about our past has been nothing short of incredible. "You've been studying hard. I think it's time for a test."

I go on stroking her folds, and her breathing grows heavier. "W-what kind of test?"

"To see how much you've learned. Every time you get an answer right ..." I swirl the tip of my finger around her entrance. "I'll give you a reward."

Her pupils blow wide. "What if I lose control in the library?"

I let out a laugh. "Oh, I won't be making you come. I value my head too much to disobey the professor."

Her lower lip trembles. She's been denied orgasms since the night she set Alexandros's office on fire, and my girl is on the edge. "But I can still make it feel nice. And every moment is a learning opportunity, right? If you can control yourself while I'm finger-fucking you in the library, I'm sure that will impress the professor."

Her blush creeps down her neck, and I stifle a groan. I want to jump on her and fuck her into that leather chair. I want to make her come so fucking hard she screams this entire mountain down. And fuck, she'd feel so good squeezing around my cock while I did. "So, a test, Ophelia. Are you ready?"

She presses her lips together and nods.

I wink at her. "Good girl."

Her heart rate spikes, and I suppress another laugh. "I'll start easy. What must a witch have in order to channel magic?"

"Access to the element they have mastery over and a spell," she announces proudly.

"Good girl," I repeat, dipping my finger inside her.

She lets out a moan as I slowly slide in and out of her. "What are the three situations when a witch's magic may not be effective, even if they have a spell and an element?"

She sucks in a breath. "When they're on hallowed ground. When they're surrounded by a magnetic field, and ..." She bites on her lip, and I still my hand.

"And?"

"When there's a counterspell in place," she breathes out.

"Good fucking girl." I push my finger deeper inside her, and she coats me in a rush of her cum. "Focus on your light, baby. I won't let you lose control, okay?"

She nods. "Okay."

"Can a witch give birth to a demon?"

She narrows her eyes. "We aren't covering demons today."

"I know, but we are covering witches." I pull out and sink into her once more, and her pretty eyes roll in her head. "So answer me, or I'll stop doing what I'm doing."

She blows out a breath. "No. Only demons can give birth to

demons. But witches can give birth to elementai, provided that their mate is a powerful demon."

"That's my smart girl." I swipe the pad of my thumb over her clit when I drive back inside her this time. She trembles from head to toe and whimpers, clinging onto my arm. The air around us grows thinner and warmer.

"I gotta stop now, Ophelia." I slide out of her, and she sinks back against the chair, her hands still gripping my forearm.

"Please, Malachi." A tear rolls down her cheek. "This is torture. I need to ..." A sob steals the rest of her words.

My heart throbs along with my cock. I pull her onto my lap and wrap my arms around her, nuzzling the sweet-smelling skin of her neck while I stroke her hair. "I know, sweet girl. Soon, okay? I want to give you what you need. You have no idea how badly, baby. But I can't."

She sniffs. "I know."

"You want to finish up here and go home for some snuggles in bed? Axl and Xavier are out of town, so it'll just be me and you. I'll put your favorite movie on, and we can go to bed early so we can be ready for Thanksgiving tomorrow."

"You'll watch *The Princess Bride* for me?"

I run my nose over her throat. "I'll watch anything for you."

WHEN WE GET BACK to the house, Axl and Xavier are in Axl's room, lying on top of the covers in only their boxers.

I shrug off Ophelia's backpack. "What are you two doing back so soon?"

"Got everything wrapped up quicker than expected. Our new recruits are pretty solid," Axl replies, looking past me at the TV.

"Yeah," Xavier agrees before he shouts obscenities at the ref.

Ophelia wrinkles her nose. "Ugh, basketball."

"I promised our girl we could watch a movie, guys." I kick Axl's feet and peel off my T-shirt.

"As long as it's not some sappy chick flick," Xavier grumbles.

"We could always go to your room, Kai," she says, fluttering her eyelashes. Axl's bedroom is bigger than both mine and Xavier's, so his has become everyone's room now. Not including the professor, who still sleeps in his room downstairs alone. Except for the rare—but still too frequent—occasion when he sleeps with Ophelia.

"The fuck," Axl says. "Get your ass into this bed, princess." He pats the spot beside him. "Now."

Xavier rolls onto his side, his eyes raking hungrily over my body as I pull off the rest of my clothes. "Yeah, I'll watch whatever sappy shit the cupcake wants. I got something else to keep me occupied for at least half an hour."

"I'm watching the movie," I insist, but my cock, only just softened after fingering Ophelia in the library, is already hard again at what Xavier has in mind.

"I haven't fucked you for days, Kai." His eyes drop to my dick. "And looks to me like you need a little relief too."

I glance at Ophelia, seeking her permission. After I left her on the edge, it doesn't seem fair to get my rocks off right in front of her. "It's okay. I'll watch the movie with Axl. We can snuggle when you're done."

Axl opens his arms wide. "Yeah, come snuggle with me. I've missed you today."

She jumps onto the bed and curls up beside him, and he wraps one arm around her while he grabs the TV remote with the other.

"Get your ass on the bed, Kai," Xavier commands.

After getting completely naked, I crawl onto the bed and lie on my front next to Ophelia. Xavier grunts his approval as he climbs on top of me and drags his teeth down the back of my neck. I twist my head to face Ophelia and Axl. They watch us while Xavier takes my hand. He runs his nose over my fingers before sucking three of them into his mouth. "Why do you taste like the cupcake?" he asks with a growl.

A smile spreads across my face at the reason why. But Ophelia mutters something unintelligible, her embarrassment seeping through her pores. If only to spare her blushes, I tell Xavier to go to hell.

He pins me to the bed by the back of my neck, pressing down hard. "Why is that, Malachi?"

"Because we fooled around in the library," I say, groaning. His dominance over me already has my body alight with desire.

Axl shifts onto his side with our girl still in his arms while Xavier keeps me pinned in place. "Did you make her come?"

I'm too distracted by Xavier's rock-hard dick pressing against the seam of my ass to answer, but Ophelia does it for me. "No!"

"Dammit," Xavier grumbles, running his nose down the side of my throat. "I thought the curse was lifted."

I buck my hips, trying to hurry Xavier up, but he's taking his sweet time, leisurely trailing his teeth along my skin.

"What curse?" Ophelia asks, snagging my attention.

My eyes lock on hers. "Not making you come isn't only a ball-ache for you, sweet girl." I twist my neck to get a view of Xavier. "A literal ball-ache for me right now. Could you get on with it?"

He growls and nudges my thighs apart with his knees. The head of my cock swells as he slips his fingers between my ass cheeks. "Love your hot ass, Kai."

"Oh, god," Ophelia rasps, and her face and neck are flushed bright red, her heart racing double-time. And fuck, the scent of her wet pussy isn't only on my fingers now, it's filling the whole room. "I d-don't think I can watch. I can feel you both, and I'm so on edge and ..." A deep, rasping breath stops her babbling.

"You gotta stop," Axl warns.

I press my face into the pillow and groan.

"But everything's a learning opportunity, right?" Xavier pushes himself off me, and I groan louder.

"Yeah," Axl replies warily.

"Then switch with me," Xavier says to him.

I'm so on edge, I don't care who fucks me as long as one of them does, but what the hell is he doing?

Axl looks as suspicious of Xavier's motives as I am. "Why?"

He takes Ophelia's hand in his. "We've been doing some work on closing ourselves off from other people's feelings, haven't we, Cupcake?"

"Yeah." She catches her lip between her teeth.

"So let's let these two fuck, and we'll work on tuning them out, okay?"

Axl's eyes blaze with fire, and he grins at me. "You ready to be fucked good, Kai?"

Xavier punches him in the arm, but they switch places without waiting for my response. They know my answer already. I'd take either of them anytime and anywhere, especially while my girl gets to watch.

Ophelia's heart races so fast, I'm sure it's going to pound straight through her ribcage.

I lean back against the headboard and pull her with me so her back is on my chest and her legs are outstretched between my spread thighs. Resting my chin on the top of her head, I band my arms around her waist and press my hand over her heart. Its quick yet steady rhythm thumps against my palm. "Relax, Cupcake. We've got this."

She sucks in a deep breath that has her juicy tits shuddering against my palm, and I screw my eyes closed and concentrate on anything but the feel of her soft body. I can't fuck this up for her. I've tuned out Axl and Malachi having sex hundreds of times before. This is a breeze. It's tuning her out that's going to be my undoing.

"I c-can't, Xavier. It feels ..." She sucks in another raspy breath. "So good. Please!" She drops her thighs open and grabs at my hand, trying to pull it away from her chest and no doubt shove it between her legs. And fuck me, I want to let her. I want to slip my hand inside her drenched panties and drive my fingers into her tight little cunt.

My cock twitches against her back, and she mewls like a wild alley cat.

Malachi turns his head, his green eyes searching my face as he chews on his lip. "You think we should stop?"

"Not a fucking chance." Axl grits out the words as he thrusts his hips, driving his cock into Malachi and making the latter's eyes roll back in his head.

Malachi and Ophelia groan at the same time.

I hiss out a breath. "Just slow down for a second, Axl. Let her take a few beats." I leave out the fact that I'm having as much trouble tuning them out as she is right now. Her presence magnifies everything. Every touch, every taste. Every single moment of ecstasy is amplified a thousand times over because of her.

I spread out my fingers so my hand covers almost her entire chest and pull her back to me. "Take a breath, Cupcake." She nods and sucks in a lungful of air. It does nothing to calm her racing heart, but it gives me a moment to clear my head.

Her skin burns, sizzling with pent-up sexual energy. "Why is this happening?" she whimpers. "What's wrong with me?"

I kiss the top of her head and inhale her scent, then wish I hadn't. "There's nothing wrong with you. You're on the edge because you have four vampires obsessed with you. We feed on you every day. We share our blood, and that's a powerful fucking aphrodisiac. And we're constantly touching you or thinking about you. We're permanently hard for you, and you're feeling all of that with us. All four of us wanting you *all* the time." I press another kiss against her hair. "And all that energy has nowhere to go because, until you get your powers under control, we can't let you come. Your orgasm might well bring about the end of days, and we can't have that."

She gives me a soft little laugh.

I press my lips to her ear. "You remember what I taught you about the doors?"

"Y-yes."

Thinking of people like rooms with doors was one of the techniques that worked best for me when I first learned to shut people out, and it seems to work well for Ophelia too. "That's my good girl. Now find the ones that are for Malachi and Axl. You gave them a color, right?"

"Yes. B-brown for Axl and green for Kai."

I remember. Blue for me and black for the professor. The color of our eyes, she said. I take another breath, and my pulse slows a little more. Axl and Malachi remain unmoving beside us, giving us the space I need to get our horny elementai's raging hormones under control.

"So find their doors and close them."

She nods, inhaling deeply, and I match my breathing with hers, murmuring words of encouragement in her ear. I've already learned that she focuses better with that than with silence.

"I've found them," she whispers, her eyes tightly closed. "They're wide open. Full of bright light."

She's already so good at this. My clever little cupcake. "Pull them tight until not a sliver of light is showing. Not even a crack beneath the door."

"But they're so heavy," she whines.

I flash my brothers a warning glare.

Axl shakes his head. "We're not resisting her."

Malachi shoots her a sympathetic look. "It's the bond. It's because of how strong it is."

"You're the most powerful person in this room, Cupcake. Now close the damn doors."

She presses her lips together, her pretty face screwed up with concentration. "I ... They're closing, Xavier."

The delight in her voice has me grinning like a goofball. "Keep going. All the way, Ophelia."

She nods, a smile on her face now. "They're closed."

Pride grows warm in my chest. "Good girl. I knew you could." I hug her tighter, resting my lips on top of her head, and she sighs, her soft body melting into mine.

I nod to Axl and Malachi, letting them know it's safe to resume their fucking.

Axl grunts with satisfaction, and judging by the loud groan that comes from Malachi's mouth, he's sinking back inside him. I can almost feel Kai's tight ass and taste his salty skin. My mouth waters.

Ophelia moans, but her pulse is steady and her skin is no longer blistering with pent-up desire. "You'll still feel them, but is it easier now?"

She blows a strand of hair from her face. "Yeah." Her voice is a soft purr, and it bypasses my brain and travels straight to my aching dick, which now twitches against her back.

"Dammit, Kai, your ass is so tight," Axl growls, and the bed rocks gently as he sinks into him over and over.

"Fuck!" I grit out, watching the two of them and wishing I could bury my cock inside my girl and fuck her right now.

"You can join them if you'd like." Ophelia's sweet voice does little to ease the desperate need racing through me. I swallow down the desire to flip her onto her back and fuck her so hard she screams my name, regardless of the consequences.

Instead, I inhale the sweet scent of her shampoo and squeeze her tighter. "I'm staying right here with you."

"I'll be okay." The tremor in her voice is slight, but it's there. She has a handle on her emotions and her raging hormones now, but I promised I'd be here for her. So that's exactly what the fuck I'm gonna do. Hold onto my girl for dear life and think about the least sexy thing I can while Axl and Malachi fuck each other senseless.

She wraps her hands around my forearm and presses a tender kiss on my skin, but it's enough to have my blood pumping harder through my veins. "Thanks, Xavier."

Oh fuck, give me strength.

You did well. Alexandros's voice echoes in my head, and if I wasn't sitting down, I'm sure the surprise would have knocked me on my ass. Or is he talking to Ophelia? That must be it. Not that she gives any indication that she's heard him. Cupcake is a slut for praise, especially his.

I am talking to you, Xavier, he says, sighing. *You have more patience and restraint with Ophelia than you do with yourself.*

My throat grows thick with so many different emotions. *She needed me.*

You did well. The deep timbre of his voice resonates through my entire body, and I close my eyes, basking in the warmth of the connection that's only for the two of us, if only for this brief moment in time.

He leaves as quickly as he appeared, and I'm left with an ache in my chest. Ophelia surely feels it because she nestles her head into the crook of my shoulder.

"You okay there, Cupcake?"

If she notices the crack in my voice, she doesn't mention it. But she does turn on my lap and faces Axl and Malachi. They continue fucking like we're not here, and she places her warm hand on my cheek and looks up at me, her blue eyes sparkling.

"I'm way better than okay. Thank you for helping me find my center." Then she presses her lips softly against mine.

A smile spreads across my face. I helped her find her center. Well, she is my fucking center. She makes everything brighter, more vibrant—just better. "I love you, Ophelia Hart." I murmur the words against her hair because, despite them being truer than any words I've ever spoken before, they sound so alien coming from my mouth. In my long life, I have never told a single soul I loved them. Not even Malachi. And definitely not Axl.

She brings her knees up to her chest, curling herself into a ball on my lap and rubbing her cheek against my bare chest. "I love you too, Xavier Adams."

I scoot down the bed a little with Ophelia still in my arms, cherishing the gentle weight of her on my chest. I watch Malachi and Axl, and although I've spent nearly every day of almost the last two centuries with the two of them, the sense of belonging I feel in their presence is so much stronger now than it ever has been before. With the full knowledge that it's undoubtedly futile, I search for Alexandros with my mind. *Why does everything feel different because of her? Stronger?*

To my surprise, he answers immediately. *Because her bond with me is unique, and therefore her bond with my sireds is too.*

But we bonded with her first. And it was like this before you two … Confusion clouds my thoughts. It's true that our bond grows stronger each day, but this feeling of belonging has been with me from the moment I bit her.

He gives me time to process before he answers. *There are bonds. And then there are other kinds of connections. I believe the one that Ophelia and I share is more, and as my blood runs through you, your connection to her is also deeper.*

What kind of connection? What can be more than a bond?

"Are you talking to the professor?" Ophelia asks sleepily.

Can she hear us? I ask him. This channel is only supposed to be me and him.

She can hear us talking, but she cannot hear the words. Consider it like her listening through a wall.

I brush a lock of pink hair behind her ear. "Just talking about how incredible you are."

She laughs softly, and I can't help but smile, both envying and admiring the trust she places in us by not prying any further.

More than a bond? I ask him again.

It is complicated.

So uncomplicate it for me. Please.

There's another moment's pause before he speaks again. *I have some business to attend to. Look after Ophelia.*

I always do, I say, swallowing down the sting of his rejection.

He's quiet once more, but I feel him lingering in my consciousness like he wants to say something more.

He doesn't, of course. He never does.

CHAPTER

SIXTEEN

ALEXANDROS

T rub my throbbing temples and screw my eyes closed until the swell of voices in my head calms to silence. How is it that my gift grows both weaker and stronger at the same time? I am less able to tune out all of the noise, but when I focus, I can hear so much more than I could before. It has been two weeks since I bonded with Ophelia, and the shift in my power since the moment I claimed her is surely no coincidence.

I lean back in my chair and stare out at the gray clouds rolling in. For once, it is merely the weather changing in Haven-wood rather than anything to do with Ophelia's mood. I stare at the sky and nothing else for a few moments, recalling the long-ago days of my youth when some of the most fearsome and powerful creatures who ever lived roamed those skies. As a child and later a man of House Drakos with the gift of communicating with such powerful beings, I was considered blessed beyond all others. Such a shame I have not been able to use that gift for almost a thousand years.

A shudder runs down my spine like a dark shadow passing over my soul.

Is that really you, old friend? Her voice is as familiar to me as if I had heard it only yesterday. But it cannot be. It is impossible.

Are you here in the netherworld?

I ignore her question. *Elpis, is that really you?*

Who else would it be, Dragon Whisperer?

An unexpected laugh falls from my mouth at that name. *Time has done nothing to dull your razor-sharp wit, I see.*

Her deep, rumbling laugh echoes around my head, reminding me of happier times when dragons roamed this earth as freely as any creature.

I have thought of you often, my old friend, she says, her voice tinged with sadness.

And I you.

Tell me who sent you to the netherworld, and I will tear off his head on your behalf. Or is it a she?

I rub a hand through my beard. *I am not in the netherworld. I am still here in the mortal realm.*

So your powers are now capable of traveling beyond the veil that separates the world of men from the damned?

I cannot fathom why that would be, but as surely as we are having the conversation, it must be true. *It seems so.*

The question I need to ask her sticks in my throat, so I clear it. I already know the answer, for it resides deep within my soul. Yet still, I must hear it from her, or I will forever wonder. *I had a wife and two daughters, Elpis. Are they—*

They are not here, friend. They were pure of soul and took their rightful place amongst the stars.

My relief is tinged with despair. I knew they were not in the netherworld, for if I had believed they were, I would have followed them without a second's hesitation. Yet her assurance is a balm to a wound I have nursed for over five hundred years. *Thank you, Elpis.*

Now there is the other question I am loath to ask, for the answer may destroy me.

I also had a son. Lucian? I hold my breath as I await her response.

There is no child of the Dragon Whisperer in the netherworld, my friend. I assure you.

Cool air floods my lungs. I knew in my heart that he was not dead. It is a bittersweet feeling to have irrefutable evidence that my son is not in the netherworld. He lives, and that is both profound and terrifying.

Even more concerning is that his hatred for me somehow allowed him to sever our bond centuries ago. The sting of his betrayal is never far from my thoughts; however, Elpis's voice stops me from falling into that particular black hole. *I was so very sorry to hear of the demise of the elementai, Alexandros. But the blind arrogance did not surprise me. To think they could vanquish an entire species and not suffer the consequences.* She snorts, and I can almost see the thick black smoke curling from her giant nostrils.

Your kind knew better than most of the foolishness found in so many of the younger generations, Elpis. The foolishness that set sons against mothers, brothers against sisters. The mangled pieces of my heart twinge with a fresh wound.

I once hoped that we would one day return to the mortal realm. She sighs. *Alas, things do not seem to have improved since the last of the dragons left over nine centuries ago.*

No, they have not.

The door to my office bursts open, and Ophelia bounds inside, her blue eyes wide and shining and her hair mussed like she just got out of bed. Her excitement vibrates through the room, so palpable that even if I were not so in tune with her, I would nevertheless feel it. She closes the door with a soft click before turning back to me and whisper-shouting, "Are you actually talking to a *dragon*?"

Once more, I slam shut the door to the vault containing my memories of Lucian. Giving her my attention, I cannot help the small smile that curves my lips. I should not be surprised she can hear me. It requires more energy than I anticipated to block her out, and I am painfully aware that I have no desire to do so. "What have I warned you about staying out of my head, little one?"

"I wasn't in your head," she insists, crossing the room before perching herself on my lap and snaking her arms around my neck. Instinctively, I wrap my own arms around her, pulling her close. "You were in mine. Or at least Elpis was."

I frown. "You heard her in your own head?"

She nods, her bright-blue eyes so full of trust and innocence that my heart aches.

Elpis, did you talk to anyone else in the mortal realm this morning?

Only you, Dragon Whisperer, comes her swift reply.

I brush Ophelia's hair back from her face. "Say something to her."

She blinks. "Like what?"

"Anything, Ophelia. Just speak to her."

She presses her lips together. *Um, hi, Elpis. It's very exciting to meet you.*

Well, who is this delightful creature, Alexandros?

So she can talk to dragons. I should not be surprised by this given all I have learned about her extraordinary abilities, yet I am. It is such a unique gift, one that I have not shared with another living creature since my uncle died over a millennium ago. *This is Ophelia.*

I can feel the excitement in her. See her in my mind's eye standing to her full height and shaking her scales. *And she shares your gift? She is a vampire too?*

She shares my gift is all I tell her for now. I trust Elpis with my life, but the fact that both Ophelia and I can communicate with her when she is in the netherworld ... whilst interesting, it is also unnerving.

"Dragons are real!" Ophelia squeals. "And I can talk to them?"

I press my finger to my lips, signaling her to be quiet before she wakes the boys. She presses her lips together and nods.

It was wonderful to hear your voice, old friend, I tell Elpis. *And we will speak again soon, but right now I have some business to attend to.*

She snorts a laugh. *Vampires!* And then, as quickly as she arrived, she is gone.

I focus all my attention on Ophelia. "Dragons?" she says, her voice quiet yet exuberant.

I nod. "Dragons."

"So they're real? Why haven't I ever seen one? Why don't people know they exist?"

Always so many questions. I am distracted from answering by the fluttering pulse in her throat, and I trail my tongue over it, letting the taste of her sweet skin flood my senses. My fangs protract.

"Alexandros!" She admonishes me even as she tips her head back and tangles her fingers in my hair. "The dragon?"

With a sigh, I stop short of biting her so I can answer her questions instead. "Dragons roamed the earth long before humans or demons. Even dragons themselves cannot say how long they dwelled here. Human measurements of time are meaningless to creatures of such age. But it is certain that they survived their dinosaur cousins. They possess a great magic. Some believe they were the cradle of where all magic began." I tuck her hair behind her ear as she listens with rapt fascination. "And that made them the targets for creatures who wished to use their magic, to exploit it for their own ends. Almost a thousand years ago, they grew tired of being hunted and manipulated, and they emigrated to the netherworld, where they have remained ever since. Until today I was never able to reach them through the veil that separates our worlds."

"So today was the first time you spoke to Elpis in almost a thousand years?"

I nod.

"Wow! How long do dragons live?"

I shrug. "Nobody truly knows, but Elpis was born centuries before I was."

She blinks, and questions race around her head at such speed I am surprised we are not both dizzy. "So can all vampires talk to dragons?"

"No. It is a unique gift of a chosen few vampires from the line of House Drakos. A gift that very few beings have ever possessed. The last man I knew who shared my gift was my Uncle Antony."

"So nobody else that you know can talk to dragons?"

I shake my head. Her unrestrained awe is so pure that it makes me smile in spite of the lingering melancholy from my conversation with Elpis. I have not thought of her kind for so very long, choosing to erase their existence from my conscious as much as possible. Their loss was almost as painful as that of the elementai, albeit less bloody and not marred by the same soul-obliterating betrayal.

Ophelia sucks in a breath, drawing my attention back to her, and more specifically to her chest and the hard nipples protruding through the fabric of Xavier's faded red Montridge T-shirt. His scent combined with hers is intoxicating, and I suppress a growl of frustration as my patience for her questions, as well as my resistance, grows weaker by the second. My restraint is never so uncharacteristically close to snapping as it is when I am with her. "So why can I?" she asks.

I stare into her eyes and wish I had more answers for her, whilst also wrestling with my base desire to distract her from further questions by sinking inside her. "It seems you are able to channel the powers of the vampires you bond with. That is why you could hear the boys' thoughts even before your powers were unlocked. Whether that is temporary or permanent has yet to be seen."

"Is that normal?"

I drag the pad of my thumb over her lips. "No, but then nothing about you is normal, Ophelia. You are extraordinary in every possible way."

She smiles, and the simple act has my cock twitching with the desire to take her right now. "And dragons live in the netherworld? Where is that? Is it like hell?"

"Not exactly. The hell humans are taught about does not exist. Nor does heaven."

She blinks. "Oh. So do we all go to the netherworld when we die? Is your family there? Can Elpis get a message to them for you?"

I screw my eyes closed as pain lances through my chest, and she places her soft hand on my cheek. "I'm sorry."

I dust my lips over her cheek. "You have no reason to apologize, agápi mou."

She curls her body into mine.

"No matter what kind of being they are, when pure souls

like those of my wife and daughters die, their energy rejoins the universe, and they live for eternity in the cosmos. But when the damned die, they go to the netherworld. A place of darkness and despair where memories die and only the cruelest thrive. It is the twisted joke played on vampires and elementai that they can never be together in the afterlife because one is eternally damned and the other is inherently pure."

Her nose scrunches up, and she tilts her head. "But why are vampires eternally damned?"

"It is our nature."

"But it doesn't have to be. I mean, you're good. I know you must have done bad things, but that doesn't mean you're not a good person."

That she surely believes that is concerning, yet it also pleases me more than I would care to admit to see myself through her eyes. "Make no mistake, little one, I am as far from good a man as you will ever meet."

She places her hand over my heart, and it thumps against her palm. "I think you're one of the best men I've ever known."

I rest my hand over hers. "I will always be a good man for you, agápi mou, but any kind of goodness in my heart begins and ends with you. I would sacrifice every soul in this world to protect you and not give it a second thought. Every. Single. One."

Her eyes glisten with unshed tears, and her fingers twitch against my skin. "I hope you never have to sacrifice a single soul for me, sir."

"As do I." But I surely shall and will. I do not voice that last part. There will be time enough to contemplate the sacrifices we will all certainly have to make, and that time is not now. Not when she is warm and soft in my arms.

"What about Lucian?"

133

Another piece of my heart is ripped away. "He is not in the netherworld."

Her eyes grow wide. "So he's alive?"

Alive and avoiding me. "It would seem so."

"But how?" She shakes her head. "Can't you feel him through your bond? Don't you know where he is?"

"I cannot, Ophelia, and before you ask, I do not know why that is, nor do I wish to discuss it any further right now."

She presses her lips together, and I am thankful she respects my wishes by suppressing her curiosity. Instead, she asks a question almost as heartbreaking to me. "So if you're eternally damned and I'm inherently good, that means we don't get to have eternity together?"

If she tears another slice from my heart today, there will be nothing left of it. "No, but we can still have a lifetime. As long of one as we can survive."

Tears well in her eyes. "That's so heartbreaking."

I nod. "I know. And that is why we try to live forever. And why to bond with an elementai is such a profound decision for any vampire to make."

"So biting me was a huge deal for you?"

I bark out a harsh laugh. "Ophelia, there are no words to accurately explain the enormity of my decision to bond with you." Sorrow clouds her features, and I cup her chin in my hand. "But know that I was aware of the inevitability of our union from the moment I first saw you in my basement. And it took every ounce of strength I had to resist you for as long as I did."

"So you don't regret it?" Her voice is small and quiet, everything she should never have to be.

I shake my head. "Not for a fraction of a heartbeat. I would choose you in every single lifetime, little one. Every single one."

She melts into my arms, nestling into me until her body

molds perfectly to mine. Until I cannot be sure where she ends and I begin.

After a few moments, she hops up and grabs my hand. "Time to go decorate the tree that Kai picked out for the den. It's huge!"

I bite back a laugh and follow her from the room. In all my years on this earth, I have never decorated for a holiday. When I had a family to celebrate with, the traditions were vastly different. However, when Ophelia revealed that she had only celebrated Christmas one time, five years ago, I allowed the boys to convince me we should do all in our power to make this year special for her. I try not to give too much attention to the notion that it may be the last peaceful Christmas she will know for a long time.

Instead, I recall the childish delight on Malachi's face earlier when he proudly declared he was going to choose the largest tree on the lot. Axl and Xavier rolled their eyes at his exuberance, but they were unable to hide their own excitement. Ophelia Hart has already brought such joy to our lives—so much that I cannot even bring myself to be mildly annoyed by the fact that I am about to spend several hours hanging tinsel and garland.

SEVENTEEN

ALEXANDROS

"Thank you for meeting with me again, brother."

Giorgios arches one thick eyebrow. "I have seen more of you these past three months than in the last three decades, Alexandros."

He is not wrong, and sooner or later, someone else will notice that too. A weary sigh escapes me, and he places a reassuring hand on my shoulder. "Nobody knows about my coming here. We are safe here in these walls." He glances around the faculty library.

I nod before dropping into the armchair. He sits opposite, hands clasped between his spread thighs, and his eyes staring into mine. "Is it about the girl? I have not yet discovered any more information about her past. It has only been a little over a week since you asked me, brother."

"If the information were easy to come by, I would already have it. I do not expect answers immediately."

He tugs at the shirt of his collar and rolls his neck. "Then has something happened with her powers?"

"No. I have not summoned you here to discuss Ophelia." I scrub a hand over my face.

He leans forward, his concern evident in the wrinkling of his brow. "Then what?"

The bitter memory of betrayal clogs my throat, stealing my words and my breath. I drop my head into my hands, willing my emotions to not betray me. Not now, after all these years.

"Alexandros, please." Giorgios's worried voice washes over me.

I swallow everything down and suck in a deep, raspy breath before I lift my head again and force myself to look him in the eye. "Lucian is alive."

His eyes narrow, and his blue irises darken. I have no need to feel our bond to experience the rage that seeps out of his pores at the mention of my son's name. "What?" he barks, the single word sounding like an accusation.

"He is alive."

He snarls, his shoulders drawing up toward his ears. "You have seen him? Spoken with him?"

Guilt and regret snake their way through my chest. How could I have gone all these years without knowing that my own son was alive? I should not have been so quick to assume him dead. I should have tried harder to find that truth for myself. That I did not eats away at my insides. "No."

"Felt him?"

I shake my head. "I only wish that I had."

His features twist in confusion. "Then how is it you know he is alive, brother?"

I take a moment to stem the raft of emotions that learning of Lucian's survival has stoked within me and carefully consider my choice of words. It is not yet clear why I was suddenly able to breach the veil between the mortal realm and the nether-world. Nor do I know whether this is a temporary state of affairs. And until I learn more about why this has happened, I will share it with nobody other than Ophelia and the boys. "I just know that he did not die. Trust me on this."

"But you felt his death." His scowl deepens. "I felt your pain at his loss, not that he was much of a loss to this world." Each word is clipped, dripping with the full force of his ire.

"No matter what he did, Giorgios, he was—he is still my son." I fight the growl that wants to seep into my voice, deter-mined to control my own anger. "Watch your tone when you speak of him."

His hands clench into fists atop his thighs, and he emits a deep, rumbling sound that communicates his frustration. "Son!" he spits. "What kind of son ..." His nostrils flare, and he inhales a sharp breath. "Betrays his own father. His mother and grandmother. His innocent sisters."

Each word is a honed blade aimed at my heart, and I again fight against Lucian's betrayal as it threatens to swallow me whole. That he was instrumental in the genocide of the elementai is the source of my greatest anguish, and no amount of time can dull the edge of that pain.

Despite my best efforts to maintain control, my lip curls back, baring my teeth. "I know what he did, Giorgios."

He hisses out a breath. "And you felt him die."

That is not true. I felt the severing of our bond. We only assumed it meant his certain death. "Perhaps I was wrong."

He leans back in his chair, his jaw clenched as he stares at the rows of books to the left of us and refuses to look me in the eye.

"What if he knows about Ophelia?" I say, needing to speak the questions that have haunted me since I learned that Lucian still lives. "What if he is somehow the one behind her attendance here?"

His eyes snap back to mine, and the horror of that realization clouds his features. "If that is true, Alexandros ... If the Skotádi—"

"We do not know if he is still connected with the Skotádi after all these years. Surely if he were, we would have learned of his survival before now." The implications of the Skotádi being aware of Ophelia and her powers are too horrendous to contemplate.

"He was their leader, Alexandros!" My name is a hiss from his tongue. Fury radiates from him like the heat from an open flame.

I roll my neck until it cracks, trying to tamp down my frustration. I was never fully convinced of that claim despite the overwhelming evidence to the contrary. "That does not mean he remains so. Perhaps he ..." I run my tongue over my top lip, and the lingering taste of Ophelia soothes the beast inside me more than anything else on this earth ever could.

"Perhaps he what? Suddenly grew a conscience and left the Skotádi to make the world a better place?" He scoffs.

I suppress my fatherly instinct to tear out my brother's throat, surprised by how quickly and easily it has returned, solidifying in my bones as though it never left. Yes, Lucian betrayed us all, but he is still *my* son. Instead, I growl a warning.

"Do not pretend that he is not drenched in the blood of thousands of innocents, Alexandros!"

I bang my fist on the table, and the sound of the wood splintering echoes through the expansive library. "I know, Giorgios!"

I grit out the words through clenched teeth. "Of all people, *I* know how much blood is on my son's hands."

The memory of the last day I saw him forces its way up from the innermost recesses of my mind. I try to force it back down where it belongs, but it emerges from the depths, relentless in its pursuit of being witnessed after five long centuries.

Lucian. My firstborn. My pride and joy, holding his dead sisters in his arms. Covered in their blood. Their still-beating hearts held in his hands. His mother, her body torn to pieces behind him. In our own house. In the same parlor where he sat at her feet as a little boy and listened to her sing whilst she stroked his silken black hair. Where he played with his sisters. Where I told him tales of dragons.

And he wept. He had the nerve to weep for what he had done.

"Alexandros!" Giorgios pulls me from the vortex that the memory yanked me into. I shut it away, locking it behind the walls of granite that I built for fear it would swallow me whole if I ever gave it too much attention.

I rub my throbbing temples. "If he were still the leader of the Skotádi, I would know. They are the enemy of every organization we provide pledges to. If my son were still one of them, certainly if he were their leader, I would have come across his signature by now."

"Unless he goes by a different name."

I twist my neck and train my icy glare on my brother once more. "I am not talking about that signature, brother."

His eyes twitches. "You mean the one that you and he share?"

"Precisely."

Giorgios licks his lips. "The Skotádi grow in power, brother. The heads of all four vampire houses are growing anxious. Six of our number were slaughtered in an attack in Vienna, two of them bloodborne. The Order remains steadfast in their refusal to interfere in anything despite their part in the creation of the very organization that threatens all vampirekind. You must feel the seeds of contention spreading their roots."

One of the reasons I remain behind the walls of this institution is to distance myself from politics and the age-old battles of magical beings. Here at Montridge, all species work in a harmony of sorts to ensure the survival of all. It is easy to forget that, outside these walls, my kind will always be seen as the enemy. The Skotádi seek to create chaos in an otherwise ordered world. It is why organized crime groups have made enemies of them—they disrupt merely for the purpose of disruption. The Skotádi also aim to erase most of the bloodborne vampires from the world, at least the older and most powerful generations. And the knowledge that my only son, a pure-blooded heir of House Drakos—the most powerful house in existence—joined their number is incomprehensible and unforgivable. That he did not even have the compassion to spare his innocent sisters is beyond any comprehension I am able to see.

"Why do they grow in power now when they were decimated and have been weakened in the last five centuries, as have all species? Who joins their number, Giorgios?"

He shakes his head. "That I do not know, brother. Perhaps as it was before, there are a few bloodborne vampires who sire armies for the Skotádi cause."

I know he is thinking that it is Lucian's sireds who grow their numbers once more. "Do you have contacts in the old country still?"

He nods.

"Then seek him out. But do it quietly."

"Of course."

I bristle at the ease with which he acquiesces to my request, given his obvious hatred of his nephew. "If you take his head, I will take yours, brother."

His blue eyes flicker with dark intent.

"I mean it," I bark. While he is the older brother, I was a foot taller than him by the time I was sixteen and have always been the stronger one of the two of us. And as our father's chosen heir, I outrank him. It was a source of great dishonor for him in our younger years, but one I hope no longer plagues him. He possesses other talents that I do not, and his lessened responsibility to House Drakos has granted him a measure of freedom that I will never experience.

He dips his head in a show of respect. "I would not dare take that honor from you, brother."

I sit forward and place my hand on his knee. "I value your counsel more than any other, Giorgios. Thank you."

A half smile quirks his lips. "You are most welcome, brother."

For all our differences, this is the man I trust more than any other. I know of his pain. Of losing Elena. Even though she was my wife and my bonded mate, I believe she was the only woman he ever truly loved. There has never been another before or since who captivated his heart in such a way. Lucian took her from both of us.

Thus, I understand his need for vengeance. But Lucian took my innocent daughters too—a crime so heinous that my brain shuts down every time I try to make sense of it. Yet still, I cannot bring myself to denounce him as my son. My love for him, though charred and blackened by his evil deeds, is still rooted within the deepest recesses of my heart. There is only one creature in this entire universe who could make me turn my back on him, and she is far too kind and pure to ever ask me to.

CHAPTER

EIGHTEEN

MALACHI

Thucydides Library is quiet as usual. In all my years at Montridge, I don't think I've ever seen more than five or six people in this cavernous space at any one time. I crane my neck to peer at the gold embossed titles on the books on the top shelf, certain I will find the one I'm looking for here. Since Ophelia's revelation that she and Alexandros can talk to dragons, I've found myself fascinated with discovering why they left the mortal realm to live in the netherworld.

"It has been a long time since I've seen you in here, Malachi." His voice sends goosebumps skittering over my forearms.

I spin around, my teeth bared in a snarl.

He leans against the bookshelves, legs crossed at the ankles and arms folded over his broad chest, a smug grin on his face. He always was an arrogant asshole. Star quarterback and next in line to be Alpha of the Brackenwolf Pack, one of the oldest and most powerful packs in North America. But I was willing to overlook his massive ego because he was also smart and funny and insanely hot. "You're not still holding a grudge?" He narrows his eyes. "It was sixty years ago."

"Sixty-two actually. And it could be six hundred years ago, Osiris, and it still wouldn't change what you did."

He shakes his head and sighs. "I thought that at least now you would understand."

What the fuck does that mean? "Understand how we were almost inseparable for two years, and then you just fucking left without so much as a goodbye?"

His dark brow furrows in a deep scowl. "I graduated, Kai. I had responsibilities. My father needed me."

The memory of him leaving still feels raw, but it wasn't his actual leaving that broke me. It was how he did it, and what happened after. "You ghosted me for six fucking years. Six years when I didn't hear a single word from you."

He takes a step forward. "Kai."

I move back, wanting as much distance between us as possible. "Don't fucking call me Kai."

He snarls now too. "Do you think it was easy for me to walk away from you? You were my best fucking friend. I ..." He licks his lips.

"You what?"

"I loved you too." He takes another couple steps so he's standing directly in front of me. Regret and sadness ball in my throat, and I force them down on a hard swallow. "But wolves and vampires do not bond."

I take a deep breath through my nose. "You broke my fucking heart, Osiris."

"I know." His voice is gentle. Tender, almost. "But when I left, know that I broke my own too. And I don't think it has ever been the same. Maybe it never will be."

I glare at him, wanting to stay pissed, but seeing the pain in his eyes, plus knowing he speaks the truth about wolves and vampires ... We are not a natural pairing, and wolves only mate for life with their fated mates. "Why did you come back? Why didn't you stay with your pack?"

He shakes his head. "Pack life was never really for me. At least not the life my father imagined. My brother was much more suited to it, so I stepped aside after our dad died. I prefer life here on campus. Teaching new wolves, an endless supply of fresh warm bodies." He nudges my arm. "And you're here. Even though you've barely spoken a word to me in the past sixty years."

"You never tried to speak to me either. You never apologized."

He laughs. "Maybe because whenever I so much as looked at you, Axl and Xavier threatened to rip out my heart."

A smile tugs at the corners of my lips. I can just imagine the hard time they gave him, and he fucking deserved it too. "I guessed they might do that."

"And I knew what I'd done. Our kinds were never meant to be together, and I knew that if and when I met my fated mate, I would have to break your heart again. I couldn't do that to you."

He's right, but that doesn't make his rejection hurt any less. "We could have been friends."

He cocks his head to the side. "I'll remind you of the aforementioned ripping out of my heart." His smile fills my head with so many memories. So many good memories that I buried beneath the pain of him leaving. A pain that I realize I no longer feel when I look at him.

"You were right to end it," I admit.

"But not to ghost you the way I did. I took the easy way out, and I'm sorry."

Wolves are obnoxiously strong-willed and guarded, but Osiris's openness with me now is all too apparent. He's letting down his walls, and I know how much it takes for him to do that. "Thank you." I already feel a little lighter. I have carried this hurt around unnecessarily for too long. And yes, I loved him, but it was nothing compared to what I feel for Ophelia. Unlike me, Osiris understood all along that a bond would be different. That it would separate us eventually. He has numerous children with various wolf mothers, but he's never settled with a single one of them. "I understand the whole fated mate thing now."

"I see the way you are with your girl. Why do you think I finally plucked up the courage to speak to you?" He winks, further dissipating the tension.

"I see you still haven't met yours yet."

He shakes his head. "Perhaps I don't have one."

I frown. My research tells me otherwise. "Don't all wolves have them?"

"Maybe she died before I got a chance to meet her. Who knows." He shrugs. "I'm happy as I am though."

I arch an eyebrow. "Fucking anything that moves?"

He bumps his shoulder against mine. "It's a tough job, but someone's gotta, right? Especially as Axl and Xavier are off the market now too."

"Yep. Now you have no competition at all."

He runs his tongue over his teeth, his eyes flickering with a hint of yellow. "They were never any real competition."

I shake my head. "You never had any problem with confidence, did you?"

He shrugs. "I was blessed with good genes. Why not take full advantage?"

I dip my head so he doesn't see my goofy smile. He's so much deeper than he pretends to be. In fact, he is one of the smartest men I know. It feels good to have cleared the air, and I only wish we'd done it sooner because I've missed his friendship more than I've missed his perfect abs. "Wait until you meet your fated mate, buddy. You're going to be in for a rude awakening."

"Nobody will ever tame me, Malachi. You know that."

Even he knows that's not true deep down, but I don't call him on it. Now that I have Ophelia, I can't imagine having to wait around for my soulmate to show up or enduring the agony of not knowing if they ever will.

"Hey, sorry I'm late. Axl and Xavier were—" Ophelia stops talking when she notices Osiris standing on the other side of the bookshelf, previously out of her line of sight. An adorable blush spreads over her cheeks.

Osiris arches an eyebrow. "They were ..."

"Um, hi Professor Brackenwolf," she says coyly.

He smiles. "It's a pleasure to formally meet you, Ophelia, although I have heard many good things about you."

I slip my arm around her waist and pull her to me, burying my face in her neck and growling when her scent floods my senses.

"Malachi, stop," she whispers. "Not in front of the professor."

I pull back and blink at her. "Why not?"

She chews on her lip. "Because he's a professor. It would be disrespectful."

Osiris lets out a barking laugh, and I pull a face at my girl.

"You know I'm older than him, right?" *And you let me do all kinds of stuff to you in front of your history professor*, I add privately.

Before she can chew me out for that, Osiris says, "I've seen all his moves already, anyway. Experienced them firsthand, in fact."

Ophelia's mouth drops open. "You two? No! When?"

I press a kiss on her cheek. "A long time ago, baby." Then I glare at him. "And you don't know *all* my moves." I flick my tongue piercing against my teeth. "I picked up a few new ones for my girl."

Ophelia clears her throat, but I can feel the way her body heats and see the direction her thoughts turn. One of my favorite things to do is flick this stud against her swollen clit. It never fails to make her whimper like a kitten. "Don't we have to study?" she whispers.

Osiris smirks. "I'll leave you two to your studies. But it was nice talking to you, Kai."

I nod, and this time I don't correct him from using my nickname. I guess I can let it slide.

"Always a pleasure, Ophelia," he says, and then the arrogant fucker winks at her.

I'd tell him to back the hell off, but he flirts with every creature that has a pulse. Besides, my girl only has eyes for me right now, and she's staring at me like she wants me to prove my tongue-piercing claim.

When Osiris leaves, I pull her to me and seal my lips over hers. Sliding my tongue into her warm mouth, I take what I want. At least some of what I want.

She moans. *We should be studying.*

I forget about my new fascination with dragons for now. *We will, baby. I have a book I want you to read about the Order, and while you're reading, I'm going to have my head between your pretty thighs so I can reward you for being such a good fucking girl.*

We can't. Not here. She protests, but she grinds herself against me.

There's a real quiet spot in the corner. Your chair will be facing the wall. Nobody will see.

Despite her objections, she allows me to take her hand and lead her to the corner of the library where I set our things before she got here. I push her down into the large wingback leather chair and angle it so that nobody has a chance of seeing what I'm about to do to her.

I drop to my knees. "Malachi, we really shouldn't," she says, looking around like we're about to get caught, but the delicious scent of her wet pussy is already thick in the air.

I hand her the book I found about the Order of Azezal. "You remember our tests, sweet girl. You're going to learn, and I'm going to reward you for every question you get right."

She nods and sinks her perfect white teeth into her pillowy bottom lip, her tits heaving in her hoodie.

"Good girl."

I glide my hands up the outside of her thighs, enjoying how her supple flesh yields to my touch. Her legs tremble and her breath hitches.

I press a kiss on the inside of her thigh. "Start reading."

She opens the book, and I resume my attention elsewhere, trailing my lips up the inside of her thighs while my hands skate higher until they find the band of her panties. Slowly, tantalizingly so, I peel her underwear down her legs, and with each inch I drag them lower, her breathing grows shallower.

I laugh, and my breath rushes over her skin. "I haven't even gotten started yet."

"I-I know, but if we get caught doing this ..."

A smile spreads across my face, and I pull off her panties and stuff them into my pocket. "We didn't get caught last time, did we?"

"No, but that was a little more ..."

I slip the tip of my finger inside her as a reminder, and she whimpers, one hand gripping the arm of the chair and the other still holding onto the book.

I push her thighs wider apart and then flick up her tiny skirt, exposing her glistening pink pussy to me. My mouth waters and my fangs throb. "More what?" I bend my head and slide my tongue through her wet center.

"C-concealed," she cries, pressing her head back against the chair.

With my mouth too busy tasting her to speak, I switch to our bond. *Read your book, baby.*

"O-okay," she whines.

I lap up her sweet juices before slipping my tongue inside her. Her arousal floods my tastebuds. Fuck, I want to eat her whole. *When was the Order founded?*

"S-sixty-seven BC," she gasps.

I flick my tongue piercing over the swollen bud of her clit. *Good girl.*

She presses her thighs flat to my head, but I push them apart again, needing more room to tease her. "K-Kai."

And why was the Order established? I continue feasting on her delicious pussy and ignore the desperate ache in my cock because I have no hope of fucking her and not letting her come. I'm too weak to hold back when my cock is inside her.

To protect the knowledge of magic. She sucks in a breath. *And to observe.*

My clever girl too. I graze my teeth over her sensitive flesh, and her hips almost shoot off the chair, making me chuckle against her skin. I go on teasing her, never giving her enough to get close to the edge, all the while keeping a careful check on her heart rate and the blood pumping through her body. If she comes in the faculty library and alerts anyone to her power, Alexandros will surely take my head.

And what do magical beings get in return for devoting their life to the Order?

She doesn't answer, but I hear her flicking through the pages of the book.

Ophelia?

"I'm l-looking." She rifles the pages more frantically.

I swirl my tongue over her pulsing clit. *You have ten seconds before I stop.*

She groans with frustration, and I count down in my head.

"Your counting is distracting," she moans.

Aw, pity. Four. Three. Two.

"Just give me—"

One. I push myself back and immediately miss the taste of her in my mouth. She glares at me, blue eyes dark with desire as she pants for breath. I swipe my hand over my jaw, cleaning her juices from my chin.

"That wasn't fair."

"I told you ten seconds." I tilt my head and smirk. "And I'm still waiting on that answer."

Her eyes narrow, but the corners of her mouth twitch. She grabs her skirt and goes to pull it down, but I snatch her wrist and shake my head. "Nuh-uh. I still want to look at what's mine while I wait for my answer."

"Ass," she mutters, but she goes back to the book. Her eyes scan over the text, and mine dart between her face and her glistening pussy. "Those who joined the Order were granted immortality for their devotion." She blows a strand of hair from her forehead and slams the book closed with a triumphant smile. "Now hand me my panties, fiend."

I press my lips together and stare at her for a few more seconds before I take her panties from my pocket and help her put them back on. Before I get them all the way up, I press one last kiss on her swollen, pink flesh, and then I look into her sparkling eyes. "Just know that I want nothing more than to finish what I just started."

"I know." She lifts her hips, allowing me to fix her underwear back in place. Staying on my knees, I pull her to the edge of the chair and push myself between her thighs, spreading them wider to accommodate me. And then, before I continue our lesson, I kiss her. Long and hard and deep, pouring everything I am into her and wishing that I could give her so much more. Because she is everything I am, everything I ever was, and all I will ever be.

NINETEEN

AXL

Xavier runs his fingers down the back of my neck, causing goosebumps to scatter along my forearms. What the fuck is wrong with him lately? He's almost *nice.* I shudder at the very word and throw him a look. "You want to stop that?"

His lips twitch in amusement. "But I like the way it makes your heart beat that little bit faster when I touch you."

I jerk away from him and scowl. "What the fuck is wrong with you?"

He leans back against the sofa, crosses his arms, and sighs contentedly. "Don't have a fucking clue." I follow his gaze to the other side of the room. Underneath a lighted garland, Malachi and Ophelia sit side by side on the sofa, each of them with their heads buried in a book. Malachi always used to love studying and reading anything he could get his hands on. But over the decades, he lost the joy of it somewhere along the way. Having been given the responsibility to teach Ophelia all about her magical side has reignited his unquenchable thirst for knowledge.

And then there's the professor. He has also joined us in the den on this dreary Sunday morning, which was previously a rare occurrence. I glance sideways at Xavier, who now has that goofy but fucking adorable grin on his face. And yeah, I guess I know exactly how he feels.

Alexandros looks up from his book, his eyes fixed on the window and a scowl darkening his features. Before I can voice the question on my lips, there's a heavy banging on the front door. He places his book on the coffee table and stands immediately, his scowl now replaced with a puzzled expression. "Osiris."

Malachi's eyes widen. "Brackenwolf?"

Alexandros nods. "Something is wrong." He screws his eyes closed and announces, "Enora is with him."

The most powerful wolf and witch on campus are outside our house on a gloomy Sunday morning. Yeah, something's wrong. What the fuck is going on? Ophelia opens and closes her mouth, but she doesn't ask a question. Malachi slips a protective arm around her shoulder.

Without another word, Alexandros heads for the front door, and muffled voices precede the three professors into the room. Enora's heart rate is elevated, her breathing shallower than normal. If I had to guess, her body is reacting in fear, but I have no idea what she could be afraid of.

Osiris is calmer, his pulse solid and steady. He glances around as he always does when he enters a room, his keen wolf eyes scanning the space quickly for any sign of threat. The only threat he's likely to find in here is Malachi's anger, but I can't feel any bubbling beneath my brother's skin the way it usually does when he's in the wolf's presence.

Enora steps up beside Alexandros. "Perhaps we should talk in private?"

He shakes his head. "Anything you say to me can be said in front of everyone here."

Her eyes skip over the people in the room. The creamy skin of her slender throat turning a fraction of a shade darker is the only outward sign of her annoyance. She's incredibly skilled in the art of masking her emotions from vampires, but blood never lies, and it continues racing through her veins.

"Is everything okay?" Ophelia breaks the silent tension in the room.

At the sound of my girl's voice, Enora's eyes fill with tears. She shakes her head.

"What has happened?" Alexandros asks in a gruff, commanding tone.

Osiris places a hand on Enora's forearm, and she offers him a nod like she's giving him permission to speak. "A young witch was killed last night. One of Silver Vale's."

Ophelia's hand flies to her mouth, and her next breath gets caught in her throat. "Who?"

"Meg," Enora says solemnly.

My gaze remains fixed on Ophelia, whose eyes now swim with tears. *Did you know her, princess?*

"Yes. I met her at the activity fair before school started," she answers aloud on a sob.

Osiris growls loudly, his annoyance palpable.

Alexandros shoots me a look of warning. "Do not talk through your bond when we have company."

I nod my head, signaling my compliance even as I ask, *Since when?*

He directs his outward attention to Enora, guiding her to sit. *They are both guarded this morning. That means they are suspicious.*

So you mean just don't make it obvious we're talking through our bond? Got it, Xavier says.

Once Enora is seated, Alexandros speaks again. "What happened to your witch?"

Enora clears her throat. "She had her heart torn out."

Ophelia presses her lips together, and I feel another sharp stab of pain in her chest. *Our girl has so much fucking empathy for other people.*

Xavier rubs his chest. *It would be adorable if it didn't give me constant fucking indigestion.*

Stop! Ophelia internally admonishes us, her wide eyes still fixed on Enora.

"Torn out?" Alexandros asks.

Enora sniffs and then rolls back her shoulders. "Yes."

Alexandros's jaw tightens with the telltale sign that he's pissed, but his voice remains eerily calm and controlled. "Are you here to accuse me—"

"No, old friend," Osiris says. "Nobody is accusing you."

Ophelia shakes her head, her eyes darting between the three professors. "What? Why would you think that? Why would they ...?"

Alexandros twists his neck until it cracks. "Tearing out a witch's heart was my ..." He pauses like he's searching for the appropriate word.

"Calling card?" Enora offers.

Your what now? I can't help myself from asking.

He offers a low growl in response, and I'm not sure if his ire is directed at me or Enora. Perhaps both. "It was much less than they deserved."

A tear rolls down Enora's face, and she brushes it away and turns her face from him.

Alexandros lets out a weary sigh. "What happened with the girl? Where did you find her?"

Enora gives him her attention once more, her jaw set and her shoulders rolled back. "She was found in her bed this morning."

Alexandros frown of confusion mirrors my own. "This happened inside the Silver Vale house?"

She nods. "It was made to appear like a vampire attack. There was a bite on her neck, and her body was almost completely drained of blood."

"Vampires cannot enter Silver Vale unless invited by you, Enora."

I thought that was all a myth—vampires not being able to enter buildings? Ophelia asks through our bond.

The Vales are all protected by magic that prevents demons and vampires from entering, I explain.

But not wolves?

No, Malachi says, his eyes boring into Osiris. *Nobody ever suspects the wolves.*

"I know this, Alexandros." Enora's voice is slightly raised. "The only vampire I have ever invited into Silver Vale was you."

Ophelia's eyes blow wide as Professor Enora's accusation ripples around the room. "He would never!"

Enora directs her fierce glare toward my girl, and my hackles rise. "Yes, child, he would. You have no idea of the things he is capable of."

Both Xavier and I growl a warning, poised to act if anyone so much as looks at her wrong or throws out any more wild accusations about Alexandros ripping out some witch's heart. While Enora is right that he is capable of such a thing, he wouldn't disrespect House Drakos and Ruby Dragon by breaching university policy and vampire law that way. All society members are protected. Untouchable unless they have broken an oath or a rule.

Relax. Alexandros's calm, commanding voice fills my head. *If she actually believed I had done this, she would not be sitting here.*

I sit back with a grunt. Ophelia sits back too, leaning against Malachi as he wraps an arm around her.

"What else is it, Enora? What have you not told me?"

"When I found her—" The curve of her throat thickens as she swallows. "She looked like all the others, Alexandros. I admit that I suspected you."

If he's bothered by that, he doesn't show it. But all the others? What the fuck is she talking about? She pauses like she's waiting for him to react, but he goes on staring at her, his expression still unreadable. "So I called Osiris to see if he could determine whether it was your scent." She looks to the wolf.

Osiris rubs his right temple and frowns.

"And?" Alexandros asks, his tone so cold and calm that it sends a shudder down my spine. If Enora and Osiris aren't careful, they're going to end up with their throats torn out, and they won't even see it coming.

"It was your scent, and also not your scent," Osiris says.

"What does that mean?" Malachi asks. "How can it be him and not him?"

"It wasn't him!" Ophelia insists.

Alexandros holds up a hand, silencing them both. "Explain to me how that is possible, Osiris."

The wolf blows out a breath. "It was as though someone used your scent to mask their own. I don't know, old friend. It was just off."

Alexandros begins to pace the room, his brow furrowed, not in anger but in concentration. "So how was a vampire able to get through the spell that protects Silver Vale and somehow have my scent?"

Enora's face grows paler, and she sucks in a deep breath. "I do not think it was a vampire."

Well, this just got way more interesting.

Alexandros stops pacing and stares at her. "Then who or what do you think is responsible for the witch's demise?"

"Well, not merely a vampire in any case. When Osiris told me about the scent, I ..." She swallows. "It is forbidden, Alexandros."

He crouches before her and takes her hand in his. His tenderness shocks me to my core, and I grab Xavier's thigh, my fingers digging into his taut muscle. I guess he's equally as shocked because he doesn't move my hand or call me a dickface.

"I promise you can trust everyone in this room, *fili mou*."

My friend? You two are friends? In all our time here at Montridge, I have only ever seen him and Professor Green treat each other with a modicum of civility.

Our acquaintance is a complicated one, he replies, keeping his eyes fixed on Enora.

How complicated? Ophelia asks.

Jealous, Cupcake? Xavier teases.

Enough. Alexandros's warning comes at the same time he speaks to the woman before him. "Enora. You are amongst friends here."

She nods. "I cast a spell from the *Book of Skoteiní Xórkia*."

What the fuck is the Book of Skoteiní Xórkia?

It's a book of dark magic, Malachi says. *Witches are forbidden from using it.*

Well, fuck me. This day keeps getting more interesting, and it's not yet noon.

"And?" Alexandros probes, seemingly unperturbed by her admission.

"Whoever killed Meg used the same magic. She was killed with dark magic, Alexandros."

Our sire is adept at masking his emotions and even better at blocking himself from us, but the spike of fear that hits him like a bolt of lightning makes it difficult for me to breathe. As quick as a flash, he composes himself, but it's too late. One look at Malachi and Ophelia opposite me and the sound of Xavier's heart beating double-time beside me tells me we all felt it. Yet his voice is cool when he speaks. "The Skotádi?"

Enora nods, and Osiris growls in agreement.

Alexandros stands and begins to pace the room once more. "The Skotádi were here. Are here? On campus?"

"I believe so," Enora says solemnly, her head dipped so I can no longer see the tears in her eyes.

"Who else knows about this?" he asks.

"Nobody but us."

Osiris runs a hand through his beard. "We should alert the heads of the other societies."

"What if I am wrong?" Enora asks.

Alexandros's dark eyes narrow. "Are you?"

She presses her lips together and shakes her head.

The Skotádi are here? Malachi asks.

Is this because of me? Because of what I am? Ophelia asks in a quiet, sad voice.

Alexandros sucks on his top lip, his brow furrowed the way it does when he's thinking, but he still takes the time to reassure her. *This is not your fault, little one.*

Is Ophelia in danger? I ask.

His jaw tenses. "Perhaps we should keep your findings between us for the time being, Enora. There is no sense causing panic when we have no way of knowing for sure who or what is behind this. It could be a rogue Skotádi attack or something more sinister."

Osiris folds his arms across his chest. "We need to also consider why they tried to frame you for this crime."

Enora dabs at her cheeks with the back of her hand. "And why they targeted Meg. She was such a sweet girl. Not overly powerful, but a promising young witch."

"Who found the girl?" Alexandros asks.

Enora looks to Ophelia, sorrow clouding her features. "Her roommate. Cadence," she says softly.

Ophelia's sob fills the room before she covers her mouth with her hand. Malachi pulls her closer and murmurs words of comfort in her ear.

It was not your fault, Ophelia, Alexandros repeats, and she nods, letting him know she understands. But whether she believes him is another matter. I wish I could take all her anguish away, and I hate that I can't. This feeling of powerlessness is unnatural and unwelcome.

Alexandros clears his throat. "Did she witness any of what happened?"

"She saw nothing that would help. She woke to find Meg dead and summoned me immediately. She is a bright young witch. She dealt with everything admirably, but she was understandably distraught. I gave her something to make her sleep. She will be out for a few hours."

He sucks on his top lip, deep in thought. "She will need to forget what she saw."

Enora nods her agreement. "That would probably be for the best."

Ophelia looks between the two of them, her eyebrows pinched together in confusion. "And how will you make her forget?"

I already know she's not going to like the answer.

Enora stares at the professor, blinking. "To make her forget such an event, one that leaves an indelible mark on a person ... You are the only one powerful enough to do such a thing."

He looks back at her for a few seconds before he gives a nod. "I will ensure it is done."

Ophelia jumps up, her pretty cheeks pink. "Are you going to bite her?"

"It is the only way to ensure she recalls nothing of this morning. To ensure her safety." *And yours, Ophelia,* he adds through our bond.

"No. You can't bite her. She's my friend," she shouts, and while it's clear her overriding emotion is compassion for her friend, she's unable to mask the tiny flicker of jealousy sparking within her. And that has my dick twitching to life.

Enora's brow furrows. "She will not come to any harm, Ophelia. A vampire's bite can be very pleasurable."

Despite the circumstances, I suppress a snort. Yeah, our girl knows that, Professor, which is part of the reason she's acting out.

"Ophelia." Her name leaves Alexandros's lips on a heavy sigh. "This is simply to—"

"What is she going to think happened to Meg?" She crosses her arms over her chest and taps her foot on the floor. "That she just upped and decided to leave?"

"I plan to tell all the girls that she had to go back to Vermont for personal reasons, which are to neither be discussed nor speculated over." Enora straightens her spine, her tone brooking no argument. "None of them will question my word."

"But I'll know the truth. And every time Cadence wonders where Meg is and if she's okay, I'll know. I'll have to lie, and I don't want to have to do that."

Enora tilts her head, regarding Ophelia intently. "The truth can be a burden to even those who are strong enough to carry it.

We are doing Cadence a favor by removing such a painful memory. But the truth can also be a gift. Consider yourself privileged to be allowed into this circle."

My girl lifts her chin. "Cadence is my friend. She can be trusted, Professor. And you know she can."

Enora purses her lips as though she's considering Ophelia's words. She looks to Alexandros and shrugs. "I do believe Cadence has a balanced head on her shoulders. She quietly notified me this morning, whereas someone else likely would have immediately descended into hysteria and alerted the entire house. We could allow her to remember the truth of Meg's demise and omit my theory about the Skotádi. It is your decision."

I am fascinated by their exchange. Why is it his decision? And more importantly, is he going to give in to our little pink-haired dictator? "It is safer if she has no recollection of these events," he says.

"If you bite her, I'll ..." Ophelia presses her lips into a thin line, her little hands balled into fists by her sides, and the entire room becomes hypercharged with tension. Alexandros trains his glare on our girl while everyone holds their breath, awaiting his response. Even Ophelia. She blinks at him, her mouth clamped firmly closed, probably so she doesn't say anything else to incur his wrath.

After what feels like an eternity, he finally speaks. And while he directs his words elsewhere, he keeps his gaze fixed firmly on Ophelia. "Wake the girl, Enora, and tell her what you think she needs to know. Summon me at once if she refuses to keep quiet. Otherwise, I will be there soon to speak to you about our next move." The menace in his voice has the hairs on the back of my neck standing to attention. Ophelia's pulse races.

Enora voices her agreement and stands, eager to leave the

room. The professor's growing rage is so palpable that it begins to fill the den like a thick cloud of smoke.

"Xavier, please show our guests out," Alexandros commands.

Xavier arches an eyebrow at me before doing as he was asked. Without pausing to see if Enora and Osiris have left the room, Alexandros grips Ophelia's chin between his thumb and forefinger. "If I bite her, you will do *what*, little one?"

Her throat works as she swallows, drawing my attention to her fluttering pulse. "I don't want you to bite her," she says, her voice barely audible.

He doesn't wait for any further explanation, moving so quickly that I hear her yelp before I see what he's done. Her feet dangle a few inches from the floor, her blood trickling down her neck as he feeds on her. With a hand now palming the back of her head and his free arm around her waist, he crushes her to him and drinks from her.

She wraps her arms around his neck and her legs around his waist, holding onto him as he takes what he wants. The sight of him doing that to her, while brutal and animalistic, is also fucking beautiful. Seeing him so feral and desperate ... There is a submissiveness in his dominance over her that is spectacular to watch unfold. And despite the savageness with which he feeds on her, her satisfied moans and the way she clings to him for dear life tell me that she needs this as much as he does.

TWENTY

ALEXANDROS

What will you do if I bite her, Ophelia? I ask again as her sweet, coppery blood slides over my tongue. Her power rages through my veins, and my heart beats so violently that it feels like it is trying to hammer its way through my ribcage.

I d-don't want you to bite her.

Why? I growl, sinking my fangs ever deeper into her creamy skin.

She continues to fight me. Fighting the truth. But why? I probe inside her mind, but she brings down a wall that shuts me out—a feat that even Axl, Xavier, and Malachi are incapable of. I pull her closer, so close that it feels like my body is absorbing hers. She grinds herself against the hardness of my cock, and the needy whimper that purrs in her throat drives me mad with the desire to claim her.

I have never wanted to devour any other being so much as I do Ophelia Hart. Every single thing about her is addictive and exhilarating and so desperately intoxicating that I can barely stand to be near her and not touch her.

Stop fighting me and tell me. I change my tone, making it less commanding and more soothing as I flick the tip of my tongue over the wound on her neck. *Why do you not want me to bite Cadence?*

She resists me still—at least she tries. But I force my way into her mind, probing deep inside the darkest recesses even as she tries to close off parts she does not want me to see. *Why?* I ask once more.

She tips her head back, a loud moan falling from her pretty mouth. *Because she doesn't deserve to have her memory wiped. That belongs to her. She should be allowed to keep the truth.*

I stifle a growl. *I know you care deeply for your friend, and that is admirable. But there is something more. Something you are hiding from me, little one, and I believe you are also hiding it from yourself.*

She whimpers, giving her body entirely to me, though she continues to fight the truth I am determined to seek out in her mind.

There's nothing more. I just care about my friend ... Sobs accompany her insistence, but she is still burying some truth deep within her psyche, and I will not stop until I uncover it.

My fangs sink farther into the tender flesh of her throat. Her blood thunders through me, and I probe deeper, trying to break through the last of her defenses. *Tell me, Ophelia!* I demand.

Hot tears roll from her cheek and onto my jaw. *I told you, sir.*

No. You did not. Why do you not want me to bite her? My tone is harsh and demanding. All the fight leaves her, and if I were a better man, I might feel a moment's guilt at forcing her to confront whatever truth she is so intent on hiding. But I am not, and I do not.

Because you're mine!

I stagger back a step with her still in my arms, my ears ringing and my cock aching from her words. The possession and strength in her voice have every cell in my body driven mad by the desire to show her who she belongs to.

I snarl. *I am yours?*

Yes! Another hot tear drips onto the side of my face, right beneath my ear. I picture myself carrying her out of the room and straight to my bed. Laying her down on it with my teeth still embedded in her throat whilst I unzip my pants and take out my aching cock. She must feel what I am imagining because a series of whimpers leak from her mouth and the thick scent of her arousal fills my nose. I cannot see straight with the strength of the yearning that courses through me. Right here in front of Axl and Malachi, whose eyes I can feel boring into my skin as they watch me with her. But given what we just learned, now is not the time for this, regardless of how the ravenous need to be inside her is driving me half crazy.

Mine! She says the word again, and it makes my blood scream in my ears.

I want to sink inside her tight, wet heat until the screaming stops. Until soul-affirming relief rushes over me, flooding every cell of my body. *Yes, I am yours, Ophelia.*

She wrenches her lips away. "Mine." She whispers the word aloud like a prayer.

I press my forehead to hers and unwrap her legs from my

waist so she is once more standing on her own two feet. My heart beats an erratic rhythm in my chest, its intensity mirroring hers as she stares at me with those huge trusting blue eyes. "Always yours."

Axl presses his chest against her back and pulls her hair aside before nuzzling her neck. "We're all yours, princess."

Malachi hums his agreement as he flanks our right side, wrapping one arm around Axl's neck and resting his lips on Ophelia's bare arm.

"Are you guys having a party without me?" Xavier's deep voice fills the room, and it makes Ophelia smile.

"Just showing our girl who she belongs to," Malachi says. "So get over here."

Xavier obliges, coming to stand on our left and resting his lips on top of Ophelia's head. I wrap an arm around Malachi and rest it on Axl's shoulder as I rest my free hand on the back of Xavier's neck. It is a possessive gesture and reveals much more of myself than I usually would with him, and whilst he softens at my touch, his focus remains on the beautiful creature in the center of our circle.

"Ophelia." Her head snaps up, and she stares into my eyes. "It is vital for our survival that we feed on others, little one. As delightfully addictive as you are, you alone cannot sustain four hungry vampires." She opens her mouth to speak, but I silence her with a warning look. "Sometimes it is necessary to bite people for many reasons, such as erasing their memory, but it does not in any way lessen what we have. So you will curb this jealous streak you are developing." I tuck a lock of pink hair behind her ear. "Before I am forced to curb it for you. Do I make myself clear?"

"Yes sir." Those words on her lips never fail to invoke a reaction in my groin area.

Sweet demons, give me strength. "Stop that!"

She sighs and presses her cheek to my chest. "Four hot, hungry vampires, and a girl still can't get an orgasm around here." She makes a feeble attempt at laughter, but her sadness is overwhelming. We all understand her need for something to lighten the somber mood. This day is only going to become more difficult for her.

Xavier swats her ass, making her yelp. "You should be careful getting four horny vampires riled up, Cupcake, or you might find yourself tied to a bed for the rest of the week."

Axl hums his agreement. "Being edged because you're not allowed to come."

Malachi chuckles. "Aw, my poor, sweet girl."

I inhale the scent of her, and I am unable to stop the images of her tied up and at our mercy from pervading my thoughts. "Perhaps we will tie our little troublemaker up later. First we must pay a visit to Silver Vale and speak with the young witch."

The boys voice their approval.

"Her name is Cadence," Ophelia says with a huff that has her warm breath penetrating my thin shirt.

"Whatever her name, we need to go speak with her." Not to mention find out as much as I can about what happened and figure out why someone tried to frame me for her roommate's death. Tearing out the hearts of witches was my calling card. Albeit, it has been a long time since I have left it.

"Shall we come too?" Malachi asks.

My eyes dart between the three of them. They are trustworthy, loyal boys, and I have not been the sire any of them deserve, though my reasons for turning each of them were very different.

Perhaps we should all pay a visit to Silver Vale. The time for secrecy is coming to an end.

~

OPHELIA RUNS to her friend as soon as we enter the parlor room of Silver Vale. Pale-pink and gold holiday decorations cover every available surface, and I had to duck to miss hitting my head on the mistletoe hanging from the doorway.

Enora, Osiris, and the young witch have been awaiting our arrival. At my request, Enora has permitted the boys to enter the house.

"Cadence, are you okay?" Ophelia asks.

Cadence wipes tears from her cheeks and steps into Ophelia's warm embrace, resting her head on her shoulder. She sniffs. "It was horrible, Ophelia. She was ..." She sucks in a harsh, rasping breath, and her grief mingles with Ophelia's and pervades every inch of the heavily decorated space.

"I'm so sorry," Ophelia murmurs, stroking her friend's auburn hair.

Cadence steps back, scrubbing at her cheeks once more. "Why Meg, though? She was so nice. Not even that powerful. Why ...?" Her question is swallowed by her grief, but I have no need for my mind-reading skills to know what she is thinking. It is the question every survivor asks themselves: Why not me?

"I suspect we will never know the true reason for this senseless act. For now, let us chalk it up to a random act of savagery," I say, drawing the witch's attention.

She blinks at me. "But why come to Silver Vale? Why ..." She breaks off, a sob stealing the rest of her sentence.

Cadence is too astute to believe that someone randomly chose Silver Vale and that the same someone was powerful enough to breach Enora's protective spells.

I cross the room so I am standing close enough that her grief seeps into my own pores. But her pervading emotion is fear. Fear that it might happen again and that next time she will be the victim of such a savage assault. "It appears that someone tried to frame me for Meg's death, Cadence. As of yet, we do not know why. And until we do, we must ask you to keep the details of her demise between only the people in this room. To reveal the truth would only cause panic and hysteria, and that will neither help the situation nor anyone involved in it."

She licks a tear from her lip and regards me with suspicion.

"Or, if you would prefer, I can make you forget. If you choose that option, you will be made to believe the same as everyone else—that Meg has returned to her family in Vermont."

She swallows hard but maintains the same level of steady eye contact. I am unsure whether to be impressed by her nerve or annoyed by her insolence, but when she speaks, the latter nearly wins out. "Why wouldn't you just do that anyway?"

I rock my head from side to side. Ophelia's eyes burn a hole in the side of my face, encouraging me, none too gently, to stretch my patience for her friend a little further. "Because both Ophelia and Professor Green assure me that you are a capable, sensible witch who can be trusted. But if that is not the case ..." I level her with the stare that has made kings, emperors, and ruthless dictators alike fall to their knees before me.

Her pupils blow wide, yet she still does not look away. "I don't want to forget," she whispers.

I search her face for signs of deceit and find none. My instincts are rarely wrong, and they are telling me that she is every bit as trustworthy as Ophelia and Enora believe her to be. "Good girl."

Ophelia scowls at me, and her unguarded reaction reminds me to be more cautious with my choice of words. I am unaccustomed to dealing with jealous lovers as I have never tolerated such behavior from those I took to my bed. It is a surprise for me to realize that I am not annoyed by her display of such a primitive emotion. Rather, I am quite pleased.

"Cadence." Enora wraps her arm around the young witch's shoulder. "You should go join the others in the den. They are all upset at Meg's sudden departure. I know I ask a lot of you, but it will lessen their suspicion if you speak to them of her leaving." She places her hands on either side of Cadence's face and talks her through the story she has told all the other witches.

After hugging Ophelia once more—and with a determination that I admire—Cadence rolls back her shoulders and heads out of the room to play her part in the charade.

As soon as she is gone, Osiris speaks. "So, what do we do now? President Ollenshaw has been alerted to Meg's death. He is in agreement that we should keep the truth of the situation from the students, but he has called a faculty meeting." Osiris checks his watch. "It begins at eleven. That means we have less than an hour to decide what to tell them."

"We tell them as much of the truth as we can afford to," I reply. "The girl was found dead. An intruder of unknown origin and motive tore out her heart."

"Does that not implicate you, old friend?" Osiris asks.

Malachi comes to stand beside me and pulls Ophelia into his arms, and she nestles against his chest. "I don't understand. Why would that implicate you where the president is concerned?" he asks.

"Because after my wife and children were murdered, I tore out the heart of every witch I could find who played their part in the genocide. And there are few magical creatures at this university who have not been made aware of that fact."

Osiris's dark eyes narrow, flickering with amber because his wolf is near the surface. "I think there are a fair few who had no idea you had a family. I knew about your history with witches, but I always assumed your quest for vengeance was about your mother."

I shake my head. "My wife and two daughters were elementai." I still keep Lucian's name out of it, unable to admit to the boys that I have a son and that he is alive.

Osiris's face remains clouded with suspicion. "You never told me."

Axl folds his arms across his chest. "He never told us until a few weeks ago either."

Osiris raises an eyebrow. "So many secrets, old friend."

I twist my neck. "We all have our secrets, do we not?" *Enora?* I say that last word to only her, and she visibly bristles. "For now, we will keep our suspicions about the Skotádi from the rest of the faculty. It would only cause unnecessary hysteria, and there is no suggestion there is any threat to the humans at this stage. But I suggest we alert the society heads so they can take the appropriate steps to protect their students."

"Dr. Ollenshaw would lose his mind and have the whole campus on magical lockdown at the mere hint of Skotádi," Enora says, her voice full of disdain. She holds him in as low a regard as I.

"We definitely don't tell Jerome," Osiris agrees.

I check my watch. It was a full moon last night, and the wolves will all be sleeping off their hunt. I cannot imagine they were happy about being called to a faculty meeting on a Sunday morning, and most of them will no doubt miss it. However, having Osiris's counterparts there is imperative. "There is not much time to spare. Can you round up the Crescent leaders and have them meet us in the history building before the faculty meeting begins?"

He nods. "Wish me luck."

With a brief goodbye to everyone in the room, Osiris leaves, and I direct all my attention to Enora. She tilts her chin defiantly, aware of the information I require. The information I have been gracious enough to allow her to keep to herself for too long already.

"Who is the witch you are keeping secrets for?"

Her brows knit in a frown, and she makes a good show of pretending she has no idea what I am referring to, but she cannot fool me for a second.

I breathe deep, channeling calmness. My patience is never so close to snapping as when matters of Ophelia's safety are concerned. "Do not toy with me. Who is the witch that asked you to keep a watchful eye on Ophelia?"

Her slender throat convulses. "I cannot say."

Ophelia takes a step forward and stands beside me, but her gaze is focused on Enora. "Someone asked you to keep an eye on me?"

Enora ignores the question and instead glares at me.

"A witch is dead, Enora. Someone clearly tried to frame me for the crime. Now is not the time for secrecy." The irony of that statement is not lost on me, but now is also not the time for self-reflection.

Her jaw tics. "I am unable to tell you. I wish that I could, but I cannot."

I take a step forward, and she flinches. "Has time softened your memories of me, witch? If you refuse to disclose their identity, I *will* bite you and discover that truth for myself."

"It is forbidden to bite a faculty member without their consent."

"As forbidden as it is to use dark magic from the *Book of Skoteiní Xórkia*? I think we are all aware that following the rules of this institution is no longer my priority."

She takes a step back, eyeing me warily, as she should. "If I allow you to bite me, then I would be breaking my oath, Alexandros. Besides, it would take you years to search my memories."

I suspect that was true as recently as three weeks ago, but not any longer. Not since Ophelia Hart snaked her way into every fiber of my being and somehow magnified my power with her own. "I am willing to test that theory."

Before she can blink, my hand is on the back of her neck, fisting in her hair. I drag her to me, pressing her slight body against mine, and sink my teeth into the soft flesh of her throat. Her lifeblood flows over my tongue. Ophelia's shock followed by a pang of jealousy spiking in her chest are the first sensations to hit me, and I take a second to remind her that I take no pleasure in biting anyone but her, even if I am about to make this entire experience much more pleasurable for Enora.

She struggles, muttering a spell that almost wrenches my teeth from her neck, but I hold fast, searching her memories as I deepen my bite. Finally, her body complies even if her mind does not. She goes limp in my arms, but she chants another spell, and I am forced to hold her tighter as I resist the external forces of the incantation that try to pull me from her.

The quicker you allow me to get what I want, the sooner this will be over, filis mous, I remind her.

"I cannot allow you access to those memories," she rasps. "I swore an oath."

You simply have to stop fighting me. I will find them myself, and then this will be less painful for all of us.

"But you cannot find them. It will take too long." A tear rolls down her cheek.

As if they are stills from a movie, I easily comb through her memories, flicking through them at lightning speed. And although her mind is as strong as it always was, it takes me but a few moments to find the memory I am searching for.

I stop feeding and take a step back. Enora blinks at me, her body seemingly frozen to the spot.

"Nazeel Danraath." A sliver of fear snakes its way through

the anger inside my chest. Never would I have expected her name to be the one I found inside Enora's memories. What was Nazeel's motive?

"Y-you found it. But how?" Blood trickles from the wound in her neck, which I did not take the time to heal. She mutters a spell, and the torn flesh begins knitting back together.

I have no desire to explain the rapid increase in my powers. "Why is a member of the Order asking you to keep a watchful eye on Ophelia?"

Ophelia gasps. "Like the Order of Azezal? That Order?"

Pride swells within me, and I suppress my smile. She is learning so fast, but I never should have expected anything less from my curious scholar.

Not now, little one.

She presses her lips together and mumbles an apology through our link.

Enora pays Ophelia no mind. "She did not make me aware of her motives, Alexandros. But you know as well as I do that Nazeel would mean no harm to any witch. She simply asked me to take an interest in the girl and determine whether she had any magical ability," she explains. "As you are aware, having accessed my memories." Heat blooms across her cheeks.

A better man would offer an apology for violating her trust and privacy, but I am not that man, and I would do it again—a fact she is well aware of. Her family swore an unbreakable oath to the Danraath witches centuries ago as penance for their involvement in the elementai genocide—a crime which Enora played no part in but for which she still had to pay.

"Who is Nazeel?" Ophelia asks, the words bursting from her as though she cannot contain them. "Do you know her? Can she be trusted?"

My ironclad control is being pushed to its very limit today, but I, too, have questions that I wish someone could answer.

Pinching the bridge of my nose, I bite back my frustration and take the time to reassure Ophelia. "She is a member of the Order. A powerful witch. And yes, I know her." I lick my lips. "I have never had reason not to trust her," I admit. But why does she have an interest in Ophelia? Does she know the truth? If she did, surely she would ... She would do nothing. Members of the Order do not act. They observe, or they do not remain part of the Order for long.

"The Order is no threat to anyone, Ophelia," Enora says reassuringly.

I screw my eyes closed and concentrate, certain that all the pieces of the puzzle are within my grasp. If I could only connect them properly ... But the answers I seek continue to elude me. "You must be curious, Enora. Has Nazeel ever asked such a favor of you before?"

The witch shakes her head. "No, and of course I was curious. But you witnessed the memory. She simply told me that she believed the girl had been overlooked and needed a chance to unlock her potential. And has that not happened?"

I rock my head from side to side, simmering rage growing hot and tight inside my chest. "I beg your pardon?"

Enora gives me a wry smile. "Do not toy with me, Alexandros," she says, repeating my own words back to me. "The girl's powers have been unlocked. I sense it in her." Her gray eyes sparkle with undisguised glee. Understandable, considering her incorrect assumption that Ophelia is a witch. "You must pledge for Silver Vale, Ophelia. The closing ceremony has passed, but for someone with such potential, we can bend the rules."

"Not a fucking chance, Cupcake." Xavier's growl of warning is echoed by his brothers.

Enora huffs indignantly. "I believe that is for Ophelia to decide." She glares at me. "Surely you will allow her to pledge, Alexandros. It is cruel to deny her the opportunity to learn from her peers. She already fits in so well here at Silver Vale. Your ..." Pausing, she wrinkles her nose and scrutinizes my three boys. "Offspring will be permitted to visit, provided they can behave themselves with the expected decorum."

So unaccustomed to flattery, Ophelia's cheeks turn a brighter shade of pink than her hair.

Do not even think about it, little one. You are ours, remember? I warn her. I do not believe she is tempted by the offer, but it is important that she knows her leaving us will never happen.

If Enora knew my boys and I were bonded with Ophelia, she would not dare suggest such a notion, but since the extinction of the elementai, vampires rarely choose to bond. And whilst I trust Enora more than most, the risk of her knowing about our bond is too great.

"Thank you so much for the invitation, Professor, but I love where I live." Ophelia offers her signature sweet smile. "And Malachi has been helping me learn about magic and spells and things. He's actually really knowledgeable about witchcraft."

Enora shudders, no doubt appalled at the very idea of a vampire teaching a witch, and her youthful veneer slips for the merest fraction of a second. Once she has recomposed herself, she says, not unkindly, "It is not the same as being amongst your own kind and learning with your sisters, sweet child."

"She will learn with her brothers instead. Together, we are more than capable of giving Ophelia what she needs." I grab Ophelia's hand and thread our fingers together.

Enora's expression lights with awareness upon seeing my overt show of possession. "Oh. I see."

"Ophelia will remain at Ruby Dragon," I declare, not bothering to hide the nature of our relationship. "She will not be pledging to any of the Vale houses."

"It is selfish to keep her from her kind, Alexandros, and you know it. And one day, she will resent you for it," she says, not unkindly, but I do not need her warning.

"No, I won't," Ophelia snaps, finally showing the feisty side that she typically keeps buried in favor of respecting her professors. Until now, I have only ever seen her speak to me in such a way, and even then, only after I pushed her beyond what any other person could deem reasonable.

"You are too naive to see it now, child," Enora says in that soft, singsong tone she uses to lull people into her web. "But one day, you will see that these boys are not what you need. Vampires and witches are not a good match."

Axl, Xavier, and Malachi growl, all of them edging forward. I raise my free hand, stopping them in their tracks, and allow an edge of danger to tint my otherwise aloof tone when I speak into her mind. *Just because you could not keep me in your bed, Enora, do not dare to assume you know anything about me or my boys.*

Her face flashes with the pain of rejection, but it is nothing less than she deserves.

You and Professor Enora? Ophelia's hurt-filled voice floods my thoughts now too. Perhaps it was cruel to allow her to hear, but I do not wish for there to be any secrets between her and me. *You have much to learn about vampires and witches. We all seek the pleasures of the flesh, but that is very much in the past.*

She tries to pull her hand from mine, but I refuse to allow it. *Behave yourself, or I will bite you right now to ensure your submission.*

Her hand goes limp in mine, her jealousy assuaged, and I focus on Enora once more. "I do not wish to dredge up our past mistakes, *filis mous*. That is long buried in the distant past where it should remain. We were always better friends than lovers, you and I. Trust me when I tell you that Ophelia's needs will be well taken care of at Ruby Dragon."

"Yeah, we got everything she needs. Isn't that right, Cupcake?" Xavier says.

Ophelia gives him an adoring smile and nods before turning back to Enora. "I do appreciate you looking out for me. And I do really like it here, it's just that Ruby feels like my home."

Enora smiles, and her obvious genuine affection for Ophelia is reason enough alone for my gratitude and loyalty. "You are welcome here any time. Cadence will be needing her friends around her these next few weeks."

Reminded of the reason we are here, I add, "If there is any indication that the girl cannot cope with the burden we have placed on her this day, let me know immediately, and I will erase her memory."

Enora nods. "I will keep a careful eye on her."

As soon as we have left the vicinity of the Vale houses and are sheltered by the cover of trees, I draw to a stop. Confused, Ophelia stops beside me. With slow, deliberate intent, I wrap my hand around her slender neck and press the pad of my thumb on the underside of her jaw, tipping her head back until her pretty blue eyes are locked on mine. Axl, Malachi, and Xavier stand to either side of us, devious grins on their faces.

Ophelia narrows her eyes. "This is either where you bite me or reprimand me. So what have I done wrong?"

I brush my lips over her jawline. "I do love having you in this position, little one. Feeling your pulse flutter beneath my hand makes me want to strip you naked right here beneath these trees and sink my cock inside you inch by inch until you are begging me to fuck you." Her pupils blow wide, and she sucks in a deep breath that makes her breasts heave. "As adorable as it is to see your little fists balled with rage, you have no reason to harbor such petty jealousies."

Her throat works like she is ready to speak, no doubt to come back with some feisty retort, but I squeeze my hand and cut her off. "I have lived for over two thousand years, Ophelia. I have enjoyed many pleasures of the flesh. I have bedded at least half the faculty of this university, but all of it was merely in pursuit of momentary pleasure. I have only ever bonded to one woman before you. She grew three of my children in her womb, but still *nothing* compares to the feelings I have for you. Our bond is unique. Not just with me, with all of us. No one will ever take your place, agápi mou. And the sooner you realize that, the easier all our lives will be."

I relax my grip on her and rest my hand at the base of her throat, allowing her to speak freely. "I'm sorry. I'll try to do better, Professor." Her sultry tone coupled with her warm breath dancing over my face has me on the edge of finishing what we started earlier in the house. Is that her end game here? She is incredibly submissive, perhaps because she knows how hard it makes all of us. The boys are as desperate for her as I am, and the wicked smirk playing on her lips tells me she knows it. What happened to her friend today has her nerves understandably on edge, and perhaps she is seeking comfort in the best way she has learned. Whilst that saddens me, I am also painfully aware that it would be a comfort to all of us.

"Are you simply looking to get yourself fucked, Ophelia?"

Her legs tremble, and the scent of her arousal grows thick around us. She sinks her teeth into her bottom lip. "Maybe."

I trail my fingertips over her cheek and suppress a smile. "Not right now."

Axl and Xavier each let out a dark laugh, and Malachi utters an unintelligible word that sounds full of sympathy. "So unfair," Ophelia mutters.

I drop my hand and walk away, striding ahead and leaving her and the boys to make their way back to the house at a slower pace behind me. Yes, it is unfair. I wish I could spend every waking second with a part of me inside her, but there is too much to lose. Too much at stake if she unleashes her powers before she has a hold on them. If it would not draw my suspicion from my father, I would take her and my boys far away from this place and never return.

I squash the idea before it takes root and begins to grow. There is no simple answer to the paradox of Ophelia Hart. And if I were a man prone to wasting time, I might wish that there was.

TWENTY-ONE

AXL

Alexandros is pacing his study and runs a hand through his hair while muttering in Greek. We got back from Silver Vale a few moments after him, and he summoned us in here as soon as we set foot through the door. I've never seen him so rattled before, and it's unnerving.

"I don't understand why Meg having her heart ripped out would be an attempt to implicate you, Professor?" Ophelia says, her nose wrinkled in confusion. "Surely you are not the only vampire ever to have committed such a crime?"

He stops pacing and stares at her, and there is a look of something like regret etched on his face. But I know that can't be right because my sire is made of granite. He is sure and iron-willed, leaving no space for all-too-human emotions like regret or guilt.

Alexandros's eyes don't leave Ophelia's face. "To tear out a witch's heart ..." His tongue darts over his bottom lip. "In ancient times, witches believed that their hearts were the root of their power." His eyes flicker over her face as though he's searching for something. Her disapproval, perhaps? But our girl simply maintains that same curious expression she often has. "Like their elementai cousins, witches' emotions have always been linked to magic. Therefore, even after their ancestors discovered that the heart was simply another vital organ, the heart remained a totem of a witch's power for a long time. To remove their heart is to desecrate their body, and some believe this prevents them from taking their place amongst the cosmos after their death."

"So by taking their heart, you also take their soul?" Ophelia asks.

He nods, his eyes still fixed on her. "That is why removing a witch's heart is so barbaric and why it is considered too heinous a crime for most to be capable of."

"But not you?" Her voice is little more than a whisper.

A low, instinctive growl rolls out of him, and before I can blink, he's standing right in front of her, a large hand cradling her face. "No, not me. And make no mistake. I would do the same again if I had to."

Unease permeates the room, so heavy I can taste it, but I can't decipher it entirely. Perhaps because it is something I've never experienced before from Alexandros. I pay careful attention to the way his heart pulses a little faster than normal, his breathing a fraction shallower, his eyes imploring her. Is he seeking her approval? Or her forgiveness?

Ophelia's heart rate picks up now, and I tune into her feelings, surprised at how much more easily I can do that since he bonded with her too. Perhaps it has something to do with her powers being unlocked, or maybe it's because the five of us are one entirely connected unit. Whatever it is, I like it, and I don't have the desire to dissect that any further right now. But she doesn't disapprove of him. Not even a little. She feels sadness. His and her own. And she's anxious too, much like the rest of us, but not because of anything he's done.

"I hope you never have to" is all she says. She tips her head back, submissively displaying the pale skin of her throat.

The air grows thick with sexual energy as he runs the pad of his thumb over her lip. My brothers watch them every bit as intently as I do, and all five hearts in the room beat to the same steady rhythm, a cacophony of blood pulsing through each of us. The symphony of our bond. "Enora will cast new spells which will strengthen the protection at Silver Vale, and I will have her cast a similar incantation preventing anyone uninvited from entering this house too, but as we discovered today, they are not failproof. We will all need to be more cautious."

He keeps his hand around Ophelia's throat. "And you will no longer go anywhere on this campus unaccompanied." She licks her lips but doesn't reply. "Do you understand me?"

"Yes sir," she whispers.

"Why do you think someone from the Order is interested in Ophelia?" Malachi asks, cutting through the uncomfortable silence. "Do you think this Nazeel knows what she is too?"

Alexandros sighs. "I cannot be sure. There are far too many unanswered questions, but we cannot discount the possibility that there are others who are aware of Ophelia's powers. At least some of them."

My frustration mirrors his. Unlike Malachi and Ophelia, I'm not naturally curious by nature. I have lived the last two hundred plus years operating on instinct. Taking what I wanted and following my sire's lead without hesitation. But now I find myself plagued by questions that have no easy answers. One thing I am sure of, however, is that my pink-haired princess is at the center of it all.

She inhales a shaky breath. "Do you think what happened to Meg might—"

"I will never allow anyone to hurt you," Alexandros says. He rests his forehead against hers. "We would all die to protect you."

Xavier, Malachi, and I voice our agreement. She sniffs, and a fat tear rolls down her cheek. "I don't want any of you to be hurt because of me. For anyone to be hurt because of me. Meg was ..." She chokes on a sob.

"You are not responsible for any actions other than your own, Ophelia Hart," Alexandros says, his tone so authoritative that it leaves no space for challenge. "Promise me you will always remember that."

She sniffs again, and he swipes a tear from her lip. "I promise."

"I have to go speak with the faculty heads." His voice is steeped with regret, and he glances between Xavier and Malachi. "You two will stay with Ophelia." He checks his watch and looks at me. "You will accompany me."

I'm torn between my sense of responsibility and my desire to stay with Ophelia and comfort her, but while Xavier, Malachi, and I are all commanders of Ruby Dragon, I am the unofficial leader, and I don't underestimate the importance of what he's about to do. There is a fine balance between curating allies while still keeping Ophelia's identity a secret, and I'm honored that he trusts me enough to allow me to stand by his side.

But I feel Xavier's acute frustration at not being chosen. He is no doubt as capable as I am, and it's too bad his fiery temper all too often lets him down. His rage simmers beneath the surface, but he keeps a lid on it, his blue eyes fixed on Ophelia. "Come here, Cupcake."

Alexandros releases his grip on her, allowing her to go to him, and Xavier wraps her in his arms. Seeing the way she nestles against his body makes me jealous that he gets to stay behind.

"We will update you with any pertinent information upon our return," Alexandros says stiffly before striding from the room. I give my girl an all-too-brief kiss before I hurry out after him.

THE TENSION in Alexandros's classroom is so thick, I could pierce it with my fangs. The various society leaders sit in the front two rows, their eyes focused on the front where Alexandros stands alongside Osiris and Enora. Anxiety and suspicion radiate from the faculty heads with an intensity that makes my mouth dry. What if they ask too many questions about Ophelia? What if they suspect?

Relax, Axl. Do you think I would ever allow them to learn of who she is before we are ready?

I know you wouldn't. They just look so fucking suspicious of us.

As they should be. We called them to a clandestine meeting immediately after the president called a last-minute faculty meeting.

"What is this about?" Nicholas Ashe is the first to voice what everyone else is undoubtedly thinking. As the faculty head of Onyx Dragon, our biggest rivals, he's the last person I'd trust with any secrets. But Alexandros is right. If there is a threat to nonhumans on campus, they need to be given the information necessary to protect their students.

Enora motions for Alexandros to take the lead, and he steps forward. "Some time last night, a young Silver Vale witch was killed in her bed. She was found this morning with her heart torn from her chest."

A chorus of gasps and curses ripples around the room. Professor Collins from Iridium Vale sobs loudly.

"I am aware of only one vampire known for tearing out the hearts of witches," Nicholas says, his beady eyes twinkling with amusement. He's such a fucking prick.

Alexandros levels him with an icy glare, and Nicholas heeds his warning and leans back in his seat, but the seed of suspicion has been planted, and now nine pairs of questioning eyes are focused on the professor.

"Nobody said it was a vampire who killed Meg," I say, unable to resist leaping to his defense. Nicholas bares his teeth at me, and I would love nothing more than to tear his throat out. It might provide some welcome relief for all the pent-up emotions hurtling through my body. Too bad it would also earn me a reprimand from Alexandros and the other society heads, so I refrain, shoving my hands into my pockets.

You are here only to observe and learn, Axl, Alexandros reminds me through our bond, but his tone isn't harsh. In fact, I think I hear his appreciation.

"There is no suggestion that Alexandros was involved, Nicholas," Enora says, shooting him a withering look. "If you would allow him to continue, he will enlighten you all further."

Nicholas grinds his jaw, but he doesn't speak again, and the next voice to fill the room is Alexandros's. "We know very little about the attack so far. We do not know what creature killed the girl, or their reason for doing so, but we do know that it appeared to be an attempt to implicate me."

There's another round of grumbles and curses, but most of them are now in support of my sire, who despite his ruthless and cold reputation, is highly respected among his colleagues.

"Is there a reason why Silver Vale was targeted? Why Meg in particular?" the head of Gold Vale asks.

"Are all witches at risk?" her counterpart from Iridium chimes in, which is the catalyst for a barrage of questions.

"Are our students safe?"

"Do we need to do anything about the humans?"

"What does this have to do with the wolves?"

"Are all vampires implicated or only Ruby Dragon?"

My ears ring. So much heightened emotion in one room is overwhelming, and I struggle to keep a lid on my temper. Why can't they just listen?

"Enough!" Alexandros barks, and the room falls silent.

"We do not know why the witch was targeted." He lies with such ease that not even the most well-trained eye could pick out a hint of falsehood in his expression or body language. I had almost forgotten how skilled he is in the art of deception, and I must admit that it's impressive to see him in action. "Nor whether there was a definite attempt to implicate me or any other vampires, or whether it was a purely random attack."

"Only a powerful being could break one of Enora's protection spells and enter that house uninvited," Professor Collins says.

There are mumbles of agreement.

Alexandros clears his throat. "That brings us to our other suspicion. We believe dark magic was used."

Another chorus of gasps, mostly from the witches. "H-how can you possibly know that?" Professor Collins asks.

"I am not here to reveal my methods, Raquel," he says, protecting Enora without having been asked to. Again, I'm struck by their obvious deep friendship which I was entirely unaware of. "My intent is simply to alert you all to the possibility that Skotádi have breached the grounds of this campus. And if so, then all of our houses are potentially at risk. So do what you need to strengthen your perimeters and protect your students."

"The Skotádi? Are you sure?" This question comes from the youngest of the Crescent Society heads, James Black.

Alexandros scowls. "We cannot be sure of anything yet. That is why we are only warning you and not bringing this to the attention of Dr. Ollenshaw."

"So you're keeping Ollenshaw out of the loop?" Professor Morrone from Opal Dragon raises his eyebrows.

"Do you think it wise to alert the university president to a potential Skotádi threat, Phillipé?" Alexandros asks.

"Ollenshaw is a fool. He would have the entire campus under lockdown and in a state of panic before the day is out," Nicholas declares, and for the first time I can recall, I find myself agreeing with the head of Onyx Dragon.

"We all know he is little more than a figurehead," one of the Crescent leaders adds.

"Useless," someone else mutters.

Professor Benedictine, head of Lapis Dragon Society, stands. "Everyone knows that the true power of this school sits within this room. I agree with Alexandros. There is no need to alert the rest of the faculty at this time. Mass hysteria is not productive for any of us."

"Wouldn't want to lose access to those tasty snack bags of yours if the humans got a sniff that their kids may be in danger, huh?" James Black says, folding his arms and grinning.

"James!" Osiris warns his counterpart, but Alexandros has already moved, and he stands directly in front of the young wolf. He cracks his neck, and the room falls deathly silent.

"My family built this university before your grandfather was even a pup. It exists for the benefit of all nonhuman species who wish to seek refuge here, you insolent little fuck." Each word is sharp and colder than ice, and the wolf's face blanches, but he has the audacity to growl anyway. "That is why each society bears a part of my family crest. Should you feel like challenging the status quo here, then I would be more than happy to *discuss it* with you in full when I have more time."

James drops his head, avoiding my sire's eyes. "My apologies, Alexandros. I spoke out of turn."

Without acknowledging his apology, Alexandros addresses the room once more. "You will each do whatever is necessary to ensure the protection of your house. We will keep you abreast of any new developments as they come to light. In the meantime, we will attend Jerome's faculty meeting. We will assure him that our defenses are being fortified and that this was a random attack. There will be no mention of the Skotádi."

It's a command, not a question, and everyone in the room knows it. Everyone voices their agreement, but there is still a small undercurrent of suspicion rippling through a few people in the room. I can't help but worry about Ophelia and how long we're going to be able to keep her secret.

"I WAS HOPING to speak with you in private, Alexandros." President Ollenshaw's tiny eyes narrow further as he regards me with disdain.

"There is nothing you cannot discuss with me in front of my sireds, Jerome. I trust them implicitly, as should you."

I roll back my shoulders and look the president in the eye, pride swelling my chest.

Jerome gives a furtive glance around, but most of the faculty members have already left the English lecture hall, and only a few stragglers congregate near the coffee machine in the small kitchenette in the corner of the room. "You seem convinced this was a random attack on Silver Vale." His voice is little more than a whisper.

"Why are you speaking in such hushed tones, Jerome? This is what we just discussed openly in front of all of our colleagues, is it not?"

He purses his lips. "But I have ... well, there are parents and the school board to answer to."

"A fact of which I am well aware." Alexandros sighs. "But what exactly would you tell them, Jerome? That a student was murdered? To what end? This was an isolated incident, one which we will ensure will not happen again."

Ollenshaw smacks his lips together, and his brow pinches in a frown. "But was it? Or is there more to this witch's death than we have been led to believe?"

Alexandros scowls. "Enora told you what occurred. If you do not believe her account, I suggest you take that up with her rather than me."

Jerome sputters, seeming to choke on his own breath. Enora Green is a powerful witch from an even more powerful family, and Jerome is clearly averse to getting on her bad side. "I did not say I don't believe her account."

Alexandros clenches and unclenches his fists beside me, and my annoyance mirrors his. There's a pink-haired elementai I'm anxious to get home to. I felt her pain all too acutely when she learned of Meg's death. Guilt threatened to overwhelm her when she thought herself responsible. Her expression when she saw Cadence at Silver Vale and the empathy that seeped from her pores at her friend's distress told me what I already know. She makes me feel more than I've ever felt in my life, even as a human, yet it is only a fraction of what she experiences. I need to hold her in my arms and do whatever I can to take away her pain.

"Do what you feel is most appropriate, Jerome. But know

that if you disrupt the delicate balance of this institution by encouraging hysteria and panic amongst the students and faculty without good reason, then there will be consequences."

Jerome swallows hard, visibly blanching. I suspect he is as aware as we are that he holds no real power within these walls —that he's a figurehead and nothing more. And the man standing before him wields more power than he can even dream of.

TWENTY-TWO

OPHELIA

"Focus, Ophelia," Alexandros snaps as his frustration with me grows deeper.

Asshat. Like I'm not frustrated too. "I am focusing! But we've been doing this for hours. I'm tired and I'm hungry." And I want a hug.

He closes the distance between us with a single step. "Your enemies will not care if you are tired." He dusts his knuckles over my cheek, and there is a tenderness there that does not translate to his harsh tone. "Nor will they care if you are hungry."

I fold my arms across my chest. "Surely we've done enough for today."

His lip curls, revealing a hint of his fangs and sending a shiver down my spine. I flutter my eyelashes. "There are much more interesting things we could be doing than lessons."

He runs his tongue over his fangs, eyes raking hungrily up and down my body. "Do not try to use your body to bargain with me, little one. It will not work. If you flutter those pretty eyes at me again, I will force you to your knees and have you suck my cock." He grips my jaw tightly. "And then we will resume our lessons."

He releases me, and my lip juts out in protest. It's so unfair that I'm the only one who suffers because of my stupid powers. Powers I didn't even ask for.

His eyes darken, piercing into mine while anger radiates from him in a fierce wave. I swallow a knot of trepidation. I'm not sure I will never get used to his ability to read my mind. "Your powers are a gift, Ophelia. There are people who would die for even a fraction of what you possess. Do not disrespect the universe by wishing them away. Do you think that we do not suffer with you? That every day I do not wish we were not burdened with this knowledge?"

Resentful tears burn behind my eyes. "You think I'm a burden?"

He sighs, and it does nothing to soothe the anger currently burning inside me. Anger, Frustration. Lots of frustration. I lived without mind-blowing orgasms for nineteen years, so why can't I function for more than a few weeks without one?

"I never—"

"I don't care what you were going to say," I cut him off, and he snarls at my impertinence, unused to overt displays of disobedience. "I am not one of your sireds. You don't get to push me around and act like I'm your responsibility, because I'm not. I looked after myself just fine before I met any of you."

I spin on my heel and march out of the room, half expecting

him to come after me and irrationally growing more annoyed when he doesn't. I head straight for the fridge and root around for something that will sate my hunger, except that I'm not hungry anymore. I'm boiling mad. My skin is on fire. My palms sweaty. I lean into the refrigerator, letting its cool air rush over my skin as I blow a strand of hair from my damp forehead.

"Looking for something in particular, sweet girl?" Malachi's hand appears on my shoulder as he peers inside the fridge with me. "You want me to make you something?" he asks upon seeing the limited contents.

A tear rolls down my cheek, and I swat it away. "Hey, what's wrong?" he asks, his deep voice so soft and soothing that it makes me want to cry even more.

"I think the cupcake is feeling a little *frustrated*," Xavier says with a wicked chuckle.

I slam the fridge closed and turn to him, giving him the fiercest glare I can muster. "Not everything is about sex, Xavier."

He arches an eyebrow. "No?"

I fold my arms across my chest while he stalks toward me, my breathing growing heavier and a dull ache building between my thighs. "Haven't I already explained how this works? Having all of us in your head ..." He places his palm over my hammering heart. "Running through your veins ..." His free hand slides to the back of my neck, and he dips his head until his mouth is close to my ear. "Would be enough to drive anyone insane with sexual frustration, Ophelia." His lips dust over my neck. "You know if we could simply make you come that it would all feel so much better, right?"

My legs tremble as heat floods my core. "Y-yes," I pant.

"Can't we do something to help ease her suffering?" Malachi's pleading tone ignites a spark of hope in me.

"I have an idea," Axl says, joining us in the kitchen.

Oh, please let it be a good one. "What is it?" I peer over Xavier's shoulder and see Axl smirking.

He grabs the keys to his Mustang from the counter. "How about we all take a ride? Get away from campus for a few hours?"

Xavier laughs darkly. "Hell yes."

Malachi presses a kiss to my temple. "Sounds good to me, baby."

Getting away from campus—getting away from the professor and his rules sounds like the best idea I've heard all week. "Me too."

Axl winks at me. "Then let's get out of here."

A few minutes later, I'm squeezed between Xavier and Malachi in the back seat of the Mustang while Axl drives as fast as the car will go. I have no idea where he's taking us, only that he's headed away from where we were, and that's good enough for me.

Xavier slips his hand beneath my skirt and tugs at my panties. "I know we don't need these, do we, Cupcake?"

I bite down on my lip, my heart racing like a prize-winning stallion, and nod at him. I am so close to the edge that I'm worried I might explode as soon as he touches me, but I'm way too desperate to stop him.

"Good girl." He tugs my underwear down my legs, then holds the material to his nose and inhales deeply. A loud, feral-sounding growl rumbles in his chest. "Fuck me, Cupcake."

Malachi chuckles and wraps an arm around my shoulder, nuzzling my neck while he lifts my leg so it's resting on his. His rough hand glides up to the sensitive skin of my inner thigh, and I whimper as he edges closer to the place where it feels like all my nerve endings have converged into a singular point.

Xavier hums his approval and does the same to my other

leg, and now both their hands coast tantalizingly closer to my aching core.

Axl adjusts the rearview mirror, angling it so he has the best view of me spread open for his two best friends in the back seat. Their hands edge closer. Axl winks at me in the mirror. I'm going to fall apart.

Malachi slides a finger through my center, and my moan fills the small space. "You're drenched already, baby," he groans.

"I love this fucking car. Don't let Ophelia set it on fire," Axl commands.

"Naw." Xavier's breath dusts over my neck. "We won't let her come yet. Still just playing." He flicks the tip of his forefinger over my clit, and my hips buck off the seat, but I'm quickly pushed back down by the two giant vampires on either side of me.

My entire body quivers at their touch, and I whimper, shamelessly desperate for more. I want them inside me. On me. All over. "What the hell is wrong with me?" I gasp out the words as I pant for breath.

Malachi's lips brush my ear. "Our horny little elementai."

Xavier continues teasing my sensitive flesh. "You think you can handle a little more? You won't set the car on fire if I slip my finger inside you, will you?"

"No!" I shake my head, frantic for him to do just that. "I need you to."

He hums, his mouth dangerously close to my skin while he lazily circles my clit. Malachi kisses my neck and squeezes the tender meat of my thigh, massaging it in his powerful hand and giving me just enough of a distraction from Xavier.

Xavier slides his finger through my dripping center, so close to where I want him. I try to buck my hips, but they hold me in place. "Naughty, Ophelia."

"Please!" I whimper.

"We're all going to be inside you as soon as we get out of this car," Malachi says softy in my ear.

Pleasure spikes through my core. "That's n-not helping."

"Will this help?" Xavier asks as he dips his finger inside me.

"Oh my—"

Xavier sinks his finger in to the knuckle and growls, baring his teeth. "Do not say his name while I'm inside you. I told you he doesn't exist."

I bite down on my lip, trying to focus on keeping a hold on the gamut of sensations rushing through my body and sending burning heat down my limbs.

"Her skin's on fire, Xavier," Malachi says, concerned. "Take it easy."

Xavier drags his fangs over the pulse in my throat and slowly slides his finger in and out of me. "You underestimate our little cupcake. She's got much more control than anyone gives her credit for."

I whimper at his praise, and he winks. Then he presses his sinfully hot mouth to my ear while he goes on lazily fingering me. "I hope you're ready, because you've got all three of us desperate to fuck you."

Every cell in my body feels like it's about to explode into a million tiny fireworks. I close my eyes and focus on my light, watching the dazzling white orb flickering, growing brighter with each passing second as I channel all the feelings coursing through my nerve endings into it.

Malachi runs his nose down the column of my throat, a low growl emanating from his chest and vibrating through me. He swipes the tip of his finger over my sensitive flesh, and my thighs tremble violently. "So desperate to eat you and fuck you, baby. Axl says you get stronger every day, and you're gonna need your strength." He grabs my hand and places it on his dick, which is currently harder than granite. "Because we're all on the edge as much as you are."

I don't think that's possible. I speak through our bond, unable to string that many words together with my mouth right now.

"It's possible, princess. You're gonna find out exactly how possible as soon as I stop this car," Axl replies.

Oh dear lord. I can see my headstone now:

Here lies Ophelia Hart. Cause of death: multiple orgasms. But at least she died with a smile on her face.

TWENTY-THREE

MALACHI

Axl brings the car to a screeching halt. "This place looks good. Secluded and far enough away from campus that no one will notice if our girl starts a fire or causes a sinkhole."

We're on a dirt road near the edge of the woods that border the school, and nobody comes this far out except the wolves on a hunt, and the full moon was days ago. Before Ophelia can voice any kind of protest, Xavier and I open the car doors. I'm faster than he is and reach in and pull her out, scooping her into my arms and making her yelp.

"We should still head for the cover of the trees." Axl jerks his head toward them, and I follow him into the woods.

Xavier falls into step beside me and yanks Ophelia's head back by her hair. "Can't wait to fuck you in the dirt, Cupcake."

She whimpers, her body heating with desire.

Axl comes to a stop in a small clearing where spongy brown and orange leaves carpet the ground and spins to face us. "This place looks good, yeah?"

I'm practically salivating with anticipation to eat and fuck my girl. Anywhere would look good to me. I set Ophelia down on her feet.

"Get her naked, Kai," Axl orders.

She covers her body with her hands. "Out here? I don't need to be naked."

I move her hands out of the way. "No one comes out here, sweet girl. And we'd never let anyone hurt you."

She sinks her teeth into that juicy-as-fuck bottom lip, but her body is trembling.

Xavier runs his fingertips over her cheekbone. "You're our little fuck-toy. Not a chance we'd ever let anyone near you. Not to touch, taste, or even look at what belongs to us."

Axl leans against a tree, his features illuminated by the dappled light of the fading sun. "Yeah, princess," Axl adds. "So be a good girl and let my brothers undress you."

She nods, but when we both crouch to take off her sneakers, Xavier catches my eye and smirks. "Actually, I think we should leave her clothes on."

I glance beneath her skirt at her bare pussy and then back at him. I have no idea what he has in mind, but the wicked look on his face has my blood pumping.

"Leave them on?" Axl steps up beside us.

"Yep." Xavier curls her hair around his fist and tilts her head back. "Because I have a much better idea. You know what you're gonna do now, Cupcake?" he asks, his voice dark and dangerous.

"W-what?" she pants, shivering in the cold.

"Run."

Oh fuck yeah.

Axl grunts his approval as his eyes rake over Ophelia's body.

She blinks at the three of us. "Run?"

I bite down on my lip, willing my cock to stop throbbing so I can think clearly. Is this too reckless? What if we lose her?

Ophelia gasps. "Yeah, what if you lose me?"

She can read fucking minds now too? Dammit! "How can we lose you when you can read our minds? And we can talk to you the whole time."

"But I'm cold." She shivers again.

Axl growls. "You won't be soon."

"And what happens when you catch me?" The scent of the sweet cum already dripping from her pussy fills the crisp air around us.

Xavier laughs darkly. "Then we fuck you."

She sucks in a deep breath that makes her tits jiggle, and subsequently, my cock jumps in my pants. "You won't let me get lost?"

We all shake our heads. "Not a fucking chance, baby," I assure her.

She glances over her shoulder. "It's getting dark."

Axl shrugs. "So use your powers to make some light."

"Every day's a school day, Cupcake."

She looks at me as if seeking my reassurance. I could throw her to the ground right now and fuck her here, and no one would be mad about it. But there is something insanely fucking hot about hunting her. Tracking her unique scent. The most difficult part will be making a sport of it. She'll be way too easy to find.

"Do I get a head start?" she asks.

Axl snorts. "Of course. You've got two minutes to get as far away from us as you can before we hunt you down ..."

"And fuck you," Xavier finishes for him.

The slender curve of her throat convulses, and after a few seconds, she nods her agreement. Then she spins on her heel and takes off into the trees, a streak of color disappearing into the night.

I impatiently tap my foot on the ground.

"Who's gonna catch her first?" Axl asks.

"Me," Xavier proudly declares.

"Don't care as long as I get to her eventually," I say, but the thought of being the one to catch her and sink into her tight little pussy while they wait their turn has my blood thundering through my veins.

I can still feel her close by. Still smell her scent. She's going to be too easy to catch. Her time is almost up, and we're getting ready to move when my heart bottoms out of my chest.

She's gone.

The look on Axl's and Xavier's face tells me they feel it too.

Ophelia!

Yeah?

Relief washes over all three of us. *Where are you, sweet girl?*

Her musical laugh fills my head. *Why would I tell you that?*

But we felt you, Xavier says. *We could track your scent, and then it disappeared like you fell off a cliff.*

She laughs again. *Oh, yeah. A little trick I read about in a spell book. Do you know witches who can channel air can mask their scent by manipulating the air around them? It works on emotions too. Like a forcefield. Cool, huh?*

I suppress a smile. That's my clever fucking girl.

Axl growls and yanks off his shirt. *You just earned yourself the spanking of your life, princess.*

You'll have to catch me first comes her giggling reply.

"Fuck me, I'm gonna blow my load before I even get to her," Xavier says with a chuckle before he pulls off his shirt too.

I do the same. "Looks like we have a hunt on our hands, boys."

THE CRACKING of a twig has my head spinning to the left of me, but an animal scurries off into the distance. We've been tracking Ophelia for over half an hour now, and despite our many underhanded tactics to get her to drop whatever magic shield she has in place, including some of the dirtiest promises to fuck her senseless, she has refused to yield.

But now I've found a set of footprints in the mud, and I'm onto her. As smart as she is and as difficult as it is to track her with no scent, we are far more familiar with these woods than she is. And there are other ways to track prey.

I get close enough to hear her soft breathing and the frantic hammering of her heart. I fist-pump the air as the sweet triumph of victory grows nearer.

I can hear you, baby. I'm gaining on you.

Not close enough, Kai. She giggles.

Don't you want to come tonight? Because the longer you make us chase you, the less likely that is to happen.

But you guys wanted to chase me. And now you're sore because I didn't make it as easy as you thought I would.

Yes, I am sore. My dick is fucking aching.

I trail my fingertips over the bark of the tree, squinting into dim light and waiting for a glimpse of her. A flash of pink directly ahead makes the beast inside me ravenous. I lick my lips and sprint ahead, and two seconds later, she's in my arms. I throw her to the ground and cover her body with mine.

She shrieks, and her scent fills my nostrils once more. Her

fear and excitement slam into me, nearly knocking me sideways, but there's no chance in hell I'm relinquishing my prize after working so hard to win her.

You found her, Kai? Xavier asks.

Yeah, you can track her scent now.

And yours, Axl growls. *We're on our way.*

Ophelia looks up at me, her blue eyes wide and her heart thumping in her chest. "I got you."

She bites on her lip. "But it took you way longer than you thought it would, right?"

"Yeah. I'm proud of you, baby." I'm already tugging open my jeans, and once I'm done, I push her thighs apart with my knee and press my mouth to her ear. "So fucking proud. I respect you so much, sweet girl. Remember that"—I flip her over and hold her down by the back of her neck before driving my cock inside her with one smooth motion—"when I'm fucking you like I don't."

She moans my name, calling out into the darkness as I thrust into her, feral with the need to claim her right here in the dirt. "Your pussy is too fucking sweet."

"Kai, please?"

The sound of her begging makes me fuck her harder. "Is this what you want?" I pull out slowly before pushing back in with one deep stroke that elicits a hoarse, keening scream. We're suddenly bathed in a warm orange glow as the trees around us catch fire. The sound and smell of burning leaves fill the clearing.

"Are you on the edge, Ophelia?"

"Y-yes."

Heat coils at the base of my spine. I'd let her burn down this entire forest before I'd stop fucking her. "Put out the fire and I'll make you come, sweet girl."

"Promise?" she whimpers.

I press a kiss on her temple. "I promise."

She closes her eyes, and I slow my pace a little, allowing her to focus. The orange glow quickly fades, and the smell of smoke drifts through the air, but the fire is extinguished.

I rock my hips, hitting her sweet spot. "Good girl."

She groans.

I'm vaguely aware of Axl and Xavier standing nearby, but they're drowned out by everything that is Ophelia. Her scent, her blood thundering around her body. Her tight pussy squeezing me and threatening to hurtle me into oblivion.

I lie over her, the weight of my body pressing into hers as I sink my teeth into her neck and let her intoxicating blood flow over my tongue. And it sets off a chain reaction in her. She throws her head back, her walls rippling around my cock, and lets out a throaty cry. Her orgasm rips through her like a tidal wave. My head spins, and my eyes shutter closed. When I reopen them, there's another small fire nearby.

I rest my lips against her ear as we both pant for breath. "Put out the fire, baby." This time she does it with the smallest nod of her head.

"That's my clever girl."

TWENTY-FOUR

Watching Malachi fuck Ophelia face down in the dirt might be one the hottest fucking things I've seen in my long life. It's got both Axl and me so worked up, and I swear I could get off just watching them. A single tug on my rock-hard cock and I'd lose it. But I'm gonna lose it inside Ophelia's sexy little body—my absolute favorite place in the universe to come. And we can keep a handle on her out here in the woods. She's already learning so fast. So she set fire to a couple of trees. No big deal. She put it out straight away. Smokey Bear would be proud—no forest fires today. And that means I get to make my girl come.

I glance at Axl, and he grins at me. "You want to take her together?"

He nods. "Fuck yeah."

"Our turn, Cupcake."

Malachi presses a kiss on her temple before he pulls out of her, and as soon as he's out of the way, Axl and I drop to our knees on either side of her. She pants, breathless from the orgasm she just had. The one she's needed for so long now. It burns me up with jealousy that Malachi caught her instead of me, but the sweet smile she gives me dissolves that feeling as quickly as ice in boiling water.

"We need you on all fours, princess," Axl says, grabbing her hips and maneuvering her into position for us. Her face is inches from my bulging cock, and I pull down my zipper, groaning with relief as I release the pressure. She looks up at me, fluttering her long dark lashes. I run my fingertips across her cheek. "Do you know what we want now?"

She licks her lips, and my cock jumps in my boxers. "To both fuck me at the same time?" she whispers, her cheeks turning a deep shade of pink.

I cup her jaw and squeeze, desperate to have her pouty mouth around my shaft. "You're such a quick study, Cupcake. So smart."

Axl hums. "So fucking smart." He pushes her skirt up, bunching it around her waist, and then he circles the tight ring of muscle of her asshole.

I snarl at him. "Don't you fucking dare. That's mine."

He laughs wickedly, his finger still teasing her there while he sinks another finger into her pussy. The wet sound of her and Malachi's cum has me growling with need. "I know, just teasing. You like it too, huh, princess?" he says.

She arches her back, and her mouth falls open on a loud moan. I free my dick from my boxers and take the opportunity to slide the tip into her open, waiting mouth. She immediately sucks on the crown, sweeping her tongue over my weeping slit and filling my entire body with white-hot pleasure.

Unable to hold off any longer, Axl takes his dick out and sinks into her pussy, and the moans of pleasure that he pulls from her vibrate around my entire length, making a shudder run down my spine.

I look down at my girl and brush a tear from her cheek. "I promised you I'd fuck your ass one day, and I meant it. Kai got your hot little mouth." I wipe a drop of spit from her chin while she goes on sucking me. "Which is very talented by the way."

She flutters her eyelashes, delighting in my praise. "And Axl got your sweet pussy. So it's only right that I take your virgin ass. I'd do it here, but I'm thinking we should at least have a bed for your first time."

Malachi snorts. "You're such a romantic."

I ignore him and the sounds Axl makes as he fucks our girl from behind and focus all my attention on her. She rewards me by gazing up at me adoringly while I fuck her throat. "I'm going to make you nice and wet first. Get you all loose and pliable so you can take my entire cock inside your tight little hole. You'd like that, wouldn't you?"

Yes, she says clearly in my head while she mumbles around my cock.

"You're a naughty girl, Cupcake. A bad fucking girl running around the woods with no panties just so you can get yourself fucked by three vampires."

She mewls, her orgasm drawing closer.

"Make her come while she's sucking my cock, Axl," I tell him.

He smirks at me before reaching between her thighs and playing with her clit while we both fuck her. The sounds she makes have my cock leaking precum down her throat. She's so compliant and needy for us. This tiny little powerhouse who could mask her scent just because she read about it in a book.

Axl pulls out and slams back inside her, and she moans so loudly it vibrates through my cock, sending white-hot pleasure through every cell of my body. I have been so desperate for this all day and then after chasing her through the woods, my adrenaline pumping and my fangs and cock aching for her—it all makes this relief all the sweeter.

The ground shakes beneath us, and I should tell her to focus but can't find the words because I'm too lost in my own pleasure. Thankfully, Malachi speaks to her instead, coaxing her through her orgasm with soothing words. "That's it, sweet girl, you can do it. Feel it all and channel it inside."

His commanding voice only adds to the sensation of euphoria hurtling through my body right now. I come hard and heavy, filling Ophelia's throat with my release. She comes too, swallowing every drop of me as her body shakes instead of the ground with the strength of her orgasm.

And when we're both spent and have filled her with our cum, Axl and I pull out of her. I swipe the mess on her chin with my thumb and place it in her mouth, and my good girl sucks it clean. "You did so good, Cupcake."

She smiles at me, so fucking sweet.

OPHELIA CURLS up on Malachi's lap in the back of the car, her legs draped over me and one of her hands clasped in mine while my other rests on her thigh beneath her skirt. The feeling of dread that balls itself in the pit of my stomach is sudden and violent.

Malachi glances at me. "You feel that too?" I ask.

"He's so mad," Ophelia whispers.

"Shit," Axl mumbles in the front seat.

"We didn't do anything wrong," I insist. "We were careful. No one would have felt Ophelia's power out there."

"So why is he so mad?" Ophelia asks, squeezing my hand tighter in hers.

"We could ask him?" Malachi suggests.

I shake my head. "No fucking way. We got five minutes until we're back. I'd rather spend them in blissful ignorance, thank you very much."

"Or fucking torture," Malachi groans. "I'm gonna ask him."

"He won't tell you anyway," Axl interjects. "When the fuck have you ever known him to take it easy on us?"

"True," I mutter.

Ophelia clutches her stomach. "I feel sick."

Malachi presses a kiss to her forehead. "He can't hurt you. He'll be pissed, but he'll get over it just as quickly, I promise."

Liar.

"I heard that, Xavier," Ophelia says.

I brush my fingertips over her cheek. "Because I can't fucking block you out anymore. You're already too powerful for me, so you just remember that when you're getting your ass handed to you in a few minutes, okay?"

Her sweet little giggle breaks the awful tension in the car.

Alexandros is waiting in the den when we get home, his rage so palpable I could take hold of it and fashion it into a weapon to punish us with.

"Exactly how stupid are you all?" he asks, his tone so even and controlled that it makes every hair on my body stand on end. His cold brand of anger is worse than shouting. At least him raging would dissipate some of his temper. Instead, he directs every single ounce of it at us.

I shoot a worried glance at Malachi and Axl while I keep Ophelia's hand clasped in mine.

Ophelia speaks first. "It was my f—"

He holds up a hand and glares at her, and she clamps her mouth shut. "I asked you all a question."

I take a deep breath. "Not stupid at all, sir."

He scowls, his dark features appearing murderous. "Pardon?"

Ophelia trembles beside me, but I tip my chin. I'll take his wrath for her. "I said not stupid at all, sir. We made sure that no one was around. There was a small fire, and the ground moved a little, but—"

"I am not talking about you animals fucking in the woods!" He roars now, the lid on his temper well and truly blown. I guess I was wrong about the raging thing. I'm certain the entire house rattles on its foundation.

I blink in confusion and see Malachi and Axl glancing at me in my peripheral vision. Meanwhile, Ophelia drops her head, embarrassed. Fuck him for making her feel like that. "Don't you ever call my girl a fucking animal."

His eyes turn blacker than the darkest pits of hell. Oh sweet motherfuck, he's going to kill me. He inches forward, and I flinch.

"It was my fault, sir," she blurts. "I was so tightly wound after our lesson, and we ..."

He trains his fierce glare on her, and she trails off. "I am not talking about you all having sex, Ophelia," he growls, but his tone is much softer for her.

"So what did we do wrong?" she whispers.

He rolls his neck, the thick vein on the underside of his jaw throbbing. His eyes dart between me, Axl, and Malachi. "You *hunted* her?"

Oh shit.

"You allowed her to run from you without any thought as to what would happen if you could not find her, just for the sole pleasure of you hunting? Yes?"

"Yes sir," Axl replies.

Ophelia shifts from one foot to the other. "But I—"

"And you!" he barks. "You thought it would be fun to mask your scent and your emotions to stop them from being able to track you?"

Her heart rate doubles. "Yes sir."

His cracks his neck, and the noise makes me wince. "And none of you thought this was a terrible idea that could put Ophelia in considerable danger? Not even for a second?"

We all shake our heads, chagrined.

"I have never been so disappointed in any of you as I am this day."

Ophelia swallows a harsh sob.

"Sorry, sir," Malachi and Axl say in unison.

But not me. Why can't I fall into line with the rest of them? Why can't I just be the person he wants me to be? Because I'm not, that's why. And I never will be.

"Fuck this. I'm not sorry!"

He focuses all of his considerable rage squarely on me. His eyes shutter closed as he visibly works to stop himself from removing my head, and when he reopens them, he seems to have regained control. He cups Ophelia's jaw in his hand. "We are all animals, little one. I did not mean to cause you any shame."

She offers him a faint smile. "I know."

His sigh is deep and weary. "Go to bed."

The relief that floods the room is like a wave. But before I can move, he puts a hand on my shoulder. "Not you."

Double fucking shit.

My co-conspirators cast me a worried glance.

"I said go to bed," Alexandros orders.

"But what about Xavier?" Ophelia asks, her hand still clasped in mine.

"Xavier and I have something to discuss. Now leave us."

A second later, we are alone. I stare at him, wondering if this is it. Did I finally push him over the edge? At least with me out of the way, he only has to share Ophelia with Axl and Malachi.

"That you believe me capable of such cruelty does not surprise me, Xavier." He cuts through my thoughts. "However, that you believe me capable of such cruelty toward you and to Ophelia and your brothers by depriving them of you ..." He draws a deep breath through his nose. "That saddens me."

"So you're not going to kill me?"

He inches closer, and I feel the heat radiating from his body. It warms me in ways that it shouldn't. "If I were going to kill you for defying me, it would have happened a long time ago, would it not?"

I shrug, feeling too vulnerable under his scrutiny. "I guess."

"Tell me what she did in the woods. How she evaded you all."

I swallow. "She read about a spell that manipulates air to mask scent and emotions, and that's what she used."

He hums. "You could not trace her at all?"

I shake my head. "But we could still speak to her. We knew she was safe."

His anger threatens to boil over once more, and he sucks in air between his teeth. "Anyone could have been masking themselves in those woods. All it would have taken was a moment, and she would have been gone. Within the grounds of this campus, there is a measure of protection, but outside of the boundaries of the university, Xavier ..."

I swallow. He's right, and I hate admitting that we put her in danger simply for the thrill of chasing her. But I don't need to admit it aloud for him to know.

He sighs. "Her powers grow quickly, and soon she will be teaching you how to control your mind."

"Yeah, she's too smart for me." I give a self-deprecating laugh.

"No." He shakes his head. "She is powerful and smart, but you underestimate yourself, Xavier. You always have."

I regard him with suspicion. This feels like a test rather than a punishment.

"Oh, this is a test." He runs a hand over his beard. "*And* a punishment."

He grabs my throat, pulling me close so our chests are pressed flush together. "But if you ever openly defy me like that in front of your brothers again, Xavier, I will not be so lenient."

I swallow nervously. "Yes sir."

"Close your mind to me," he orders.

I frown. I wish I fucking could. "I can't. You know that."

"Try."

I close my eyes and feel him inside my head, searching my thoughts. And now my memories. He flicks through them like images on a cell phone. Going back to my life when I was a human.

My heart rate spikes. "No." I don't want to see even a snapshot of that time.

"So stop me."

I shake my head as he searches deeper, into the darkest recesses and the memories I keep hidden. "I can't," I insist.

"Because you are not trying," he snaps.

My mouth goes dry. My blood screams in my ears. And then I see him. My father. "No!" I shout. Alexandros has seen these memories before, but I feel a sense of shame in allowing him to see them again.

"These are the memories you refuse to relive, Xavier."

"Yes." I grit out the word.

"Perhaps we should relive them now?"

My eyes fly open, and I find him staring at me. His expression is entirely unreadable. I shake my head. "I'm sorry, sir. I'll never question you again. Please don't do this."

"Stop me, Xavier. Close the door, and I will not be able to force you to relive them."

I screw my eyes closed again as images of my father swim through my mind. His face twisted in disgust. The hateful bile he spewed at me. The way he couldn't even bear to hit me that time, too disgusted to lay a hand on me again. My heart is racing so fast it's going to beat out of my chest.

"Stop!" I plead with Alexandros, but he keeps pushing, forcing me to replay that horrible day over and over.

"Stop me," he growls.

I drop to my knees, rubbing at my temples as I try to scrub away the images. "I can't."

And he's there again, screaming at me and telling me how disgusting I am. An abomination he should have smothered at birth. I feel a splinter of wood spearing my skin as he beat me with the leg from the dinner table.

"No!" I scream the word aloud while chanting it over and over in my head, no longer sure who I'm screaming it at—Alexandros or my father. Did I simply swap one monster for another? But at least Alexandros has always been clear about what he is. He's never pretended to be something he's not.

You can fight it, Xavier. His voice fills my head.

Tears run down my face. "I can't."

I'm being pulled to my feet. Strong hands rest on my shoulders. "Yes, you can. Close the door and shut me out."

But I'm too weak. Too weakened by the man who haunts my nightmares. The man I called father a long time ago. I'm falling forward, but I don't hit the floor. Instead I face-plant into solid muscle. Alexandros is no longer in my head, and the memories disappear, locked once more inside the vault I kept them in. Only I didn't put them back there this time. He did.

I open my eyes, and he's holding me upright. Disappointment threatens to swallow me whole. I'm such a fucking failure. Maybe my father should have smothered me when I was born.

"You did well, Xavier." The deep timbre of Alexandros's voice soothes the tremors in my body.

I didn't. I let him down. Just like I eventually let everyone down.

He runs a hand over my hair, pulling me close to his chest, and I drink in his unique scent. It is both comforting and intoxicating at the same time. "Next time," he says quietly. Then his arms are gone, and he walks out of the room.

When I'm sure my legs will carry me, I leave the den and head to find her. To find the comfort that only she can bring me. I crawl into bed and wedge myself between Malachi and Ophelia. Wrapping an arm around her waist, I bury my face in her hair.

"Are you okay?" she whispers.

"I am now."

"What did he do?" Her voice quivers.

"He just taught me a lesson, that's all."

"What kind of lesson?"

Pursing my lips, I will my voice to remain even. "A valuable one." I drape one leg over her, pulling her into my body like a pitcher pulls his arm into his chest before his best pitch. Pain and regret still linger at the edge of my consciousness. "Tell me you love me, Ophelia."

She wriggles in my arms, turning until she faces me, and rests her hand on my cheek. "I love you, Xavier."

I smile, and she does too, pressing her nose to mine. "Love you too, Cupcake."

TWENTY-FIVE

ALEXANDROS

Ophelia blinks at me, fluttering her eyelashes and feigning innocence when she knows exactly what she does to me. I brush the back of my knuckles over her cheek, and she presses her face into my touch like a puppy desperate for affection. I have been rough on her these past few weeks, and whilst that has been a necessity, it still weighs heavily on me. I wish we had more time.

"Ready for lessons, little one?"

Her shoulders droop, and she drops her head with a heavy sigh. I felt the excitement buzzing through her when I called her to my office. She has already partaken in all of her lessons today, and perhaps it is expecting too much of her to do this as well, but she is much stronger than she was when I first claimed her in here three weeks ago.

And it is time. I can wait no longer. Placing my finger beneath her chin, I tip her head up and force her to look at me. "You will enjoy this one more. I promise."

She narrows her blue eyes like she cannot quite believe me, but her lips curve. "I will?"

I rub the pad of my thumb over her full bottom lip and pull it down, parting her mouth and imagining sinking my cock inside its warmth. "Yes."

I guide her across the room and take a seat, positioning her on the edge of my desk directly in front of me so she is perched between my spread thighs. After sliding my hands up the supple skin of her legs, I reach beneath her skirt until my fingers curl around the waistband of her panties. When I tug them down, her pupils blow wide, and she sucks in a shuddering breath.

"I think I am going to enjoy this lesson," she says with a sexy laugh that warms me from the inside.

Suppressing a dark laugh, I tug her underwear over her boots and stuff them into the pocket of my pants. "I *know* I am."

She presses her lips together and hums. The scent of her arousal is already thick in the air, making my mouth water to taste her. I roll my chair forward a few inches, spreading her thighs wider with my shoulders. "So wet for me already, Ophelia."

Her cheeks flush the same shade of pink as her hair. I slip my hand beneath her skirt once more, glide it up the soft flesh of her inner thigh, and drag the tip of my thumb through her dripping center.

She shivers, her bottom lip trapped between her teeth as she tries to stifle a groan. I sink a finger into her tight heat, and her back bows, her head tips back, and her loud moan fills my office. She plants her palms on my desk and rocks her hips.

"Look at me, Ophelia," I command. She lifts her head, and her gaze fixes on mine as I slowly inch out of her before easing back inside. She sucks in deep breaths, her chest heaving with the effort. "Today, you are going to learn to control your emotions when in a state of high arousal."

The slope of her throat thickens as she swallows, and I continue working her gently, her eyes locked on mine.

"The ability to control your emotions when in a state of intense fear, anger, or pleasure is one of the most difficult lessons to learn, agápi mou, but before we leave this office today, you will have mastered it. Do you understand me?"

She gives a single nod of her head. "Sounds like a lot of fun."

With my free hand, I trace my fingertips over her cheek. "Oh, it will be." I add a second finger to her heat, and she mewls with pleasure. "For me, anyway."

Her lip trembles as her orgasm builds quickly and urgently. The skin on her neck turns a deep shade of pink. The air crackles with energy. "Find your light, Ophelia."

She sinks her teeth into her pillowy lower lip and nods. I grind the heel of my palm against her clit, and her legs begin to shake along with the desk.

I ease out of her slowly, leaving her teetering on the edge. "Focus!"

Pressing her lips together, she gives me another nod, and I sink my fingers inside her once more.

"You get so beautifully wet for me." Her pussy squeezes around me. She moans my name, so close to the edge now it makes her whimper with desperation. "Do not come, Ophelia."

"I c-can't help it." She pants out each word.

I slow my movements, gently massaging her sensitive flesh. "Yes you can. Focus."

Her chest rises and falls with each heavy breath. A single flame licks along the edge of the bookshelf.

"Ophelia!" I growl. "If you set my office on fire again, I will edge you like this for the next ten years."

She squeezes her eyes closed, and the flame is extinguished.

I sweep the tip of my finger over the sensitive spot inside her, and her back bows. A husky, satisfied moan pours from her throat, and it is enough to have my cock aching to be inside her.

"Please, can I—"

"No!" I add a second finger to her dripping pussy and have to stop my own eyes from rolling with how good she feels gripping me the way she does.

"B-but—I c-can't ..." She holds her breath, and the air becomes thinner like it is being sucked from the room by a vacuum.

I slip my fingers out of her. "Breathe," I command, and she sucks in a breath that allows air to fill the room once more.

She opens her eyes just in time to see me unfasten my belt. A hungry expression claims her face.

I free my aching shaft from the confines of my zipper and grunt with relief. "Is this what you want, little one?"

She nods, and a shy smile spreads across her face, making her eyes sparkle. I find it adorable that she thinks me teasing her with my cock will be any more tolerable than using my fingers. What I do know is that it will be much more pleasurable for me. I am burning up with the need to be inside her.

"I would like you naked for this next part." I pull her tank top off and over her head. Her bra and skirt quickly follow until her clothing lies in a pile on the floor beside my desk. I grab her hips and pull her onto my lap, hissing out a breath as her bare pussy skims the head of my cock.

I growl and yank her down, seating myself fully inside her

in one smooth stroke. She groans out a plea, begging me to allow her to come.

I rest my mouth on the shell of her ear and lick my lips as the scent of her blood calls to my soul. It is not the time to bite her. Not yet. As soon as I sink my fangs into her sweet flesh, I will be done for and the lesson will be over. She could shake this entire building to dust, and I would not care enough to stop her.

Instead, I fuck her, repeatedly bringing her close to her climax and easing her back down each time her powers threaten to overwhelm her.

Every cell in her body vibrates with pent-up energy. Her hair is stuck to her forehead, her skin coated with a thin sheen of perspiration. Her eyes roll back, and she shakes her head. "P-please, no more."

"Almost done." I ease myself inside her once more. "And you are doing so well."

She buries her head in the crook of my neck, her hot breath rushing over my skin. "I c-can't."

"You can, Ophelia." I lift her head and have to maintain a firm grip on her jaw to hold it upright. She is beyond exhausted. "Look around. Nothing is on fire. The air is as it should be. The walls are not shaking. There is no rain or any hint of a storm brewing. You can do this because you already *are*."

She sniffs, and a single tear rolls down her flushed cheek.

"One last test, little one." I rub a finger over her throbbing clit, and her body spasms before it melts into mine. I release my grip on her jaw and allow her to rest her head on me once more so that I can press my lips against her ear. "Would you like to come?"

"Yes," she whimpers.

"Are you going to be a good girl and not incinerate me or my office when you do?"

"I'll try."

I growl. "No, Ophelia."

She groans. "I won't burn down your office."

I band one arm around her waist and place my free hand on the back of her head, crushing her body to mine. "Focus on your light. Do you see it?"

"Yes."

I rock into her, sinking my cock deeper and maintaining a firm pressure on her sensitive clit. "What do you do now?"

She takes a deep breath. "Channel everything into the light."

"Good girl."

She whimpers at my praise, her walls fluttering around my cock as I bring her closer to the edge. "What if I can't?"

"Then we will keep practicing until you do."

She wraps her arms around me, clinging to me like I am the only thing tethering her to this earth.

I rest my lips on the top of her head. "Are you ready, agápi mou?"

Her pussy squeezes my cock in a death grip. "Y- yes."

"Then come for me, Ophelia." I pull her down onto me and sink my teeth into her neck. Her orgasm implodes inside her core with the force of a neutron bomb. She screams my name, and like a chain reaction, that sets off my own release. The force of both our climaxes renders me immobile for several long moments. Her taste floods my being, and the smell of her surrounds me. A series of moans soothes all the fractured slivers of my soul.

Her body is molded to mine as she comes down from the aftermath of her orgasm, every inch of her shaking. I glance around the room and note the lack of damage. Whilst my entire world just rocked on its axis, she did not in fact make the walls or the ground shake. There is no sign of rain in the cloudless night sky, and my breathing is fine, albeit labored from my exertions.

You did it, little one. I speak through our bond to save my much-needed breath.

I did? She burrows her face deeper into my neck, and I rub a soothing hand over her back.

Yes. Would you like me to take you home now?

No more lessons?

Not tonight.

Will you stay with me?

I press a gentle kiss to her temple. *Always.*

I mean—

I know what you mean, and yes, I will stay with you tonight.

Did Ophelia just …? Did you make her come? Is the curse lifted? The voices of all three of my boys come at once.

Yes. She was incredible.

We need to celebrate, Malachi says, and both Axl and Xavier voice their agreement.

They begin to make plans for how they might do that, and I listen for a moment, allowing their elation to sit in my consciousness before I block them out once more.

She smiles against my skin. *I really did it?*

Take a look around and see for yourself.

Gingerly, she lifts her head and scans the room. A slow, triumphant smile spreads across her face. She still has no idea how truly powerful she is, and a part of me is honored that I get to be the man to show her. But the rest of me … that part is terrified to have such responsibility sitting upon my shoulders.

I DRESSED A STILL-TREMBLING Ophelia and carried her home to my bed after her lesson was done. Now she lies contentedly beside me, her head nestled in the crook of my shoulder and her arm draped over my chest.

"I can't wait to tell the boys that I'm allowed to have orgasms again," she says with a yawn.

"I think we should keep it to ourselves for now, Ophelia."

"But why?" she asks quietly.

"In case your powers are not fully controllable yet. What you did was incredible, but we still need to exercise some caution." The ease at which I lie to her concerns me, but I do not wish to spoil the boys' plan to mark the occasion. "Just for a day or two," I offer as reassurance when sadness clouds her thoughts.

That seems to satisfy her, and she sighs contentedly.

I trail my fingertips along her spine and suppress a satisfied smile when her resulting shudder presses the soft curves of her body farther into mine. "I know that I have been hard on you."

"Understatement," she huffs, and her warm breath dances over my skin.

I am amazed by how much I enjoy her feisty side. I cup her chin and tip her head back, forcing her to meet my gaze. "You understand why it is necessary for me to push you so hard?"

She nods. "Because my powers could be dangerous if I don't control them."

Is that what she thinks this is? Her being a danger never crossed my mind for even a fraction of a second. "No, Ophelia." I sit up and pull her with me so she is straddling my thighs. "This is to protect you. Everything I do is to protect you. Do you not understand that?" She flinches at my tone, which comes out sharper than I intended. "You must know why I push you. Why all I desire is to keep you safe."

She blinks. "Because you love me?"

Love? How ill-fitting a word. "I do not love you, little one."

Her eyes fill with tears, and the sharp stab of pain that

lances through her chest is like a dagger to my own heart. She can feel everything I feel; how can she not know the truth? I draw a deep breath and try again. "I do not simply love you."

"I don't understand." She wraps her arms around herself as though she is trying to make herself small and disappear.

I untangle her arms from her torso and drape them around my neck. Her shining blue eyes bore into mine as I brush a lone tear from her cheek. "Love is not enough."

She blinks, still confused. I pull her close and press my lips against hers. And as always, I find immense pleasure in the way her mouth yields so easily to mine. *This is so much more than love, Ophelia. More than a bond. More than I have ever felt. Love cannot endure a thousand lifetimes. It forgets and it fades. You and I are eternal. You have conquered my heart and stolen my soul. Do not insult what we have by calling it love.*

She whimpers, and I swallow the sweet sound. *But love is all I've ever wanted.*

Her taste overwhelms my senses, scrambling my thoughts until she is all I can see, taste, smell, hear, and feel.

I would give her anything. *Then I will love you for eternity.*

But we can't have eternity. The light and the dark, remember? Another tear rolls down her cheek, finding a home on her soft lips.

I lick it off with a swift flick of my tongue before resuming our kiss. *I will either burn in the light or drag you into the dark, little one. And whenever Death should come for you, I will offer Him one thousand souls in return for yours so that you will remain in this mortal realm with me for the rest of time.*

Her heart thumps against my own, reminding me of the powerful ambrosia coursing through her veins. *Forever?* The word is full of hope, and perhaps it is cruel to promise what I have no hope of delivering.

Or perhaps it is crueler still to admit the truth.

So I tell her what we both need to hear. *Always.*

P *lease sir.* Ophelia's soft groans fill my head and rouse me from sleep, but when I open my eyes, I'm in bed alone. Axl and Malachi left some time in the night to set up another operation for our Ruby recruits, and Ophelia is clearly with Alexandros somewhere nearby. I stop myself from replying to her as I feel her climax build to a crescendo.

If I let her know I can hear her and feel her, the surprise we have for her later will be ruined. And as much as I'd like to talk her through whatever Alexandros is doing to her, I'm stopped by the thought of the look on her face if we pull off what I'm planning for later. Without either Malachi or Axl to provide me any relief, I wrap my hand around my aching shaft and squeeze hard, whispering her name like a prayer.

Her keening moan rips through me. *What the hell are you doing to her, Alexandros?* I ask the question rhetorically.

Eating her beautiful pussy. His deep growl shocks me to my core and also serves to magnify the need throbbing through my cock. I stroke up and down my length, imagining they're both watching me. Pleasure coils at the base of my spine.

I didn't expect you to hear me.

I always hear you, Xavier.

I don't want her to know I can feel her. We want to surprise her later.

He doesn't reply, and I close my eyes. Pressing my head back against the pillow, I let her ecstasy meld with my own, her moans mingling with mine as I work my cock and wish it was her. Or him. And maybe it's the pleasure circling in my chest, or maybe it's feeling her connection with him that makes me bold enough to say it. *Tell me how good she tastes.*

She tastes just as she always does. Like heaven.

Fuck. *How wet is she?* I push my luck a little farther.

Soaking. She is dripping down my chin.

Goddamn fuck! I can feel her. She's so close. I'm so close. Precum beads on the slit of my crown.

And he knows how close I am too. How close we both are, but still he doesn't lock down the connection between us. He lets me feel it all. Her pleasure. His need. And when she comes with a silent cry of his name, I hear her in his head and fall off the edge right alongside her. Gasping and panting and wondering why my sire allowed me to experience that with him. Before I can ask, he's closed me off once more.

～

MALACHI IS CHAPERONING OPHELIA TODAY, and they left five minutes ago for class. Axl went to shower, leaving me alone with the professor.

"I can't believe Ophelia managed to keep her exciting news all to herself."

He takes a sip of his coffee. "I asked her not to tell you yet. I heard a little of your plans last night, so I warned her that she may have to proceed with caution for a day or two."

His uncharacteristic magnanimity shocks the hell out of me. "You did that for us?"

"And for her. I am sure she would love whatever surprise you have planned for her."

I picture the kitchen filled with pink girly unicorn shit and a giant sickly sweet cake, all for her—and Kai. She's gonna fucking love it. "I was thinking a party. We only have a few hours to pull it together, but some cake and some balloons should do it, right?"

"A congratulations-you-are-allowed-to-orgasm party?" he asks, and I am sure I see the hint of a smirk on his lips.

"Can't think of a better way to celebrate."

He arches one dark eyebrow. "No?"

Is he kidding around with me? Like actually cracking jokes? This alternate reality I've stepped into is fucking bizarre. Despite my confusion, I smirk. "Well, obviously making her come as many times as possible before she melts into a puddle of cum is top of the list, but cake is a good way to start proceedings, right?"

He offers me a casual shrug. "And how do you intend to keep it from her for the rest of the day? Once you tell Malachi, he will be unable to stop himself from letting his emotions spill over. She will read his mind, and your surprise will be ruined."

"Shit," I mutter. That is a flaw in my plan. Unless we simply don't tell Malachi. But he knows we want to do something special. We discussed it before he left this morning. "I guess we're gonna have to keep him in the dark. Although he's the one who'll know where to get all the soppy girly shit."

"So why not have him arrange the party, and you accompany Ophelia for the day?"

I shake my head. "I know all the plans. If she reads my mind, she'll know it all."

He licks his lips and takes two steps toward me until we're standing only inches apart. "I believe you can block her from your thoughts."

Is he serious? "Even you can't do that."

He scowls, and I almost regret saying that and ruining whatever this pleasant interaction is between us. "I can. I choose not to, partly because I like her in my head and partly because it requires the kind of effort I am not used to exerting on a regular basis."

"If it requires effort for you, there's no way I can manage it."

He tilts his head, eyeing me with curiosity. My heart rate spikes, and I know he feels it, but his scrutiny always has this same effect on me. I'm vulnerable and exposed and turned on all at once. "I have already discussed with Ophelia how impolite it is to read another's mind without permission unless they are in danger. I believe she would respect your wish not to probe if you asked her. And I also believe you could withstand any accidental attempts by her to read your thoughts if you so desired."

"I didn't do so great the other night." Fresh, hot waves of shame roll over me. Images of my father flash through my mind.

Alexandros places his hand on the back of my neck. His touch grounds and soothes me, and a few seconds later, the negative emotions ebb away. "When I tested you the other night, you were in a state of high emotion, Xavier. Everything is more difficult to achieve when we are in fight or flight mode.

And whilst you will need to learn to lock down your mind under those circumstances eventually, perhaps it was not the best environment for you to begin to practice that particular skill."

Nervous anxiety crackles through my veins. "So what would be?"

His hand drops from my neck, and I shiver at the loss of his touch. "Here, now. No threat. No danger. You are going to block me from your mind."

Immediately, my heart rate doubles, and I shake my head. "I can't. I don't want to see him again. Please, Alexandros ..."

"I am not going to delve too deeply, Xavier." His tone is so calm and soothing that it eases the trepidation enveloping me. "I will simply search your memory of the last twenty-four hours." He presses his forehead against mine. "To block someone effectively, it is helpful to know when they have breached your mind. Are you able to distinguish that?"

"S-sometimes. When I'm expecting it."

"The more accustomed you become to identifying a breach, the easier it will become. Until you no longer need to be on alert for it. But the only way to do that is with practice."

He's such a good fucking teacher. So patient when he wants to be that. I wonder if he was like this with his kids. Did they get a part of him that we never will?

I glance down at his bare chest and the hard ridges of his muscles. It's also insanely fucking hot when he's in professor mode. "Yes sir."

"Concentrate," he orders. "Tell me when you feel it."

So I do. I listen to the sound of our breaths and the rhythmic ticking of the clock, waiting for the moment when he breaches that boundary of my consciousness. Minutes pass, and I wait so long that I'm sure I must have failed. And then I feel him. Like a tiny electric current above my left ear. It would be impercep- tible if I were not searching for it. "I feel you."

"Good. Try again."

I wait, and this time he acts much more quickly. "Now?" I say.

"Why are you unsure?" His voice is gruff and laced with frustration.

"I don't know. It felt the same, but ..."

"But what, Xavier?"

"It felt too easy," I admit.

He lifts his head from mine, and his smile is like a sucker punch to my gut. "Again."

I catch my breath, and we go through the process a half a dozen more times. Each time, I'm able to identify the precise moment when he enters my mind. And I feel something monumental radiating from him. Something I am not entirely sure he's ever directed my way.

Pride.

"Now that you have learned to identify the sensation you feel when your mind is breached, it is time to block me."

I nod, feeling much more confident than I did ten minutes ago. And he said he won't try to access the memories I don't want to relive. Alexandros Drakos is a lot of things, but a liar isn't one of them. I trust him. And as I stare into his dark eyes, I realize something.

He is nothing at all like my father.

CHAPTER
TWENTY-SEVEN
OPHELIA

M alachi and Xavier have their heads close together and are engaged in a conversation that I'm too far away to hear. I am vaguely aware of Dr. Underwood telling me I'm capable of better grades, but I'm too distracted, wondering what the boys are up to. They appear way too conspiratorial for my liking.

"I don't want to see you waste your potential, Ophelia." Dr. Underwood raises his voice an octave, dragging my focus back to him.

I nod my appreciation. "I won't, Professor. I'll study harder. Promise."

The corner of his mouth lifts like he doesn't entirely believe

235

me, but he dismisses me with a wave of his hand, and I head immediately for the boys standing in the corner of the classroom. "Hey." I bump my arm against Xavier's. "What are you doing here?" Malachi is my designated chaperone today. "I thought you and Axl had some super important Ruby Dragon recruit business to take care of?"

Xavier flashes me a smirk, his deep-blue eyes raking over my body in a way that makes me squirm. "We did. It's done."

I glance between him and Malachi, and my stomach flutters. "So you're both with me today?" The excitement in my tone would be embarrassing if I didn't know how much they enjoyed being with me too.

Malachi winces. "Nope. I have to go, sweet girl. Xavier is spending the rest of the day with you." He avoids my gaze and instead glances at Xavier.

"Oh?" Something feels very fishy here. "What were you guys just talking about so intently?"

Xavier slings an arm around my shoulder and starts to guide me toward the exit. "Nothing for you to be concerned about, Cupcake."

Malachi still won't look at me, and the flutters in my stomach turn into an anxious churning. Xavier dips his head and presses his lips to my ear. "And remember, it's impolite to read our minds without permission, Ophelia."

Dammit, he's right. It would be so easy to tune into their thoughts and find out what they're keeping from me. "Except if I think any of us are in danger," I remind him with a triumphant grin.

"Nobody is in danger." He drops a kiss on the top of my head before tipping his chin at Malachi. "You'd better go."

Malachi offers me a smile and does his best to hide his disappointment, but even without reading him, I can still tell from the slight droop to his shoulders and the lack of shine in his bright-green eyes. "Catch you later, sweet girl."

I give him a halfhearted wave. "See you later, Kai."

Without another word, Xavier guides me down the hallway to my next class, and I'm left wondering what just happened. It doesn't feel like anything bad is going on. Xavier is humming softly to himself, and I don't feel any fear or anxiety from the others, but still ... "What's going on? Why did Kai have to leave?"

Xavier laughs and shakes his head. "Because he's too much of a sap for you."

I elbow him in the ribs. "No he's not."

He responds by laughing harder and wrapping me in a loose headlock. Then he presses another kiss on the top of my head but still doesn't answer my question.

"What does that even mean, Xavier?"

"There's nothing for you to worry about, Cupcake. Let's just get your classes done with so I can get you home."

There is no mistaking the change in his tone when he says those last few words, and it's enough to send shivers of excitement racing down my spine. The boys don't know that *the curse* is lifted yet, and I cannot wait to tell them. I have it all planned out. I try to tamp down my excitement before Xavier feels my giddiness and tickles the truth out of me. I'm so wrapped up in my own plans that I almost forget he's hiding something from me too.

I don't intend to read his mind, but I kind of can't help it, and I probe inside for a clue. Casually, without breaking a step, he wraps his large hand around my throat and squeezes gently. "Rude, Cupcake."

"Wait! You could tell I was—?" Embarrassment at being caught out heats my cheeks.

"Yes." He gives me yet another kiss.

"I'm sorry. I can't help it. Sometimes I just ... I'm sorry."

He stops walking, and a second later, I'm pinned to the wall of the hallway. Students move past us, throwing amused or concerned glances our way, but I guess the fact that I'm not struggling prevents any of them from stepping in. "There's no need to be embarrassed. And I like you inside my head. But you're not getting in there today."

"You can block me out?" I ask, awed. I know how much the professor believes in his abilities and how my lessons have been helping him develop his own powers too, but I didn't realize how far he'd come.

He caresses my throat with his thumb. "As long as you don't push too hard. I think, anyway."

My cheeks hurt with the force of my smile. "I'm so proud of you!"

"Yeah, well, you can show me just how much later, Cupcake." The playfulness in his tone is enough to assuage any fears I had about something bad going on. Now I'm simply more curious than I have ever been in my life. I open my mouth to ask a question, but before I can, Xavier seals his lips over mine and kisses me.

No questions either.

So unfair, I grumble. Well, as much of a grumble as I can muster while Xavier is kissing me the way he is.

I STAYED out of Xavier's head for the rest of the day, but I did bombard him with questions, all of which he skillfully avoided answering while somehow also managing to stoke my excitement. We reach the porch, and my curiosity is so heightened that I feel like I might burst.

"Am I going to find out what you've been keeping from me soon?" I ask, bouncing with the effort of containing my glee.

He lifts my hand to his lips and brushes them over my knuckles. "I have no idea what you're talking about, Cupcake."

"Liar," I huff as we walk into the house. Malachi's energy hits me as soon as we step inside. He's almost as giddy as I am. "What the hell is going on?" I whisper.

Xavier jerks his head toward the kitchen. "Go see for yourself."

I practically run down the hallway and burst into the kitchen. The sight that greets me has me both stunned and deliriously happy. A giant unicorn balloon sits in the middle of the table, and pink glittery balloons are strewn around the room, clashing with the classic red and green Christmas decorations that I insisted we needed. A congratulations banner is strung from the upper cabinets, and paper plates and cups that match the balloons are set out in each of our places. The over-the-top unicorn cake is decorated with colorful lollipops and sprinkles, and I can't wait to dig in. But best of all, Malachi, Axl, and Alexandros are here too. Malachi almost knocks me over with the force of his hug, and I struggle to catch my breath. "W-what is all this?"

"It's your party, princess," Axl says, pulling me from Malachi's arms and into his.

Xavier stands behind me, his chin resting on my head. "Congratulations, Cupcake."

"Congratulations for what?" I look to Alexandros for some clue. He remains seated at the table but watches us all with an unexpectedly tender smile on his face.

It's Malachi who answers. "You controlled your powers. The curse is lifted." His joy makes me laugh.

"You already know?"

Xavier laughs. "Fuck yeah, we know."

Axl gives me a hard squeeze before releasing me. "We knew as soon as it happened, princess."

I look to the professor and do my best to appear indignant, but I can't keep the smile from my face for longer than a second. "You told me they didn't know. You said I should wait to tell them," I say accusingly.

He shrugs. "The boys wanted to do something special to mark the occasion, and I ..." He draws a breath through his nose and pushes himself to his feet. "It has been too long since we had something to celebrate." He holds out his arms, and I walk into them, allowing him to wrap me in the comfort of him. "And what you achieved last night is worth celebrating, little one."

I rest my head against his chest, my eyes landing on the cake and the unicorn balloon tied to the back of my chair. This is so out of his comfort zone. A laugh bubbles from my lips. "You secretly hate this, don't you?" I whisper.

He rests his chin on the top of my head. "More than you can ever know," he says with an exaggerated sigh that has his breath ruffling my hair. "I expect you to make this up to me tenfold."

"Time for cake!" Malachi shouts, and I untangle myself from Alexandros's embrace.

"And then orgasms," Axl declares.

Xavier fist-pumps the air. "A metric fuck ton of orgasms."

I mouth a thank you to Alexandros and then take the seat Malachi pulls out for me. "Is this what you guys have been doing all day?"

Malachi nods eagerly. "Yep. We thought of doing something last night, but I had no idea of the full plan until Xavier came to get me after your geology class."

Xavier laughs. "Yeah. Axl and I came up with it after you left for class, and we knew we couldn't tell him about it because he would have spilled."

Malachi punches him on the arm. "Fuck you!"

"It's true." Xavier throws his hands in the air. The boys start to squabble, and I bask in the normalcy of the moment. After a few minutes, Alexandros tells them to behave, and they fall silent.

"You each have your own unique talents, but it is only Xavier who is currently powerful enough to block Ophelia from his mind." The overwhelming feeling of pride in Xavier ripples through all of us. Then Alexandros turns his attention to me. "That is why he had to accompany you to your classes today."

My eyes dart between all four of them, and I'm overcome with so much positive emotion that I feel like I could quite literally burst into a cloud of glitter. I can't believe they did all this. Tears fill my eyes, but they are tears of pure joy. "I've never had a party before. Thank you all so much."

"Anything for you, sweet girl." Malachi brushes a tear from my cheek.

Axl places a slab of cake in front of me. After taking the seat next to mine, he rests his hand on the back of my neck. "Eat your cake so we can get to the good stuff."

Xavier groans his agreement.

"How many orgasms do you owe our Ophelia, boys?" Alexandros asks, a wicked glint in his eye that I've never seen before. Seeing this side of him is a rare gift, and I feel so incredibly lucky to witness it.

Malachi has a huge bite of cake in his mouth that he tries to speak around, but all that comes out are sprinkles and unintelligible mumbles.

"At least twenty-one," Axl answers.

"Twenty-one?" My legs are shaking at the mere thought of it.

He shrugs, a smirk spreading across his face. "It's been three weeks. That's only one a day, princess."

"Not even one from each of us," Xavier chimes in.

Warmth ignites in my core, and suddenly the giant piece of cake in front of me looks much less appealing. All I can think about are their expert hands and their sinful mouths and their naked bodies.

Malachi licks his lips. "Twenty-one multiplied by three is sixty-three."

Oh my god, I'm definitely going to die from orgasms.

Alexandros cups my jaw, his dark eyes burning into mine. *You deserve all of this and more, little* one, he says to only me before speaking aloud. "Perhaps not all in one night, boys." Then he presses a soft kiss on my forehead and walks out of the room, leaving me alone with the three of them.

Axl looks down at my plate. "Not hungry, princess?"

I shake my head. Not even a little. "Not hungry for cake at least."

He pushes my plate away and lifts me onto the table so I'm sitting in front of him. Then he edges forward, spreading my thighs apart with his broad shoulders. "Shall I tell you what I'm hungry for?" He flicks his tongue over his fangs, and heat pools between my thighs.

I already know the answer, but I whimper a yes anyway.

One corner of his mouth lifts in a smirk, and he wordlessly pushes me back until I'm lying on the table with the unicorn balloon hovering ominously above me. I let out a giggle that earns me a nip on my thigh.

"How many times do you think we can make her come in one night?" Xavier asks while Axl removes my panties.

I suck in a shuddered breath.

"I dunno. Is there a limit before we have to stop? I mean, burning down the house wise?" Malachi asks.

No. She is more than capable of controlling herself now. There are no limits. The professor's voice fills our heads and also seals my fate. I am surely going to leave this mortal realm tonight, and I'm not even mad about it. My legs are already trembling violently, and Axl has barely touched me.

"Has anyone ever actually died from an orgasm?" Malachi asks, letting me know I've been communicating all my thoughts to them.

Xavier lets out a wicked laugh. "I guess we'll find out."

I shoot him a warning glare, but it loses all its heat the second Axl's mouth meets my flesh. He licks a hot, wet trail along my center that has white-hot pleasure spearing through my core. I cry out, trying to buck my hips, but I'm held down by Xavier and Malachi while their brother feasts on me.

"This is your favorite way to come, right, Cupcake?" Xavier asks.

I press my lips together, screw my eyes closed, and nod furiously as I try to maintain a handle on my powers. The incredible sensations delivered by Axl's skilled mouth require me to focus. When he flicks his tongue over my clit, I explode like a firework at the stroke of midnight on New Year's. Quick and fast and electric.

And I smile because I'm in heaven, but also because my powers remained in check with minimal effort on my part. Which is good, considering that was the first of many orgasms tonight. Xavier and Malachi are already arguing about who gets to make me come next, and perhaps I should hate it, but I can't. Not when I feel their devotion and their loyalty coursing through my veins along with my pleasure.

～

"Can you feel your legs, princess?" Axl's low voice drifts into my ears.

I murmur something unintelligible, unable to open my eyes as I lie nestled in a cocoon of their warm bodies. I have no idea how many of their sixty-three orgasms they delivered, having lost count after six. But they ate and fucked and fed on me over and over again until the morning sun broke through the dawn.

Malachi laughs softly, his breath dusting over my shoulder. "I think we broke her."

"Naw. She's fucking invincible, aren't you, Cupcake?"

I smile and murmur my agreement as sleep threatens to take me under, and I let myself fall with the sound of their hushed voices surrounding me. In the comfort and protection of our bond, I know that nothing will ever break this. Nothing will ever break us.

This is home.

TWENTY-EIGHT

OPHELIA

"This is the talented young witch I spoke of." Enora's voice drifts into the room, and I lift my head from my textbook to see her walking through the open doorway, followed by another woman with flaming-red hair that seems to glow under the strand of lights strung around the room. The latter may be the most striking creature I've ever seen. But who is she, and what is she doing here?

"Cadence Callander. Members of her family have attended our school for generations," Enora adds, gesturing to my friend sitting on the bed opposite me.

Cadence jumps up from the bed and greets her guests. The woman with the red hair gives me a light smile in greeting before she introduces herself to Cadence as an old friend of Enora's, but she doesn't reveal her name. I go back to my book —or at least pretend to. My innate curiosity won't allow me to not listen while they discuss Cadence's family and her dreams of becoming a professor at Montridge herself one day.

They go on chatting openly like I'm not even here, and while some people might find that impolite, I quite enjoy fading into the background. Especially after having been able to do so little of that these past few weeks. It feels like I'm always the object of someone's attention lately, and while I mostly love it, I sometimes miss being able to disappear without anyone noticing I'm gone. It's why I enjoy visiting Silver Vale so much. Here, I am simply Ophelia. Not Ophelia, the only elementai in existence who is likely to soon bring about the apocalypse.

"Cadence." Enora grips my friend by the elbow. "Come help me make our guest some tea." Cadence nods eagerly, her eyes not leaving the redheaded woman who seems to have captivated her completely. So much so that Enora has to practically drag Cadence from the room, and I am left alone with the strange, enigmatic woman whose name I still don't know. She takes a few steps toward me, and I swing my legs over the edge of the bed and plant my feet on the ground in preparation to run or fight should I need to.

The woman with the red hair is smiling, but there's something about her that unnerves me. Each step she takes toward me feels like the lowering of a veil, as though she was shielding her power but for some reason is no longer doing so.

"You have nothing to fear from me, Ophelia." She smiles sweetly, her emerald-green eyes sparkling like they're made of actual gemstones. And while her vibe feels genuine, I no longer trust my instincts. I have come to recognize the metallic taste of powerful magic, and its flavor now coats my tongue.

"How do you know my name?" I ask, closely examining her

to see if I can find some clue as to who she is and whether she's a threat to me. Surely Enora wouldn't have left me alone with her if she were. Alexandros, a man who has faith in so few, trusts Enora. Surely that means something.

"I know a lot about you, Ophelia Hart. I was there at your birth, after all."

Her statement is like a sucker punch to my solar plexus. "Y-you—You what?"

She nods and takes a seat on Cadence's bed. "Yes. I was one of the beings who saved you."

"Y-you saved me?"

She nods again.

My head is spinning, and I place my hand on the back of my neck and try to cool myself down, but it doesn't work. "From who? Who are you?"

She arches an eyebrow. "I truly do not know who was hunting you and your family, child. They were scorched to death by the time we arrived, and only the most intense fire can kill a vampire. It is a myth that their heads must be removed to kill them. If a fire rages hot enough, it can burn them faster than they can heal."

"They were vampires?"

"Yes. They killed your mother and father, and we saved you from her womb and left you on the steps of the church. I recall it like it was yesterday. Your eyes were that same electric shade of vibrant blue."

My natural curiosity is drowned out by the fear and uncertainty snaking through my veins, curling talons around my heart and squeezing tight. The dresser begins to rattle.

"Calm your mind, Ophelia. I am no threat to you." Her voice is soothing, but I can't trust it.

Ophelia? Alexandros's commanding voice rings through my

head now, the complete opposite of the musical tone of this charismatic witch sitting before me.

The walls go on rattling, and heat blisters my skin.

Ophelia! Alexandros calls once more.

The woman stares at me. She's still smiling, but her green eyes burrow into my soul. I shake my head if only to tear my gaze from hers. So many emotions flood me, and I can't focus on any of them.

Where are you? Alexandros shouts, frantic. *I cannot find you!*

I vaguely hear Axl, or perhaps it's Xavier, tell him that I'm at Silver Vale. My blood is rushing in my ears. I gasp for oxygen, but it's sucked from the room, and I know that it's undoubtedly my doing, but I can't stop it. However, the green-eyed woman is unaffected.

"Use your light, Ophelia," she says calmly.

"H-how do you know—" The next words are stolen from me by the lack of air in my lungs.

"If it is Alexandros who calms you, then reach out to him and have him guide you before you shake the walls of this house to the ground."

Alexandros, I call desperately.

I am almost there, little one. I will never let anyone hurt you.

Nobody is hurting me. But I can't control my power. I can't focus. Tears leak from the corners of my eyes.

Yes you can. Close your eyes and find your light, agápi mou.

I try to focus, but there are too many questions and feelings racing through my head.

Listen to my voice and nothing else, he says, much calmer now, the deep timbre of his voice washing over me in a comforting wave.

I do as he says, listening only to him as he utters words of comfort and praise. I see the dazzling orb of light that is my center. As though it were as simple as flicking a switch, I can breathe again and the house goes still.

When I open my eyes, the witch is still regarding me with curiosity. "You are powerful, Ophelia. But ..." She presses her lips together.

"But what?"

There's a loud commotion downstairs, and I recognize Alexandros's voice in the melee. Anxiety spikes in me once more, but I control it. He's demanding to be let into the house. "Why can't he come inside?"

"Because I have cast a spell to prevent him from doing so."

I fold my arms across my chest. "Why?"

"Tell him you are safe and that I will allow him inside in but a few moments," she says. "And then we can talk."

"Can I give him your name?"

Her eyes sparkle with delight. "Nazeel. He will know of whom you speak."

I'm even more confused now, but I do as she asks, if only to stop him from tearing the house apart to get to me.

"Nazeel!" Alexandros's roar echoes through the house. With a wave of her hand, she drowns out all sound, and we're shrouded in complete silence. I can no longer hear him in my head either.

"Who are you?"

"An old friend of Alexandros's. An ally." She rests a hand on my knee and squeezes.

I frown, still unsure of her motives. "He doesn't seem to think so."

"He is simply afraid of what will happen when the world finds out who and what you are. But there is no stopping that from happening."

Terror washes over me at the casual way she speaks of my

inevitable demise. "We could stop it though. Why does anyone have to know?"

The spot between her brows pinches together, and she purses her lips. "They must know, Ophelia. Who you are cannot be hidden."

"I know I'm supposed to be the last of my kind and all that, but—"

"No." Her green eyes darken, and she leans forward. "You are so much more than that."

I open my mouth to speak, but Nazeel flinches back and rubs her temples. "He is much stronger than he was."

My pulse spikes once more. "What? Who?"

"I must leave."

"Wait! No." I have too many questions, and she seems to have several of the answers I need. "Who were my parents? What do you mean I'm more than that? Who are you?"

Her eyes fill with tears, and she takes my hand in hers. "I did save your life, sweet Ophelia. I knew from the moment you were born that you were special. Many will try to use your power for their own ends, but do not let them, my child. Always trust your light."

She lets my hand go, and before I can ask another question, she has disappeared. Not even a trace of her power lingers. But the sound of Alexandros storming through the house like a bull charging at a matador fills my ears, and I blink when he rushes into the room, his eyes wild as he glances around Cadence's room.

"Where is she?" he growls.

I glance at the space where she was just five seconds ago. "She disappeared. Literally disappeared."

Enora races in behind him, and he turns on a dime, wrapping his hand around her throat and hoisting her into the air. "I trusted you." The rage in his voice is unlike anything I've ever heard before. The temperature in the room seems to drop below freezing.

Panic covers my flesh in goosebumps, and I run to him and take hold of his free hand, threading my fingers through his. "Let her go."

He ignores me, keeping his glare fixed on Enora. "I trusted you to protect her."

She tries to speak but can't. Her eyes bug out, and her face turns a deep shade of crimson. I tug on his hand. "Please let her go so she can explain."

For a few heavy seconds, I'm worried he's going to snap her neck. But he finally releases her and wraps me in his arms. His hands run over my body as if checking for injury. "Are you okay?"

No, I am not okay. I'm confused and scared, and I have three billion questions I need answers to, but I know that's not what he means. "I'm fine. I promise."

He keeps one arm around me and turns back to Enora. "How could you? The Order … Nazeel?" He seems unable to string together a complete sentence, and I'm left wondering why he's so angry, not to mention seemingly afraid of the woman with the red hair. She was incredibly powerful, but I didn't sense any danger from her.

"I'm okay," I assure him.

He ignores me and keeps his glare trained on Enora.

"She asked to meet our most gifted witches, and also to meet Ophelia. You know she would not cause her any harm. What was I supposed to do?"

His breath dusts over my forehead as he grips me tighter. "You should have told me immediately."

"She swore me to secrecy, and you know that my family's oath to the Danraath witches prevents me from going against her wishes. You also know that she is no threat to Ophelia."

"Wait. Is she the one who asked you to look out for me?" I ask.

Enora nods.

"She said that she saved me when I was born. She said she was there."

Alexandros turns to me, his eyes narrowed. "She told you that?"

I nod. *She also said I am more than an elementai, Alexandros. What does she mean?* I ask him through our bond because I'm not sure I fully trust Enora after she left me alone with Nazeel. Plus, there are some things I'd rather keep between us, at least until I know what they mean. Not that I can discount the question of whether Enora knows what I am, given her connection to Nazeel.

He doesn't answer me. Instead, he retrains his glare on Enora. "You have broken my trust, and for that, I will never forgive you."

The pain on Enora's face is so acute that it winds me. "Alexandros, I never meant to—"

"I trusted you with the most precious thing in the world to me." His body vibrates with the strength of his rage.

"But Nazeel would never hurt her," Enora insists.

He lunges, his fangs bared, and Enora flinches back against the door. "That is not the point, Enora. You have set in motion a chain of events that cannot be undone!"

She hardens her gaze. "No, Alexandros. Whatever is meant to be will be. There is nothing either of us can do to change even our own fates, let alone the fate of another. If Nazeel has an interest in Ophelia, there must be a good reason."

My stomach churns. Why do I always feel like I'm out of the loop in my own life?

Alexandros grabs my wrist. "You are not to come to this house again."

I struggle to keep up with him as he marches me toward the door. "What? No, you can't—"

He stops in his tracks and grips my jaw between his thumb and forefinger. We're standing in the hallway now, surrounded by a dozen scared-looking witches. "You will not come here again, Ophelia."

"You can't stop her. She's my friend," Cadence yells from the peripheral of the circle surrounding us, and my heart warms at her sticking up for our friendship.

With a vicious roar, he bares his teeth, and a couple of the nearby witches yelp and scurry back.

"Girls, that will be enough for now." Enora's calm voice coasts down the hallway. "Alexandros, must you discipline the girl in front of her friends?"

There's a single snigger from somewhere behind us, and he releases his grip on me. *I have barely even started*, he warns me through our bond.

I bite down on my lip and close my eyes. My cheeks burn with shame, but the spot between my thighs is also inexplicably warm. He's enraged and dangerous, and this is definitely not the time or the place. Yet I can't seem to help myself.

"Say goodbye to your friends, Ophelia," he commands. "You will not be coming back here."

I want to tell him to go to hell, but the look in his eyes is murderous, and I don't want to test out his "barely even started" threat in front of all these people. So I turn to my friend and give her a small but warm smile. "Bye, Cadence." Her eyes fill with tears. "We can still meet in the library," I offer, my heart breaking.

Alexandros growls. "No, you will not."

Before I can protest, he hoists me over his shoulder like a firefighter rescuing someone from a burning building and marches out of Silver Vale.

"Will you put me down?"

He ignores me and breaks into a run, and by the time we get back to the house, I feel dizzy and a little sick. He sets me down in the entryway, and I sway on my feet.

"Are you okay, baby?" Malachi says, stepping up behind me and stopping me from rocking backward.

"No," I snap, directing all my anger at the man standing in front of me.

Alexandros flexes his palm. "Do not push me, Ophelia, because I *will* punish you, and I will make the boys watch me turn your backside redder than your blood."

"Uh-oh." Axl steps up beside us now. "What did you do, princess?"

"I didn't do anything!" My indignation takes a sudden turn into sadness, and tears fill my eyes. This is so unfair. I just lost my best friend, and I didn't do anything wrong.

Alexandros wipes a tear from my cheek. "How many times do I have to tell you that everything I do is for your protection?"

I bite down on my lip. He's told me that many times, but still ...

He dusts his lips over my forehead. "But you do not get to question me in front of the witches, Ophelia."

So that's what this is about? Me challenging his authority in front of other people? "Okay. But I—"

"Ophelia!"

Xavier's dark laugh rings out behind me. "Please piss him off some more, Cupcake. I would love to see that spanking."

Axl and Malachi murmur in agreement, and my cheeks heat. Alexandros cups my jaw again, much more gently than he did at Silver Vale. He sweeps the pad of his thumb over my bottom lip, tugging it down, and grazes his mouth over mine until I whimper. "We can save the spanking for another time. I have a witch to track down."

"Are you going to find Nazeel?"

"If she is not long gone by now." He drops his hand from my face and directs his attention to the boys. "Do not let her out of your sight."

Xavier gives a mock salute that makes Alexandros scowl. Malachi wraps his arms around my waist and rests his chin on my shoulder. "We'll keep our girl on lockdown, sir."

I sigh. I should fight, but I don't have the energy, and lockdown with my guys isn't all that bad. Food and a movie followed by lots of cuddles—not to mention all the orgasms. Lots of orgasms.

Alexandros must have read my mind, because he was headed for the door, but now he turns on his heel, and quicker than a flash, his hand is at the back of my neck, his hot mouth resting on my ear. "When I get back, little one, I do not care how exhausted you are or how much you have already given. I am going to feed on you whilst I fuck you, and you are going to moan my name as I do it."

I swallow the needy whimper that tries to claw its way from my throat. He's the same asshole who plans to stop me from seeing my friends, and I'm still mad at him for it. But I also know that to argue now, when he's intent on having his own way, is futile. So I fix him with my sweetest smile and say, "Yes sir."

CHAPTER
TWENTY-NINE

ALEXANDROS

"Your tracking skills have not dulled over the centuries, old friend." Nazeel's feminine voice contains a hint of amusement that only further feeds my fury. She is somewhere nearby, cloaked in the shadows, glimmering in and out to throw off my senses. But her powers are lessened here. There is something about hallowed ground which affects witches' magic, making it less potent. That is what makes a cemetery the perfect place to disguise a portal to another continent. The energy is dulled enough to not draw attention.

Luckily for me, my eyes are more accustomed to the dark than hers, and therefore all I need is a little patience to find her.

Unfortunately, my patience is in short supply when it comes to all matters of Ophelia.

"A witch with your power is easy to find, Nazeel. It leaves a scent behind."

Her musical laugh rings in my ears. "Only for those clever enough to decipher it."

My frustration grows. "You flatter me, witch."

I skirt the edges of the mausoleum, focusing in on her scent and picking out the unique notes of the rare orchid which only grows on the foothills of the mountain where the Order makes their home. "I had thought this portal decommissioned a long time ago."

"I resurrected it but a few years ago. It seemed pertinent to have a quick route to Havenwood." Her breathing is quiet but easily detectable. Her heartbeat is steady, but her pulse thrums against the pressure points on her body.

I lick my lips, tasting the air as I edge closer, staying between her and the portal. Waiting. Patience.

My hand snaps out and wraps around her throat. "Nazeel Danraath. What brings you to Havenwood, so far from home?"

I tilt her head up so her bright-green eyes sparkle in the moonlight. "You already know, Alexandros Drakos. That is why you are here, is it not?"

I squeeze her throat a little tighter, but she offers no reaction. She is too powerful to show weakness. "You resurrected the portal to have direct access to Ophelia?"

She nods.

A growl rumbles from deep inside my chest. "Why? What is your interest in the girl?"

"If you let go of my throat, it would be much easier to tell you."

I stare into her eyes and look for signs that she is not to be trusted, but I find none. Nazeel is cunning and underhanded, but she has never given me reason to doubt her. She was an ally during the elementai genocide, even saving Giorgios's life despite not being permitted to interfere. For that, my family will always owe her a debt. I release her from my grip, and she steps back, giving her neck a soothing massage.

"I first came across the child when she was a babe."

I recall what Ophelia told me earlier. "It was you who found her?"

She tips her head and presses her lips together. "Not exactly. Kameen was summoned by her parents."

Kameen Nassari does not allow himself to be summoned, unless ... Another piece of the puzzle falls into place. "His brother, Jadon. He was Ophelia's father?"

She nods. "Yes."

Jadon and Kameen, the only sons of Artemis—one of the heirs of the most powerful demon who ever lived. "So she is a descendant of Azezal?"

"Yes. And Kameen's niece."

I scrutinize her familiar features as though they will offer more than what she has already disclosed despite knowing the futility of such an endeavor. Even with my newly enhanced powers, it would take me a century to break down Nazeel's walls. "Then it was you who bound her powers." It is not a question. She is one of the few who still lives with such knowledge and strength.

But there is no mistaking the hurt that flashes in her eyes. Binding a child's powers is barbaric and cruel, and Nazeel comes from a long line of witches who use their magic to heal. I have no doubt that it was not a painless undertaking for her. "I did. It was necessary for her protection. There were others who surely knew she was a powerful being. Others who would have stopped at nothing to get to her. The same ones who sent the creatures that killed her parents would have come for her."

"Who was Ophelia's mother?"

She brushes a speck of dirt from her cloak. "A common human. Nothing special." There is no disdain in her voice, simply the truth of her observation. However, it grates on me that she would call the mother of the other half of my soul *nothing special*. I suppress a growl and allow her to continue. "At least half a dozen vampires lay burned to ash in the surrounding wood. The baby was removed from her mother's womb with fire after the human took her final breath. Ophelia survived without even the slightest mark on her skin."

A thick coil of trepidation snakes its way through my gut. I refuse to believe in prophecies, yet the words are a chant in my head all the same, like a disembodied voice from a long-suppressed memory.

"Many souls were lost that night, Alexandros. Her mother perished before Kameen set fire to her corpse, and her father bled out from a wound poisoned with painite." I take a step backward, no longer wishing to hear what I know is coming next. Her hand grips my forearm with astonishing strength, and I am unable to pull away.

The events of that night unfold before me like I am standing there witnessing it firsthand. An infant Ophelia is lifted from a burned-out corpse, her tiny body covered in a film of blood and ash, her piercing cries of declaration ringing through the night air. "She was borne of fire and blood, Alexandros."

I grit my teeth and shake my head. "Do not quote prophecy to me, Nazeel."

Her frustration grows palpable. "I do not have much time." She glances at the portal entrance behind me. "Kameen will come searching for me."

"All the more evidence that you should not be here, meddling in matters that do not concern you."

Her emerald-green eyes narrow. "You only know part of the prophecy, Alexandros. If you knew the full verse—"

I growl a warning. "Do not hold your knowledge over me like some kind of bait for me to snap at, witch. I do not believe in prophecies."

"You cannot deny that she has the ability to be the most powerful being of our time. Of our entire history. And you are—"

"I said do not!" My roar reverberates off the stone surrounding us in the otherwise empty cemetery.

She presses her hand to her temple and winces. "Kameen is searching for me. I must leave."

"I have many more questions, Nazeel."

She shuffles, her eyes darting to the portal and then back to me. "I have no more time."

I press on, uncaring about what she needs. I need answers, and she has them. "Was it you who led her here? To Montridge?"

She nods quickly. "To you, Alexandros."

My eyes narrow. "Why?"

"To fulfill your destinies." She hitches up her cloak like she is about to make a run for it, but we both know I am faster. "I must go."

"I will let you leave if you give me your word that you will stay away from Ophelia."

She licks her bottom lip, contemplating my offer and no doubt wondering whether she could get by me. She cannot. Not without the full strength of her magic, which she does not have access to on this hallowed ground. Were she a demon or an elementai who could channel without the need for spells, she would stand a chance. Her eyes screw closed, and she staggers back a step. "I must leave. Now."

"Give me your word."

Her pulse flutters in her throat like the wings of a bird trapped in a cage. No doubt her fear of Kameen is greater than her fear of me, but I will use whatever I can get to my advantage.

She glances over my shoulder once more. "Fine, I give you my word I will stay away from the girl. But she is more powerful than you can even comprehend, Alexandros."

I step aside and allow her to pass. The concealed portal opens upon her approach, recognizing her ancient magic. Before she steps through it, she gives me one final look over her shoulder. "And she will change you."

In the blink of an eye, she disappears, and I am left staring at the crumbling wall of the mausoleum. What the hell did she mean? I resist the urge to follow her and ask. She will be long gone once she passes through to the other side, and my knowledge of that terrain is much less than hers. Besides, I am eager—no, *desperate* to return home and hold her in my arms.

And to fulfill the promise I made before I left. Her blood sings to my soul, calling me back to her any time I stray too far.

Of course she will change me. She already has.

THE HOUSE IS QUIET, but the sound of all four of their heartbeats is vibrant inside my head. I am connected to each of them, and I feel them always. Lately, the connection has been more intense than ever before, and I know the boys feel it too. Perhaps it has been opening my heart to Ophelia that has allowed the bond with them to take root there too. Or perhaps it is something entirely different.

Malachi steps out of the shadows at the top of the stairs. "You're back. Did you find Nazeel?" he asks quietly.

"I did." I climb the stairs, and with every step I take toward her, to all of them, my blood grows hotter.

"Is everything okay? Is Ophelia in danger?" He still speaks quietly, his velvety rich voice thick with sleep. His innocence and curiosity serve to pull a halfhearted smile from me. I place my hand on the back of his neck and squeeze as I press my forehead to his. "Ophelia is always in danger, Malachi. That is the reality of the burden we all share now."

"She's not a burden." His warm breath mingles with mine.

"No, she is not. She is the reason that our hearts beat."

Gingerly, he rests his hand over my heart, where it beats a steady rhythm against his palm. He has always been the most sensitive of souls, even though he refutes such assertions. "Is she sleeping?"

"Yes."

The thought of crawling over her sleeping form and slipping inside her warmth as she slumbers has my fangs protracting and my cock stiffening. "Were you all gentle with her for me?" They heard the promise I made to her before I left, and whilst I did not order them to take it easy with her, I hope that it was implicit.

His fingertips flex against my shirt. "Yes sir."

"You are good boys." I press a kiss on his forehead before I brush past him and go to her.

The door to Axl's room is ajar, and she lies curled up to Xavier's chest with Axl pressed up against her back. Her soft breathing soothes the beast inside me that wants nothing more than to climb on top of her and claim her. Rut into her until she feels nothing but me. Instead, I shrug off my coat and crawl onto the bed. Xavier wakes first and, upon seeing me, rolls away from her, giving me room. I nudge Axl out of the way, and he opens one eye before rolling onto his back. I should carry her to my own bed, but her arousal and her blood are already thick in the air, and my body physically aches for her too much to wait any longer.

I pull the comforter down, revealing her pale skin, and dust my mouth along her arm. She shivers. My cock hardens, pressing painfully against my zipper.

I hold myself up on one forearm as I trail my lips up her body until my mouth is close to her ear. "I am back, little one."

"Alexandros," she mumbles sleepily, her eyes still closed.

With my free hand, I push her onto her back and allow my eyes to rake over her perfect body. Her naked skin is covered in the scent of my boys, but that does nothing to detract from how good she smells. My fangs ache, and my mouth waters with anticipation to taste her.

I trail my fingertips across her collarbone. "So sweet, little Ophelia."

She murmurs, stuck halfway between a dream and waking. I slide my knee between her thighs, pushing them apart. "Shh. You can stay asleep if you must."

Her lips curve in a smile, her eyes remaining closed. But she is not closed off from me. Her mind is open. Her thighs spread wider until I drop between them, fitting against her like I was always meant to be here. I am vaguely aware of Malachi climbing back onto the bed beside Xavier and feel all three sets of eyes on me, but it does not matter. We are all a part of this. A part of her. I will take her whilst they watch and show them how beautifully she moans my name when she comes for me.

"Need to eat," she mumbles, still dreaming.

I hum against her skin, my lips vibrating against the soft skin of her throat. "You are right. I do need to eat." I drag my mouth lower and flick my tongue over the turgid peaks of her nipples, then move down to her stomach. She moans, and the lower I get, the louder her needy little sounds become. Finally, my mouth is at the apex of her thighs, and I suck the swollen bud of her clit into my mouth. She gasps, threading her fingers in my hair and rocking her hips against my face.

You awake now, little one?

"Y-yes." She grinds herself onto my lips and tongue as I lick and suck at her delicious pussy.

So close to the edge already. Were you dreaming of me? I chuckle against her, and the vibration makes her whimper.

I was waiting for you to come home and d-do this. She speaks through our bond, her breathing becoming raspy and labored. I lick her to her first orgasm, taking care of her swollen, tender flesh with my mouth before I fuck her because, as careful as I intend to be, I can never hold back as much as I should.

"Alexandros!" The breathy cry of my name from her lips fills me with pride, not only at the sounds she makes but also the groans that rumble from my boys as they watch us—as they *feel* her come apart for me.

You come like such a good girl for me.

She mewls at my praise, and her submission makes my length ache with the need to be inside her.

I press a kiss to the top of her inner thigh. The arterial pulse in her groin throbs like a beacon, calling me to bite her, but I move up her body, trailing my hungry mouth over her stomach and breasts until I reach the place where her lifeblood flows strongest. There is nothing better than sinking my fangs into her pretty throat whilst I am buried inside her hot, needy pussy.

Hurriedly, I free my cock from my pants and line up my crown, already seeping precum, at her entrance. She snakes her legs around my waist, and her snug entrance milks the tip of my shaft. Nazeel's words ring in my head. *She will change you.*

Jealousy—and the desire to prove to Ophelia and the rest of the world that I own every part of her—burns through me, causing a possessive growl to rumble in my throat.

Hold her open for me, I order Axl and Xavier, who obey immediately, unhooking her calves from behind my back and spreading her thighs as wide as she can comfortably tolerate.

She blinks at me, her blue eyes shining with anticipation. "I want to be so deep inside you that there is no doubt who you belong to, little one."

She nods and sinks her teeth into her pillowy bottom lip, daring me to do it. To fuck her so hard that she is forever molded to the shape of my cock.

And the sweet relief I feel when I push all the way inside her with one possessive stroke has my eyes rolling back in my head. My entire shaft is cocooned within her pulsing heat, but it is not enough. I rest on my forearms and nuzzle at her neck until I find the perfect spot where her carotid artery runs thick and fast with her blood. Her whimpers turn to needy moans as I bite down, piercing her tender flesh with my fangs and allowing her decadent taste to flood my mouth. The fire already raging inside me is stoked to an inferno.

"I need you." She runs her hands over my back, pulling up my shirt so she can access my skin. Her nails rake down my spine, and it makes me drive harder into her, causing the bed to rock violently.

And with every stroke inside her, ancient prophecies and their vague notions swirl around my mind.

The one who will bring our ruin or our redemption.

The one who will bring balance to the world.

But the world cannot have her. She is mine. *My* ruin and redemption. I try to drown it all out and lose myself in only her. In the way her tight warmth grips me like she fears I will leave, and in the way her soft body yields to mine despite the power running through every fiber of her being. But the witch's words continue to play on repeat. *She will change you.*

I pull out and sink into Ophelia again, over and over, deeper and harder than before, suckling greedily on her neck until her lifeblood courses through me as strongly as my own. Her desperate moans anchor me back to her, to this. The moment we share is so much more than the simple act of fucking. It is the life-affirming, eternally beautiful reunion of two halves of the same soul. A soul forged from the atoms of the universe billions of years ago, when the world was still blinking its newborn eyes at the first sun. I have surely loved her before, and I will find and love her through every incarnation until the end of time itself.

CHAPTER

THIRTY

XAVIER

There's something truly mesmerizing in the animalistic way he takes her, brutal and tender in equal measure. And when she comes for him, pressing her head back into the pillow while a series of guttural, satisfied cries pour from her pretty lips, I feel it deep in the pit of my stomach. How the two of them together complete a previously broken circle. Together, we are surely invincible. Because I feel it. Stronger and faster and sharper than I have ever felt before.

He pulls his teeth from her neck, and I have to stop myself from leaning forward and licking her blood from his lips. It is so tempting to push him while his own pleasure still courses through his veins. To take advantage of the vulnerability I only ever see in him when he's with her. But there is a line I know he'll never cross. As much as I burn for his skin on mine, his hands running over my body: squeezing, kneading, taking ... I know that I burn alone.

Malachi slides his arm around my waist and kisses my shoulder like he knows. Of course he knows. They all do. It's impossible to keep anything secret from them. Especially now that our bond seems to grow stronger with each passing day.

"Did you find Nazeel?" Ophelia's quiet voice cuts through the cacophony of pounding hearts in the room and provides me with a much-needed distraction.

Alexandros pushes himself up, sits back against the headboard, and pulls Ophelia onto his lap. Sighing, he pinches the bridge of his nose. "Yes."

"And?" I ask, propping myself up on my elbow.

He clears his throat. "She is aware of Ophelia's powers. It was she who bound them as a child."

Tears well in her eyes, and profound sadness pours from her, enveloping us all. "But how? And why?"

Alexandros twists his neck and groans like he's wrestling with what to tell her. His eyes land on mine. "She deserves the truth," I say.

He blows out a breath. "It will be painful, little one."

She swats away a tear and nods, her jaw set in determination. "I can handle it."

I grab her hand and link our fingers. "Yeah, you can, Cupcake."

He shifts her on his lap so she's straddling him. "It will be easier to show you."

She tips her head back, exposing her throat, and he rests a hand on her forehead like he's checking her temperature. "How do you feel?"

She blinks at him, unsure of what he means.

He runs his hand from her forehead to the back of her neck. "Are you lightheaded? Do you feel tired? Weak?"

"No. I feel strong," she whispers.

"Your ability to heal quickly has grown exponentially." He traces the fingers of his free hand over her chest. "And your blood replenishes much more quickly too."

The smile she gives him in return has me grinning too. "I know. I can feel it."

I lick the tip of my fangs, wanting to taste her right now. We've all felt how much longer we can feed before the flow of her blood tells us to stop.

Alexandros glances between Axl, Malachi, and me before directing his focus back to our girl. "I could show them what happened too. I think it is important that they know where you came from, that we all share your pain. But we would all have to feed from you."

Holy shit. Yes fucking please. Not only because I want to know everything about my girl and her past, but also because the idea of feeding on her with them already has euphoria lighting up my veins.

"At the same time?" she whispers.

"We will stop if it gets to be too much."

Her hand grips his biceps, fingers digging into the taut muscle. "Yes. I want to show them too."

The beast inside me growls, and Alexandros shoots me a look. I'm not sure if it's supposed to be a warning, but his eyes are dark and full of desire. And while I know that the lust in his eyes when he looks at me is because Ophelia's on his lap and he's about to bite her, my body doesn't seem to be able to distinguish the difference. My dick stiffens.

All too soon, his gaze is back on Ophelia—specifically, the fluttering pulse in her throat. He licks his lips. "Are you sure, Ophelia?"

"Yes." She declares the word with such confidence that there can be no room for doubt.

He sinks his teeth into her neck, and she whimpers. Axl and Malachi move quickly, wasting no time in sinking their fangs into her perfect tits. And with Alexandros at her front and them on either side, the only place left for me is behind her. I straddle the professor's legs and press my chest against her back, then gather her hair in my fist and expose the nape of her neck. My eyes lock with my sire's, and the hunger in his gaze makes my knees weak. I maintain eye contact while I sink my teeth into the back of her neck.

He shows us everything: her birth, the fire, the blood. Her parents and the dead bodies scattered around. The conversation between Nazeel and two other members of the Order about binding her powers. We watch it unfold like a movie, and through it all, we feel Ophelia's despair. Her anguish, her pain, and her truth.

It floods my being along with her blood. And so does her power. I get but a glimpse of the raw, untapped magic that makes up her every atom, and it is enough to ensure that I will kneel at her feet for all eternity.

And when we have seen enough, drank enough, we stop feeding. I lick the residual blood from my lips and taste the salt from the tears streaking down my face. She falls back into my waiting arms, and I wrap her up so tight she must know I'll never let her go.

"Ophelia." Alexandros's voice is a plea as though he's worried he's broken her.

She sniffs. "I'm okay. Thank you for showing me."

He cups her face in his hands and brushes her tear-streaked cheeks with his thumbs, his eyes shining with unshed tears too.

Malachi kisses her shoulder. "You're incredible, sweet girl."

"Thank you for sharing that with us, princess."

She rests her head back on my shoulder. "You're all a part of me. There's nothing I won't share with you."

Alexandros clears his throat. "I should ..." He glances around, looking for the easiest way to extricate himself from the four bodies surrounding him.

"Please don't go. Stay here with us," she begs. "Just this once."

I hold my breath, wishing I had the courage to ask him too, but I doubt it would make a difference to his decision. I can practically see his armor breaking. He closes his eyes and releases a heavy sigh. "Tonight only."

She lets out a tiny squeak of delight that has me smiling. Even after watching the traumatic events that saw her entry into this world, she still has it in her to find joy in the little things, and that is one of the most incredible things about her. She must have a billion questions racing around her mind, but for once, she doesn't ask anything. Probably because she doesn't want to scare him off.

"If I am sleeping in here, little one, then you are sleeping on me or there will not be enough room."

"As long as you won't be too uncomfortable," she says meekly.

He arches an eyebrow. "How could I possibly be uncomfortable with you lying on me?"

She takes a deep breath, and I press my lips against her ear. "If you make a comment about being too heavy, Cupcake, you're going to be punished severely."

Alexandros licks his lips and nods his agreement.

"Okay then," she says.

I let her go and roll back into my spot. He lies down, shuffling her so she's lying on his chest. We lie in the dark, all of us exhausted but unable to sleep. Perhaps we're simply unwilling to close our eyes on this precious time together.

Ophelia breaks the thick silence in the room. "Now that you know Nazeel is no threat, can I go back to Silver Vale?"

That silence is replaced by tension. "I never said she was no threat," Alexandros growls.

Ophelia rests her chin on her hands so she's staring down into his face. "But she saved me when I was a baby. She's the one who's responsible for me being here, right?"

"I also never said that," he snaps.

"No, you didn't. But it makes sense. Who else could it have been? It for sure wasn't my parents who put that trust together, was it?"

Alexandros is quiet, and I smile in the darkness. The cupcake is far too smart for our own good. "I believe it was her, yes," he finally answers.

"So I can go back to Silver Vale and see Cadence?" she asks hopefully.

I roll onto my side to watch the show. He never yields to anyone about anything, but I can practically hear him wrestling with himself about this. "I do not trust Enora."

Ophelia sighs. "I think you do, but you're just really mad at her right now so you're refusing to admit that."

I press my lips together and stifle a snicker, reveling in the uncomfortable silence that follows.

"Ophelia Hart." His menacing tone sends a shiver down my spine, but in the best possible way. "One day, I am going to give you the spanking you deserve."

Oh, yes please. For the love of all the demons on hell and earth, spank her fine ass.

She sighs, resting her head on his chest once more. "But I can go to Silver Vale, right?"

He grunts.

"I'll take that as a yes. Thank you, sir."

He smacks her ass. "Go to sleep."

She turns her head my way and smiles. Smiling back, I rest my hand on her back and draw circles on her skin.

I like the way you do that. It makes me sleepy. We're the only two here, and it totally blows my mind that she's able to block people out of my head while talking to me. Even after all the practice I've done with her and the professor, I still can't block him out on my own.

Are you okay after what you saw?

Malachi breathes softly and steadily behind me, and I smile at the familiar sounds of him sleeping.

Yeah. I know it was awful, but I actually feel better, you know? Like I finally know where I came from.

I go on lazily tracing a circular pattern on her skin. *I can understand that.*

Her eyes flutter closed. *Will you always do this for me, Xavier?*

Always, Cupcake.

A few seconds later, she drifts off to sleep too. Sparks of electricity seem to engulf my hand when Alexandros strokes her skin and his fingers brush mine. I know he must have felt my reaction, but it doesn't cause him to move his hand. He leaves it next to mine, our fingertips resting next to each other. And that's how I fall asleep—touching her and him and wishing this could be how I fall asleep every night.

THIRTY-ONE

OPHELIA

"Hey, O," Sienna calls my name across the quad, and when I look up, she's waving at me with a huge smile on her face. "Get over here."

I offer a wave before glancing at Axl, my bodyguard for today. The professor kept to his word. I don't leave the house without at least one of the guys accompanying me. Classes, the library, dining halls. Axl gives me a kiss on the cheek and leans against a tree, his arms folded over his broad chest. "Go talk to your friend, princess. I'll be right here watching."

"Thanks." Skirting my way around the giant Christmas tree in the middle of the quad, I keep my head dipped low, aware of people's eyes on me as I head over to one of the most popular girls on campus. I'm still not quite used to having the attention of someone like Sienna. She literally turns heads when she walks by, and I swear her skin shimmers when she moves. She tosses her long, thick braids over her shoulder. "You want to come to a party tonight?"

"A party?"

She props a hand on her hip. "Yeah." Her laugh is warm and friendly. "You know, those things most college kids go to? Maybe dance? Get a little drunk? You know, if that's your deal. It's not mine but ..." She shrugs.

"But it's Monday," I say, then immediately wish I could call those words back when I see her amused expression. How big of a nerd do I want her to think I am? "Not that it matters. Um ... Could I, uh ..." I press my lips together. "Bring a friend?"

"Sure."

"Or three?"

Her eyes sparkle, and she glances over my shoulder at Axl. I follow her gaze to see him still leaning against the tree, his tight T-shirt straining against his biceps. Girls check him out as they walk by, but he keeps his attention focused on me, and I can't help but smile.

"Oh, you mean the Ruby Dragon commanders? You're their girl this year, right?" Sienna says, directing my attention back to her.

Despite not getting any judgy vibes from her at all, my cheeks burn with embarrassment. I'm not sure I'll ever get used to everyone on campus knowing I have three boyfriends. Technically four, but the professor and I are still not common knowledge. But wait, did she say— *"This* year?"

She twirls a dark braid between her fingers. "Sure. They usually have a few regular girls they hook up with every year."

My heart almost falls through my chest. "They do?"

She nods. "Yeah. It's no big deal. You know what they are, right? It's kind of their nature to need a few people to sustain their needs."

I try to keep a lid on my growing temper. "And this year?"

Need me to come over there, princess? Axl asks, sensing the change in my emotions.

No. I refrain from snapping at him, even though I want to. *I'm fine. I promise.*

Sienna licks her lips. "Well, this year they seem to have gone exclusive. Word on campus is they're off the market for good." She inches closer. "So actually, I was wrong. I guess you're just their girl. Period."

I swallow down the swell of jealousy that rolls up from my chest, which is dampened by her last statement. "I guess I am."

"That's a whole swath of broken hearts out there. Because those boys ... Well, you know better than anyone, right? They're not exactly my type, but I can see their appeal."

My only response is to stand here and blink at her like an idiot.

Her lovely green eyes shine, and she tilts her head, scrutinizing me. "Hey, I'm sorry if I made you feel uncomfortable. Sometimes I speak before my brain's engaged. I've always thought vampires got a bad rap. We're all driven by instincts, and there's nothing wrong with that. Those boys have it bad for you, O. And I can't say I blame them."

I shift from one foot to the other. She's being nice to me. Paying me a compliment even, so why do I feel so intimidated?

Because you do not believe yourself worthy of her friendship or her adoration, little one. But I assure you that you are. Of that and so much more. His voice, warm and strong and reassuring, fills me up.

I feel a smile spreading across my face. *Were you just listening in on my thoughts, Professor? Aren't you supposed to be teaching?*

He growls softly, and the sound has pleasure snaking through my limbs and my toes curling in my boots. *You are a constant distraction, Ophelia.*

"So, what do you say?" Sienna asks, reminding me we're also having a conversation.

"Um, to the party?"

She laughs, rolling her eyes. "Yeah, girl."

Sienna Brackenwolf wants me to go to a party later, I tell Alexandros.

Are you asking for my permission to attend? His tone is light and amused.

No. I just ... Can I?

He laughs now, and the sound is so alien yet so sexy. My knees threaten to buckle. *So long as you finish your lessons first, and the boys will have to accompany you.*

Thank you.

He hums. *Stop distracting me. I have a class to teach.*

You spoke to me first, I remind him, but he's already gone. I give Sienna my full attention. "I'd love to come."

Her smile grows wider, but before she can respond, Cadence joins us. "Hey, guys. What's up?" There's been a sadness around her since Meg's death that wasn't there before, and I guess it's totally understandable, given what happened and how I'm one of the few people she can talk to about it.

I link my fingers through hers and squeeze, trying to convey all my understanding and empathy in that one single gesture. She gives me a smile in return.

"I was just inviting O to a party at Amalthea Crescent House tonight. It's gonna be fun. You should come too."

Cadence shakes her head. "I don't think so. I should probably study for my algebra test on Monday."

I squeeze her hand tighter. "If you change your mind, we

could go together. I'll be bringing the guys too, but they'll be on their best behavior. Promise."

"I dunno. Maybe." She chews on her lip.

Sienna bumps her arm against Cadence's. "I heard Jake will be there."

Cadence's cheeks flush pink, obscuring her smattering of freckles. I remember Jake, the son of the chief of police. He and Cadence invited me to a party a couple months ago, and she seemed to like him.

Cadence checks her watch. "I really do have to study for my test though."

"How about I help you study? I was just gonna go to the library for an hour before I head home." A reminder that I'm supposed to meet Malachi and study with him makes me groan inwardly. He's not going to be happy about me canceling on him. Plus, I did just promise the professor I'd do my lessons before the party. But Cadence is my friend, and she needs me right now.

"I can help too," Sienna adds. "Three heads are better than one, right? My classes are done, and I have an hour free. Besides, algebra is my jam."

Cadence's eyes fill with tears. "You'd both do that for me?"

I link my arm through hers. "Of course we would."

Hey, I'm going to go to Silver Vale to help Cadence study for an hour, I tell Axl.

No. You're coming home with me, and then you have to meet Malachi.

I glance back at him. He's no longer leaning against the tree, but he remains at a distance. Watching. Always watching. *If I help her study now, we can all go to a party later.*

Don't care much for parties comes his gruff reply.

It could be fun. I've never been to a party. Please!

He grunts. *As long as I get to feel you up in a dark corner.*

Sienna stands on Cadence's other side and links her arm through hers, and we begin to head in the direction of Silver Vale. *So I can go study?*

I can think of better things to do than hang around Silver Vale while you study with your girlfriends. Let me check with the professor.

I listen in on him asking the professor if I'll be safe at Silver Vale. After some grumbling, Alexandros reluctantly agrees that Enora's new protection spells will be sufficient protection, provided Axl drops me off and picks me up after.

I'll walk you there, and then I'll come back to pick you up in sixty minutes. No arguments.

Thank you, Axl. I'll make it up to you.

Damn right you will.

Cadence sniffs, wiping a tear from her cheek and redirecting all my focus back to her. "I really appreciate this, you guys."

"Sure, girl. It's just a little studying. No big deal, right?" Sienna shoots me a look over the top of our friend's head that is equal parts concern and empathy. A look that tells me she's aware that this is about so much more than studying, but she doesn't press for details, and I admire her so much for that.

Sienna's right. This is about so much more than studying. It's about the fierce kind of friendships that I only ever dreamed about. And although I barely know Sienna and have only known Cadence a little while, I have an instinctive feeling about both of them. It comes from deep inside me, perhaps the same place where I find my light. And it tells me that I can trust these girls with my secrets and my life. It tells me something more too, but that is something I don't want to think about right now. I consciously ignore the gnawing in my gut telling me that one day I won't have a choice.

THIRTY-TWO

ALEXANDROS

Alexandros. The concern in Ophelia's voice sets every nerve in my body on edge.

I pause in the middle of my lecture, leaving the hundred or so students sitting in front of me waiting with anticipation for me to finish my sentence.

What is it, little one?

I'm still with Sienna. She said something's happened in the woods. Her father needs you.

My pulse spikes with adrenaline. *Osiris? What happened?*

She doesn't know. He wouldn't say. He asked for you.

Is this some kind of trap? *Where are you?*

At Silver Vale with Cadence and Sienna.

Is Enora there?

She's on her way to the woods. Osiris asked for her too.

I draw in a breath, trying to drown out the sound of my heart pumping in my ears. *Stay where you are. I will send Xavier and Malachi to come stay with you.*

But I—

Stay, Ophelia! My tone is harsh but necessary, even as I sense the hurt in her.

A student from the front row reminds me I am supposed to be teaching by raising their hand. "Uh, Professor Drakos?"

"Class is done for today," I call as I exit the classroom. I am making my way out of Clio Hall when I reach out to the boys and instruct Xavier and Malachi to go to Ophelia and Axl to meet me. Once I reach the cover of the trees, I break into a run.

I search out Osiris's energy to pinpoint his location. It is not an exact science, but today, I feel his anger and despair so keenly that it makes him easy to track. Heavy emotions radiate from him with such ferocity that they guide me to him like a beacon. I give Axl directions to my location as I grow closer and sense him moving through the trees not too far behind me. Osiris's pain grows heavier as I get closer.

I breach the thick clearing of trees and immediately see why. My old friend kneels on the ground, his head bent low over the remains of a young wolf. However, it is only her scent that tells me she was a wolf; her body has been torn to shreds. There are other scents here too. Vampires, witches. My nose twitches, trying to determine whether any of them are familiar.

Osiris lifts his head at my approach, but a growl from beside me snatches my attention. A meaty hand darts out, aiming for my throat, but I dodge it easily. A second later, I have my hand wrapped around my would-be assailant's neck. I recognize Osiris's nephew from my history class as he claws at my forearm, futile and desperate.

"Mack. Enough. He is not the enemy." Osiris's commanding growl vibrates through the air around us and is enough to make Mack stop fighting against my hold.

With a weary sigh, I release my grip on his throat. His tear-filled eyes narrow as he rubs the red skin of his neck.

"Forgive him, old friend." Osiris's voice is calmer now. "She ... Esme is ..." He clears his throat. "Was his girlfriend."

I offer Mack a nod of condolence, and then make my way to Osiris. Crouching down, I inspect the body more closely. Her torso has been torn open from pelvis to neck, her internal organs pulled out and ravaged. Her nose and lips were ripped from her face, leaving it unrecognizable. "You knew her well?"

He nods. "She's a senior Amalthea Crescent member. And she's been Mack's girlfriend for two years."

I place a hand on his shoulder and squeeze. "I am sorry, old friend."

He jerks his head in the direction of the river. "Those animals were feasting on her when Mack got here."

I follow his gaze and find the object of his and Mack's fury. The two vampires who look vaguely familiar are bloodied and beaten and being watched over by two very angry wolves. My hackles rise. Vampires drink blood; we do not eat flesh. At least not ordinarily.

The sounds of a scuffle breaking out come from behind me, and I do not need to turn around to know that Axl has arrived. His growl and scent are too deeply ingrained in my mind. No doubt he, too, has been accosted by Mack. Without taking my eyes off the two vampires, I yell, "He's with me."

"Boys. Enough," Osiris says with a weary sigh.

A few seconds later, both boys join us beside Esme's body, and I drag my gaze from the vampires to Mack. "What happened? How did you find her?"

Mack scrubs at the tears running down his cheeks. "I heard

her howling for help. And when I got here, those two ..." He bares his teeth in their direction. "*Animals* were eating her. They were fucking eating her."

I glance at Osiris, and his skeptical expression mirrors my thoughts. "Vampires do not eat flesh, old friend."

He nods solemnly.

"They do. They were. I fucking saw them," Mack screeches.

Axl snarls in warning.

I keep my gaze fixed on Osiris as I speak to Axl through our bond. *He is upset. They are no threat to us.* To accuse either me or one of my sireds is not what Osiris has brought me here for this day.

Osiris puts a steadying hand on his nephew's arm. "Nobody is disputing what you saw. But this"—he glances down at the girl's ravaged corpse once more—"isn't natural vampire behavior. That's why Alexandros is here."

The lacerations covering almost every inch of her limbs suggest not only immense rage, but also a hunger that would be unusual for any vampire within a hundred-mile radius of a town full of humans. Not to mention this happened in a forest filled with deer and other wildlife.

"Do you recognize them?" I ask Axl, jerking my head in the direction of the vampires and the wolves still holding them captive. Everything about this situation has my nerves on edge. Nothing adds up. Vampires who devour a body like this are feral. Driven mad by blood lust that does not abate no matter how much they consume. Yet the two vampires accused of this crime stand idle under the watch of their wolf guards.

Axl sniffs the air and trains his eyes on the accused. "Two of the Onyx recruits. Sophomores, I think. Definitely not this year's."

"Esme was a senior, but she was taking a couple classes

with sophomores because she changed her major last year," Mack offers, his voice thick with grief.

"Did you ever see her hanging out with those guys? With any vampires?" Osiris asks his nephew.

Mack shakes his head. "She was shy. Only ever mixed with other wolves."

"So what the hell was she doing out here with a pair of nutsacks from Onyx?" Axl asks with a snort.

"What the fuck are you implying, you stupid fuck!" Mack leaps on top of him, and a second later, the two of them are rolling around in the dirt, throwing punches at each other.

Osiris pinches the bridge of his nose and shakes his head.

"Axl," I say, the cold warning evident in my voice. *Have a little respect for their grief*, I add in private.

He wrenches free of Mack's hold and dusts off his clothes before crouching by my side once more. Mack grumbles and goes to lean against a nearby tree. He stares off into the distance, no doubt avoiding looking at his girlfriend's body any longer than he has to.

Osiris's dark eyes meet mine, and they are clouded with sadness and anger but mostly fear. "Why would they do this, Alexandros? Is this linked to what happened to the witch?"

"It is more likely than not," I admit, stealing another glance at the two vampires and the wolves guarding them. They were once two of Osiris's finest students, and now they are part of the faculty here. They both appear ready to tear off some vampire heads at their pack leader's command. "Is that why you spared them?"

He swallows harshly and gives a shaky nod. "Mack found her. He called for me ..." His eyes darken. Wolf packs can communicate with each other much like vampires can. "When we got here, he was fighting the two of them off." He glances down at his bloodied knuckles. "We pulled them off her, and it was like ..." His brow furrows. "Like they were fucking rabid one second, and then they were just ..." He shakes his head.

"Just what?"

He jerks his head in the direction of the two vampires who killed the girl. "Like that."

Another quick glance in their direction finds them standing in the clearing. One leans against a large rock; the other stares at the horizon. Both of them appear distinctly vacant.

Using the tip of my index finger, I collect a sample of Esme's blood and hold it close to my nose, inhaling deeply. Whilst there is the distinct scent of vampires, there is something more. Something darker. Ancient.

I wipe the blood on my pants and make my way over to the accused with Axl close behind me. The wolves, bristling with pent-up rage, step aside and allow me to inspect the two suspects.

The one staring off into the distance has remains of Esme's intestines stuck to his clothes. The pink twisted meat obscures part of the silver skull motif on his T-shirt, making it appear like brain matter oozing out in some kind of bizarre three-dimensional image.

"You know their names?" I ask Axl without taking my eyes off the young vampire in front of me.

Axl hums. "Pretty sure they call this one Bones."

Tall, skinny, dark circles under his eyes. Makes sense. I take a quick look at his accomplice. Shaved head, heavyset, square jaw. His eyes have the same glassy look as Bones's, but he looks directly at me. Or more likely through me. He wears a dog collar, adorned with red and black spikes. "And the other?"

Axl snorts. "Bad Dog, or some stupid shit like that."

"Watch him," I order, and Axl and the wolves step in front of him, but Dog shows no indication of registering their presence.

Tightly gripping Bones's jaw, I tip his head back, and I am

unsurprised when he offers me no resistance. His fangs are still protracted and coated with Esme's blood. A growl rumbles from his chest, and if I had to guess, it is more instinct than anything else because he remains otherwise compliant. I twist his head from side to side, examining his throat for any sign of a bite mark but finding none. "What is your name?"

He blinks in response, his gray eyes almost lifeless.

"Alexandros." Enora's breathless voice comes from behind me. She can teleport only short distances and must have run most of the way here. "What happened?"

I take a few more seconds to appraise Bones. His eyelids look heavy now, shuttering closed. I shake him roughly, and they flicker open once more. "What is your name?" I repeat.

Still nothing.

Enora's arm brushes mine as she reaches out and plucks a strand of long dark hair from Bones's T-shirt. She twirls it between her fingers. "Dark magic was used here, filis mous."

I hum my agreement.

She leans closer to the accused. "Can you read his mind?"

"I can search his memory, but I will only know what he knows, and I suspect it will be little more than we do."

Osiris stands beside me now too. "Do it."

Searching another's memory, even their recent memories, without biting them takes time and focus. Blood never lies. And drinking another's blood connects me to their mind with precision, allowing me a level of control while we are connected. But to read another's mind without that connection is not as simple as opening them up and plucking out what you want to see. It is akin to searching an archive of thousands of books with no reference to guide you. But it would leave my own mind vulnerable to invasion if I bit him without having any idea as to who is pulling his strings or what type of powerful magic he may be under the spell of. It makes Ophelia vulnerable, and I will not put her at risk.

Placing my hands on either side of Bones's head, I close my eyes and concentrate. My mind penetrates his easily. Although it is fogged with confusion and terror, I move without resistance even when I probe deeper, combing through his most intimate memories. I flick through them at lightning speed, the images flashing by so quickly that they make my own head spin. I draw a deep breath and will them to slow. When they do, I concentrate on the events of today, and as easily as if I had bitten this vampire standing before me, the memories that I want to see come to me as though I summoned them through him.

Esme running through the trees. Bloodlust, his heart racing. The overpowering urge to devour her flesh. I search further back, to the events that happened right before. Bones and Dog walking on the edge of the forest, tossing a football back and forth. Then there is fog. Darkness. Bones's fear. A hooded figure draws closer. Are there two? Maybe three? The memory lacks clarity, swimming with uncertainty and plagued by darkness. Ancient dark magic is whispered in his ear, the voice low and soothing, even as it speaks of spells so dangerous they were forbidden before I was born.

Bones's inner turmoil makes the memory too difficult to see clearly. Such is the problem with memories—it is only possible to see what the person recalls themselves. There are more cloaked figures. Hundreds swarming around him now. The Skotádi. I know this cannot be real because we would have noticed an army of Skotádi invading the campus grounds. But Bones's terror is real. I can taste it as clearly as if I had tasted his blood—the dark magic snaking through his veins and permeating every limb and organ, forcing him to submit to a master that he cannot see. Then one hooded figure draws closer. He snarls, tipping his head and revealing the lower portion of his face. Lips curled back. Fangs bared. He drops his hood.

Lucian!

My heart stops beating. I stagger back, dropping my hands from Bones's head. It cannot be true. If he were here, I would feel him. If he had done this ... Why would he do this? I ask the questions despite knowing my son is capable of much worse.

Opening my eyes, I half expect my companions to be pointing accusing fingers my way, somehow knowing what I just saw. But they watch me with concern. Osiris, Enora, Axl, and the two wolves, all eyes fixed on me as they wait for an explanation.

"What did you see?" Osiris's voice cuts through the chaos that rages inside my brain.

"The Skotádi." My voice is firm and even, disguising the terror and betrayal that is burning me up from the inside.

Axl's dark-brown eyes narrow. *Is everything okay?*

We need to speak with Ophelia and your brothers urgently.

Enora grabs my arm, her grip tight, conveying the tension that vibrates through her body. "Then it is true. They are able to infiltrate the campus grounds."

My jaw clenched, I offer a brief nod. "We need to call a faculty meeting."

Osiris growls, his nostrils flaring with unsuppressed rage. "I'll speak to Ollenshaw."

Although I have no idea how, I am certain that the death of the wolf girl is somehow linked to Ophelia. Perhaps others sensed her powers awakening. Ollenshaw cannot know of her existence, nor can the rest of the faculty. Her safety is paramount. Osiris and Enora watch me intently, waiting for me to speak. The Skotádi are another field of expertise of mine, even if I wish with all my heart that I did not possess such intimate knowledge of their kind.

I feel the weight of my colleagues' concern. Their uncertainty. It has been a very long time since I have needed allies, but I am now painfully aware that this thing grows bigger than all of us. And both Osiris and Enora have proven that they can be trusted. Enora may have sworn an oath to Nazeel, but I do not believe that either of them would ever cause Ophelia any harm.

"Before we speak to him and the rest of the faculty, I need to discuss something with you both."

Osiris frowns. "So speak of it."

I suck on my lip, tempering my frustration. "I must speak with Ophelia and the boys first."

Osiris scowls. "If this is something to do with my pack, Alexandros ..."

"I suspect this is something much bigger than all of us. I am asking that we delay bringing this to others' attention for no more than an hour. I implore you to trust me."

Enora nods and loops her hand through the crook in Osiris's arm. "It is in all our interests to discover what happened here tonight and why, my friend. If Alexandros thinks he can find some answers, we should let him do what it takes to locate them."

Osiris's nostrils flare, but he eventually gives me a nod. "Let us all meet at Silver Vale at the top of the hour, yes?"

As soon as they have assured me of their agreement, Axl and I sprint through the woods and head to the house.

Are we going to tell them about Ophelia? he asks.

Perhaps. But first, I need to tell you all something.

We continue sprinting in silence, but I feel his mind racing with questions. I focus on getting back to them as quickly as possible. It seems there will be several truths revealed before this night ends. Whether I am ready for that or not.

THIRTY-THREE

AXL

Ophelia sits between Xavier and Malachi on the sofa. I lean against the fireplace, and together, we watch Alexandros pace the floor of the den. There was definitely something off about him on our way back to the house, something bigger than what happened to Esme. And it seemed to have something to do with whatever he saw in Bones's memories. I filled Xavier, Malachi, and Ophelia in on what we found in the woods, and now we're waiting for the professor to tell us our next move.

"What will happen now?" Ophelia asks.

Alexandros stops pacing and stares at us, his face unread-able. "Osiris will alert President Ollenshaw, and he will call a faculty meeting. But before that, there are things we need to discuss."

I twist my neck until it cracks, feeling tense and unsure. Whatever it is that he has to tell us doesn't seem like a good thing, at least from where I'm standing. We wait with bated breath, and I am sure that in all my two hundred years with him, I have never seen him so seemingly lost for words.

"I told you all that I had a family once. Two daughters. But before their birth, I had a son."

A son? What the fuck? It's not enough that he kept his family from us for over two hundred years, he couldn't even come clean all at once? And a son? For some reason, that hits harder, and the bitter flavor of betrayal coats my tongue. Too stunned to speak, I stare at him in silence.

"You had a what?" Xavier asks.

The thick column of his throat works as he swallows. "I had three children. Two daughters and a son."

"How old was he?" Malachi asks.

"He is seven hundred and sixty-two," Alexandros answers matter-of-factly.

Back the fuck up. "He *is*? Not was. Is?"

Alexandros nods, his face a mask of granite.

I growl instinctively. "So you have a son who's still alive, and you never thought that was worth telling us?"

Xavier snorts. "We're just the stupid fucks he sired. Haven't you learned by now that he owes us nothing?"

"Xavier!" Alexandros sighs.

"Please let him explain," Ophelia says, her eyes brimming with tears.

Oh, hell no. Please don't tell me she was in on this too. "You knew about this, princess?"

She bites on her lip, her cheeks turning pink with shame, and nods.

"Fuck, Cupcake!" Xavier shakes his head.

Malachi jumps up, his fists balled in anger. "Leave her the fuck alone. It wasn't her secret to tell."

I grind my jaw to stop myself from saying anything I may regret. Malachi is right, although that doesn't make it hurt any less. That she kept such a huge secret from us stings like the cut of a thousand blades. Still, I direct my anger at the professor where it belongs.

"Ophelia found Lucian in my memories when we bonded. I did not consciously choose to tell her about him, but I was unable to stop her from discovering him. And I asked her to let me tell you myself when the time was right."

Lucian? That's the name of the professor's son? His real son. Unlike us, the three idiots who idolize him despite everything.

"The time would have been right four weeks ago when you told us about the rest of your family," Xavier snaps.

Alexandros shakes his head, his frustration growing more evident. "I had my reasons."

Xavier sits back in the armchair and huffs. "Yeah, I bet."

"Xavier," Ophelia says softly, reaching for his hand, but he shrugs her off.

I glare at my sire. He has a son. A living, breathing son, and he never told us. "I can't believe you kept this from us. Do we mean anything to you at all?"

Based on the veins bulging in his neck and face, Alexandros's temper is approaching its boiling point, but I don't care. I want to push him. Goad him until he explodes because that's what I feel like doing. And if he comes at me, then I can fight back, and maybe that will make me feel better.

"Why are you telling us this now?" Malachi asks, frowning.

Xavier answers for him. "Probably because the prodigal son has learned his pop bonded with an elementai, and now he wants to come home and try to take what's ours. Am I right?"

Alexandros's body is little more than a blur crossing the room, and a split second later, he has Xavier hoisted in the air by his throat. Rage radiates from him like heat from the sun, and I take a step back for fear I'll burn if I get too close. "I did not tell you about him because up until two weeks ago, I thought he was dead. And before that, you insolent little fuck" —he shakes Xavier, who claws at our sire's arm for him to let go, but he takes no notice—"I never spoke of him because he destroyed my heart and shattered my soul. He killed his own mother and his little sisters, and he probably did it with a smile on his face. Is that what you wanted to know? Does that satisfy you?"

He throws Xavier onto the sofa and stalks back to his spot on the other side of the room, far away from all of us and, I can only assume, away from the temptation to rip someone's head off.

"I'm sorry, sir," Xavier chokes out, rubbing at his throat.

Malachi drops his head and refuses to look at any of us.

I can't imagine living through that kind of betrayal, and although the words seem hollow now, I murmur my own apology.

Alexandros twists his head from side to side and closes his eyes, visibly regaining his composure. Ophelia goes to him, the only one of us brave enough to comfort him right now. "Does Lucian have anything to do with what happened to Esme?"

He clears his throat. "I believe he is connected to that and to the attack on the witch at Silver Vale."

Malachi lifts his head, his mouth gaping open. "That's why there was a trace of your scent?"

Alexandros nods. "Perhaps."

Xavier stands, his sore throat already forgotten. "What do you think his angle is? I mean, the first attack seemed like an attempt to frame you, but this one was aimed at the Onyx Dragons, right?"

Alexandros blows out a long breath. "I have no idea. Perhaps to cause chaos with the vampire houses. Maybe they hope to destabilize the entire institution of Montridge."

"Possibly to get closer to Ophelia?" Malachi suggests, and a chill runs down my spine. Lucian is a bloodborne vampire; he'd want her for himself too.

Alexandros nods. "It is possible he is aware of her existence, yes."

Something the professor said earlier fills me with terror. "But he wants to kill elementai, right? He killed his own mom and sisters?"

"We cannot rule anything out." He wraps a protective arm around Ophelia's shoulder before pressing a kiss on top of her head. "I will never let him hurt you, agápi mou."

She nestles her cheek against his chest and brushes a stray tear from her cheek.

Xavier snarls. "None of us will let him hurt you, Cupcake."

I couldn't agree more. Just give me an excuse to rip Lucian's head off his shoulders, and I'm there. "So what do we do now?"

Alexandros stares at me, his dark eyes boring into my soul. I want to look away, but I can't. It's ridiculous, but I always felt special, thinking of myself as his first son. But now I realize I'm not even his son at all, and that hurts like a knife to the heart. "I believe that, as the threat toward Ophelia grows, it would be in our best interests to curate some allies," he says.

Malachi blinks. "Allies?"

"People whom we can trust to learn of Ophelia's identity and protect her secret."

"And you think such people exist?" I ask.

"Enora and Osiris," Ophelia answers for him.

He drops a kiss on her head. "Yes, little one."

"I think we should tell Cadence and Sienna too."

The fuck we will. "No, princess." I growl a warning.

She untangles herself from his arms and steps into mine, and despite the raft of negative emotions still hurtling through my body, some of which are unfairly directed at her, I soften for her immediately. "They're my friends, Axl, and I trust them."

I bury my face in her hair, inhaling her comforting scent.

She plays you like a fiddle, you know that, right? Xavier says.

"I heard that, Xavier," she huffs.

He laughs darkly. "I know, Cupcake."

I glance over her head at Alexandros. No matter how pissed I am at him, I still seek his reassurance, and he offers it with a single nod. "I guess we tell them our girl's an elementai then, huh?"

She melts into me, her body molding into the shape of mine like she's a part of me. And I think she always has been a part of me—a part of us—and I have spent the last two hundred and forty-seven years simply waiting for her.

CHAPTER

THIRTY-FOUR

ALEXANDROS

O siris paces the room, and Enora regards me from her armchair. "Do you recall me asking you to look into the person responsible for Ophelia's attendance at this institution, Osiris?"

He pauses his steps and nods. "And I found nothing. I used all my usual resources and couldn't get anything more than what I gave you. Like I told you before, whoever was responsible hid their tracks expertly."

"Nazeel Danraath admitted that it was she who was responsible for Ophelia coming here, but I believe there are others who wanted her at Montridge as well."

His piercing eyes narrow. "But what does this have to do with Esme?"

"I believe it is all connected. The witch being killed here last week, Esme today, the poorly disguised attempt to frame me and then the Onyx vampires. All of it is linked to Ophelia."

I feel Ophelia bristle beside me, but when I glance sideways at her, she has her shoulders rolled back, and she meets the suspicious gazes of both the wolf and the witch with a fiery determination that makes pride swell inside me. Such a fearsome creature, but nobody would ever suspect it.

"How? Why is everyone so interested in this girl, Alexandros? You, Nazeel Danraath?" Osiris takes a step toward her.

I growl a warning at him along with Axl, Xavier, and Malachi, which increases the tension in this small room one hundredfold.

"We are all on the same side here, aren't we?" Ophelia says, her jaw tilted defiantly. "And I would also love to know why anyone would take an interest in me, Professor Brackenwolf."

Her confident tone does something to soothe his anger. "You may call me Osiris."

She offers him a single nod and a faint smile that has the possessive beast inside all three of my boys wanting to break free. I warn them to control their tempers and focus on my old friends. Two people at Montridge who are amongst those I trust most in this world. As much as I would prefer to keep Ophelia's identity to myself, I meant what I said earlier—we need allies to help us ensure her safety.

"It's a question that begs to be answered," Osiris goes on. "Why are people being killed for this girl?"

An intense wave of guilt washes over her, so profound that she sways on her feet. I place a steadying hand on her arm. "Nobody is being killed *for* her." The warning in my tone is abundantly clear, and Osiris doesn't push further.

"Can't we just ask this Nazeel woman why she wanted Ophelia to come here?" Axl asks. "If she's interested in Ophelia, maybe she knows who else is."

Enora shakes her head. "You cannot simply speak to a member of the Order. They are supposed to remain hidden away. Their identities are a closely guarded secret. At least they are supposed to be."

"There is nothing I would keep from any of my sireds," I remind her. "You can trust them as you would me." I am aware that the first part of that statement is a lie. I kept Lucian from them for years, and even now I keep part of him from them. At least what I saw in the Onyx pledge's mind earlier.

"Regardless, it's not that simple," Osiris tells Axl before he turns his attention to me. "You have known there was something different about Ophelia since the start of semester. I have never known you take an interest in any witch before, old friend."

I tip my face to the ceiling and suck in a deep breath, the weight of what I am about to disclose sitting heavy on me. As though sensing my hesitation, Ophelia reminds me that this decision is not mine alone. *I want them to know, and I think you're right to trust them*, she says in her gentle, soothing voice. *Cadence and Sienna too.*

She is not wrong. In the coming months, Ophelia will need as many friends as she can get. Cadence has proven her trustworthiness to a degree, and Sienna is Osiris's daughter. He will ensure her compliance. Things are happening at a faster pace than I anticipated, and we no longer have the luxury of time to determine who we can and cannot trust. But if I am forced to rely on the intuition of another, I cannot say I am displeased that Ophelia's are the instincts we must listen to. Elementai are known for their skills in this area, and she has proven herself no exception. "Are the girls here? Cadence and Sienna?"

Enora gives me a suspicious look. "Indeed they are. Are they important to this discussion?"

I glance sideways at my fearless elementai. "They are important to Ophelia, so yes, they are."

Osiris regards me with curiosity, his wolf glimmering in his eyes, not far from the surface. "I will summon Sienna."

Less than a moment later, the two girls walk into the room, and after a quick greeting to Ophelia, they sit on the sofa. Their eyes lock on me, cheeks lined with the tracks of their tears. Osiris must have told his daughter what happened to her packmate.

"What I am about to tell you must stay within this room," I begin. "*No one* is to know. You must swear me a blood oath."

Osiris scowls. "You cannot ask such a thing of us. We have people who depend on us. Those we need to protect from harm. May I remind you that it was a wolf who was killed tonight, Alexandros? A member of my pack. I cannot hush this up like we did with the witch." Crescent packs are unlike the typical familial wolf packs that exist outside of Montridge. The bond each member feels is manufactured and lasts only as long as they remain here, whereas a familial pack bond lasts for eternity. However, the fleeting nature of the bond does not diminish its intensity. Manufactured bond or not, I am aware that the loss of a member is felt keenly by every wolf within the pack, and I am not unsympathetic to their pain. I merely do not have time for it at the moment.

"Dad!" Sienna says, her eyes pleading with him to let me finish.

Enora lays a hand on his arm. "I have known this man for six hundred years, and he has never asked me to swear such an oath, Osiris. I can only imagine he has good reason for doing so now."

I doubt that he thinks me foolish enough to have not

considered all the consequences and it is likely his grief speaking, so I permit him his outburst without rebuke. "I do not expect you to break your word, Osiris. If I thought it would put your pack in jeopardy, I would never ask you to make such an oath. Your loyalty lies, as it should, with your pack, and I would not endanger Ophelia by foolishly asking you to forsake your responsibility."

He does not respond right away, but Cadence and Sienna glance at each other and then at Ophelia. "I'm in," Cadence says. "I don't know what it is, but I'm in."

Sienna nods. "Me too."

Osiris glares at his daughter. "If you swear a blood oath and break it, he will know you have broken it, and according to ancient vampire law, he will have every right to tear off your head."

Sienna shrugs and glares back at her father. "Then I guess I won't break it."

Osiris throw his hands in the air, and Ophelia tries to suppress a snort but fails. I scold her with a look that she simply shrugs off. She is becoming far too feisty for my liking. My palm twitches, desperate to take her in hand right now, but I focus on the current situation.

"Fine." He takes a breath and continues. "I, Osiris Brackenwolf, in front of these witnesses present, swear you, Alexandros Drakos, a blood oath." He slices a cut in his hand with his razor-sharp teeth and allows a drop of blood to fall into my outstretched palm.

Sienna, Enora, and Cadence repeat the oath, the latter with the assistance of Enora's spells to cut and heal. Satisfied I have secured their compliance, I lick my palm clean. Then I clear my throat, giving myself no time to reconsider my decision. "Ophelia is an elementai."

Enora claps her hand over her mouth, her gray eyes filling with tears.

Osiris folds his arms across his chest. "Prove it."

I suppress the urge to snarl a warning. "She does not have to prove anything."

"You're telling me this girl is one of a species that died out—"

"That was exterminated," I remind him with a growl.

He offers me a slight nod to indicate he has heeded my warning. "That were exterminated over five hundred years ago. I believe we are entitled to a little proof of such a claim."

"It's okay," Ophelia says. "I mean, I get it. I didn't believe it either at first."

"Ophelia, you're really an elementai?" Cadence asks, staring at her friend in awe.

Ophelia nods, embarrassed at being the center of attention. Her eyes drop to the floor for a moment. "At least I think so."

I fix her with a glare. "You are."

Enora moves over to Ophelia and takes her hands. She peers closely at them, turning them over and inspecting her palms and then her fingertips. "I knew there was something very special about you, child, but I had no idea." Her tone is full of wonderment. "I have not been in the presence of a being such as you for longer than I care to admit. Would you be so kind as to demonstrate your power?"

Ophelia looks to me for permission, and the plea in her eyes is the only thing that makes me acquiesce. *Show them, little one. It is time they knew of your power.*

She nods. "I'm not that great at it yet, but ... here goes."

She waves a hand at the fireplace, and a fire bursts to life, flames crackling.

Osiris narrows his eyes. "She could have used a spell."

Enora claps her hands together, an uncharacteristic squeal

of delight falling from her lips. "She did not use a spell, Osiris. I would know if a spell had been cast in this room."

Ophelia smiles appreciatively at the giddy professor, and I already know that Enora is going to be one of our greatest allies. My old friend fans her face, seemingly overwhelmed. "Mastery of fire. Extraordinary."

Ophelia closes her eyes, and the ground begins to shake beneath our feet.

"That's our girl," Malachi murmurs as a round of gasps ripples around the room.

"Earth and fire?" Enora shrieks.

Even Osiris is looking suitably impressed now, as he should.

A flush creeps over Ophelia's cheeks. "Shall I show them more?" she asks me.

I nod, pride filling me as they watch her with astonishment. My three boys stand beside me, arms folded across their chests, and we all bask in the glory of our perfect elementai. Ours. That word vibrates through my entire being. I wish we could have kept her to ourselves a bit longer, but her destiny is moving at lightning speed.

"Okay, air is a little harder to demonstrate." She balls her hands into fists, and a few seconds later, the air has all but disappeared from the room.

"Ophelia," I gasp, and her eyes widen before oxygen floods the space once more. Everyone sucks in a deep breath. "Your powers grow stronger each day."

"Air too?" Osiris asks. "But that's impossible. No being in over a thousand years has had power over three elements."

I wonder how wise it is to reveal that Ophelia is only the second creature in existence to have mastery over four. No one in this room could be called a fool. They will all know that her rarity means something. Something more than we already know that I do not wish to contemplate. "So you see why it is so vitally important that we keep Ophelia's identity a secret?"

He nods solemnly. "I understand."

Shall I show them water too?

The quiver in her voice assuages my doubt. She is spectacular, and the time for hiding her, at least from the people in this room, has come to an end.

Xavier wraps his arms around her waist and presses a possessive kiss on her shoulder. "You haven't seen her final trick yet." The unmistakable pride in his voice makes her blush deeper.

"Show them your power over water, Ophelia," I encourage her, and the smile she rewards me with is dazzling.

"Impossible." Osiris shakes his head. "Not since Azezal himself ..." He trails off but keeps his attention locked on Ophelia. Meanwhile, his daughter jumps up from her seat, her eyes shining as though urging Ophelia to go on.

Ophelia directs her attention to the large monstera plant sitting in the corner of the room. With nothing more revealing than a twitch of her lips, a small cloud the size of a football appears above the plant—and it starts to rain.

Enora stumbles back into the nearby armchair, her hand over her mouth and her face as pale as the waning full moon.

"Alexandros." Osiris's voice contains a sensible hint of fear. "This ..." He opens and closes his mouth and blows out a breath.

"Is fricking epic!" Sienna squeals.

Cadence stares, wide-eyed and open-mouthed. "Wow, Ophelia. All four elements!"

"The plant, sweet girl." Malachi brings all our attention back to the monstera with its own rain cloud, which has almost doubled in size in the past minute.

"Oh, damn," Ophelia mutters, and the cloud disappears. "It's all still so new. I'm getting used to everything."

"How long have you had your powers, child?" Enora asks, regaining her composure and climbing to her feet.

She glances at me, her teeth sinking into her luscious lower lip and making me long to take her from this room and have her to myself. I motion for her to answer.

"Almost four weeks now," she whispers.

Enora shakes her head in disbelief. "Four weeks? Surely not."

Ophelia wrings her hands together. "I know I'm not great, but Alexandros and the guys are teaching me. I have lessons every—"

"Ophelia." Enora goes over to Ophelia once more and places her hand on her perfectly smooth cheek. "My sweet child. The fact you have mastered such powers in four short weeks is extraordinary."

"Ophelia is extraordinary," I say, my eyes darting between Osiris, Cadence, and Sienna before coming back to Enora. "Which is why the secret of her identity and the magic she is capable of must not leave this room."

I take Ophelia's hand in mine, lacing her nimble fingers through my own. Xavier does the same with her other hand. Malachi and Axl stand behind us.

Osiris continues to stare at her like he is witnessing a miracle, and I suppose that he is. "You cannot keep her a secret forever, old friend. People will realize what she is. Power like that cannot be hidden for long. It is possible that the Order is already aware. It's almost certain that the Skotádi know something if they've been here on campus."

Sienna rubs her hands on her jeans. "But why did they come for Esme? If they know about Ophelia, why not come for her?"

"We are not yet sure of what the Skotádi do or do not know. I am certain they are not aware of the full extent of Ophelia's powers. Otherwise, they surely would have made some attempt to get to her. But there are still far too many unanswered questions. Such as why the Skotádi made both the murder of the young wolf and that of the witch at Silver Vale appear as though they were committed by vampires."

"What witch at Silver Vale? Meg?" Sienna asks.

Her father nods solemnly. "I will explain later."

I rub my temples and try to drown out the growing cacophony of questions racing through the minds of everyone in this room. Tasting their blood has permitted me entry to their innermost thoughts. "We are aware that there will be a time when we cannot conceal Ophelia's identity any longer."

"But you saw how good she is already," Xavier adds. "The more time we have to help her learn to control her powers, the stronger she'll be when that time comes."

"She's already more powerful than everyone in this room," Axl says.

"I am not." Ophelia blushes, so self-deprecating in spite of what she just showed us.

You are, little one, I tell her through our bond.

Malachi drops a kiss on the top of her head. "And her powers keep growing every day."

"We are going to do what we can to give Ophelia as much time as she needs to learn to control her powers, and we are asking nothing of you but your loyalty. My boys and I will keep Ophelia safe. We will take care of her training. The five of us will leave this place if and when it becomes necessary."

"The five points of a pentagram," Enora murmurs, a knowing smile on her face.

"You can't leave," Cadence says, jumping from her seat.

Ophelia brushes a tear from her cheek, and her sadness causes a dull ache in my heart. "I don't want to."

I give Ophelia's hand a reassuring squeeze. I wish I could tell her that we will never have to leave here, but reality closes in on us more with each passing day. "This is bigger than all of us."

Enora clears her throat and nods. "Bigger than anything we have ever dealt with before. Cadence and I will do all we can, Alexandros. I know an elementai's powers are channeled differently, but the fundamentals of use are the same. If there is anything I can do to assist in Ophelia's lessons, it would be an honor."

Cadence nods eagerly. "I'm here whatever you need, Ophelia."

Osiris wraps an arm around his daughter's shoulder. "Ophelia's secrets are safe with us, old friend."

Sienna rolls her eyes. "My new bestie is the most powerful being who ever lived, and I can't even tell people. That sure as hell sucks." She flashes Ophelia a smirk that makes her giggle.

Ophelia leans against me, and I wrap an arm around her, pressing her into the crook of my shoulder.

They know, and they didn't freak out, she says.

Not too much anyway, Axl replies.

They've got your back, Cupcake.

But not as much as we do, sweet girl.

I inhale the scent of her, letting it flood my senses. *Never as much as we do, little one. Never forget that.*

Whilst I take some comfort in knowing that the people in this room have sworn an oath to protect her identity, and I have no doubt they will stop at nothing to protect her as well when the time comes, the events of this day continue to feed my unease.

Lucian was here at Montridge. He used dark magic to control the two Onyx recruits and, for reasons I still cannot fathom, to target a young wolf girl. Does he know Ophelia is an elementai? Does he know of how truly powerful she is? Or is this all one big coincidence?

I hold her tighter, sure of only one thing. My son or not ... I would end him and every other soul in existence to protect her.

THIRTY-FIVE

ALEXANDROS

T he faculty meeting has devolved into a catastrophe of muttered accusations, murmured anxieties, and suspicious looks.

Osiris addressed the room first, briefly outlining the circumstances of Esme's death earlier this evening—a version of events as akin to the truth as we can allow that was agreed upon before we left Silver Vale. Under the watchful eye of my boys, Ophelia stayed behind with her friends. I am grateful for the two young women who have shown Ophelia unwavering loyalty even in the face of their own fears.

"So it was two vampires from Onyx who killed the girl?" Professor Yakon rubs a weary hand over his face. The werewolf is nearing retirement, and he tends to lack patience for anything outside of the biochemistry curriculum he pioneered at Montridge. "And where are they now?"

More mutters and glares are directed at Nicholas Ashe. As much as I enjoy seeing my counterpart as the object of our colleagues' disdain, I feel obliged to speak up on behalf of the Onyx pledges. "They were physically responsible for committing the act, yes, but they cannot be held responsible."

"What?" Yakon barks, and many other faculty members voice their own disapproval.

Eugene Jackson casts me an anxious look from where he sits a few feet in front of me. Perhaps I should have alerted him as to what was going on before this meeting, but despite our kinship and his role as sire to many of the Ruby Dragon pledges, he has never been a man I particularly trust or admire. "What the hell is this, Alexandros?" he mutters.

My attention remains fixed on the crowd of professors that grows more agitated by the moment. There is no reason to respond. I do not have an answer that would be satisfactory in any case. Everything he needs to know will be revealed to everyone in this room before we all leave.

Arrogant asshole. Eugene's voice is as clear as if he spoke those words aloud, but I know he did not. He would not dare. He remains staring directly ahead, lips pressed tightly together and his jaw ticking.

His insolence makes me want to teach him a lesson, but this is not the time. I have never bitten Eugene, and we are distant cousins at best; therefore we have no connection that would allow me to so easily read his mind.

"Professor Drakos!" Jerome shouts, and I realize they are awaiting an answer from me.

I roll my neck and suppress a growl. Keeping my frustration in check is becoming increasingly tiresome.

Don't mind me. I'm just the president of this entire goddamn university, Jerome says, but his lips do not move. *Any time today would be good.* His tone drips with sarcasm, but outwardly he simply repeats my name again. I can read his mind; I can read all their minds. When did that happen?

I work my way through the minds in the room, picking out the pertinent points. Most of them are simply waiting for me to explain the statement I just made about the Onyx pledges. Some of them are wondering why I would cover for House Onyx, and the humanities professor is wishing this meeting would end so he can go back to the young witch currently keeping his bed warm.

Aware I currently lack the time necessary to unravel this curious new development, I set it aside and return to the conversation. "The Onyx Dragon pledges were acting under someone else's orders."

"But they still killed that girl, even if someone else told them to do it," someone yells.

I shake my head. "They were under the spell of dark magic."

A round of gasps and accusations rumbles throughout the room. I hear Nicholas Ashe's silent words of relief.

"You're just protecting Onyx," a witch accuses me.

"Do not be ridiculous," Nicholas shouts. "Why would he do that?"

"Because if your kind is going around murdering students, it doesn't look good for any of you, does it?" the witch retorts.

The meeting descends into chaos. Wolves and vampires and witches all hurl insults and accusations at one another.

Ollenshaw remains frozen at the front of the room, silently pleading for this to all be tied up as quickly and cleanly as possible so he will be saved from having to deal with any fallout. Looks like it might be too late for that.

I work my way through the minds of the Crescent Society

heads. Two are loyal to Osiris, and knowing that he has my support is enough for them. The fourth, however, is angry and suspicious. All the witches, with the exception of Enora, do not believe me, but that is to be expected given my history with them.

Osiris catches my eye and throws his hands in the air. *For the love of fuck, get a grip on this lot, Alexandros.* I am astounded that I hear his thoughts as clearly as all the rest after the decades he has spent building a wall against me. But he is not wrong, and his words are what I need to hear to pull myself together.

"Enough!" My bellow reverberates from the walls, causing the noise level to drop first to a hushed murmur and finally silence. I take a moment to shove back my instinct to tell them all to get the fuck out of my way and go rot in the netherworld before standing and addressing the room. "I have no desire to cover up wrongdoings at this university. If the two vampires of Onyx had killed the wolf girl in cold blood, then I would not hesitate to ensure they met with swift justice. And whilst Nicholas and I have had our differences"—I glance at him—"I know that he would demand the same." He nods his agreement. As much as we disagree on a lot of matters, vampire law is not one of them. "I read one of the vampires' minds, and I can assure you that he was under the influence of dark magic."

A new professor, a witch I believe, raises her hand. "But who would do such a thing?"

"We believe it was the Skotádi," Enora says, her tone soft yet full of gravitas.

Again, audible disbelief trickles through the room, this time more hushed than before. However, I also hear the society heads voicing their relief to themselves that they no longer have to keep this secret.

"But Skotádi? Here on campus? Why, Alexandros?"

"I have no idea, Jerome," I say, lying with ease. "Probably a random attack. The Onyx vampires and the young wolf from Amalthea were in the woods. It is possible that the Skotádi realized their proximity and chose to cross onto campus grounds."

"But I thought the campus was protected?" another witch asks.

"It is, Indigo," Enora replies. "But the Skotádi are powerful enough to breach such protective spells."

"Then we must bolster our defenses," Nicholas Ashe declares. "Prevent this from happening again."

"Whatever we do, we must do it quietly and without fuss," I remind them. "We do not want to cause unnecessary panic across the student body."

Jerome grimaces. "How do we keep this from them? A girl was murdered in the woods."

Osiris steps forward. "I am speaking with Esme's family tonight and will deliver the news myself. They are long-standing patrons of Montridge and do not care for human interference. They will wish to deal with their daughter's death privately and will likely seek assurance that her killers are dealt with." He glares at Nicholas Ashe.

Nicholas licks his lips. "They will be expelled and transferred to their posts within the day. But if they were not of sound mind, that is all the action I am prepared to take."

Osiris glances at me. *It is the best course of action*, I tell him.

He nods his understanding, and we spend the next twenty minutes fielding a barrage of questions from the faculty, giving and repeating all the information we agreed to disclose.

Finally, I hold up a hand and silence the room. "There is nothing more to add. All of you know what must be done."

"If that is all, I must go make arrangements to meet with Esme's parents," Osiris announces. He strides from the room, and I follow, ignoring the pleas from Jerome to stay and assist him in assuaging the concerns of the staff.

I have much more pressing matters to deal with.

I walk down the hallway with Osiris, and Enora scurries up beside us. "All four, Alexandros," she whispers.

"I know, Enora."

"Do you not wonder if she could be ...?"

"No." I spin to face her, and she finishes the question in her mind. "I do not believe in fairytales."

She hisses out a breath. "Then you are a fool."

Realization dawns on Osiris's face. "The child borne of fire and blood. You read her admission essay, Alexandros. What if she is?" He glances up and down around the empty hallway as if suddenly aware he is being indiscreet.

Enora places her hand on my arm. "I saw it too, file mou." She lowers her voice. "And now she has powers that would rival those of only Azezal himself."

"And did they not make such claims about him? Except that he was not the chosen one because the Prophecies of Fiere are nothing more than the ramblings of an ancient sage, probably high on some sort of mushroom."

Enora gasps like I have committed the most heinous of crimes, but Osiris, much younger than either of us, rolls his eyes.

"She is incredible, Enora. And unique." *And she is mine.* There is no need to voice the last part. "But she is not some chosen one from an archaic prophecy."

"But if you knew the entirety of the prophecy, Alexandros, if you—"

"I will have no more talk of prophecies." I inject my voice with all the authority and ice I can muster and bring my face closer to hers. "She is in danger enough without you adding to that burden with such preposterous notions."

She swallows nervously, her gray eyes narrowed. "As you wish."

Yes, I do wish. But more than that, I wish I could take Ophelia and my boys away from here, someplace nobody would ever find us. And with each passing day, the desire to do exactly that grows ever stronger.

THIRTY-SIX

XAVIER

Our heartbeats are the only sounds in the room, hers a steady rhythm that mirrors mine. "You're getting better at this every day."

I've spent the past half hour trying to speak to her through our bond, using every trick I can think of from tickling her to kissing her neck, but she's closed me out completely. The wall in her mind is impenetrable. Given the thin sheen of perspiration on her brow and her trembling lip, I suspect she might cave if I pushed much harder, but we have spent long enough on her training today, and now I have something much more enjoyable in mind.

She gives me the sweetest fucking smile I've ever seen, and I can practically feel her heart swelling with pride. "Thanks, Xavier," she purrs.

I lick my lips and stalk toward her. Her juicy tits heave against her thin white tank top. "What's that look about?"

I arch an eyebrow. "What look?"

She tips her chin up. "That one right there. Like you have something deviant on your mind."

I shake my head and take a step closer. "Not deviant, Cupcake. But you've been such a good girl for me today, I think it's time we both claimed our reward."

She backs up until her body hits the wall, making her gasp. "Our reward?"

I nod. "You remember how Axl was the first to claim your virgin pussy? And Kai got your hot little mouth?"

She bites on her bottom lip, driving me wild with lust. "Y-yeah."

"I think I've waited long enough for my first, don't you?"

Her blue eyes blow wide. "But ..." She chews on her lip now, her back flush against the wall of the den.

I step closer, pressing my chest to her perfect tits. "But?"

"What if it hurts?"

I brush my fingertips over her cheek and grin. "I would never hurt you."

"What if I don't enjoy it?"

I run my nose over her jawline. "Oh, you will. I can fucking promise you that." She swallows hard. "Do you trust me, Ophelia?"

She replies without hesitation. "Yes."

I skate my fingertips across her shoulders and pull down the straps of her tank top and bra, exposing all her creamy skin so I can lick an uninhibited path from her shoulder to her jawline and along the length of her collarbone. "Then you have nothing to worry about."

She curls her fingers in my hair and tugs my head back, even as she arches into my mouth. I yank her bra down farther, exposing the full roundness of her breast before sinking my fangs into her juicy flesh. The sweet taste of her blood floods my mouth and sends wildfire through my veins.

"Xavier," she moans.

I hum against her skin before pulling away and licking her blood from my lips. "You gonna let me fuck your perfect ass, Cupcake?"

Her heart is still racing. "Y-yes."

"Good girl." I palm her juicy ass cheeks and lift her with ease. With her legs wrapped around my hips, I carry her to the sofa and take a seat.

I make short work of her clothes until she's exactly how I like her best—naked and straddling me.

The door to the den swings open, and Alexandros walks in. "Is everything okay? I felt Ophelia ..." He licks his lips as his eyes rake over her undressed form.

I suspect he knew exactly what was going on in here before he walked in. Yeah, she's trembling, but it's mostly from anticipation tinged with a hint of anxiety, and I know he feels all of that. I press a kiss on her neck. "Yeah. Cupcake is just a little nervous because her ass is about to be fucked for the first time."

Her skin heats, and she burrows her face against my neck as embarrassment washes over her.

She has zero reason to feel like that in front of either of us. And the sexy-as-fuck growl that comes from his mouth is proof enough that he's not about to miss this show.

His reaction makes me grin, and it also prompts me to push my luck a little. I arch an eyebrow at him. "You could always help me ease her nerves, sir."

His eyes grow darker as he makes his way toward the sofa. "A tempting offer, Xavier."

Ophelia whispers, "How will he do that?"

He kneels behind her. I have never seen this man kneel for anyone. "Turn her around," he orders.

I arch an eyebrow, not entirely sure what he has planned or whether he's about to claim this particular prize for himself, but I grab Ophelia's hips and obey him. "You heard him. Turn around."

Her eyes go wide, but she sucks in a breath, and I help her turn so her back is to my chest and she's facing the professor. He flicks his tongue over his fangs, and she quivers against me.

His eyes narrow on her face. "This will be your first time, yes?"

She nods.

He glances over her shoulder at me, a wicked smirk tugging at the corner of his mouth. "You will need plenty of lubrication."

Sweet mother of fucks. Yeah I will. "What do you suggest?"

He places his hands on the inside of Ophelia's thighs and spreads them wide before running his nose through the folds of her wet pussy. She groans and bucks her hips, but he holds her in place. "I think we can make use of our sweet Ophelia's propensity to be soaking wet when any of us have our hands on her." He lets out a wicked chuckle and then licks the length of her. *And if that is not enough, we can always use some blood too.*

Ophelia's pulse spikes. "Blood?"

He lifts his head, licking her arousal from his lips. "Not yours, little one. That is far too precious to waste."

She sucks in a shaky breath that makes her tits tremble, and my cock twitches against her ass. "Then whose?" she whispers.

"Mine." Without giving her a chance to respond, he goes back to licking her. She whimpers as he eats, working her into a frenzy, and I feel every bit of her desperation and pleasure. I feel his too, and I'm surprised by how much. Ordinarily, he closes his feelings off to us, but now I experience his desire for her, and it mirrors my own. That desperate need to be inside her rolls through me in wave after unending wave. My cock is harder than granite, and I'm half rabid with the need to be inside her.

I free my cock from my sweatpants and rest it on the seam of her perfect, untouched ass.

I need to take her. Now! I plead with him through our bond.

She is almost ready.

Ophelia trembles in my arms, and her pleasure vibrates through my body too, warm and euphoric as she comes with a loud moan, her body bucking against his mouth and her hands in his hair as she rides his face. I slip my hand between her thighs and rub soft circles over her swollen clit, prolonging her orgasm until she's soaked his face in her cum.

Alexandros sits back on his heels, his dark beard glistening with her. He winks at me, and something more than her pleasure flares hot in my chest. "Now she is ready."

With a grunt, I lift her a little and slide my dick into her dripping pussy. She sinks her fingernails into the sides of my thighs, crying out from the overstimulation of her sensitive flesh. Her cum slicks my length—hot, thick, and silky. I rest my lips against her ear. "That's my good girl."

She whines when I pull out of her, but I quickly shift her into position and line the crown of my cock at her tight ass. I glance over her shoulder at my sire, his eyes dark with unrestrained lust as they rake hungrily over her sexy little body. My cock and fangs throb to the same beat, aching. I graze my lips over her neck.

"If you bite her now, Xavier, she will be unable to tell if it hurts," Alexandros warns.

"I want him to bite me. Both of you." She gasps out each word.

His eyes narrow. "Xavier is desperate to fuck you, Ophelia."

As am I, he adds through our bond, and I smirk. "If we bite you, then there is a possibility the pleasure from that will override any potential pain and we will not be able to tell if he is causing you any harm."

"Let me inside you, and once I'm in and you're okay, we'll bite you too, okay?"

She nods, trapping her bottom lip between her teeth.

"Good girl," I whisper.

She mewls at my praise, and I take the opportunity to push the crown of my cock against her until I feel the tight ring of muscle squeezing the tip. "Oh, wow," she breathes.

Alexandros massages her thighs and begins to feast on her sensitive pussy once more. She throws her head back, torn between pain and pleasure as I inch deeper, breaching past her resistance and sinking into her ass. Fuck, she feels so good. Hot and tight and so inviting.

"You're doing so good for me, Cupcake. How are you feeling?"

"G-good. It feels so ..." She sucks in a ragged breath. "Strange."

"Because nobody has ever done this to you before. Nobody but me." I inch deeper, and she cries out.

Careful, Alexandros warns.

"Yeah, I know." My muscles vibrate with the effort it takes to not drive my cock all the way inside her.

Do you need something more to ease her discomfort? Even the voice in my head is a deep growl, and there is something about his tone that resonates to the frequency of my soul. My balls ache with the need to come, and the idea of using his blood to fuck my girl's virgin ass has the depraved beast inside me snapping its teeth to get out.

I nod. "Y-yeah."

He hums against her flesh, and a few seconds later, a warm

liquid is running between Ophelia's thighs, one that feels different from her cum. I peer over her shoulder, and his mouth remains on her pussy, but he glances up. Upon catching my eye, he winks, and I almost pass out from the lightning bolt of ecstasy that shoots through my veins. He's cut his lip or his tongue, and his blood flows down the seam of her ass, coating my cock and allowing me to inch deeper and deeper inside.

"Xavier," she groans.

"I know, Cupcake. You're being such a good girl for your first time. Taking my cock in your tight ass so fucking well."

She whimpers, her body going lax in my arms.

You can bite her now, Alexandros says.

I sink my teeth into her throat and let her blood flow freely over my tongue. A moment later, I feel her blood being pulled elsewhere too, and I peer down to see Alexandros suckling softly on her thigh. We feed on her while I fuck her, rocking my hips into her until her tight muscles squeeze my cock so hard that I feel like I'm about to pass out.

The pressure increases when he adds his fingers to her pussy while my dick is in her ass, and we take her together. Feeding on her and fucking her, we are both lost in the exquisite ecstasy that is Ophelia Hart. And when she comes, she cries out both our names and trembles in my arms as we work her through another.

My head is spinning so rapidly that I can barely see, and Ophelia comes again. Her pussy walls ripple so violently around his fingers that the aftershocks travel straight to my dick. I am lost, emptying myself into her and holding her close as she takes everything I can give.

When we're both done, I gasp for breath, resting my forehead between her shoulder blades. "Fuck, Ophelia, that was spectacular."

She murmurs, her body molded into mine. But all too soon,

I feel the loss of her warmth as Alexandros plucks her from my lap and into his arms. "You have some work to finish up with your brothers, Xavier," he says, his tone cold and detached. As though we didn't just share something incredible. My eyes drift to Ophelia curled up against his chest as he holds her bridal style. I flick my tongue over my fangs and swallow down my frustration.

His eyes narrow. "I will get Ophelia cleaned up."

But I want to take care of her.

You have responsibilities, Xavier.

I know that I do, but the only thing I'm interested in is her.

Maintaining the status quo is important for Ophelia's safety. If we fail in our duties to the university and to my family, then we will draw unwanted attention.

I stand and tuck my dick back in my pants before pressing a kiss on her forehead. She almost takes me out with a smile. "Thank you," she whispers.

Wanting to prolong this moment as long as possible, I tuck a lock of her hair behind her ear. "No. Thank you, Cupcake. It was an honor."

Alexandros watches me intently, a look in his eyes that I cannot read. "And thank you for letting me have this." Because he could have taken this for himself had he chosen to. I know that he wanted to. I could feel him longing for her and wishing it was him buried inside of her instead of me. Magnanimity is not a trait he displays often, and I have no idea why he did so today. But whatever his reason, I am grateful.

He gives me a nod. *Go find your brothers.*

THIRTY-SEVEN

ALEXANDROS

Every hair on my body stands on end as though I have been electrified. His presence has always had the same effect on me, but that sensation is magnified times one hundred today. I have no idea if that is a result of the changes in my own powers, or if it is because the stakes have never been this high before.

I close my eyes and suck in a deep, calming breath, but it does little to ease the raging swell of anger and anxiety that swirls within my chest. He is here. On campus. And I have too little time to warn her properly.

I concentrate on her alone, blocking out all other noise. Blocking out everything but her, and that simple act already does something to calm the storm inside me. I find a peace in her that I have never experienced, and the irony of that—given the turmoil she has already caused and will surely bring in my future—is not lost on me.

Ophelia! My tone is sharp, too harsh for her, but we have no time for pleasantries.

Alexandros? She is surprised and more than a little annoyed, but her innate curiosity makes her answer me anyway.

You must go to Thucydides Library. Take all the boys with you, and do not leave until I tell you it is safe to do so.

What? Why? Are—

They are all safe, I assure her, knowing she is thinking of the boys and her friends. *You will all be safe. Just do as you are told. I do not have time to argue. Go. Now!*

I think Axl and Malachi are sleeping. I'm in class with Xavier. I'll ... Her anxiety seems to swallow the rest of her words.

I change my tone, aware I need to soothe her, if only to prevent her powers from showing up in the middle of class. *We are in no danger, little one. Just do as I say and all will be well. Go with Xavier immediately. Tell your professor you feel unwell.*

My father's energy grows closer. I feel him probing the edges of my consciousness, and a shudder travels down my spine.

I'm leaving right now.

Thank you. And Ophelia? This is of the utmost importance. You must stay out of my head. Do you understand me? I can block out my father, having done so for most of my life, but I have no idea how her powers affect mine or, more importantly, whether he will be able to detect her somehow. The sooner we learn the full extent of her power, the better off we will all be.

I understand.

Good girl. I wince at my choice of words when the current of desire ripples through her and into me. But there is no time to give it any more thought. He is here, standing outside the door to my office.

I block Ophelia out and shout for him to enter before he gets the chance to walk in uninvited, which he surely would have done. He steps inside, and his huge frame fills the doorway. I inherited his height, his build, and so much more from him. His dark-brown eyes that smolder almost black when he is angry. His cruelty and his impatience. I constantly fight to tamp the former down, and for a long time, I succeeded beyond what I imagined myself capable of. But those parts of me—of him—are always there, beating within my chest as vibrantly as my own heart.

He snarls. "Son."

"Father." I give him a cursory nod and indicate the chair opposite mine. "It is a surprise to see you."

His response is another snarl, but he takes the proffered seat, crossing his legs and resting his ankle on his thigh. He glances around my office. "You were supposed to be the president of this institution, not a mere *professor*."

"We built this place to ensure the continued survival of our house and of our kind. Whether I am the president or a janitor, the results would be the same. Do I not provide you with an ample supply of pledges to be turned every single year? Do Houses Chóma, Elira, and Thalassa not get the same? Are they not forever in our debt and our servitude because of it?"

He avoids my glare, choosing instead to inspect his fingernails. After seeming to find them to his satisfaction, he lifts his head, and his dark eyes burn into mine. "House Drakos built this institution to ensure the legacy of all magical beings, and *you* were supposed to be at its head."

I bang my fist on the table, sending a stack of term papers to the floor. "I am. Jerome Ollenshaw is a mere figurehead. Everything of importance that is handled within these walls is overseen by me."

He runs his fingertips through his thick black beard and brings them to a point beneath his chin, his nostrils flaring as he works to reign in his temper. The last time we fought, I tore out his throat. It was almost five hundred years ago, but I am sure that memory still stings as keenly as if it were yesterday. It was the first time I bested him and the last time he laid a hand on me.

"Your walls are stronger than ever, Alexandros. Have you labored on them all these years?"

I twist my head from side to side. "From the moment I learned how, I have always kept my walls strong where you are concerned, Father."

He shakes his head. "This is different. You are ..." He sucks on his top lip as though deep in thought. "Impenetrable."

I lean forward and rest my hands on the desk. That he finds my mind impenetrable is surely the best thing he could have said to me and reason enough for me to endure his visit without too much resistance. I can only hope it is as brief as all his others have been these past five centuries. "Why are you here? All the pledges for this year have already been turned."

He dismisses me with a wave of his hand. "I have no interest in the pledges. Not until you find me one with a little more backbone."

"That most eighteen-year-old humans are not cruel enough for you to turn is of no surprise to me, Father."

He shakes his head and snorts. "You have always thought me cruel, yet look at the man you have become. All of this"—he motions at the four walls surrounding us—"because of me."

"Or in spite of you," I retort. "And only a moment ago, you were berating me for not being enough."

His eyes narrow. "You are one of the most feared and

respected creatures to walk this earth, Alexandros. Choosing to waste your time as a history professor locked behind these walls does not change who you are. It does not erase your past victories." His voice is tinged with pride now, and of course it is.

"You speak of victories, but all I recall is vengeance and pain and a darkness that would have surely swallowed me whole had I let it."

He bares his teeth again, and his fangs glisten in the dim light of the bulb hanging overhead. "You did what was necessary. What I expected of you. What your mother, your wife, and your daughters would have expected of you."

Anguish threatens to steal my next breath. "Do not speak of them in my presence."

"I will speak of who I want to. They were my blood too. She was your mother, but she was my *everything!*" His roar rattles the arched window behind me.

Fury surges through my veins like wildfire. "You think I do not know what it is like to lose everything?"

He shakes his head and licks his lips, visibly working to control his ire. "Your children were a great loss."

I leap to my feet. "A great loss? Are you—" I lack the words necessary to convey my outrage, so I grind my teeth together.

He stands too and plants his fists on my desk. "Yes. A great loss. And Elena was your wife. Your bonded mate, but she was not ..." The muscles in his throat convulse. "She was not what your mother was to me."

I struggle to maintain my composure, astounded by his arrogance although I know all too well the man he is.

"Very few vampires have a fated mate, Alexandros. It is a curse I almost wish had never been inflicted upon me. I was never a good man. Born to rule in a time when cruelty and vengeance were the only way of life. And she was the only one who could unlock the tiny sliver of goodness that I had buried inside my black heart. That she could only bear me two children was not enough to dull my devotion to only her. But she took that goodness with her. I made peace with the monster I am a long time ago."

I had no idea he and my mother were fated mates, and in the two thousand years I have known him, I have never understood my father more than I do in this singular moment. "Would you change it? If you could?"

"Your mother and I were carved into the fabric of the universe when it was merely a collection of particles. Our story is a fixed point in time. It cannot be changed. It is an inescapable truth."

Frustration and realization take root inside my core. "But would you change it? If you could go back and not bond with her, would you?"

His eyes darken further, but it is not anger I see in them. "What if you were told that you were merely sleepwalking through your life, but that for a brief period of time, you could awaken and experience everything in its fullest splendor? Everything you tasted and touched and felt would be magnified one million times over, and you would finally know, deep in your soul and down to the tiniest atom of your being, the true reason for your existence. But what if I also told you that this awakening would not last forever? Once you returned to your dreaming state, everything would hurt all the more. But you would be forced to remain in that constant purgatory of a life without her because the netherworld would claim all your good memories, and then you would truly lose her forever. Would you still choose to be woken?"

I can do nothing but stare into his eyes and feel some of the deep-rooted pain he has laid bare before me. I know the answer to his question without having to consider the alternative.

"Well?" he prompts.

"I do not know." I lie with ease but avert my eyes before he can see what I am hiding. Before he sees my feelings for her and recognizes them.

I drop back into my seat. "What are you doing here?"

He rocks his head from side to side, and his nostrils flare. "You are keeping something from me."

My adrenaline spikes, but I keep my voice calm and steady as I hold his gaze once more. "I keep many things from you. I have kept myself guarded from you since I was a child."

He nods, and there is an unmistakable look of pride on his face. He retakes his seat. "You have, but your brother ..." He sneers. "Giorgios is not as skilled as you. He never has been."

I actively work to breathe normally and maintain a steady pulse. While I can mask my emotions and block him from my thoughts, blood never lies. Staying in the moment and focusing on each measured inhale and exhale stops me from spiraling about what my brother may have inadvertently revealed about Ophelia. If my father thought for a second that an elementai was here, he would not be sitting in my office having a conversation. He would be tearing this campus apart to find her.

"Giorgios is skilled in different ways," I say, gratefully changing the subject and coming to my brother's defense in the age-old argument.

He snorts. "Teleportation."

I scowl. "It is a gift I wish that I possessed."

"The Drakos power is in our minds, not in teleportation." His tone drips with anger. "If I did not know for sure he was my son, I would have sworn he was a bastard child."

The way I used to allow our father's disdain to egg me on and would taunt Giorgios for his lack of abilities as a child is a source of great shame and is a big part of the reason I cannot help but defend him now. Nobody was as shocked as I when his teleportation power developed long after he became a man.

Latent powers are unusual in vampires. "He has developed his gift of mind control too. I would have thought you would be proud to have a son with such diverse and unique gifts."

His eyes narrow. "I was proud of my son who could talk to dragons. That is why you were chosen to marry into the most powerful elementai family that existed. The son who summoned two of the most powerful beings who ever roamed this earth to serve by his side when he was only a boy. *That* is the son who made me proud. Until you let them leave."

I cannot believe the gall of this man. "You think that I could have persuaded the dragons to stay? When their numbers were decreasing so rapidly they were all but extinct?"

"You could have convinced them, Alexandros, and yet you chose not to."

This is another age-old argument that neither of us will ever win. "Why are you here?" I repeat.

"I told you."

I shake my head. "I am hiding nothing from you."

He leans closer, regarding me with both curiosity and disdain. "As you said, you are always hiding something, but now Giorgios is too. I could always read him so clearly, and now ..." He flicks his tongue over his fangs. "I cannot."

"So go speak to Giorgios." Fortunately, our father does not have the power of teleportation that he holds with such blatant disregard, so I will have plenty of time to warn and prepare my brother for a visit. And despite our father's disdain for Giorgios's skills, his ability to control his own mind and block his thoughts from others is considerable. Otherwise, I would not have trusted him with Ophelia's safety.

My father runs his fingertips through his beard again, sizing me up. He will get nothing from me, and of that I am certain. "Be sure that I will. But he has been here four times these past few months alone."

"He is my brother."

He scoffs. "A brother you had not seen for almost two decades until recently."

"I thought there may be a pledge that would suit him. That is all."

He regards me with undisguised suspicion. "Perhaps I should extend my stay here for a little while in the event he visits again. It would make for a splendid family reunion, would it not?"

Even if I were hiding nothing from him, that would be a terrible idea, and he knows it. But if he does stay, I will be forced to take Ophelia and the boys and travel somewhere he can never find us. Perhaps that is what I should do in any event. "Whatever you decide is best, Father. But your rampant killing sprees will not go as unnoticed across America as they do in the dark corners of the earth you usually frequent."

As powerful as he is, even he would not be foolish enough to bring such unnecessary attention to our kind. Plus, he is too set in his ways to exist for extended periods of time in civilized society.

"I go where the Skotádi are. It is they whom I seek out and destroy. Should any humans or witches or any other kind of beings get in my way, then I cannot be held accountable. I do what I do for the greater good."

His mention of our common enemy has my interest piqued. "And just how many Skotádi have you actually killed these past hundred years?"

A growl tumbles from his lips. "Too few. They were born to hide in the shadows. I know not how many remain, but I will not rest until I find them all."

His immense hatred for the Skotádi is the reason I cannot tell him about their recent activities. He would stick around, and his investigation would inevitably lead him to the two people who need to be protected from him more than anyone—Ophelia and Lucian. My desire to protect the latter takes me by surprise. As much as I tell myself it is because I want to deal with him in my own way, I know that is not entirely true. And like with anything to do with my son, I refuse to unpack it and instead push it behind the wall of granite I keep him behind.

"Then I have nothing further to offer you. I got all the vengeance I needed a long time ago."

"That is not quite true, is it, Alexandros? You got all the vengeance you could stomach because, despite your strength, you are weak. And that is why you will never rule House Drakos."

His contempt snaps something inside me. Rage bubbles beneath my skin like it is bursting to be let out. "I killed too many of our kind. Tore off their heads and watched them turn to ash. And the witches." Their screams of terror are as piercing now as they were so long ago. "I killed hundreds. Tore out their hearts whilst they were still beating and fed them to the wolves before I slaughtered them too."

I ball my hands into fists, my knuckles cracking with the effort. "I took enough."

"It will never be enough." He shoves his chair back. "They took our only chance of survival, Alexandros. There will never be enough blood spilled to make up for what we lost. No more vampire children will ever be born. Do you understand what that means?"

I lick my lip and taste her. A lingering trace of her arousal from when I had my face buried between her thighs a little over an hour ago. Fire ignites in my veins. I need to be more careful. Had that been a drop of her blood, he would have smelled her on me and known she was something different. I clear my throat and recompose myself. "Of course I know what that means, but all those lives I took brought me no peace. If it had, then I would surely go on killing until every trace of any bloodline that had anything to do with their deaths was erased from existence, but it did not."

"If we cannot live in peace, then we should thrive in anarchy," he says, recounting part of an ancient prophecy that I thought I had forgotten long ago. It was one we quoted often as children. Having little understanding of its true meaning, Giorgios and I used it to justify our reckless adolescent behavior.

I reply with the response my mother would give us every single time. "If we only feed chaos, then there is no hope of finding peace."

He falters at her words, but only for a fraction of a second. "Hope." He snorts. "Hope is for fools. Those who believe in prophecies and that all things must be in balance. There is no balance. The strongest and cruelest of us will always survive, and that is the simple truth. The destruction of the elementai was proof enough of that."

Only a few months ago, I would have agreed with everything he just said. But now, I remain silent. Now I know better.

"I will find out what you are hiding from me." With that, he stalks out of my office, leaving me to stare at his retreating back as dread settles deep in the pit of my stomach.

THIRTY-EIGHT

ALEXANDROS

I t takes me not even a moment to find Giorgios amongst the cacophony of voices that fill my head these days. It seems as though my mind can tap into every person I have ever connected with, and all at once. And I can isolate each one as quickly as pressing a button on a remote control.

Giorgios.

Good evening, brother. His familiar voice fills me with a sense of nostalgia and, despite my reason for reaching out to him, I feel a smile tugging at the corners of my mouth.

It disappears quickly. *Our father paid me a visit me today.*

He is silent for a moment, no doubt as shocked as I was. *For what purpose?*

He knew of your visits to me these past months. He asked what we were hiding from him.

I assume you told him nothing.

I told him I had a pledge that I thought you may be interested in siring.

Good. Smart thinking, he says. *Do you think he suspects anything close to the truth?*

If I did, then I would already be long gone, not calmly having this conversation. *No. But it is a grave concern that he suspects anything at all. We will have to limit your visits from now on.*

I agree, brother.

I am sure he will pay you a visit shortly.

He groans. *What a pleasant surprise that will be.*

I smile in spite of everything. He is a good brother, and I have seen far too little of him the past several years. And now it looks like we will not be able to see each other for the foreseeable future.

He will learn nothing of the girl from me, Alexandros. I may not have your skill, but I can hold my own. I have had many years of practice.

I know, Giorgios. I believe in you.

Thank you, brother. I must go. I have some business to attend to, and she does not like to be kept waiting, he says with a dark chuckle.

After bidding him goodbye, I close my eyes and tune out the voices that once again fill my head. They slowly fade to a quiet hum of white noise. The voices are so much louder and more vibrant than they used to be, and I am surprised at how easily I can tune them in and out.

And the walls that I built to keep out those I am bonded with, both through choice and through family, are stronger somehow. There is no escaping the fact that the shift occurred when I bonded with Ophelia, although I have no idea why. When I bonded with Elena, I never experienced any shift in my powers. But she did not channel any of mine either.

She was one of the most powerful elementai of her generation. We met when she was only sixteen. She was a powerful and alluring elementai even at her tender age, but it was my brother who found her beauty intoxicating. They would spend hours reading the old philosophers and speculating about the Lost Prophecies of Fiere.

But it was I, the son of House Drakos, who could communicate with dragons and was therefore chosen as her suitor. Her father and mine deemed it the most appropriate match, and being the obedient children that we were, we did not question it. Vampire and elementai can choose to bond, or not, with any of our respective kinds. There does not have to be any kind of attraction for the bond to take root. And my bond with Elena was a strong one. We were as committed to each other as any vampire and elementai before us. And we were happy. Even for the seven hundred years before we had our first child. A healthy vampire boy, who looked just like me but had her hazel eyes. He was an only child for almost two hundred years until his little sisters were born.

Painfully bittersweet memories of the way he would carry them both on his back, how they would wait at the castle door, eager for his safe return, unfold in my mind like pages from a book. A tear runs down my face, and I swat it away, closing the book and shutting down my grief before it can take root.

My bond with Ophelia is so very different. Was our story also written billions of years ago when the universe was new? I have always known of the possibility of vampires having fated mates, but it is so rare an occurrence that I never considered it a possibility. Until today, I had no idea my parents were fated mates. Never would I have thought that I had one or that I would wait over two thousand years for her.

Knowing what I know now, I would wait two million years for Ophelia. She is different from any being I have ever known before, and as her powers grow, so do mine. And what better way to test them ...

I clear my mind and focus on him, and as I breach the veil between our worlds, my mind grows sharper.

Alexandros Drakos. His deep growl is even fiercer than I recall.

My pulse spikes. *Anikêtos.*

He snorts, and I can practically feel the heat from his fire. *Elpis told me you had spoken.*

I expected that she would.

I am surprised to hear from you. The last time we spoke, you called me ... What was it now?

I pinch the spot between my brows and sigh. *You burned my wife's face, Ani.*

She got in my way.

Fury burns inside me as raw as the day in question, but I swallow it down. He never accepted her part in my life. *You are a dragon with a three-hundred-foot wingspan. Everyone is in your way.*

I was by your side for over a millennium, Alexandros.

And then you left! I remind him. *And when my entire world was burning, you still did not come back. I needed you.*

Do you think that we could have done anything to stop what happened?

Grief, acrid and hot, balls in my throat. *You could have tried.*

And risked the elimination of my entire species too? Do not be so arrogant as to assume that dragons owe your kind anything, Alexandros. We stalked this earth long before any of you, and when you all destroy each other, as you surely will, we will return once more.

337

I am not talking about what your kind owes anyone, Ani. I am talking about you and me.

He snorts again. *You think that I owe you something?*

A familiar rage swirls inside me once more, only now it is tinged with guilt and regret. I should have known this would be a mistake. The door of my study opens, and Ophelia pokes her head inside. The mere sight of her is enough to soothe the raging vortex of emotion that churns inside me.

I hold out a hand and beckon her to me. Closing my eyes, I listen to the sound of her soft footfalls as she crosses the room. Her slender fingers curl around mine, her touch sending a gentle warmth through my veins rather than the electric current I usually feel in such close proximity to her. She shuffles onto my lap and curls her small body against mine. With my arms around her, I rest my lips on the top of her head. She fits so perfectly here, as though she is precisely where she was meant to be. As though our atoms were forged from the same piece of the same star.

Hello Anikêtos, son of Herôs, first of your kind, Seer of truths and Keeper of the cradle of magic. It's an honor to speak with you, Ophelia says in a calm, clear voice.

I blink at her.

And you are? Ani responds, but I can already tell that using all of his titles has gone a long way toward ingratiating herself to him. Dragons are known for their large egos, and none can compare to that of Anikêtos.

I am Ophelia Hart. I'm bonded to Alexandros.

I narrow my eyes in warning so she knows not to reveal too much, but she simply smiles sweetly at me.

You are not a vampire. His tone is much less harsh than it was a moment ago, full of curiosity now rather than disdain.

I am not, she admits.

He is no threat to her, but I still find myself banding her

within the tightly protective circle of my arms. *You are a curious creature, Ophelia Hart. So few are able to talk to dragons.*

I know. I consider it a great honor, sir.

He snorts a laugh, probably because he knows how much her calling him sir will enrage me. I tip her jaw up with my forefinger. "*You* do not call *him* sir, little one."

She flutters her eyelashes. "Sorry, sir."

I stifle a groan and shift her on my lap so she sits squarely over my aching dick. It seems I become a slave to my desires whenever she is around. It is a distraction I could do without given the grave situation we all face, but it is one I relish all the same.

Is she your fated mate?

Ophelia's blue eyes widen as she stares at me, both of them awaiting my answer.

There is no denying this truth, and I am no longer sure why I did not admit it sooner. *Yes.*

I told you, Dragon Whisperer, Ani says.

Ophelia gasps, and her heart flutters. I am certain she did not hear his reply, although it seared itself into my brain. Condescending egomaniac. He told me many times that Elena was not the one meant for me, and I rebuffed him every single time.

She blinks at me. *I thought only wolves had fated mates.*

No. Other species do too, although it is very rare.

Ani snorts. *Not for dragons.*

No, not for dragons, I admit. *But your kind are so few in number that my statement still holds true.*

Ophelia's eyes spark with fascination. *How many of your kind are there, Anikêtos?*

We have so few left. Less than twenty dragons remain in the netherworld. Our food supply is not so nourishing here.

They have more than halved in number, which is a feat for

creatures who can live for many thousands of years. *I am sorry for your losses, Ani*, I tell him sincerely.

He offers me only a growl of acknowledgment.

Ophelia wrinkles her nose. I find her curiosity so annoyingly endearing. *What do dragons eat?*

We do not eat. We consume. He snorts again, and I see the thick plumes of dark smoke in my mind's eye, and a pang of regret and longing lances through my chest.

Is that not the same thing?

He remains silent. Knowing him, he considers it beneath him to answer such basic questions, so I tell her. "Dragons feed on energy. There is energy everywhere in the mortal realm, but it is not as abundant in the netherworld. Whilst they have an ample supply of souls to feast on, they are not so filling, diverse, or, I imagine, as pleasant as those in the realm of the living."

Would you ever return to this realm, Anikêtos? she asks.

I brace myself for a diatribe about how dragons are superior to every race on earth and how we do not deserve them. As true as it may be, it is a sermon I have heard too many times.

But he surprises me and speaks in a tone as gentle as I have ever heard from him. *Perhaps one day, if there is a strong enough reason. And you, Clandarrah, may call me Ani.*

"Ani." She says his name aloud and repeats it in her head. *What does Clandarrah mean?*

I brush the pad of my thumb over her full lips. *It is dragon speak. Roughly translated it means Choice.*

Chosen, Ani snorts.

Dragons have such few words unique to their kind, but Ani taught me all of them. I suppose my dragon is a little rusty after a thousand years.

I like this one, Dragon Whisperer, he says. Then he is gone, closed off to me once more.

My heart beats erratically in my chest. So many fond memories interspersed with the bitter ones. I met him, the most feared and respected dragon to ever roam the skies, when I was only a boy. He was my ally. My most trusted friend. Ophelia places a hand on my cheek. "Why are you sad?"

I stare into her bright-blue eyes. "I am not."

She frowns. "You can't lie to me. I feel your sadness as strongly as I would my own."

I sink my teeth into my bottom lip and tip my face to the ceiling, avoiding the scrutiny of her gaze. My annoyance is irrational, but her ability to see me so clearly—to know me so intimately—makes it impossible to keep up the facade that has served me so well for half a millennium.

"And you don't have to hide anything from me, Alexandros. It's true that we're fated mates. I felt it the moment you claimed me, but I didn't know the words to describe the feeling."

I brush her hair back from her face. "There are parts of me I should hide from you, agápi mou. Parts you should never have to see."

She shakes her head, her eyes brimming with tears. "You never have to hide any part of yourself from me. I love all of you. Your darkness, your shadows, your light. Everything that makes you uniquely you. I feel like I have loved you since the beginning of time."

I rest my forehead against hers and drink in the scent of her. Everything feels like too much to experience all at once. My love and obsession for her, guilt and regret over Ani and Elpis, Elena and our beautiful daughters. Lucian. My heart aches with such a profound sense of happiness and loss at the same time, and it is tearing me apart. My hands ball into fists. I need to do something that will sate the raging beast inside me. Feed him until he falls silent once more.

She turns on my lap and straddles me. "I will be whatever you need," she whispers, her breath dusting over my forehead.

My fangs ache. My cock throbs. "I will not be gentle, little one."

She brushes her lips over my cheek. "I'm an elementai. I'm sure I can handle it, sir."

I growl, reminded of the jealousy that raged in me when she said that word to Ani a few moments ago. "If I ever hear you call another sir again, I will punish you severely."

Her nimble hands glide over the collar of my shirt before she fists her hand in the soft fabric. "And I'm sure I'll handle that too. But what do you need right now?"

I run my nose over her throat, stopping at the pulse that flutters beneath her skin. "All I ever need, Ophelia. You."

She drags in a breath and grinds herself against my shaft. "So take me. I'm already yours."

Yes, she is mine. A fact I remind her of when I fuck her on my lap and then on my desk. Over and over until she is the only thing I can taste and see and feel.

And I will take the few blissful hours of mindless oblivion that being inside her provides me before all the pain of the past and the fear for our futures comes crashing down around us once more.

THIRTY-NINE

NAZEEL DANRAATH—GRAND HEALER OF THE
ORDER OF AZEZAL

"Thank you for meeting me here, Giorgios," I say in a quiet voice, glancing up and down the empty street. Whilst my magic is powerful enough to deceive most beings, Kameen will not be fooled about my absence for very long. He is already suspicious after my trip to Havenwood last week. But my visit to the girl was a necessary one. She is not yet ready for the war that comes, and she must be.

Giorgios dips his head in the usual mark of respect for a grand lieutenant of the Order. "It has been too long since I visited my birthplace." He smiles, his eyes flitting to the old stone church a few meters behind us. The figure of Pegasus sits atop one pillar of the original gateway, the other having fallen a long time ago and become a part of the earth.

"Corinth was always such a beautiful place," he says with a wistful sigh, his eyes brimming with tears.

"Neither you nor your brother has been back here since your mother died." I pose it as a question despite knowing it to be fact.

He shakes his head. "It has been too painful. Even five hundred years later, her death still haunts me."

I bow my own head in respect of Magdala Drakos. One of the most powerful elementai who lived, she was the one being capable of keeping Vasilis, the head of House Drakos, in check. Since her passing, his cruelty and rage have known no bounds.

Giorgios clears his throat, and I am reminded that I have little time. Unlike the vampire standing before me, I can only teleport a couple hundred feet if I expend a great deal of energy, which means I will need to make my way the two miles back to the mountain fortress of the Order on foot.

"I must ask something of you."

"I owe you a great debt, Nazeel." He rubs at the scar on his neck. The one he got when he fought against the elementai genocide when he almost lost his head. The one I healed despite Kameen's orders not to interfere. And at the time, I had no idea why I was so drawn to the save the life of a vampire I knew only as an acquaintance, but now I understand. Viewing that moment through the eyes of history, he was saved for a greater purpose. This purpose.

"And what I must ask of you will repay that debt one hundredfold, Giorgios. Know that I ask it of you only to serve the greater good."

His Adam's apple bobs. "What is it?"

"A scholar such as you must be aware of the Prophecies of Fiere, yes?"

He nods.

"There is one in particular that speaks of a child."

"Who shall be our ruin or our redemption," he says quietly, as though he is afraid the words may grow wings and fly into the night, thus alerting others to this most clandestine of conversations.

I have read the prophecy so many times, the words that come next flow effortlessly from my tongue. "Bringing balance to the new world order."

"Be it through peace or total annihilation."

"I refuse to believe that such great power can be gifted to one who would choose to use it for evil, Giorgios."

He runs his tongue over his bottom lip, revealing a glimpse of his fangs, and his eyes seem to sparkle. "Does the prophecy not allude to the child being a ..." Pausing, he frowns. "A blank canvas?"

"It refers to her powers being neutral until she is forced to make a choice."

"She?" His frown deepens. "I do not recall the child's gender ever being specified."

My haste has made me reveal too much too soon, but I will scold myself later. "I believe the chosen one will be a female," I reveal. "An elementai."

His right eye twitches. "Elementai no longer exist. They were—"

"Giorgios!" Time moves rapidly, and there is no more of it to waste talking in riddles or fearing the inevitable. Ophelia's powers are not fully awakened, and that is a danger to us all. "I know about the girl. I know about her and your brother. You have met with him four times these last months, Giorgios, so I know that you know too."

He shakes his head, his eyes darkening and his fangs protracting farther. "I have no idea what you are talking about."

He makes to walk away, but I grab his forearm, gripping him tightly through his thick coat. "The Skotádi grow in power. If they find her and have the opportunity to corrupt her before her powers are fully developed, then all hope will be lost. She must claim her power. All of it. And she must do it now."

"*If* you speak the truth, Nazeel, then know that my brother would never allow that to happen. They have a bond. She will not fall prey to the Skotádi so easily."

My fingertips dig deeper into the taut muscle of his forearm. "You know they are master manipulators, Giorgios. You know they are capable of breaking bonds. If they should find her before she reaches her full potential ..." I let that thought hang in the air.

He wrenches his arm from my grip, but I know I have gotten through to him by the way his shoulders slump. "What is your favor?"

"I need you to help unlock the full potential of her powers."

"Me? Why?" He scowls. "How?"

I wet my lips and tip my chin, prepared for him to try to tear out my throat when I tell him what must be done.

I am unsurprised to find Giorgios already in the library waiting for me. His request to meet was full of urgency, so much so that I stopped feasting on Ophelia to answer him. Whatever he needs to see me about must be of the utmost importance, given our father's visit the other day and our subsequent agreement that we would limit our face-to-face interactions.

I take a seat across from him and study his face. The lines of worry marring his expression make me wary. "What is it, brother?"

His eyes dart nervously around the almost-empty library. "I believe I know where Lucian is."

I rear back, feeling like I have taken a hit to my solar plexus. Surely I misheard him. "Lucian?"

He nods solemnly, his tongue darting out to moisten his top lip.

I screw my eyes closed for a second, trying to fight off the barrage of questions that immediately plague me, or at least get them into some semblance of order. "Where is he?"

"Europe. In the old country."

I am eager to find my son, but I know that Giorgios cannot be right. "The old country? No. He would not risk living under the nose of the Order. He is many things, brother, but he is no fool."

He rubs his fingertips through his beard, the simple action one of the few things about him that reminds me of our father. "Believe me, I thought that too, but what better place to hide than in plain sight?"

I shake my head. It cannot be true, although I wish it were. "Where did you come by this information?"

"From someone I trust. Someone who still has ties to the old country. After you told me he was alive, I reached out to some of them—"

"You did not mention Ophelia, correct? The wrong words in the wrong ear could have grave consequences."

"I said nothing of the girl. Nor of my meeting with you. I simply told some old friends that I suspected he was still alive. I believe I know where he is, Alexandros."

A seed of suspicion is planted deep inside me. I search his face for the truth. His mind is unavailable to me within these walls, not that I would search it without his permission. "So why are you telling me this?"

He jerks back like he is stunned by my question. "Why would I not?"

My hands curl into fists. "Because your hatred for my son—"

"Is not stronger than my love for my brother."

I twist my head from side to side and pull at the collar of my shirt. "And what if we find him, Giorgios? You expect me to take his head?" I have no idea how I will respond when I come face-to-face with my son again. I may well take his head for his betrayal. I should. But I might also kneel at his feet and beg him to forgive me for being such a terrible father that he became more monstrous than any creature I have ever known.

He clears his throat and leans back in his chair. "I will leave it up to you to decide his fate. But if he is a risk to the girl ..." The rest of the sentence hangs in the air, coating my tongue with bitterness. I cannot risk him discovering Ophelia. I would tear Lucian's head from his shoulders with my bare hands before I let him harm her.

"If we can find him, perhaps he can lead us to the Skotádi." My brother's tone is almost a plea. "He must certainly play a role in all of this, Alexandros. Surely it is fate that we have learned of his survival at the same time we learned of Ophelia and what she is."

Fate! Instinct makes me want to dismiss his notions, but I cannot. Because the more I learn, the harder it becomes to ignore the fact that something much bigger than any of us is at play here. And as for what Ophelia is ... A shiver runs down my spine. "I spoke with Nazeel Danraath."

His blue eyes widen, and her name must throw him for a loop because his lip trembles. We have never really spoken about the night he almost died or Nazeel's choice to go against the rules governing her position in the Order by saving his life, and now is not a good time. But I make a mental note to be a better brother and find a way to talk to him about that night when things settle down a bit.

A laugh threatens to bubble from my throat at how much Ophelia has changed me, but I school my expression and lock back into the conversation. "Alexandros, are you okay? What did she say?"

"She met with Ophelia. Behind my back and against my will." My rage comes hurtling back at the memory, but I suck in a breath and soothe my temper. "It was she who saved her at birth. It was also Nazeel who was responsible for Ophelia's attendance at this college."

He leans closer, hands clasped between his spread thighs. "Why did she have such interest in the girl? Did she know who or what she was?"

I wrestle with my conscience, battling my desire to protect Ophelia against the need for answers that will surely help to keep her safe. I lower my voice. "Nazeel spoke of the Prophecy of Fiere. The one mother used to recite to us as children."

I do not miss the spark that ignites in his eyes. "The child borne of fire and blood?"

I nod. He was always eager to believe in such fairytales. And I suppose that I was at least open to the idea once, but that was a long time ago. Before the Skotádi stole my faith in anything that I could not touch with my own hands.

"What does that have to do with the girl?" he asks, although he surely knows the answer.

I simply scowl at him, refusing to say the words aloud.

My brother shifts in his chair under the scrutiny of my gaze and whispers, "She thinks that Ophelia may be the one?"

I snort. "It is ludicrous." But perhaps it is not. In fact, it makes more sense than anything else I have considered up to this point. Still, I refuse to admit it. Refuse to allow her to be the one the world has been waiting for because she is who *I* have been waiting for—even if I had no idea that anything was missing. She belongs to me and my boys.

Undoubtedly recognizing the stubbornness stamped on my

features, Giorgios does not say anything more on the subject. Instead, he returns the conversation back to the reason he is here. "We need to find Lucian, Alexandros. Before he causes any further harm."

My jaw tenses. I told nobody of seeing my son's face for the first time in five hundred years when I searched that young Onyx vampire's memory, and I have no intention of starting now. "What harm do you speak of?"

"The harm he caused our family, Alexandros. Our mother. Your wife. My nieces." He hisses the last word. "And I have no doubt that his black heart is responsible for many more crimes against our kind since."

I swallow down the retort on my tongue and inhale a deep breath through my nose.

"Come to Corinth with me," he pleads. "We will use the witches' portal. It will take us but a day at most."

A day during which I will be away from her. Thousands of miles away.

"You can use the portal to be by her side at a moment's notice," he says, reading my mind without actually needing to.

I lean back in my chair, a heavy sigh leaving me. If Lucian is in the old country, then he could have used the portal to get to Montridge. The portals are monitored, but he is gifted enough to have found a way to remain undetected.

"Alexandros?"

"I will go." There is no other choice. I must find Lucian, although the thought of confronting the son who betrayed me brings me nothing but anguish.

CHAPTER
FORTY-ONE
OPHELIA

The syrup drips down the tines of the fork, slow and thick and sickly sweet.

"Come on, baby. This is your last bite, and you need to keep your strength up." I lick my lips and open my mouth, allowing Malachi to feed me the final bite of the waffles he made me. "That's my good girl," he says, his face breaking into a wicked grin because he knows what those words do to me.

Xavier's arms loop around my waist, and he nuzzles my neck. "Yeah, you gotta finish your dinner so we can eat ours, Cupcake."

I giggle, squirming in his arms.

"Put her down." Alexandros's deep, sexy voice fills the room, and I squirm for a different reason. But I look up and see that he isn't alone, and the energy in the room shifts on a dime.

"Giorgios?" Xavier sounds surprised.

Alexandros's brother? I ask through our bond.

Alexandros gives me a brief kiss. "Ophelia, meet my brother, Giorgios."

Alexandros and his brother look alike, except that Giorgios's eyes are blue, and he's slightly shorter than his brother, and a lot less ... I don't know. His presence is just a lot *less*.

Giorgios extends his hand in greeting. "Ophelia, I have heard so much about you."

I stare at his outstretched hand, unsure how I feel about this stranger, even if he is Alexandros's brother.

Alexandros presses his lips to my ear and slips an arm around my waist. "He knows who and what you are, little one," he reminds me. "We can trust him."

I force a smile. Something feels off. "Hi, Giorgios."

He takes my hand, his palm swallowing mine whole, and brushes his lips over my knuckles. A possessive growl rumbles from Alexandros, and Giorgios releases me.

Alexandros's fingers dig into my hip as he holds me closer. "Giorgios and I need to take a trip to Europe."

My heart sinks. That's why their energy was giving me anxiety. They're leaving. He's leaving. The thought of him being so far away makes my heart skip erratically. Fear, an emotion I'm unused to, curls its icy tendrils around my heart. "Europe? But why?"

He rests his lips against my hair and inhales deeply before replying. "Giorgios knows where Lucian is. I must find him and determine if he poses any threat to you."

"No." I shake my head. "You don't have to go." My eyes dart between him and his brother. "Why can't Giorgios go alone?"

Alexandros tucks my hair behind my ears. "I have to go, little one. He is my son."

I look toward Axl, Xavier, and Malachi in hopes that they'll back me up, but they remain silent, even though I feel their anxiety too. "But it feels too dangerous. What if something happens to you? What if you don't come back?" Dread coils deep in my gut. It's just a quick trip, right? So why does it feel like more?

He dusts his lips over my forehead, his breath warming my skin. "Giorgios and I can take care of ourselves. I assure you."

A tear rolls down my cheek, and I swat it away. "How long will you be gone?" It's almost Christmas Eve, and I have been so looking forward to spending it with the four of them.

His strong arms band around my waist, pressing me against his solid chest. "Less than a day, Ophelia. Perhaps only a few hours. There is a portal which will take me there immediately. And I will return as soon as I find him."

"You're going to bring him back here?" Axl asks, visibly bristling.

He shakes his head. "I do not know what will happen. But I will not allow him to endanger Ophelia." His eyes dart between the three guys. "Or any of you."

I press my cheek against his chest, inhaling his comforting scent and wishing there was some way to make him stay. But it's futile. He's already decided, and nothing we say is going to change his mind now. And how can I expect him to choose not to go find his son simply because I am going to miss him too much and having him away makes me anxious? "When do you have to go?"

"It is best if we leave now," Giorgios answers for him.

I lift my head and fist my hands in the soft fabric of the professor's shirt. His handsome face is so serious and resolute.

Solid. Invincible? "You have to go right now? Can you not wait until morning?"

His features soften a little, eyes crinkling at the corners. "The sooner I leave, the sooner I can return to you."

Another tear rolls down my cheek, and I don't bother brushing it away.

"You'll be back before we have a chance to even notice you're gone, right?" Malachi says, forcing out a laugh and trying to ease the thickening tension in the room.

Alexandros offers me a faint smile before giving me a tender kiss. "Precisely. And I will certainly be back before Christmas Eve."

"We should leave, brother," Giorgios says.

Despite wanting to cling to him even tighter, I force my hands to let go of his shirt. He holds onto me for a moment longer, pressing his lips against my ear. "Ophelia." He whispers my name like a prayer. *I will never leave you, agápi mou*, he says, finishing the thought in my head where it's just the two of us.

So why is he leaving me now? I choke on a sob and don't voice that. Instead, I say the only words that matter. *I love you.*

CHAPTER

FORTY-TWO

MALACHI

"Hey, sweet girl." I wrap my arms around her waist, rest my chin on her hair, and stare out the window with her. Together, we watch rain sluice down the glass. "He'll be back before we know it."

She leans back against me. "He just feels so far away." She sniffs.

"He's not though." I place a hand over her heart. "He's here." Then I tap my finger against her temple. "And right here."

"I tried to speak to him, but I couldn't."

"He's probably trying to concentrate on finding Lucian. You can feel him though, can't you?"

She tilts her head so she can look up at me, a smile lighting up her face. "Yeah."

I wink at her.

"I found us the perfect movie," Xavier declares triumphantly from the other side of the den.

Ophelia rolls her eyes and flashes me a grin. "What awful movie are we going to be forced to endure? Nothing scary. You know I don't like horror movies."

He plucks her from my arms and hoists her over his shoulder. "You're going to love it, Cupcake," he declares, giving her a smack on the ass that makes her squeal.

He smirks at me and jerks his head toward the staircase. "You coming, Kai? Axl's upstairs too."

I nod and follow him out, all the while trying to ignore the churning in my gut that tells me something bad is about to happen. It's simply Ophelia's anxiety I'm picking up on. Nothing more.

THE CREDITS ROLL DOWN the screen, and Ophelia sniffs, her head nestled in the crook of Axl's shoulder and her back pressed up at my side. "I can't believe you finally watched *The Goonies* with me."

"I can't believe we got through an entire movie without any of us fucking." Xavier snorts a laugh.

I take my pillow from behind my head and hit him with it. At least I try, but he ducks out of the way and laughs harder. I can't believe we did either, but I guess we're all missing the professor, and Ophelia's happiness over one of her favorite movies was infectious. But now it's over and there's no mistaking the impact his absence has on us all. Which is weird as fuck because he's left the three of us before. It's not like we've spent every hour with him since he turned us.

"You think he's okay?" she whispers.

Axl gathers her in his arms. "Princess, he is the most powerful vampire alive—probably who ever lived. He's going to be fine. Now please stop worrying."

"I'm sorry."

Xavier climbs over me, wedging himself between us, and rests his chin on his hands. "I think we need to take your mind off the professor not being here."

She raises her eyebrows. "Another movie?"

He scrunches his nose up like he's thinking, then shakes his head. "Not exactly what I had in mind."

I don't have to hear his thoughts to know what he's got in mind. It's in mine now too, and judging by the twinkle in Axl's eye, his as well.

"What did you have in mind?" she asks innocently. Like she doesn't already know.

"Well." He reaches beneath the oversized Montridge Dragons T-shirt of mine that she's wearing and finds her matching red panties. "It involves you being entirely naked for starters."

She giggles. "Of course it does."

Xavier takes off her panties, and I do the same to her T-shirt. "All the best things start and end with you naked."

"Yup," Axl agrees, rolling onto his side.

"And if I recall, I once made you a promise that we were all going to take you together, Cupcake. Do you remember?"

Her breath catches, and her eyelids flutter along with the pulse in her throat. "I d-do."

Axl hums, trailing his lips over her skin. "And I can think of no better way to distract you than by filling all three of your perfect holes."

"Oh god," she pants.

Xavier nips her thigh. The skin breaks, and he laps up a trickle of blood. "What have I told you about calling for him? He doesn't exist."

"I'm sorry. It's a reflex."

He nips her again. "Then get a new one." He trails his tongue farther up her thigh, splaying his hands on her legs and pushing them wide apart. An instinctive growl rolls out of me at the sight of her glistening and spread open. The possessive need to fuck her burns through my veins.

"Pussy's mine." Xavier stakes his claim by settling his mouth over it.

Ophelia's eyes roll back, and her mouth parts in a perfect O shape. But I don't want her mouth. Not tonight. I rest my lips at her ear while Axl nuzzles her neck. "I want to fuck your perfect ass, sweet girl."

She whines, rocking her hips into Xavier's greedy tongue.

Axl chuckles darkly. "I guess I'll take this hot little mouth then."

I glance at Xavier. We've done this plenty of times before, though never with anyone like Ophelia. Never with anyone I've felt anything remotely like this for. I'm almost feral with the desire to fuck her, but it would kill me to hurt her.

"You won't hurt me," Ophelia whimpers. "You couldn't."

I drag my fangs over the soft skin of her neck. "How long have you been able to read my mind, baby?"

She wraps an arm around my neck and claws at my skin as Xavier brings her to the edge. "I d-don't know."

"Can you read all our minds?" Axl asks.

"I think so-oh!" She cries out as her orgasm crashes over her in an unexpected wave. Xavier lifts his head and grins triumphantly before he winks at me. He lies on his back and pulls Ophelia to straddle him. She pants for breath, still riding the high as she places her hands on his chest.

"I'm gonna slip inside you first, and then Kai. Okay?"

She nods, breathless.

"Good girl." He pulls her down, impaling her on the full length of his cock, and her pussy soaks him with her juices. The wet sound of him fucking her makes my own ache.

I crawl behind her and press my chest to her back.

"We got some lube?"

Axl grabs a bottle from the bedside table and tosses it to me. After squirting almost half the bottle on my cock, I smooth the sticky gel down the length of my shaft and press the tip at her asshole. She inches forward with a guttural moan, and I press my lips to her ear. "I'm desperate to fuck you, baby, but I promise I won't hurt you."

She drops her head back on my shoulder, and I wrap my hand around her slender throat. "I know."

"Yeah you do," I growl, inching the crown of my cock past the tight ring of muscle.

"Kai," she moans as she takes me. She feels so fucking good. So warm and snug and welcoming. It takes all my strength not to drive deep inside her in one thrust.

"That's my sweet girl." I push a little deeper and feel the vibration of her pussy squeezing Xavier's cock. "You're doing so well."

"Yeah?" she whines.

"Yeah, Cupcake," Xavier groans. "Taking both of our cocks like a good little slut."

She sinks her teeth into her lip as tremors wrack her body.

"You think you can take a third, princess?" Axl kneels beside us, his hand wrapped around his thick shaft while the crown weeps with precum. I resist the urge to lick it off myself. My girl can have that pleasure.

"Yes," she pants.

I release her throat and marvel at how her lips wrap so expertly around him. The soft sucking sounds she makes coupled with her muffled moans are fucking beautiful. And when all of us are seated inside her, we fuck her to a slow, delicious pace. Each of us taking what we want while giving her what she needs.

And as my climax builds, burning hot in my thighs and at the base of my spine, so do theirs. The maelstrom of noises—Axl's loud grunts, Ophelia's muffled whimpers, Xavier's harsh groans—form a symphony in my ears. If there is a god or any kind of heaven, it's surely right here. The euphoria racing through every nerve in my body feels like nothing I've ever felt before. The world could stop turning, and I wouldn't give a single fuck. In fact, I hope that it does so I can live in this exquisite moment for the rest of eternity.

There's only one thing missing. One person. And I know we all feel his absence even as we embrace the indescribable pleasure of our climax. We each fall off the cliff, one after the other, and when we can barely breathe from the strength of the orgasm that just ripped through every single one of us like we're a single entity, we fall into a heap on the bed. One messy pile of cum-covered bodies. One unit. Missing a vital piece, but still whole. And he'll be back before sunrise.

I'm sure of it.

FORTY-THREE

ALEXANDROS

The trees flash by in a dark blur of muddy brown as we run through them toward the mountain that looms over the valley like a portent of doom.

My anxiety grows as we draw nearer. Which is surely to be expected at the prospect of finding my son and not knowing the state he will be in. In my mind, he is a grotesque version of his younger self. Dark holes where his eyes once were, crawling with maggots that feast on his soul. His black lips curled back over a snarling set of fangs, face twisted with vengeance and hatred. That is the only version of him I can easily recall. Despite him never actually having looked like that, it is all I see when I think of him. It is much harder to

362

find images of his true self. The one who looked so much like me.

Giorgios slows his pace until he comes to stop, and I do the same. He pulls up the hood of his cloak and nods to the foot of the mountain, which houses a deep cave. "That is where he is hiding, brother."

I glance around, looking for signs of guards or other protection and trying to sense any dark magic in the vicinity, but I find nothing. "Do you know if he has anyone in there with him?"

Giorgios shakes his head. "No. But at most, he will have what? An army of sireds? You and I can make our way through them without pausing for breath."

Whilst he speaks the truth, I am wary still of walking into the unknown. Albeit only a few short months ago, I would have had no such qualms. But now I have so much more to lose.

"We can at least take a look around and return with our own army should we need to. With your mind and my teleportation, we will be able to detect any foul play as soon as we enter the cave."

I swallow my trepidation, and we head to the cave entrance. It is quiet and still, and I cannot sense any sign of any life inside. We edge deeper into the darkness, our eyes able to see much better than most creatures in the dark, but as we make our way farther in, the total absence of even a glimmer of light makes it impossible to see. I search for any signs of energy but feel nothing. Not even Giorgios.

Something is very wrong. My powers do not work in here.

"Giorgios. We must leave."

"Just a little farther," he says quietly.

I reach for him, and I am about to grab onto his cloak when the room glows orange. Sizzling pain snakes around my shoulders as fiery chains of silver burn through my cloak and shirt before searing into my skin. They wrap around my thighs and chest, and I grit my teeth, ignoring the pain as I try to break my bonds, but I simply struggle against their strength.

"Giorgios!" I have no idea where he is. Has he met the same fate?

A disembodied voice speaks into my ear. "There is no use struggling, son of Drakos; those chains were forged of silver from the sacred mines of Peru, the place where dragons laid their eggs. They are imbibed with more magic than you can imagine."

"I will take your head for this!"

There is no reply, but a torch is lit on the wall nearby, followed by another and then another. My eyes adjust to the growing light, and the sight that greets me knocks the air from my lungs. At least two dozen hooded figures stand in a semi-circle around a pentagram crudely drawn on the ground with the blood of an animal. My heightened sense of smell tells me it is from a goat.

"What?" I growl. "Why are you doing this? Lucian?!" I roar my son's name, but it is not his face that appears before me.

"Giorgios?" He is not bound in chains. He is as free as the witches who stand around us. They begin to chant. My heart cracks open, and every bit of love I have ever had for him pours out into my chest, scalding like acid.

I glance quickly around the cave, looking for an escape route, but there is none. The silver chains scorch my skin, branding my flesh. My eyes find Giorgios's. "Brother, please!" I implore him.

He shakes his head, at least having the decency to look me in the eye when he says, "It is the only way, Alexandros. You know this."

"No!" I roar, the sound bouncing off the walls of the ancient chamber. "Not like this."

He takes a step closer, and I struggle against my bonds,

but they are forged with a magic stronger than any I can break. Ophelia could break them though. If she were here, she would break them all. "She is the one, brother. Your mind will always be the key to finding her. She must be protected at all costs."

"Even this? We have stood at each other's sides for over two thousand years."

He lifts his chin. "Even this."

His betrayal burns more than the silver wrapped around my limbs. Despair, fury, and grief fight for dominance but end up merging into one colossal mass of emotion. A single tear runs down my face as I stare into my brother's eyes, and my heart, which only recently felt like it had a reason to beat again, splinters into a million fragments. The only thing stronger than my own grief is the knowledge of the anguish this will cause her. Will cause all of them.

Giorgios peers into my soul as though imploring me to trust him.

But I cannot trust him on this. I have trusted this man more than any other for the entirety of my long life, but this time he is wrong. This is not the way to ensure her safety.

"Giorgios, listen to me."

"I am sorry, brother." He closes his eyes and turns away.

The irony of the fact that I am about to lose my head when it is the only time in the past five hundred years I have had a reason to keep it is not lost on me. But that I did not sense my brother's betrayal disturbs and perplexes me most. I thought ...

Rage has every cell in my body trembling. "Look at me when you are betraying me, Giorgios."

He refuses to turn around.

"Coward!" I spit.

Light flashes off the sharp edge of a sword in my peripheral vision, but my glare remains fixed on my brother. Cloying desperation overwhelms me. I fight against it as it tries to claw its way out of my chest. "Swear to me you will protect her!"

He still does not turn around. "This is all to protect her, Alexandros."

Her face flashes through my mind. Her sweet smile. Her sparkling blue eyes, always so full of trust and innocence. And then I see all my boys, and I am crushed with regret that I was never the father they needed me to be.

Giorgios finally turns and faces me once more. "Alexandros." He says my name softly, almost reverently. "*This* is the only way. At some point in the future, the history books will look back on this day as the defining moment of our future."

I growl, fangs protracted, and make a last attempt to escape my bonds. But it is futile. "That my last act on this earth was trusting you, Giorgios, shall be the fire that fuels my rage until we meet again in the netherworld."

"Trusting me shall not be your last act, dear brother."

He glances to the witch beside him. The slight figure removes the hood of their cloak, and given what has happened here today, I should not be surprised by who stands before me, but it hurts all the same. "Nazeel?" One more betrayal to carve a chunk from my soul.

"Do it," Giorgios orders.

I close my eyes and picture her. My sweet Ophelia. Whilst it is true that her life is infinitely more important than mine, what will become of her without me or my boys to protect her? "No!" I roar, fighting against the bonds once more. "No!"

But my struggle is useless against the might of the army of witches Giorgios has summoned here. I could break down the walls in their minds, but it would take longer than I have left.

"Now, Nazeel." My only brother's voice rings out, strong and certain. "It is the only way."

FORTY-FOUR

OPHELIA

T he dish slips from my fingers and shatters on the floor. Porcelain shards pierce my flesh. But that pain is nothing. Everything hurts. Blinding light flashes behind my eyes.

Inhale. Exhale. Each breath is harder than the last. The window behind me explodes.

Malachi's pained cry fills my ears. "Ophelia!" He staggers into the kitchen, his hand clutched to his chest.

"D-do you feel that?" I force out the words, unable to use my mind to speak through the pressure threatening to crush my skull.

An anguished scream erupts from somewhere. The hairs on

the back of my neck stand on end. The same sound continues, and I am certain it's coming from Axl. Xavier's agonized cries add to the cacophony inside my mind. Where are they? They left the house a few minutes ago. Was it for pizza? Ice cream? I can't focus. Everything hurts so much. A vise squeezes my heart. Crushes it. My soul is being wrenched from my body.

I stumble into Malachi's arms. "K-Kai." I choke on a sob.

His arms squeeze tighter around me. Axl and Xavier appear, their bodies joining the huddle. Our wails become one wall of sound.

At some point, we all sink to the floor in a heap. Our souls crack open as if to allow the piece that belonged to him to slither away. Leaving us mere shells of the people we were before.

He can't be gone. Alexandros Drakos is one of the most powerful beings in the entire world. He can't be ... I bury my head into Malachi's chest once more. Fist my hands in Axl's and Xavier's shirts. If I hold on tight enough, they can't leave me too.

A forgotten conversation from a cool October night rushes back to me. Xavier's voice. *"Sired vampires can't survive if their master is dead."*

A swirling vortex roars to life in the center of my chest. Like an inferno burning up everything it touches. Flames swirl around us, engulfing the room in an instant. A strangled scream like nothing I've ever heard before pierces my ears, and it takes a few beats to register that it comes from me. If I weren't holding onto the only other people in this world who mean as much to me as Alexandros, I would scorch this entire campus to ash.

The flames creep closer, licking and blistering the boys' skin, and I pull together every ounce of willpower that remains within me and douse the flames.

As if I swallowed it whole, the fire now rages inside me, sparking in every cell of my body like lightning at the very millisecond before it strikes. Their pain joins the inferno. Fear of staring down their own mortality, the inconceivable loss of their sire ... But even more, the agony of leaving me behind.

I screw my eyes closed. I will not let that happen.

I can hear his voice as if he were still here with us. *Focus on your light!*

I suck in a deep breath that begins to soothe the fiery vortex inside me.

I am an elementai.

The most powerful being that ever lived.

I will not lose them.

EPILOGUE

NAZEEL DANRAATH – GRAND HEALER OF THE ORDER OF AZEZAL

E ven through the walls of this ancient chamber, I feel it. Like a crack in the fabric of reality. A change in energy and power that reverberates throughout the universe itself.

Alexandros Drakos lies at my feet, the silver chains now slipped from his arms, leaving angry red welts in their wake. Giorgios drops to his knees at his brother's side and cradles his head in his hands, murmuring to his unmoving body in Greek.

It is a sad yet inevitable truth of this world that the quickest and surest route to power is pain. To tear Ophelia Hart from her family once more—to shred her fragile heart to pieces is both dangerous and cruel.

Although I have always thought the notion of cruelty to be so very subjective. Is it really cruel if what you do is for a higher purpose? This is why the Order exists. For objectivity and balance. Because in a world with hearts and souls and life-long bonds, men, even men as powerful as Alexandros Drakos, will always choose the bigger sacrifice. He would let the entire world burn to save her.

So whilst some may consider me cruel to allow Ophelia Hart to be torn from the only true loves she has ever known, I consider it necessary. Because Kameen was right; she has no need for our help. She is capable of everything all on her own.

I slip out of the chamber unnoticed. My work here is done, and I must return to the Order to face my fate. Kameen will know by now what I have done. A figure falls into step beside me, shrouded in the hood of their thick cloak, but I know who it is. I knew he would come. "Did you feel that?"

I more than felt it, and he does not need me to confirm that.

"What did you do, Nazeel? What happened?"

My lips curve into a wide smile. "The chosen one is here, Lucian."

READY TO FIND out what happens next? Preorder the final instalment of the Broken Bloodlines trilogy now:

Bound in Blood

IF YOU'D LIKE to know a little more about Axl's origin story and how he first met the Professor, you can find out in Born in Blood

. . .

AND JOIN Sadie's newsletter to keep up to date on all things Havenwood here

ALSO BY SADIE KINCAID

Book 1 of Sadie's latest series, Manhattan Ruthless is out now. A billionaire romance set in the heart of Manhattan, and you might just bump into a Ryan brother while you're there.

Broken

The complete, bestselling Chicago Ruthless is available now. Following the lives of the notoriously ruthless Moretti siblings - this series will take you on a rollercoaster of emotions. Packed with angst, action and plenty of steam.

Dante

Joey

Lorenzo

Keres

If you haven't read the full New York Ruthless series yet, you can find them on Amazon and Kindle Unlimited

Ryan Rule

Ryan Redemption

Ryan Retribution

Ryan Reign

Ryan Renewed

And the complete short stories and novellas attached to this series are available in one collection

A Ryan Recollection

If you'd prefer to head to LA to meet Alejandro and Alana, and Jackson and Lucia, you can find out all about them in Sadie's internationally bestselling LA Ruthless series. Available on Amazon and FREE in Kindle Unlimited.

Fierce King

Fierce Queen

Fierce Betrayal

Fierce Obsession

If you'd like to read about London's hottest couple. Gabriel and Samantha, then check out Sadie's London Ruthless series on Amazon. FREE in Kindle Unlimited.

Dark Angel

Fallen Angel

Dark/ Fallen Angel Duet

If you enjoy super spicy short stories, Sadie also writes the Bound series feat Mack and Jenna, Books 1, 2, 3 and 4 are available now.

Bound and Tamed

Bound and Shared

Bound and Dominated

Bound and Deceived

About the Author

Sadie Kincaid is a spicy romance author who loves to read and write about hot alpha males and strong, feisty females.

Sadie loves to connect with readers so why not get in touch via social media?

Join Sadie's reader group for the latest news, book recommendations and plenty of fun. Sadie's ladies and Sizzling Alphas

Sign up to Sadie's mailing list for a free short story, and for exclusive news about future releases, giveaways and content here

Acknowledgments

As always I would love to thank all of my incredible readers, and especially the members of Sadie's Ladies and Sizzling Alphas. You are all superstars. To my amazing ARC team, the love you have for these books continues to amaze and inspire me. I am so grateful for all of you.

But to all of the readers who have bought any of my books, everything I write is for you and you all make my dreams come true.

An extra especially huge thank you to my editor, Jaime Watson. This series has been a true labor of love for both of us and I could not have done this without you. I appreciate and respect you more than you can ever know.

To my author friends who help make this journey all that more special.

To my lovely PA's, Katie, Kate and Andrea, for their support and everything they do to make my life easier.

And I can't forget my (not so) silent ninja, Bobby Kim. Thank you for continuing to push me to be better and for making each book release even better than the last.

To my incredible boys who inspire me to be better every single day. And last, but no means least, a huge thank you to Mr. Kincaid—all my book boyfriends rolled into one. I couldn't do this without you!

Made in the USA
Monee, IL
13 December 2024

73501125R00225